Cooper's smile faded as he approached. Chad didn't realize he had been frowning until his friend's facial expression shifted to concern. "How goes thee? I assume there's an explanation for such a maudlin countenance?"

"Yeah. This place. This specific clearing is where it happened."

"It?"

"It."

"Whoa." Wide-eyed, Cooper turned slowly to take in the enormity of Chad's words. "Should I even venture a guess as to how weirded out you are by returning to the very spot where the biggest event in your life had taken place?"

Chad shrugged. "I'm okay. Just forgot where we were in the woods. All good."

"Well, that is certainly fantastic to hear that you're coping well with the surprise. But might I ask a question?"

"Umm, yeah. Sure. What?"

"Are you wearing Tsinel armor?"

"Yeah. I got it last week."

"That is what I had surmised. That gives you a defense of four. My sword is imbued with the charm of the Albathian Ogre, giving it plus five attack strength to the two it already has, so . . ." Slashing upward, Cooper struck Chad in the chest with his sword. "Minus three!"

"What?"

Cooper pirouetted and smacked Chad in the chest again. "Minus six!"

"Damn it!" Chad brought his sword up to block but was too slow. Another strike to his chest.

"Minus nine!"

Like the weaponry carried by all of the game participants roaming the forest today, Cooper's sword was foam wrapped in duct tape. Sure, Chad wore Tsinel armor, but that was a chest plate made from plastic-coated foam, airbrushed to look like he had defined pectoral muscles. He felt the impact of Cooper's sword strikes. "Ow!"

Chad arced his sword downward, but Cooper dodged with ease. Chad swung again, missed, but kept spinning to swing a third time. Cooper's speed made Chad feel like a clumsy kindergartener. Not only was he missing his target, but he also couldn't parry a single one of Cooper's attacks. "Minus twelve! Minus fifteen!"

"Dude!" Chad yelled as he swiped at Cooper's legs only to miss because his friend jumped over his sword strike.

"Oh, my dearest friend Chad, it's about to get so much worse for you." Cooper stepped away from Chad and tilted his head back to scream, "I have found a member of the enemy team! Gather to me! Follow the sound of my voice, and join me as we traverse the halls of victory!"

Chad didn't bother calling out to his team because Cooper had announced his position, nor could he think of anything more interesting to say other than, "I'm over here." Instead, he tried to relieve Cooper of a few hit points. His attempts were impotent at best. In less than two minutes of swordplay, he found himself down thirty-nine hit points while not even getting close to touching Cooper with his foam sword. What a shame, too. He spent quite a deal of time overlapping the duct tape to create a series of chevrons from hilt to tip and wanted to christen the new design with some imaginary blood from his fake enemies.

"Down to your last hit point, Sir Chad, Lord Duke of Yousuckington."

"The only reason you got the jump on me is because this is the first time we weren't on the same team. I forgot that and you used it against me." Their LARPing group boasted more than two dozen members when Chad and his friends joined three years ago. Today, only ten people were running around this forest, so for the first time ever, Chad was not on the same team as Cooper, Heston, or Kyle.

As if by the magic his character was purported to have, Kyle, in wizard robes—repurposed tan robes he once used to cosplay for the opening of the last Star Wars movie—appeared out of nowhere and pelted Chad with snowballs while yelling, "Fireball! Fireball! Fireball!"

"One down! Four to go! Ballyhoo!" Cooper shouted as the other seven participants rushed into the clearing. Dead for the purposes of gameplay, Chad shuffled to the edge of the clearing, relegated to spectator status for the remainder of the battle. It sucked being the first one out, but it was awesome to watch his three closest friends participate with gusto and laughter. During the last outing with the group, the quartet enjoyed themselves with smiles and chuckles, whispering any necessary words. Now, Cooper shouted poetry to glorify victory, Kyle belted out the spells he cast, and Heston swung his foam and tape war hammer while roaring. All because of this place.

Chad witnessed an atrocity here and then participated in a life-altering event. At first, he thought it was Hell, but then Cooper, Kyle, and Heston joined him. They helped him become a better person, changing the situation for the better. They would be best friends forever; Chad could feel it in his gut.

The game was over, Cooper the triumphant last man standing. Holding his sword over his head, he shouted about sailing down the Nile, visiting the Elysian Fields, and storming the gates of Valhalla, as well as a number of other mixed mythological references of dubious accuracy in a long-winded victory speech. Everyone congratulated him, and after a few minutes of small talk about what everyone had done during winter break, they dispersed until only four were left.

"I'm gonna stay here for a minute," Chad said as the other three started to leave.

"Yeah?" Heston asked.

"This is *the* place where . . . everything started," Cooper answered.

"Whoa." Kyle looked at the ground as if lava might erupt from it. "Are you okay, Chad?"

"Yep. It's all sorts of cathartic. I'll see you all at the student union before class Wednesday."

Chad grabbed Cooper by the arm as the other three started to leave. When Heston and Kyle were far enough away, Chad asked, "Have you noticed anything different about Heston?"

Cooper's eyebrows knitted as he and Chad watched their friend walk away. Heston still had a lumber to his gait, and his waist overtook his belt, but he looked different. "In what way might you mean?"

"Like . . . has he lost weight?"

Cooper chuckled. "That very well may be the case. After all, the four of us have been training hard these past few months. And I do believe our good friend is standing taller. That's a sign of pride that, too, comes with training. Do you believe there's a cause for concern?"

"Only if he's using his abilities to do it. Let's not forget—the four of us made a pact not to use our abilities unless we really have to."

The smile of a used car salesman spread across Cooper's face as he brought his hands together, then parted them. "Chad. Come now. When we train, we actively practice using our abilities. We can't adhere to a *strict* moratorium on using them. They're a part of us, in us, make us who we are and who we can become."

"We practice to make sure we can handle the jocks should they decide to attack us."

"First of all, 'jock' is such a derogatory term. We aren't fans of when someone we don't know, like, or respect calls us nerds, so maybe we should become the change we wish to see in the world and stop using that word. Second of all, the football team finished their season undefeated and won the championship, so the trio of individuals we've been wary about couldn't be any happier with life."

"That doesn't mean . . ." Chad paused to allow his brain to catch up, to process what Cooper had said. Not so much the words, but why he said them. "Wait. Have you been using your abilities?"

A fraction of an inch separated Cooper's thumb and index finger. "A tiny, tiny, tiniest of the most minute bit of a hint of one aspect of my abilities."

"Cooper! Really? Come on."

"We've been handicapping ourselves for our entire lives, Chad, so we now have the chance to grow, to learn, and all we have to do is get out of our own way. I'm not talking about running around at night in spandex and capes to fight crime; I'm just saying that we have the opportunity to create opportunities, and so what if Heston figured out a way to use his abilities to lose a few unnecessary pounds or if I use mine to . . . to . . . you know what? I'm just going to say it. I'm trying out for the lacrosse team tomorrow."

Chad felt like he chugged sour milk. "You . . . you want to become a . . . jock?" He whispered the last word as if saying too loud might summon those he didn't wish to see.

"Lacrosse players are a vastly different breed than football players. Much more civilized. And just because I want to try out for a particular sport doesn't make me a jock—it just means I want to try new things and learn more about myself through exploring the world around me. For the entirety of last semester, you went to great lengths reminding everyone that we're no longer in high school, yet when presented with new information, you reacted to it as if you learned about it in the hallways of East Bend High between gym class and geometry."

The cool air showed Chad's breath but did nothing to stop the burning in his cheeks. He dropped his chin to his chest and asked, "Do Kyle and Heston know?"

"They do. They suggested that I should wait to tell you until after try-outs."

"Fair enough." Chad nodded while struggling with the fact that his friends knew him better than he knew himself. "Okay. Good luck tomorrow. I . . . I really mean it."

Cooper put his hands in his pockets and started to walk away. "I'm sorry I didn't choose my words better, but I do appreciate your support. I'll see you Wednesday."

Chad walked the opposite direction across the clearing, his mind chugging along and hopping from one track to the next. His reaction was pure immaturity, and he wondered if that was his default setting. Cooper was his friend, and he should have been more encouraging. However, he wanted to protect Cooper, dissuade him from willingly putting himself in a situation where he'd get humiliated. Or would he? Chad and his friends based so many decisions on the odds of failure. Assuming they'd fail at most new things, they limited their exposure to trying them. Maybe Cooper would be good at lacrosse. Of course, he'd have to use some level of his new abilities. But who was Chad to stop him? Like Cooper mentioned, these abilities were a part of their persons now, like an appendage or organ or thought or feeling. And if Cooper had learned to control his ability with such precision that he could use a part of it in his everyday life, well, that should be lauded, not stifled.

Chad mulled over the idea of using his abilities in everyday life, but those thoughts evaporated when he saw the footprints again. Crouching to get a better look, he determined that they indeed belonged to a woman, and she was barefoot. There were only two girls that participated in the LARPing event today, and they both wore boots. Whose feet did these tracks belong to?

Chad thought about using his abilities but decided that they were unnecessary to follow a set of tracks. Walking next to them, he focused so intently on them that he didn't see the gazelle until he heard a branch snap.

He stopped.

A gazelle.

He pulled his phone out to take a picture, but the creature fled, bounding through the forest with great leaps, gone from view in seconds.

Confused, Chad tapped away on his phone screen to pull up images of a gazelle. He had to be mistaken. It had to have been deer that he saw, and his weird mind thought "gazelle" for no reason. The images on his phone confirmed that, for this particular instance, his mind wasn't being weird. The facial features and colorings. The horns that looked like they were twisted. The horizontal black marking. It was a gazelle, no doubt.

What was an African animal doing in the Northeastern United States? The new semester started in two days, and it would be a long one.

CHAPTER 2

The barn. Chad's sanctuary. He loved it here. Plus, he had nowhere else to go or anything better to do. He hated being at home while his parents were involved with their new hobby. Cooper was trying out for the lacrosse team, Kyle was trying out for the school's esports team, and Heston texted that he had to work for his dad today. Chad had hoped to hang out with Tyler, but he was gone, too, leaving a simple handwritten note under a half-filled ashtray on the coffee table: "Dear Lycanthrope Club. I'm out partying. *Mi casa es su casa*. Be awesome today."

"Coffee table" was a loose term describing this piece of furniture. In fact, "furniture" was a loose term for the barn's furnishings. Hay. All of it hay. Except for the main table—a large wooden spool, once used for massive industrial-sized cable, now turned on its side. Two bales of hay side by side created the coffee table. Half a dozen bales were next to the coffee table, cut up and rearranged to form a simulacrum of a couch. There were two oversized armchairs made of hay bales with one bale between them to use as an end table.

Chad plopped down on the couch and slouched as if his body were melting. He looked at the note again. Partying on a Tuesday afternoon didn't surprise him in the least. Quite the opposite—he was a little surprised that Tyler wasn't back having some intimate fun with a woman. Or a man. Or both. Or multiples of one, the other, or both. Chad wanted to be Tyler. Which led his eyes to the last part of the note. *Be awesome*. Easier said than done.

Lethargy seeped into Chad's bones and pooled within his joints. His body hummed a tune of soreness as he sat up. *Be awesome*. He wanted today to be awesome. He wanted one more get-together before classes started tomorrow, but everyone was busy—except for Chad.

Chad ran his hands through his moppy hair and stood. *Be awesome* meant "stop with the self-pity." Yesterday was an awesome day. All four of them got to participate in a fun LARPing session. That was followed quickly by the weird gazelle spotting.

Be awesome. Yes, Chad would certainly try.

There were three other items on the first floor of the barn that were not made from hay: a pantry, a small refrigerator, and a safe. There were six cubbies in the pantry, one for Chad and each of his friends, the other two for towels. A pair of nylon shorts and a T-shirt were in each of the four cubbies. While Chad was here, he decided to get a little exercise.

Snow blanketed the barn and surrounding landscape, but it was plenty warm inside for Chad to change out of his clothes into a pair of shorts and a T-shirt. Yes, a workout was a good start to being awesome.

A few sets of pushups, sit-ups, pull-ups, and burpees. Other than the sit-ups, he had yet to crack twenty reps on any exercises. But he was improving, and that was all that mattered. Ten minutes worth of punches and kicks to the heavy bag followed by ten more minutes with the quarterstaff, and Chad called it a successful workout.

While changing, he smiled, glad he fought through his feelings of being blah. He indeed felt more awesome than before he stepped into the barn. But he couldn't shake the gnawing feeling that something was wrong.

No texts from anyone in the past few hours. Not unheard of, but certainly not the norm. His thumbs were poised to send a digital "what's up?" to his friends, but he opted to put his phone back in his pocket. He didn't want to seem needy, and he was pretty confident that this feeling of unease wasn't born from his friends flying solo today. No, it was something else. The gazelle, maybe?

That had to be it. Chad knew he saw a gazelle, not a deer. Cooper had smacked him plenty with a duct tape sword, and Kyle had pelted him with a few snowballs yesterday, but there were no headshots, so he wasn't suffering from blunt force trauma. Chad's immediate thought was the gazelle was like him and his friends. If that were true, then someone must have created it. He and his friends had the means to do that, but they certainly didn't create the gazelle. Unless . . . Paranoia's squirming fingers wriggled around in Chad's gut as he ran to a large pile of hay in the far corner of the barn. He dropped to his knees and cleared away enough hay to expose the front of a small safe hidden within.

No light made it this far back into the barn, so Chad needed to use his phone as a flashlight to see the combination dial. Turn, turn, turn, then open. The safe had only one purpose—to store, protect, and hide three vials of a crimson liquid.

One, two, three. One, two, three, Chad counted, again and again, making sure that none were missing. *One, two, three.* Satisfied that his eyes and mind weren't playing tricks on him, he shut the safe and swept loose hay to conceal it once again. Now what?

Chad had a mystery to solve, and he was getting nowhere with it by himself. He needed his friends. He pulled out his phone and went to the group text. No. He put it away before typing anything. Classes started the next day, and everyone already had enough to think about without Chad dumping more on their plates. Was he really that needy?

Come on, he admonished himself as he shut the barn doors on his way out. *You can do this by yourself.* He decided to walk home via the woods and pass through the area where yesterday's LARPing session took place to look for more clues.

Nothing. Hands in his pockets, rucksack slung over his shoulder, he walked around in a few loose circles by the clearing in the woods, his mind drifting until he pulled it back to examine a broken branch or a disruption in the snow. After an hour, he decided that even if he found something like a few strands of gazelle fur or hoof prints, he really had no methodology for following up with it, so he decided to go home.

His neighborhood was like many others in the area. Two-story dwellings on either side of parallel streets, just nice enough for the middle-class families to delude themselves into thinking they crossed the echelon into the upper-middle class. Peer pressure and fear of being shamed maintained the lawns at a consistent height, and individualism was expressed by artistically crafted flower bushes, accented by stone ornaments of animals or characters that embodied the spirit of Americana. No decoration was eye-catching, save the occasional flag of a sports team. If there were something such as a stray pink flamingo, it was displayed with an eye-wink, finger-gun irony. Even the lawn gnomes were innocuous.

Chad lived with his parents, their house within walking distance to the college, so no one thought it made any fiscal sense for him to live anywhere else.

Their home was in one of the end rows, affording them a long backyard to the border of the woods. It had been a while since Chad came home via the woods, which was why it surprised him when, as he stepped from the forest to his lawn, an arrow whizzed by his face and sunk into the tree next to him.

"Oh my God! Chad!" his mother yelled. Samantha dropped a bow so compound that it had more pulleys and strings than a respectable Rube Goldberg machine and ran to Chad. "Are you okay?"

Chad's first thought was, *Believe it or not, I've been shot at with arrows before*, but he decided to keep that inside his head and instead went with, "Yeah, I'm fine."

"I'm so sorry if I scared you, sweetie."

Attempting to lighten the mood, he looked at the small target on the tree she had hit. A bull's-eye. "As good of a shot as you are, I'd be scared if I were one of the creatures you're hunting."

"I bet you would be, Chad. I bet you would be," came from Whacky Wanda, the woman teaching his mother and father the fine art of archery, among other weaponry and skillsets for hunting.

Chad's father, Rick, waved him and his mother over to the small table and two chairs—thick beige plastic designed specifically to be outdoors full-time. On the table were two crossbows and another compound bow, while four quivers of arrows and crossbow bolts rested on one of the chairs. Relaxing on the other chair as if sitting on a cushioned throne was Whacky Wanda. She earned that title from the denizens of The Bends—the colloquial appellation for the tri-borough area of East Bend, West Bend, and South Bend—by skulking around public places like malls and plazas with aimless wide-eyed fervor. Add to her visible intensity a snarl of shoulder-length brown hair streaked with gray that matched the perpetual snarl on her hard face and a wardrobe of worn jeans and an olive-green army jacket, the rumors that she was homeless, crazy, or both all but spread themselves. Chad knew she wasn't aimless, though. She was possibly crazy, but her seemingly random appearances around the towns had a purpose. She was a hunter. And she was now in Chad's backyard with her niece, Natalia, teaching his parents how to hunt and about what they were hunting. Chad did not approve.

Samantha picked up her bow and dusted away snow as she followed Chad to the table and chairs. Rick, a good six inches taller, greeted Chad with a firm hand on his shoulder. He was still in good shape but had developed the paunch of a man pushing forty, thinking he had the metabolism of someone half his age whose only exercise was walking potential customers from one car to the next on the sales lot. "Hi, son. You okay? Your mother didn't scare you, did she?"

"I'm fine, Dad," Chad replied. "Mom's a really good shot."

"She certainly has been getting better. Someday she might even be as good as me." Rick released Chad's shoulder and grabbed one of the crossbows from the table. He loaded it and brought the butt to his shoulder. One eye shut while aiming, he squeezed the trigger. The bolt sunk into the tree, but two feet above the target. Rick held the crossbow in front of him and scrutinized it, as if looking for evidence that someone had tampered with it. "Hunh. The sights must have shifted."

"That's okay, Rick," Wanda said. "That's why we practice."

Chad appreciated Wanda's intelligence, subtly appealing to the high school quarterback still lurking within his father. Rick was always quick to regale anyone who'd listen about the time he threw for six touchdowns to win the state championship. Of course, it was the same hidden quarterback that kept Chad and his father from being close since Chad was the complete opposite of Rick at that age.

"You're right," Rick said, patting the crossbow with reverence. "We definitely want to be ready for game day."

Rick and Samantha moved closer to Wanda to absorb her words of wisdom. Chad took this rare opportunity to talk to Natalia, something he hadn't done for months. "Hey. It's good to see you again."

Crossing her arms, Natalia replied with an icy stare.

Awkwardness. Chad excelled at awkwardness. In an attempt to keep from fidgeting and making the situation worse, he slid his hands into his pockets. He made a concerted effort to keep his voice even as he said, "Silent treatment. Good to know. But before you do that, could you explain to me why you and Wanda are helping my parents and my friends' parents? I know you two are mad at us, but aren't you worried they might kill your mom?"

That struck a nerve. "Neither your parents nor any of your friends' parents have the skill to kill a fly. Your mother is the best of the bunch, but I'm pretty confident she'd break down and cry should she squeeze the trigger of a crossbow during a real hunt. No, I have no fear of my mother getting killed by them."

Chad thought about her statement for a bit. "So . . . it does have something to do with your mother, though?"

Natalia was beautiful, the kind of pretty face writers would wax poetic about while painters would agonize over capturing every perfect detail. When she frowned, which was often, her face demonstrated the primal beauty found within lightning storms. When she smiled, Chad believed in the miracle of Brigadoon. He hadn't seen her smile for months. "It's not your concern."

Chad sighed. "Look, Natalia, I'm really sorry for what happened—"

"Nope." She cut him short by holding up her hand and shaking her head. "Stop apologizing, Chad. You've done it a hundred times, and it becomes less effective each time you say it. My aunt and I went against our better judgment and trusted you and your friends. You betrayed that trust. What you did wasn't an accident, so just own it." With that, she ended the conversation.

Chad wanted to say more but didn't know what. He wanted to make things between them better but didn't know how. Instead of trying and failing, he opted to stand still with his hands in his pockets while Natalia helped her aunt out of the chair. After Wanda gave Rick and Samantha a few words of encouragement, the hunters left.

While Samantha gathered the crossbows and quivers, Rick approached Chad and put a hand on his shoulder. With a bright smile, he said, "I still think Natalia is really into you, son."

"Dad, she totally hates me."

"No, son, not at all. That's just passion."

Chad didn't know much about women, but he knew her feelings for him weren't born out of passion. After all, she was helping her aunt train his parents to kill him and his friends.

CHAPTER 3

"Next."

Cooper took a nervous inhale, then puffed it out with one quick burst. This was it. There was no turning back. Fighting off one last screaming insecurity telling him to run, he crossed the Rubicon by taking one step forward. "It is me. I'm next, sir."

Unaffected by chaos swirling around the indoor sports facility, Coach Howard looked up from his clipboard, the boredom in his eyes bordering on weariness. As if not worth the energy to speak any more than he had to, he grunted, "Name?"

"Cooper Duper, sir."

Coach Howard sighed. "Seriously?"

"On more than one occasion throughout my life, I wish I wasn't serious, but for all the things I have been teased or tormented over, my name is surprisingly close to the bottom of the list, sir."

Returning his attention to the clipboard, Coach Howard asked, "What position?"

"Which position? If you're asking for the positions I've played throughout my lacrosse career, the answer would be none, because I've had no lacrosse career until this very moment. If you're inquiring about which position I'm trying out for, that would be goalie, sir."

Coach Howard was built like a pillar, his shape as undefined as any Doric column used by the bank downtown to adorn their entranceway. Once upon a time, he was a muscular man, as evidenced by the size of his arms and thighs, but time, alcohol, and larger-than-suggested dinner portions softened those muscles and turned his abs from washboard to washing machine. But when he crossed his arms over his chest and scowled, he could have made a man twice his size incontinent. "Are you punking me? Who put you up to this? Johnson? Sanders? They needed a good laugh today?"

Cooper thought about running but stood his ground. He didn't want to quit already. Being asked to leave was imminent, so why not stick it out the extra minute or two until then? "No, sir. I know neither any Johnsons nor Sanderses. I'd like to try out for goalie."

"Goalies are usually a little stouter. You're a friggin' bean pole."

"I'm wiry. And quick. I believe I'm the quickest person in the building, and I'm only asking for the opportunity to prove the validity of my beliefs."

Coach Howard pinched the bridge of his nose while squeezing his eyes shut. After a minute of making a noise akin to a blender full of nails, he re-opened his eyes and pointed to a portly man standing by a goalie net with a half-dozen lacrosse players. "Go see that guy over there."

"Excellent! Thank you for this opportunity, sir. So, when do I get fitted for equipment?"

Rolling his eyes, he huffed, "Of course you didn't bring your own equipment. Jesus Christ, I hate open tryout day." He pointed to the equipment manager and finished with, "Go see that guy over there. Next!"

Cooper jogged over to the equipment manager. "Greetings and salutations! I'm trying out for goalie and am in dire need of corresponding equipment."

Without a word, the equipment manager pointed to a chest pad, a pair of gloves, a helmet, and a stick. The chest pad and helmet were too large, the gloves were cumbersome, and a few of the connection points of the stick's pocket netting had long since failed. But Cooper jogged to the goalie coach, unable to quell the pride blooming in his chest. Even when the goalie coach accused him of being an accomplice to a prank orchestrated by either Johnson or Sanders. Even through the chuckles and snide comments by the growing number of players gathering around the goal.

"Dear God, I have lacrosse sticks wider than you," the goalie coach muttered to Cooper.

"I've heard as much, sir," Cooper replied as he took his place in front of the goal.

"All right, let's get this over with. Sanders! You're up."

Sanders wore his jersey but no helmet, so Cooper could see his future teammate's blond hair and wicked smile. He cradled a ball in the pocket of his stick, rocking it back and forth, a motion that seemed as natural as breathing, and said, "This is gonna be fun."

Adding a grunt for emphasis, Sanders shot the ball.

Cooper didn't need to move, the ball rocketing right for his chest. With the sound of a bat hitting a slab of meat, the ball ricocheted off Cooper's chest. Taking the shot hurt. It hurt a lot. But he had been hurt plenty of times at the hands of jocks for reasons far less meaningful than trying out for a team.

Sanders laughed and encouraged his teammates to laugh as well. "How'd that feel, Stick?"

Cooper shrugged. "Considering the team's top scorer has yet to score on me, I'd say I'm feeling pretty good."

The laughter didn't stop, but the tone changed, the onus of justification shifting. Sanders shook his head as he scooped up a ball from the dozens on the ground around him. "Okay, Stick. Looks like you're gonna put the 'fun' in 'funeral.'"

Sanders took another shot, this time aiming for the top right corner of the goal with just as much velocity as before.

Cooper blocked it.

Sanders stopped laughing as his teammates erupted with an explosion of hoots and hollers, wordless noises comprised of vowels. He scooped up another ball and shot it with no pretense. Cooper blocked that shot, too.

Growling in frustration, Sanders took three more shots, each one targeting a different part of the goal. Cooper stopped all three with ease.

Smiling as if enjoying the novelty of the situation, another player scooped up a ball and stood next to Sanders. He took a shot immediately after Sanders did. Cooper blocked them both.

The second player laughed, but Sanders did not. He continued to scoop and shoot, not taking a breath in between. The other player shot as well, occasionally at the same time as Sanders. Cooper didn't miss a shot.

A third player joined in, then a fourth. The cheers and jeers of the small crowd garnered the attention of the rest of the team, as well as Coach Howard. The last four balls the players had near them went toward the net at the same time. Two hit Cooper's right arm, one hit his left leg, and the fourth bounced off his helmet. Everyone except for Sanders cheered and clapped.

"We had a hundred balls laying around. He stopped them all," the goalie coach said to Coach Howard.

Coach Howard cuffed the goalie coach's shoulder with his forearm. "You have to admit that I'm a genius for believing in him. I knew he'd be great. Now, find him some equipment that fits."

Cooper jogged to the goalie coach while the rest of the team moved back to where they had started, many congratulating Cooper for his performance. Except for Sanders. He snapped his stick in half over his knee and stormed away.

——◆——

"Eyes up here."

Kyle was nervous. He was always nervous. Even when he was calm, he was nervous about why he wasn't being nervous about something else. But now, this was a normal kind of nervous. He was nervous because he was trying something new.

Three months ago, he and his friends went through a major change. Lots of unknown variables. Lots to be afraid of. Lots could have gone wrong. Thanks to their friendship, they made it through the hardships, and it was time to reap the rewards. Cooper was trying out for the college's lacrosse team. Well, the college had other teams, and there was one Kyle thought he might be good at.

"You all know me as Pixel Ronin, but my real name is Champion. I'm the Champion because I win championships. I'm the Champion because I led this school's team to the championship, and we dominated." Pixel Ronin was the captain of the university's esports team. He paced the front of the room while introducing himself. He was the same height and build as Kyle—thin and shorter than average—and had similar facial features like defined cheeks, a pointed chin, and thin lips. However, Kyle aspired to be Ronin. The team captain's brown hair swept upward into a teal-tipped fauxhawk while Kyle's was a limp bowl cut. Ronin's substantial nose looked powerful while Kyle's looked like a beak. Ronin was all confidence while Kyle was not. Ronin was everything Kyle wanted to be.

"You're all here because three of our ten-person team got busted for hacking into the college's system, trying to steal scholarship funds. Since they were stupid, we now have three spots up for grabs." Ronin used hand gestures as if giving a TED talk. Light glinted off the eight rings on his left hand; he wore no jewelry on his right hand. Even if Kyle didn't make the team, he wanted to learn from this experience, study Pixel Ronin. However, after spending many hours practicing one aspect of the abilities he obtained a few months ago, Kyle felt the odds of making the team were in his favor.

"I know, I know, we could be doing this from the comfort of our homes, but I'm old school. I like to see all your faces, see who I accept and who I reject.

And I want to make sure you all see me." Ronin stopped and extended his arms to the side as if preparing to embrace them all. His T-shirt displayed a stylized linework of his face in profile while Kanji ran vertically down the left side.

The others in the room applauded, and Kyle did as well, softly. The room was a computer lab, available to the esports team during non-class times. Each table was designed to host two users comfortably with half a dozen outlets and just as many USB ports. Each user had use of two twenty-four-inch touch screen monitors compatible with any device with a USB port. Five rows of three tables on either side of the aisle, and almost all sixty seats were taken.

"Hi," came from the seat next to Kyle. "I'm Janey."

So nervous about being here, Kyle hadn't noticed anyone else until the girl next to him introduced herself. She had a nervous smile and red cheeks. Her voice started to tremble as she continued, "I . . . umm . . . I never tried out for anything before. I'm really nervous."

Kyle blinked a few times, trying to process the fact that another human being had initiated contact with him. Her smile faded, and her cheeks flared to a shade of red reserved for crayons, so he hurriedly got the words out of his mouth before she got the wrong impression. "I'm Kyle. I never tried out for anything either. I'm nervous, too."

Janey's smile grew larger than an excited chibi character as she nodded. She glanced at the front of the room and then back at Kyle. "Okay. Looks like we're about to begin. Good luck."

"You, too."

Before Pixel Ronin took his seat in front of his monitors, he said, "Where you finish isn't necessarily how I'll judge if you make the team or not. I'll be looking at performance and strategy. The only exception is, if you beat me, you're on the team. Since that's unlikely, remember to use your best strategies! Prepare to conquer *The World of Glark*! Let's gooooooo!"

Ronin pushed his glasses back up his nose, each lens hexagonal-shaped, then sat down to start the game.

Kyle's monitors came to life. *The World of Glark* was a real-time resource-management strategy game, pitting players against each other. Each started with a town consisting of one building and one worker. The denizens of Glark were creatures of fantasy origin, ranging from buffoonish trolls to powerful dragons. Werewolves were also involved, powerful creatures in the game, though Kyle disagreed with their portrayal. The right screen gave a detailed view of the town and inside each building, more constructed as the game went along, giving the player access to specific characters to micromanage. The left screen contained a more macro view of the world.

Players must balance the building and protection of their town with exploring and conquering the world around it. Within ten minutes, Kyle reached a comfort level of the happenings within his town that allowed him to explore the map. It took twenty minutes for the first player to get knocked out of the game, their town razed and ransacked by Pixel Ronin. Five minutes later, Kyle found Janey's town. He never made alliances when he played online, but he was trying out for a team, and alliances were essential. It felt weird, but he extended the invitation for alliance. The message "Talons of Doom formed an alliance with Insaney Janey" popped up on everyone's screens. This made him smile.

For the next ten minutes, a flurry of attacks happened all over the map, soldiers from every town invading other towns. Half the players got knocked out of the game. After five minutes of regrouping, more attacks happened, but in a much more coordinated effort. Alliances attacked other alliances. Some were broken by betrayal; some were just overpowered.

Down to four teams left. Kyle and Janey set a coordinated attack against one of the towns, but Ronin took advantage and swept through Janey's town.

"Oh no!" Janey squealed as her last minotaur fell to the spears of Ronin's centaurs. She then laughed and clapped. "I finished fourth! I can't believe it!"

Kyle wiped away the town he attacked, leaving only him and Pixel Ronin in the game. Janey slid her chair closer to watch Kyle and whispered, "Wow. You're *really* good."

Kyle was very capable at this game. Unlike the others, though, he had a secret. A few of the players only used the index finger of their dominant hand to tap away at the two screens, while everyone else used both hands to issue commands. But everyone needed to glance from one screen to the other, often making mistakes due to sensory overload as the game's complexity increased the longer they played. Except for Kyle. He could independently control his eyes, focusing on both screens at once.

No matter from where Ronin's attacks came, Kyle could counter them all while effectively managing his town and making helpful upgrades. As the attacks slowed, Kyle went on the offensive. Tap, tap, tap, his index fingers danced over both monitors. He had fewer troops than he would have liked, but his battle strategies became complex and his tapping furious. Victory was swift and accompanied by a chorus of cheers.

Kyle sat back in his chair, exhausted from the experience, overjoyed at making the team. Janey congratulated him, as did a few other students close by. He was happy, over-the-moon happy, to be officially a part of an organized team. Although, from the way Pixel Ronin glared at him from across the room, he wasn't sure what that meant.

———

"Get up, loser!"

Heston recognized that voice. He hated that voice.

The door to his bedroom shook as the person on the other side kicked it.

Heston rolled over and pulled his covers over his head, hoping he was having a nightmare.

"Come on! Wake up!"

Heston was indeed having a nightmare, just one that didn't happen while sleeping.

More pounding on his door. He tossed his covers off and sat up in bed. "Coming!"

That made the pounding stop. He didn't want to wake up yet, he didn't want to leave his bedroom yet, and he sure as hell didn't want to see his brother. Ever. Why was he even here?

Heston slipped on a pair of sweatpants and ambled to the mirror on the back of his closet door. His belly rolled over the top of the sweatpants, and it took very little movement to make his arms jiggle. This upset him, but he hated his chest the most. Man boobs, or moobs, as he had so often been teased. But he was working on changing what he saw. In a few seconds, his waist shrunk by two inches while his arms and chest tightened up a bit. He could hold this shape with very little concentration or effort. He put on a plain white T-shirt and exited his room.

A piece of paneling in the hallway had popped loose again. Heston used his thumb to push the small nail back into the hole it came from. On his way to the kitchen, he glanced into the guest room. The two empty suitcases implied that the dresser and closet were now full. A swirl of anger, fear, and sadness burned in his gut.

"What's Chuck doing here?" Heston asked as he entered the kitchen.

His father and brother—*half*-brother, actually—sat at the kitchen table, gulping coffee from faded red, white, and blue coffee mugs, souvenirs from an

Independence Day street festival a decade ago. His father's jowls melted into the rolls of his neck and jiggled as he said, "Good fuckin' morning to you, too."

"Sorry," Heston mumbled. "Just surprised to see Chuck."

"Why? I fucking live here!" Chuck barked. He was a younger version of their father, without the gray stubble coating his cheeks and neck.

"You haven't for the last six months."

"Well, I do now. Is that okay with you, Klesky?"

Heston's gaze fell, taking his shoulders with it. Chuck took every opportunity to dig at Heston about his last name. Heston's parents never married, so he somehow got his mother's last name, as well as her cherubic round cheeks and large green eyes. According to his father, she should have taken her name with her when she left. But Heston decided to keep it, holding on to it like a life preserver in the turbulent ocean of his life, hoping that someday she'd sail back to rescue him. Chuck McCurdy wanted to make sure Heston knew which son was the favorite of Bud McCurdy. "Sorry. Yeah. That's fine. So . . . What'd you want?"

"What do you mean?" Chuck asked.

"You woke me up. Why'd you wake me up?"

"Just to wake you up."

"Dick."

"Hey!" Bud barked. "Don't talk to your brother like that!"

"Yeah, asshole! Don't talk to me like that!"

"If he didn't wake you up, I was gonna," Bud said. "I need you to come with me today. I'm a man down."

Doing free manual labor on his father's worksites wasn't how Heston had hoped to spend the last day of his winter break. "What about Chuck?"

"What the fuck about Chuck?" Chuck yelled.

"Why can't he fill in?" Heston asked his father.

"Jesus Christ, he just got home last night, so how about you give him a fuckin' minute to breathe?"

"Tomorrow's my first day of classes, so I wanted to be ready."

"Yeah? And who do you think pays for your school?"

"My scholarships and grants from the state and federal governments."

"Well, Chuck and I pay fuckin' taxes. Now get changed so you can earn what we give you."

Without another word, Heston stormed back to his room and slammed his door shut. He tore off his shirt and stood in front of the mirror. His skin rippled and rolled like cellophane under a hairdryer. His belly lifted over his pants and folded in on itself, disappearing to make way for his abdominal muscles. Skin tightening, the droop of his chest lifted, striations within his pectorals formed. Inflating like balloons, his shoulders swelled, the muscles stopping when each one became the size of his head. Wriggling veins played under the tight skin of his tree-trunk arms.

This was what he wanted to look like, wanted to be. This is the person he wanted to show his father and half-brother.

The concentration was too hard, the pain overwhelming. As if exhaling after holding his breath for too long, Heston relaxed and fell back onto his bed. His body went back to the shape it was this morning when he woke up. Panting, he needed a minute to get his energy back to stand up and get dressed, and he fantasized about the day he could look like that full time. He'd show Bud and Chuck who he really was. He'd show them soon enough.

CHAPTER 4

The first day of classes was over, and Chad couldn't wait to get back to the barn to confab with his friends. Nothing important or interesting happened in any of his classes today, but his friends promised stories. Last night, a text chain let him know that Kyle made the esports team and Cooper made the lacrosse team. Thanks to busy nights, they didn't go into detail. All four met up at the Student Union Center before class this morning to ply themselves with energy drinks and donuts, but there was no time for stories. Plus, Heston had bad news to share, and the busy Student Union Center was hardly the place to give him the attention and support he needed.

Chad's last class was in a building close to the sports practice field located in the far corner of the campus. All he had to do was cross the field and hike through the woods for a mile, and then he'd be at Tyler's barn. The trip had sour memories, but it was the fastest way to get to the barn from the college.

The memories of three months ago escorted him through the forest like a tour guide. *You're following the same path you took to run from Mason and his friends. Over here was where Mason tackled you. In this clearing right here, the Ink Stains attacked and killed Mason and his friends. If you concentrate, you can still hear the screams and smell the blood. Keep your hands and feet in the vehicle at all times.*

Chad's heartbeat sped up as if Mason and his friends were still chasing him, right behind him. He swore he heard their voices, their malicious laughter. Wait . . . this was no auditory hallucination. There were voices behind Chad.

As much as he hated being in this part of the forest, he had visited it enough to know it well, his most recent visit just two days ago with the LARPing group. A little past the clearing was a fallen tree trapped between the tightly grown trunks of two others. Perfect place to hide.

Chad rushed to the trees and peered around to see three figures walking through the forest. Large, familiar figures. He needed to know who they were and where they were going. What they were doing in this part of the forest. Tightening his grip on his backpack straps, he scampered from his hiding spot deeper into the forest. He wanted to get ahead of them, but he was too close to be stealthy. Once he couldn't see them, he sprinted from tree to tree, looping through the forest to get in front of them. Far enough, he slowed down, trying to determine which tree to hide behind for the best vantage point. Too thin. Too small. Too many fallen branches around that one. Too small. Too . . . Chad just realized that he lost the people he was trying to identify.

He froze and held his breath. No voices. No crunch of snow or forest floor debris. No noises other than his blood pulsing between his ears to the rhythm of his heart. Where were they? Chad turned and turned again. He looked deeper into the forest. In front of him, behind him. Up to the bare canopy, not entirely sure what he expected to see. He turned again. On his third rotation, he found them.

Three football players stood five feet from him.

Brick. Orlando. Emmanuel.

Instinct told him to run, but Chad squelched it and prepared to take a stand. In a split second, he slid from his backpack and changed into his half-human, half-rabbit form. He shredded his clothes, but if these three were hunting him, he'd have bigger problems than destroying a pair of jeans, a sweatshirt, and his tighty-whities.

Chad had metamorphosed into this form only for practice over the past few months, having no true need to use it until now, but his practice paid off. Now over six and a half feet tall, compared to his five-foot-ten human height, he curled his thick rabbit fingers into fists and shifted from one powerful leg to the next, ready to throw punches or leap into the air. It all depended on what the trio did next.

Brick frowned and took a step back. In half-rabbit form, Chad's chest was broader, more muscular than what he had as a human, but Brick's was still more than twice as wide, his shoulders so large it looked like he was trying to smuggle melons under his sweatshirt. Chad didn't care. He had fought Brick before, Emmanuel and Orlando, too. Brick was stronger, much stronger, but Chad had speed and cunning. He was prepared for anything, flipping through different scenarios in his mind faster than rifling through the papers of a filing cabinet drawer. Despite his readiness, he wasn't prepared for what happened next.

Brick looked over his shoulders as if concerned about potential bystanders, then said to Chad, "Dude. What's wrong with you?"

Chad attempted to make his voice rumble like a Harley, but instead, it sounded like a moped with two squeaky wheels. "You are!"

"I am? I am . . . what? What's wrong with you? That doesn't even make sense."

"Yes, it does!" It totally didn't.

Brick held out his hands and shook his head, admitting defeat to the concept of confusion. "Dude, seriously, what are you doing?"

"What am I doing? What are you three doing following me?"

Brick looked at his teammates and then back to Chad. "We're just heading back to our apartments."

"What?"

"Yeah, man. Our last class was in the Dexter Building," Orlando said. He added a shoulder shrug to convey there was nothing more nefarious to his explanation. One of the football team's wide receivers, he was tall and thin. Chad doubted he possessed an ounce of body fat, his muscles more corded than steel cables.

"Why?" Brick asked. "Why would you think we're following you?"

Good question. Great question, in fact. Chad had no other answer than the limp, "Because."

The trio chuckled but made no move more threatening than Emmanuel putting his hands in his pockets. Brick said, "Chad, you need to chill the fuck out, dude. You're paranoid."

"I'm paranoid because it's obvious you three are using your abilities. The football team had a losing record last year, and then this year, you went undefeated and won the national championship game."

The three football players laughed harder this time. "Of course, we are," Brick replied. "We tap into our animal sides just enough to give us a little edge here and there. You do, too, so you got no room to talk."

"No, I don't!"

"You're doing it *right now*."

"This is different. This is because I have to. To protect myself from you three."

"No offense, but we don't give a fuck about you."

This was wrong. This encounter could *not* be as innocent or random as they were proclaiming. "No? Not even to find out if we used any of our Elder Blood?"

Brick snorted. "We don't give a shit about that either. Haven't used a drop of ours."

Chad scrutinized Emmanuel. It had been three months since the fight at the coal depot, three months since Emmanuel walked away with serious injuries. Injuries that should have left scars. He was just as tall and thick chested as Brick, but as a lineman, he was thick everywhere, especially his waist, going rogue over the confines of his belt. Not a single mark on his face or wattled neck. They all could heal faster than a regular human, but Chad didn't know the full extent. Could the scars have disappeared on their own during the past few months? Or was Brick lying about not using the Elder Blood?

The three football players started to walk around Chad. Brick smiled and said, "Look, I get why you're thinking what you're thinking, but dude, all that shit happened months ago. We were all under a lot of stress from performance goals we needed to meet to maintain our scholarships. Now, we don't gotta worry about that. We won the national championship. All three of us are getting attention from NFL scouts. And we're drowning in so much pussy that we might go shopping for snorkels later. Life is too good for the three of us to worry about you or the Ink Stains or Elder Blood or any of that shit. Later."

All three gave cursory hand flips, like half-hearted efforts to shoo away a fly. They continued through the woods and disappeared from view. Chad stayed in his half-rabbit form for ten full minutes after losing sight of them, just in case they came back. They didn't.

Nothing. These were the jocks who made his life miserable months ago. No threats. No torments. They wanted nothing to do with him. That didn't sit well. They were up to something. They had to be. Chad sighed, unable to think of a single thing they'd be up to.

The cold air swept over his naked body as soon as he went back to human form. Knees together as his muscles tightened, he shivered while opening his backpack to remove his spare clothes. Sweatpants, long-sleeved shirt. It was enough to make it to Tyler's barn without freezing to death.

Just as he was ready to leave, he saw the gazelle.

CHAPTER 5

"Fuck," Chad whispered to himself. The gazelle was back.

Chad didn't move, stuck in an awkward pose of crouching with one back-pack strap over his shoulder. He didn't know what to do. Should he call to it, try to convince it that he was a friend? But was it a friend to him? It didn't attack, so that was something, right? Maybe. Hell, this animal might be one hundred percent gazelle and not a lycanthrope. Either way, a gazelle in this forest was not natural.

A picture. Or video. Evidence. He needed evidence to take back to his friends. But his phone was in his backpack. Still half bent, he reached across his body to take hold of the strap. Dropping his backpack in the snow would prob-ably scare the gazelle, and he didn't want to do that. *Easy*, he warned himself as he slid it off his shoulder and lowered it to the ground. *Slowly*. But as soon as the backpack touched the ground, the gazelle took off like a shot.

"Shit!" Chad couldn't let it disappear again. Shirt off, sweatpants dropped, he transformed into a rabbit and gave chase.

With his light brown fur and puffy tail, he looked like any rabbit found in the fields and forests of northeastern America, except he was human-sized. He assumed he was faster than a regular-sized rabbit, given that each of his strides covered a few yards rather than a few feet. Yet, for all his speed, the gazelle outpaced him.

Long, graceful strides propelled the gazelle through the forest as if it were gliding on air. Weaving among the trees, cutting from left to right to left again, was artwork. Chad pushed himself harder, farther with every leap. Snow and dead leaves rooster-tailed behind him as he strained to go faster. But rabbits weren't pursuers. There was no instinct on how to catch an animal, no adrenaline from chasing. The gazelle widened the gap every time its hooves hit the ground.

Chad gave up the chase, slowing to a stop, and instead watched the direction the gazelle ran, hoping to garner even the slightest clue where it was going. Deeper into the forest. He contemplated following the gazelle after a rest but concluded it would do nothing more than turn a small defeat into a larger one by abandoning his backpack. And clothes. And phone. His phone!

At a full sprint once more, Chad headed back the way he came, cursing himself for leaving his phone unprotected. Losing his phone four months ago had made his life, and the lives of his friends, a living hell when it ended up in Brick's hands.

His belongings were right where he had left them. Naked and not caring if there were any bystanders, he rifled through his backpack. Books. Notebooks. Writing utensil case. Velvet bag of gaming dice. Torn up clothes. Phone. Nothing was out of place. Chad exhaled, his relief visible as a blast of fog billowed from his mouth into the chilled air. Once his clothes were back on, he headed to the barn.

Everyone else was inside by the time Chad got there, exactly where he had expected them to be. Kyle sat in one of the haybale armchairs, his thin frame and the over-exaggerated size of the chair making him look like a child. Heston was sharing a beer and a joint with Tyler on the hay couch. Next to each other, they looked like opposites. Heston, overweight and wide-eyed, with a clean-shaven face and fuzz for a hairstyle; Tyler, made from lean muscle, long hair the same color as the hay and a thin goatee, a slight curl to the tips of his mustache, and eyes in a perpetual smoldering squint. The three laughed at Cooper as he gesticulated by the wooden table. While telling a story, his tall, thin body whipped about, similar to a windsock tube man found at the local car dealerships. He had thick black hair and a habit of styling it differently every month. This month's creation was a subtle fauxhawk that snapped back into place any time he ran his hands through it.

Chad resisted the temptation to run in, screaming, "Guys! Guys! The jocks are up to something nefarious because they don't appear to be up to anything at all, and there's a mysterious gazelle in the woods between here and campus." He opted to read the room instead. His friends were laughing, a nice sight.

Tyler was new to Chad's life, an acquaintance for less than six months. He didn't smile often. He wasn't an angry or depressed person by any stretch of the imagination. Quite the opposite, in fact. There was an air of relaxed stoic apathy around him, in such control of his life like he had learned all the secrets, so far above the motivations of the ignorant masses that they no longer affected him.

The other three were lifelong friends, inseparable even before memory. Sure, they could carry on and have fun like this, but only behind the emotional palisades found within comfortable walls, cutting them off from the rest of the world. They could achieve this level of zeal with role-playing dice or gaming controllers in their hands, but only after complaining about their parents or treating their wounds from the latest run-in with bullies. What Chad walked into now was different. Their world had changed, and they were now free to explore it and recount their tales of discovery. Chad didn't want to ruin that with his news of the jocks and the gazelle. The conversations would get there eventually. Plus, they would surely question why he was wearing clothing not conducive to the weather outside. Chad sat in one of the haybale chairs by the wooden table and dropped his backpack next to it.

"Looks like you're gonna put the 'fun' in 'funeral,'" Cooper said.

"Did he *really* say that?" Kyle asked, chuckling.

"He did!" Cooper answered, his eyes wide from glee. "I assure you that my self-awareness includes the knowledge that I have the propensity to exaggerate, but I'm so not making this shit up. That was an exact, unabridged quote from— Hey, Chad! I apologize for starting the tale of how I made the team before you arrived."

"No worries," Chad replied. "I'm happy for you. So, who said such a ridiculous statement?"

"One of my new teammates. Well, he was neither new to the team nor a teammate of mine at the time. He's the alpha of the team and their top scorer. But not during my tryout! I stopped all of his shots. In fact, three other teammates joined in, and I halted their siege upon the goal. Coach said I blocked a hundred shots, sometimes four at once, without a single one getting through."

"Nicely done." Chad started clapping and the others joined in with applause and whistles.

Cooper bowed with exaggerated hand gestures and facial expressions. When finished, he pointed to Kyle with both hands and said, "I deeply apologize for monopolizing the flow of joyous information, Kyle! Please regale us with your tale of victory!"

Cooper led another round of applause as he took a seat. Kyle blushed and shifted in his chair. "There's really not much to say. A bunch of us tried out for the team, like sixty, I think, but only three of us made it. I partnered up with one of the noobs and we kicked ass. She made the team, too. Her name is Janey."

Kyle's face turned such a bright shade of red that Chad became concerned it would set fire to the surrounding hay. Kyle's lips twitched as he tried to stifle a smile, which brought on a smile from Chad. Cooper and Heston grinned as well, everyone exchanging furtive glances, secret unspoken communications among friends. Everyone wanted to ask questions about Janey, but Kyle was so skittish he might burrow into the haybales he sat upon to escape the perceived embarrassment. All four of them were well behind their age bracket when it came to dating, none of them having done so yet, nor making attempts to do so because of a crippling lack of confidence. It was obvious that Kyle liked Janey, and that was enough information for everyone in the room.

Shifting the spotlight from Kyle, Cooper turned to Heston. "I apologize if I'm opening any wounds, but you mentioned you had some unfortunate news to share."

Two clouds of smoke plumed from his nostrils. "Chuck's back."

"Fuck," Chad, Cooper, and Kyle whispered in unison.

Tyler took a drag from his joint and gulp from his beer. "I, too, apologize for needing to ask, because he clearly disrupts your chi, but who's Chuck?"

"My half-brother."

"The last time he was in town," Cooper started, nervously scratching the back of his head, "he broke Heston's arm. The circumstances behind the incident were unclear and mysterious to everyone except the four of us."

Tyler nodded, his look soulful, sympathizing. "I comprehend. The next training session we have, I'll realign your chakras."

"Appreciate it," Heston said as he and Tyler fist-bumped.

The only time Cooper lacked exuberance was when one of his friends was in pain, and this was no exception. A slight furrow, his protective gaze lingered on Heston for a few heartbeats before Heston turned to Chad. "So, how was your first day of classes, Chad? Anything fun or exciting."

"Well, unfortunately, I, too, have bad news."

The furrow in Cooper's brow returned. Kyle pulled his knees to his chest. Heston sat straighter. No one needed to verbalize the question, so Chad continued, "The jocks are back."

Everyone relaxed. It was Kyle who said, "Umm . . . the jocks never left."

"True. But they're up to something."

"What makes you think that?"

"They've been using their abilities. Brick told me as much when I ran into him and Emmanuel and Orlando after class."

Cooper sat straighter and leaned his elbows on the table. "Okay, running into them could certainly be construed as a bad situation. Did they hurt you? Threaten you? What happened?"

"No. We conversed."

"Wait. Wait, wait, wait. You're saying you held a civil discussion with them?"

"Yes."

"Then why in the names of everything holy and unholy do you believe they're up to something?"

"Because Brick called me Chad."

"That's your name," Kyle said.

"He's never used my name before. It's always something derogative. The nicest name he's ever used for me is nerd."

"How is this a problem?"

"It's suspicious."

"You're suspicious of everything."

"I'm only suspicious of suspicious things. Brick calling me by my name is uber suspicious. This is DEFCON one suspicious."

"Suspicious and dramatic."

"Wait, doesn't DEFCON one mean normal?" Cooper asked.

"No, five is normal," Kyle answered.

"So, the lower the number, the worse it is? That makes no sense. You can't increase the severity of the situation from one. What if something happens that's worse than one?"

"Well, DEFCON one means nuclear attack, so there's really nothing worse than that."

"Radioactive zombies after the nuclear attack!"

"Okay, okay, okay," Chad huffed, waving his hands to erase the prior conversation. "I don't have sufficient evidence that Brick and his friends are up to something. But we still have the problem of Wanda training our parents to hunt us. In fact, my mom almost shot me with a crossbow."

"Whoa," Cooper said, eyes wide. "Were you in rabbit mode?"

"No. I was walking out of the forest and didn't see the target she was shooting at."

Cooper slouched as if weary from showing concern when it wasn't warranted. "Again, this is not a problem."

"How is it not a problem. Our nemesis is training our parents to hunt and kill us."

"Only if we run around terrorizing people in our animal selves, Chad! None of us do that. The fact that Wanda hasn't told our parents about us means she's trying to use psychological warfare. She wants to mess with our heads for the perceived sleight we perpetrated against her. We show her that we're not a threat, and she will stop thinking of us as one. In fact, if she's looking for lycanthropes and you think the jocks are up to something, then all we have to do is nothing and then we solve two birds in the bush with one stone in the hand."

"Doesn't it bother you that she's literally training our parents to kill us?"

"My mother already quit whatever little group Whacky Wanda is trying to form."

"It's not quite as harrowing for you then. The rest of our parents, along with Justin Butera's parents, are actively learning how to use weapons in preparation to hunt lycanthropes, to hunt *us*," Chad said.

Cooper sighed and stood up. "I'd love to spend the rest of the night running around circular conjecture, but I have an eight o'clock class tomorrow. Before I leave, though, let me remind you about our parents, Chad. Do you remember the 'Around the World in Eighty Dishes' club they started? We were like seven or eight. Once a month, one household would cook up a delectable three-course meal from a different, exotic country voted on by the group from the prior month. That lasted six months. When we were ten, when my dad was still around, the dads were a team in a bowling league and the women started a book club. Eight weeks until both of those ideas went the way of the *raphus cucullatus*. Let's not forget my personal favorite, the investment club they formed when we started high school. They were so gung-ho about equities and fixed income investment vehicles, motivated by looming college expenses. Each parent, including my mother, was the embodiment of determination, willing to do whatever was necessary to become market experts and reap the fungible fruits from the seeds they were planting. Everyone researched and poured over charts and graphs, ferreting out any bit of information they could to achieve the greatest returns. Until they didn't. Ten months and they sold the club assets and divvied up what they had. I'm sorry, Chad, but the only possible way I can view this situation with our parents is as a non-issue."

Kyle scooted off the oversized chair. As he grabbed his backpack and slung it over his shoulders, he added, "I agree with Cooper. His mom was the first to quit. The rest of our parents will follow."

Heston crushed his empty beer can and tossed it into the trash can. On his way to the door, he placed his hand on Chad's shoulder. "Dude. My dad's an asshole. The first time someone doesn't follow a suggestion he makes, he'll throw a tantrum and storm away like a fucking five-year-old."

Chad said his goodbyes to them as they left, all the while wondering if maybe they were right. All three of them were confident that this lycanthrope hunting cabal would dissolve soon enough. As if reading his mind, Tyler sidled up next to Chad and asked, "What about your parents, specifically? Are they known for their tenacity?"

Chad shook his head. "No. My dad constantly tries new things, but he doesn't just try them, he gets quasi-obsessed. He bought hundreds of dollars of SCUBA diving equipment to take a few lessons and then lost interest. He bought all kinds of gear when he wanted to learn to be an MMA fighter. He moved on to something else after he got knocked down a few times during a sparring match. Hundreds of dollars of hockey equipment, but he couldn't get the hang of skating. For his thirtieth birthday, he decided he loved parkour; two days later and a trip to the emergency room changed his mind. My mom will sometimes take an interest in whatever hobby he's into next, but once he stops, she stops."

Tyler slid his hands into his pockets and tilted his head. "C'mon, let's walk."

Chad walked next to Tyler as they did a lazy lap through the barn. With a tone so soothing he could relax a whirling Tasmanian devil, Tyler said, "Okay, so it seems to me that after a bit of introspection and data analysis, you've determined that Cooper might be right. As long as none of you four runs around the Bends exposing your animal selves, your parents learning new skills seems to be a non-issue."

Chad shrugged and sighed. "Yeah. Yeah, I guess you're right."

Tyler slowed his pace just enough that he was no longer next to Chad. "Okay, so that's one problem your soul can deprioritize. On to the next one. The *real* problem."

"You mean the jocks and the Ink Stains?"

Tyler squinted more than usual while casually slowing his pace just the slightest bit more. "I'm not so sure they're the problem. They're the itch that reminds you of the mosquito bite, but not the mosquito bite itself."

Chad now had to look over his shoulder to reply to Tyler's statement. "Aren't they one and the same?"

"Not necessarily."

"I'm sure you're trying to teach me a lesson here, but I'm not getting it."

"Not yet."

"Not yet? When will—" The pain of smacking into one of the wooden posts holding up the loft cut his statement short. He winced and rubbed part of his head that made contact. "Ow! Shit!"

Tyler stopped walking and smirked. "Did you figure out the lesson yet?"

It was as obvious as the lump forming on his forehead. The voice in his ringing head sounded suspiciously like Tyler's. *If you're looking behind you, you'll never see what's in front of you.* Okay, so his friends were all looking forward. The jocks and the Ink Stains were behind him, and he needed to stop focusing on them. Stop living in the past and look at the future. So, now what?

CHAPTER 6

Why in the holiest of holy hells is she here? Cooper thought as Whacky Wanda exited his house. *Play it cool, play it cool,* he repeated to himself as he walked closer.

"Hey, weasel," Wanda grumbled as they approached each other, adding a little extra lip curl to her sneer.

"It's actually ferret, thank you very much," Cooper whispered as they passed each other. "Please educate yourself on family *Mustelidae*, will you?"

"Prick."

Cooper turned the door's knob but paused and nonchalantly glanced over his shoulder. His words could have been misconstrued as aggressive and antagonistic, and he'd rather not have her view him as either. He'd rather her not view him at all, but he wanted to see if she kept walking or if there was a loaded crossbow pointed at his skull.

She was gone, and Cooper doubted he had seen her in the first place. He shrugged it off. No worries. Whatever she was selling, his mother wasn't buying. He opened the door to find everything exactly as he expected, his mother exactly where he knew she'd be.

If it weren't for her dreams never extending beyond the contentment of being a serf, she would have looked like a queen upon a throne—a yellow tweed upholstered throne. She eschewed its capabilities to recline, opting instead to sit perfectly upright, resting her hands upon the thick arms of the chair. Her right hand gripped a can of orange soda while a lit cigarette dangled between two fingers of her left hand over a small tin ashtray at the end of the chair's arm. Brows not quite furrowed, she held the sage look of concentration, as if contemplating both sides of a heated debate despite her eyes trained on the television.

"Hello, Mother. I'm home from class," Cooper said in a sing-song voice as he stood on the small linoleum patch in front of the door. The rest of the living room had beige carpeting, made darker by the brown paneling. The only place to sit other than his mother's armchair was the loveseat, angled in such a way that Cooper sat on it more like a chaise when watching television with her.

"Very happy to see you, son," she replied even though she didn't look away from the television. She tilted her head back as if pointing to the kitchen and small dining room beyond the half-wall behind her chair. "I got the mail today and sorted it out. Got a few bills."

"Awesome sauce! Thank you." Cooper approached her from the side and kissed the top of her head. She still wore her tollbooth operator's uniform—a light gray top and black cotton slacks. "Did you get paid today?"

Cooper knew the answer; he had set the back account to notify him via his phone anytime there was a deposit. He asked the question to create a semblance of conversation. She patted his hand that rested on her shoulder and answered. "To the best of my knowledge, I did."

"Excellent. I'll get the bills in the mail for tomorrow."

His mother's response was a long pull from her soda. Cooper fought the urge to smell the can's contents. He knew there was no alcohol in it. He had searched the house repeatedly over the years. No stash. If she did have one so secret he couldn't find it, she offered no signs of drunkenness. No unexplained outbursts, no abuse, no slurring or stumbling, nothing like the stories Heston shared about his father. Cooper almost wished she were a slave to the bottle, which would explain her mind-numbing apathy. She set the soda down and patted his hand again.

He gave her shoulders a squeeze of affirmation and stepped to the side to avoid obstructing her view of the television. "I also have to inform you that since I made the team, I'll now need to attend practice, sometimes, possibly, maybe even going into the evening, so there's a chance I won't be home to cook dinner for a night or two. Or three."

His mother nodded and took a drag from her cigarette. After a quick exhale of smoke, she said, "No problem. Just pick me up a few microwave meals the next time you hit the store."

"Okay, yeah, I can do that. I can do that. And speaking of me joining the team . . . I've been using some of the spare equipment they have, but the pads and sticks have long since served their useful purpose, so I'll need to venture to a sporting goods store to procure new equipment for myself. Maybe a couple hundred dollars?"

"Is there enough in the bank?"

"Yes, there sure is."

His mother tilted her head and gestured, ashes from her cigarette drifting to the floor. "Okay, then. You're good to go."

"Wonderful! Thank you, Mother. I'm very excited about this. Maybe when the season starts, you can come to see me play."

His mother turned her head and regarded Cooper as if this were the first time he mentioned he was on the team. "You'll be playing?"

"I should be. Coach named me the starting goalie."

"You're that good?"

"I think so."

She smiled. "Great job, son. Yeah, I'd love to see a game."

Too surprised to offer anything meaningful, Cooper simply beamed.

His mother went back to watching television. Cooper wanted to write up a contract stating there would be nothing on God's green Earth that would keep her from attending his first lacrosse match. Instead, he resigned himself to savoring the thought of getting her out of the house beyond her job for the first time in a long while. The last time he could remember her doing that was to meet Wanda with the other parents at Chad's house. Speaking of . . . "Hey, Mother? I saw Wanda Deveraux had paid a visit. Did anything of substance come of it?"

Another drag from her cigarette, another exhale of smoke. "Nah. Just her peddling nonsense. There's a reason everyone calls her 'Whacky Wanda,' right?"

"Very true." This was the longest conversation they had shared all week, so Cooper didn't want to sour it with any more comments or questions. He started down the small hallway to his room. "Very true, indeed. I'm going to do some schoolwork and get dinner ready in about an hour."

She held up her can of orange soda as a salute. Good enough for Cooper. He knew Wanda had visited to change his mother's mind about the "crusade." His mother had declined the offer from the start. It'd be a matter of time before the rest of the parents gave up. He didn't want to jinx himself by admitting it, but life was pretty good right now and getting better.

Life is pretty good right now and getting better, Kyle thought as he entered the Alexander Building and aimed for the computer lab the esports team used for practice. He cursed himself for that thought, no matter how fleeting it was. Since it entered his brain, it was enough to jinx him.

Gathered around the front of the room, seven team members were huddled around Declan. A senior who was probably the second- or third-best member of the team. From the first moment of meeting Declan, he reminded Kyle of Heston, with a full beard and glasses, especially how his body jiggled from the hitched breathing. Kyle felt bad. Judging by his wide eyes, Declan was upset, but Kyle's empathy was stunted by Pixel Ronin's hand on Janey's shoulder. "Hey, guys, what's going on?"

Janey turned to Kyle, a movement so drastic she removed herself from under Ronin's hand. *Did she do that on purpose?* "Declan got accosted on his way here."

"Whoa. Are you okay?" Kyle asked.

Declan nodded. "Yeah. Yeah, I'm fine."

"What happened?"

"On my way here, some guy stopped me in the hall and asked if I was a graphic design student, and when I told him I was, he started asking me questions like how good I was and if I did freelance work. I told him I wasn't interested and ran away."

"Do you want us to contact campus security for you?"

Declan's breathing steadied and his eyes no longer resembled plates. "No. No. I don't think that would do any good. I don't know anything about him. He was big, like, muscle and fat, and wore a trucker cap. No tattoos or piercings that I saw. I actually feel a lot better. Thank you all for being here for me."

Pixel Ronin clapped his hands, causing everyone else to jerk, and said, "Great job, team. That's what teamwork is all about." He pointed a finger in the air, a sign that he was busy unpacking a deep thought that could only be described as a gift to all those who heard it, as he separated himself from the group and made his way to the desk at the front of the room. "And let's make that the focus of tonight's practice."

Kyle patted Declan's shoulder and was rewarded with a thumb's up. He felt like he did all he could for his teammate, then took a seat, the same one as last time. Now, what to do about the relationship between Ronin and Janey? The question became murkier when Janey took the seat next to Kyle.

"Hi!" Janey blurted as if her mouth had forgotten how to hold words in. "That was really nice what you did for Declan."

Kyle smiled, but not too much. If she were the girlfriend of the team captain, he didn't want his interactions to appear flirtatious. "Hi. Thanks, but I really didn't do anything."

She rolled her eyes as her cheeks reddened. "And he's humble, too. Of course, you did. You created a safe space for him. He was super nervous when he came in, but you helped him feel better."

"Do you really think so?"

"I know so."

Kyle didn't know what to say next. Any topic other than Declan had the potential to veer into personal territory. Luckily for Kyle, the rest of the team had shown up, and Pixel Ronin took the floor to explain the plan. His T-shirt for today displayed his face—a rictus smile and exceedingly wide eyes—with the words "full throttle" above and "full time" below. He prattled on about the need for teamwork, explaining that their new strategy for *The World of Glark* would be to find the other teammates' settlements as soon as possible to increase the resource flow. The team worked on this strategy for the next hour and a half, Janey finding Kyle's settlement every time Pixel Ronin reset the game. Kyle didn't know what that meant either.

After practice, Pixel Ronin patted himself on the back with thinly veiled compliments to the group with nuggets of nonsense like, "If you awesome people keep following my lead in the amazing ways that you do, the championship will easily be ours."

Simple conversations flowed among the team members as they got ready to leave when Ronin came up behind Janey and put his arm around her shoulders. "Hey, Janey, glad I got a moment to catch up. So, we're in the same speech class, right? I wondered if you'd like my expertise in the subject matter sometime."

Kyle glanced around to find the quickest escape should the couple become too schmoopy for his taste. Then Janey did something that surprised him—she slid out from under Ronin's arm. She stood next to Kyle, her arm against his. His internal temperature doubled when she said, "Sorry, Ronin, but I'm going to get speech expertise from Kyle."

Pixel Ronin's smile faded into a soured pucker, the pursed-lip dissatisfaction of chewing on a lemon peel. "Okay, yeah, cool. I get it. I see it. I see it with VR goggles."

"Have a good night," Janey said, ending the conversation.

Ronin backed up, back toward the lab. "Yeah. Yeah, I can't help but not." Before he left, he glared at Kyle.

"Sorry you had to see me be so mean," Janey said, voice small and timid.

"That's okay." Kyle didn't know what else to say while processing what he had just witnessed. It was now clear she and Ronin weren't a couple. What did that mean for him, if anything? "But I had speech last semester."

"That's okay. I could use all the help I can get."

"Ummm . . . okay?"

Her cheeks brightened to a stove-top red and threatened to singe the freckles right off her face. "Great! Maybe tomorrow? Meet in the Student Union Center after class? Oh, I get done at four o'clock tomorrow. Does that work for you? If tomorrow doesn't work, we can come up with a different time. Or place. Or place and time."

"Yeah," Kyle said before she had a chance to change her mind. "Tomorrow. Four o'clock, Union Center."

"Great!" she squeaked as she started toward the closest exit. "See you tomorrow!"

"Yes! Great! That's awesome! Great!" Kyle shouted to a closed door. His cheeks burned as he looked around to make sure he was alone. He took a moment to process what just happened. *What the literal hell?*

———

What the literal hell? Heston wondered if his eyes were playing tricks on him. Was . . . was that his brother at the other end of the quad? Coming out of the Alexander Building?

Heston hastened his pace, careful not to slip on the sidewalk. The campus did a great job removing the snow from the sidewalk, but there were plenty of darker patches that could be residual dampness or ice. One could never be too cautious, but he assumed the risk of finding out why his brother was on campus. After five o'clock. Hanging around one of the IT buildings.

Heston was on his way home. Today's light class load let him hit the retro arcade for a few hours. After he had finished, he checked in with the other three to see if anyone was available. Kyle's practice started soon, Cooper needed to do homework and discuss something with his mother, and Chad had "plans" he was vague about. Heston was concerned about Chad, worried he would get himself into trouble and drag everyone along with him. It was bad enough that Wanda got their parents riled up and ready for a fight with monsters from fantasy stories, but Cooper was right—if everyone kept their heads down, the parents' interest in Wanda's craziness would subside. Chad just couldn't leave well enough alone, looking for conspiracies regarding the jocks. That was Chad, though. Always picking at scabs. All through childhood he'd need six or seven Band-Aids for even the smallest scrape or cut, always picking at the wounds, never letting them heal.

Unlike Chad's invisible threats, Chuck's appearance on campus was a real one Heston needed to investigate. As he got closer, there was no doubt it was his half-brother. Tall, aggressive, angry, as if his whole body perpetually scowled. Hands in his pockets, eyes forward, Chuck walked along the front of the building and turned the corner. Heston sped up.

Why would Chuck be on campus? Heston was surprised he even knew where the campus was. Was he looking for him? He didn't have Heston's cell phone number, but Bud did. There could be no logical reason Chuck would be here. This was Heston's world, and Chuck had zero right to intrude in it. This couldn't stand!

Heston hurried to the Alexander Building and followed Chuck's path to the rear. He thought of what he might say to his half-brother, but when he rounded the corner, Chuck grabbed him by the shirt and slammed him against the wall, hard enough to knock away all the words he had carefully pieced together.

The rear of the building had the designated delivery area and dumpsters. The smells of trash and truck fumes entered Heston's nose and thickened at the back of his throat. How fitting since he felt like garbage and exhaust, residue from some great machine chugging through the world. "Why you following me, weirdo?"

"You . . . you . . ." Heston stammered, caught off guard. Much of life had always caught him off guard. "You shouldn't be here."

"Yeah?" Chuck growled as he moved his face closer, his grip tightening. His breath smelled of lunch meat and beer. "What are you going to do? Tattle on me?"

That question propelled Heston through a decade of the past, to his third-grade self in this same situation. Pinned to a wall in the school hallway by Chuck, a fifth-grader at the time. A broken action figure had slipped from Heston's pudgy fingers. "What are you gonna do?" Chuck had asked, his childish voice laced with hints of impending puberty. "Tattle on me?"

The thought of telling a teacher that Chuck had broken his toy terrified Heston more than Chuck. There was a chance that the teacher would take

Chuck's side and punish Heston for wasting their time. Then it would be two against one. After all, his father always took Chuck's side, so why not all authority figures?

Third-grade Heston had wet his pants right there in the hallway.

Right now, familiar pins pricked away at his bladder, attempting to pop it.

Chuck was not a smart man, but he knew how to manipulate Heston.

"That's what I thought." Chuck said his goodbyes with a few slaps to Heston's face and one last shove against the wall.

Heston grit his teeth so hard his jaw hurt. His insides shifted, muscle taking the place of fat, organs rearranging for bones to change their structure. Then the fear. The fear of getting caught. The fear of someone seeing him and reporting him to a higher authority. He let his body go back to how it was a minute ago and watched Chuck walk away.

Soon. It had to all change soon.

CHAPTER 7

McClintock's was a neighborhood corner bar. The locals referred to it as "Clinty's." Of course, there were only locals in this neighborhood—a less-than-savory part of West Bend. Nothing on this street interested outsiders, just tightly packed three-story row homes. The words "faded" and "worn down" and "weathered" could be used to describe both the buildings and the people who lived in them.

A quick bit of research on the internet indicated that West Bend had the lowest crime rate of the triplet cities, and this five-square block of town known as The Flats was the lowest in West Bend. No one would have guessed by the bars guarding the windows on some of the homes, the rampant graffiti on al-leyway walls, the metal gates ready to shut over the doors of the taverns and convenience stores. Even the churches' walls, stone perimeters topped with pointed rocks, had a look of "fuck off." Chad didn't feel comfortable in this neighborhood, but this was where Clinty's was located. And he needed a drink.

He wasn't sure if "need" was the right word, considering he didn't like the taste of beer, at least what he could judge from the last time he was here. That time was for a mission, though. Now it was for . . . for . . . Chad wasn't entirely sure why he was here, but this was the one thing he had done in his life without his friends. He had become a lycanthrope without them, but they all quickly joined him in that bizarre journey. But Clinty's was his.

Chad rolled his eyes at himself. "Clinty's was his" felt like the logic of a twelve-year-old, the immature residue after a tantrum. But he couldn't help his

43

feelings. At first, he thought he was mad at his friends for moving on without him, but he realized he was mad at himself for not having anything to move on to. No matter the reason, he opened the door and stepped in.

It was an open secret that Clinty's served alcohol to minors who knew the appropriate way to order. Since its location was less than savory, the bar was never concerned about college kids ruining the status quo. This place's exception to the law wasn't for them; it was for the eighteen-year-old high school dropout with a limited future. It was for the nineteen-year-old parent so desperately focused on being a better one than they had. It was for the twenty-year-old kid working overtime in the warehouses, elbow to elbow with adults two or three times their age. Sure, a college student like Chad would wander in on rare occasions, but he had the special phrase. "I left my ID in the car."

"Oh, for fuck's sake," the bartender snarled. "You again?"

Chad shrugged. He wasn't sure if the question was trick or rhetorical. With hesitation, he answered, "Yes?"

"Get out."

"I wasn't any trouble last time, and it's not like I'm taking up valuable space."

The bartender looked around the room as if he hadn't been standing behind the bar all day. There were two other patrons, the same two as the last time Chad was here: a man at the other end of the L-shaped bar, and an older man, hair long since white, who had more gum than teeth, at a small table in the back conversing with himself. The bartender grabbed a glass and started to pour a beer as he said, "At least wait for me to ask next time."

"Got it," Chad replied as he stood straighter, an actor waiting for his cue to recite his favorite lines.

"You got ID?"

"I left it in my car."

"Well, I tried," the bartender mumbled. Chad took the beer and walked to the other end of the bar, leaving the bartender to talk to the grizzled man on the duct-taped barstool.

Feeling accomplished, Chad took a sip of beer. Yep, still tasted the way a public restroom smelled. This was his "thing" now. He took another sip of beer. This couldn't be his "thing." He had come here to figure out how his abilities could help him better his life.

Okay, so Cooper and Kyle were using their abilities in micro-amounts to help them out in the areas of their lives where they wished to excel. In which areas of his life did he want to excel? Well, all of them, of course. Cooper used his ferret-self's natural speed to aid in being a goalie, while Kyle used his pheasant-self's wide range of vision to master the happenings of multiple computer monitors. Chad was majoring in accounting and doubted a rabbit had better innate bookkeeping skills than any other woodland critter, so he had no help with his schooling. Rabbits were speedy with superior reflexes, but Chad had zero desire to participate in any kind of sportsball. Phenomenal eyesight was another gift bequeathed by nature to rabbits. Racecar driver? Pilot? Both activities generated less interest than sportsball. He had no idea how to use his abilities to benefit his life because he had no idea what to do with them. At nineteen, he was in the thralls of an existential crisis. His beer suddenly tasted better.

"I left my ID in the car," came from the other end of the bar.

Chad had been in a daze, somehow mesmerized into a trance by the carbonation bubbles in his mug, unaware of the world around him. He briefly wondered if that was what happened to the crazy, old man at the table behind him. One day he stared too deeply into the bubbles, and they were the only things he could communicate with now. Chad looked up.

Natalia.

Run. Up until three months ago, that had always been his first instinct. It took becoming a lycanthrope, killing a werewolf with his bare hands, and coming face-to-face with the Celtic triple goddess, The Morrigan, to alter that instinct. Fleeing was no longer his only option. Except when it came to Natalia.

Chad placed his hands on the bar, ready to sprint the other way. Then bravery seeped into his body. He was here first and, to the best of his knowledge, had no reason to fear her. In fact, he just learned something new about Natalia—she wasn't twenty-one yet either.

When Natalia noticed Chad, her posture slumped, deflating like a balloon and Chad was the needle. After a long drag from her mug, she joined Chad on the stool next to him. "Go home, Chad."

The exact same words the last time she saw him here. "What? No. Why?"

"The last time I saw you here, you were looking for the Ink Stains. You don't want to be looking for them now."

"Well, I'm not looking for them."

"Then why are you here?"

To find myself. To figure out what to do next. To search for all of life's answers at the bottom of a mug. To introduce myself to the raving old man at the table behind me. That would be his future anyway since he had no answers to any of life's questions. "To get away for a little bit. Clear my head. Think."

Natalia looked at him as if he said he was plotting to take over the world, incredulous at the notion and a bit dubious about the validity of his conviction. It was obvious to Chad that she had no idea what to say next. Trying to keep his tone neutral, he asked, "So, why are you here?"

Bringing the mug to her mouth, she chuckled as if one of them were a joke, but he didn't know if it was him or her. Before she drank, she mumbled, "To get away for a little bit. Clear my head. Think."

They sat in silence for a few minutes. Chad had no idea what to do or say, so he simply drank every time she did. Mimicking the actions of others was the best way to learn their motivations. Then he felt stupid for mirroring her. The heat from her growing frustration flowed over him, promising to burn him to a crisp unless he changed his behavior. Finally, his brain gave him a good idea, referencing something from earlier. "So, you said I shouldn't be looking for the Ink Stains now. Why is that?"

"Because they're dangerous."

"Well, I've always known that. You kind of implied that, right now, they're being even *more* dangerous."

Natalia frowned and took another swig in silence.

Chad tried again, leaning closer and not attempting to hide the concern in his voice. "Is your mother up to something?"

Natalia worked her jaw muscles as if chewing the words in her mouth to determine if she would swallow them or spit them out. Chad whispered, "It's okay. You can tell me."

"Yes, my mother is up to something. She's recruiting. The Ink Stains are back up to four."

This news didn't agree with Chad's stomach, a sudden churn shot an acid bubble up to the back of his throat. He took a sip of beer to release the unstoppable belch into his mug. "She turned two more?"

"I don't know. Rumor has it that one of them is a straggler who happened to wander into her territory."

If that was true, then Kat might have used one vial of Elder Blood to turn someone. The Ink Stains might be down to two vials. At the culmination of a showdown among Chad and his friends, the Ink Stains, and the jocks, The Morrigan had gifted nine vials of her blood, three to each group. Whichever group used the last vial of the nine would receive her eternal grace, whatever that meant. "So, your aunt is going to focus on your mother?"

"She's focusing on *all of you*. She's thinking about taking her new recruits on their first official hunt."

New recruits. His parents. Kyle's parents. Heston's father. The parents of a lycanthrope attack victim named Justin Butera. The idea of Wanda training the parents to be hunters made Chad nervous, but Cooper had a point. If there were no lycanthropes to hunt, the issue would be moot. "Why is your aunt doing this? I know she wants to make me and my friends nervous because she feels like we betrayed her, but what's her end game?"

"She feels like you betrayed her because you did. There were four lycanthropes in the area before you stumbled your way into becoming one. You told her you wanted to help get rid of the lycanthropes but then turned around and created six more. Which brings us to her 'end game.' She wants to kill all lycanthropes, maybe even her sister—my mother. Thanks to you, there are too many for me and her to handle, so she's training some recruits of her own. Yes, she chose your parents and your friends' parents as a form of psychological warfare."

"Well, that's wasted effort because my friends and I have no intention of using our abilities."

"Really, Chad? Isn't that why you're here right now? To figure out how to exploit your abilities like your friends?"

"What do you mean?"

"Oh, please. It's so obvious that your friends are using their lycanthropy to help themselves through life. The ferret joined the lacrosse team, the pheasant is talking to a girl, and the ox has been losing weight."

A weird steam hissed through his bones, formed by the ice of fear that she knew so much about his friends, then slammed into a wall of fire raging from her referring to them as the animals they turned into. "How . . . how do you know this?"

"The college's campus is large enough to blend in with ease."

School. She's hanging around the school. The tingle of relief tickled his chest—she didn't say anything about the barn. She knew where it was, but it didn't seem like she had been spying on them there. It was still his sanctuary. "You're watching us? Are you watching the jocks, too? They've been using their abilities more than we have. Out in the open."

"I am and they haven't."

"What do you mean? The football team went undefeated all season and easily won the championship."

Natalia shrugged a shoulder. "So? They trained hard and reaped the rewards. It's much less suspicious than a group of losers suddenly becoming winners."

Chad's glass heart shattered from the rocks she hurled at it. And Natalia knew it, her angry squint giving way to wide-eyed surprise, her features going from battle-hard to sympathy-soft. "Chad, I'm sorry. I didn't—"

He cut her off by standing, slapping a twenty on the bar top, and leaving. He couldn't bring himself to look at her or the tears would come. Every time they interacted, Chad did his best to remind himself that she had a far different upbringing than he did. Even though he spent most of his life bullied, he still had the luxury of a middle-class, suburban upbringing. She had spent her life constantly on the move, learning about the world through the myopic vision of her aunt while they hunted her lycanthrope mother and deadly associates. He tried to give her as much leeway as possible, accepting the occasional cut from her sharp edges. He thought there was a bond forming, born from loneliness and uncertainty. But she went too far. She still saw him as a loser. And the jocks as winners.

Women could be so frustrating! Women could be . . . no. Chad stopped himself. He had no right to think these thoughts because he didn't know them to be true. He had no idea because he had no relationships with women. Sure, there were plenty of female classmates he associated with, but there were no relationships beyond studying together. He had never even been on a date. Ever. This was what he wanted to change. This was what his friends realized. Now that they no longer had a bully issue, they were free to explore what life had to offer them. They weren't doing what they were doing because they matched up with their abilities; they were doing what they wanted and using their abilities to help them. Well, Chad wanted to explore the world of dating. He doubted that his inner animal would be able to help, but that was okay. He was perfectly content never to call upon his inner rabbit ever again.

CHAPTER 8

Chad took a massive pull from the straw of his sixty-four-ounce root beer. Flat, syrupy, and warm, even though ice took up more than fifty percent of the volume within the Styrofoam container. He suddenly craved a real beer.

Oh, God, am I an alcoholic already? Logic dictated he wasn't, but he couldn't stop his brain from showing him pictures of the old man sitting alone at the back of Clinty's. Chad wondered if that old guy might make a good wingman, because his brain now told him that the only place he'd ever meet a woman was at a dive bar.

Sitting at a table in the mall food court, Chad shook his head hard enough to dislodge those thoughts. It wasn't going to be easy meeting women, especially at the mall. He knew that he was at an awkward age—the term "awkward" being subjective since he had yet to feel *not* awkward at any point in his life—where he was too old to look for love at a retail conglomerate, yet not old enough for the more traditional path of the bar scene. His best bet was campus and classroom, but on a cold Friday evening, his only real choice right now was the mall. Plus, he had nothing better to do since Cooper had practice, Kyle had a date, and Heston was tied up with his dad again. He missed those guys and would love it if they were here to help.

Would having them around help? Their presence would be calming, but would there be a new pressure to perform with three sets of eyes watching him? Maybe they could be like his pit crew and give him pointers after returning to the table rejected and dejected. Or they could participate with him? Maybe do a "get shot down" bet? They'd all try to get shot down by as many women as possible. Whoever got a date first would have to buy the guy who got shot down the most a prize, something like exclusive downloadable content for *The World of Glark*. It'd be a great idea, if not for the weirdness of the person getting the date being considered the loser. Of course, the concept of the bet wasn't necessarily to get a date but to get over the nerves and shyness of doing something so foreign, like talking to women. Cooper would be all for it, maybe Heston, too. But Kyle? He was even shyer than Chad. Plus, he had every DLC available for *The World of Glark*. Double plus, he was actually on a date right now without the need for any kind of contrived bet. Kyle had a potential girlfriend before Chad. Rubbing his eyes, he couldn't stop his brain from telling him his only choice of wingman was the old crazy man from Clinty's.

"Oh, that is some serious existential crisis you got going on right there."

A voice across the table. A woman's voice. One he hadn't heard for months. Kat.

Chad had to stop himself from turning into a rabbit and bolting out of the food court. Kat was many things. Natalia's mother. Wanda's sister. The one who had turned Chad into a lycanthrope. Leader of the Ink Stains. The sexiest woman he had ever interacted with. Right now, on the top of the list, though, she was a betrayer.

Hunter had been the leader of the Ink Stains and promised Chad a way to stop his bully problem. Due to a series of unfortunate consequences stemming from incalculable variables, Chad and his friends became lycanthropes and his bully problem worsened. Then Kat gave Chad an opportunity to fix it all—kill Hunter. She lied.

Yes, his bully problem subsided, and his confidence increased, but the death of Hunter gave her more power while simultaneously tethering all of the area lycanthropes to the triple goddess, The Morrigan. Chad hadn't seen Kat since he killed Hunter. He audibly gulped and then spoke slowly, enunciating his words so his voice didn't crack or squeak. "What do you want?"

Kat played with his drink cup, spinning and tilting it from side to side. "Maybe I just stopped by to talk. It's been a while."

Her presence, her voice, turned his insides into balloon animals; the look of hunger in her eyes showed Chad that she'd gleefully pop them all. But not without reason. If she were here, eyeing him up as if he were the only piece of meat in a tofu store, then she wanted something more than conversation. "Maybe it hasn't been long enough."

"You don't mean that," she purred as she picked up his drink. Her tongue slid between the two silver hoops through her bottom lip like a welcome mat, an invitation only for Chad. She gently placed the tip of the straw on her tongue and slowly wrapped her lips around it. She took a sip and . . . her right eye involuntarily closed, and her nose crinkled. "Oh, God, this is awful."

"I agree. I think a major machine malfunction is throwing off the water to syrup ratio."

Kat chuckled, but Chad wasn't sure if it was real or part of her act. He so rarely knew the difference. She placed the drink container back on the table and slid it away from both of them. "Next time you're at Clinty's, I'll buy you a real drink."

"Okay. Sounds— Wait . . . how do you know I've been to Clinty's?"

That wicked smile again, the one that makes him sweat from both fear and arousal. "Oh, Chad. Haven't you ever noticed the stuffed crow on one of the shelves behind the bar?"

Various knick-knacks of esoteric meaning and little signs with pithy statements about the bartender's authority or the magic of alcohol decorated the wall behind the bar, accented by polaroids of the staff and customers over the years. Kat was right—on the top shelf was a taxidermized crow. He never thought about it until now. "The crow. The symbol of The Morrigan. The symbol that unites us all."

"Settle down, Lord of the Rings. We may all have her marking, but we're hardly united."

The marking of The Morrigan—a crow tattoo the lycanthropes had been branded with by the goddess herself. They all had one. Chad's was on his shoulder, meaning he had to make sure he wore a shirt around his parents. His dad would probably approve, though, viewing a tattoo as the manliest thing about Chad. Kyle had a similar need to constantly wear a shirt around his parents as his tattoo was on his chest over his heart. It didn't matter that he was legally an adult; his parents were so overprotective that they would send him to a mental hospital because a tattoo was out of character for their fragile son. Heston's was on his back between his shoulder blades, and he didn't care who knew about it. Uncomfortable about his weight, he was never without a shirt anyway. Cooper's tattoo was on his ass, and Chad still hadn't found anything funnier than that. Kat's was on her thigh, close to her hip. Chad knew this because he had seen her naked. Twice. She had a lot of tattoos, including a set of cat paws padding along her hip and pelvis and lower still. Those were

Chad's favorite. "We also have her blood within us, the whole reason we're lycanthropes."

Kat's expression hardened, her face sharp and stern. "Chad, don't make this any weirder than it has to be."

If he knew how to make things not weird, he'd do it all the time. "Make what weirder? I don't even know what we're talking about."

Kat closed her eyes and pinched the bridge of her nose. When she reopened her eyes, she leaned forward. "Okay, I didn't tell you why I'm here yet. Fair enough. I have information. There is another group of lycanthropes on their way to The Bends."

This was major intel! So big that Chad wondered what the catch was. There had to be a catch. *Play it cool*, he reminded himself so he wouldn't barf out the hundred questions he had all at once. He started with an important one. "From where?"

"A town called Mills Hook. You ever hear of the place?"

"Mills Hook? Yeah. That's like a hundred miles down the river. Why would they come here? There are bigger cities closer than The Bends."

"I don't know, Chad. Maybe this trio of towns is their Goldilocks expectation—not too big, not too small. Has plenty of resources. Not too far from a major highway and is a great pit stop for travelers and truckers. Lots of industry and retail, even has an active mine nearby, yet is surrounded by farms and forests and a goodly sized river. And don't forget about the college you attend, which is about ten thousand students, right? Hell, that's why Hunter chose this place as our hunting grounds five years ago."

There was more to this. There had to be. "How do you know this?"

"I have my sources."

"The newest Ink Stain?" Chad regretted letting her know he had information about her pack of lycanthropes, but he couldn't stop the words from flying out of his mouth.

Kat's smile changed, a flimsy disguise trying to hide her anger. "How do you know about the newest members?"

"I have my sources."

A throaty growl made its way to Chad, activating his every primal instinct, warning him that trouble was near. But he didn't budge. They locked eyes in a battle of wills, and Chad refused to turn away, even when her eyes went yellow with sickle-shaped pupils. Chad won! Though, she kept her eyes cat-like.

"You're correct. One of my new members is from Mills Hook. His name is Kicks, and his true form is an alligator."

Chad wanted to ask about the other member, but he said too much already. He just needed to listen and ask smart questions. "Alligator sounds impressive."

"It is, but not enough to stop a whole pack of lycanthropes by himself. They came into his hunting grounds of Mills Hook and attacked him, drove him out."

"So, what kinds of animals are in this pack?"

"Don't know. Kicks was ambushed and got the shit beat out of him. He said it was over in mere seconds."

"Why are you telling me this?"

Kat snorted and shook her head, incredulous by Chad's distrust. "Because there is an outside force coming to challenge us for our territory. We don't know how many of them there are, and we don't know when they're arriving. We need to prepare. And we may need to consider working together."

After every one of her statements, Chad developed ten questions. Wanda shattered his chances of asking any of them when she appeared out of nowhere and joined them at the table. "I knew it would only be a matter of time before that happened."

The air chilled so quickly that Chad expected to see snow falling from above the table. Fear gut-punched him for the second time within minutes, hard enough to cause nausea. He knew Kat was a user, someone who used her abundance of sexuality to manipulate. Whatever she offered had a price. Wanda? He had no idea what she was up to, other than an overt desire to kill lycanthropes. Worse, she had direct influence over his parents, so he wanted to make sure she didn't make assumptions that could impact him negatively. He stammered, "We're not working together. We haven't spoken in months, let alone worked together. We're definitely not working together."

Neither woman acknowledged his words. He wondered if they even remembered he was still at the table with them.

"It's been a while, sister," Kat said, her words like the water of a freezing lake. "How's my daughter?"

"Doing well," Wanda replied through her smirk. "Becoming very adept at a crossbow. If you're not careful, you may find out how good of a hunter she's becoming."

"No need to be a bitch."

"No? I think having a sister who runs around eating people gives me every right to be a bitch."

"It's so much more than that, Wanda, but you're too closed-minded to listen to me, so . . ." Kat stood and gestured for Chad to join her. "Come on, Chad. We can finish our conversation elsewhere."

Chad pushed his chair out, but Wanda grabbed his hand, and he froze. "Not so fast, Chad," Wanda hissed. "We have a conversation of our own to have."

Only capable of moving his eyes, he looked from one sister to the other. Kat was frozen in time at mid-twenties while Wanda continued her march through the years, at least fifty of them, but there were enough similarities to assume they were related. The younger woman glared at him, burning the words, *come with me, now*, into his mind while the older woman tightened her grip, threatening to crack bones. The moment stretched into eternity. Pain crawled from his hand to his wrist and farther up his arm. He couldn't move. For the second time today, Kat acquiesced. With a final squint, a wordless warning to Chad not to tell Wanda anything, Kat turned and walked away.

Now alone with Wanda, Chad's chest tightened, even after she released his hand. "So, Chad," she started as she leaned back and got comfortable in her chair, "Care to tell me what you and my sister were talking about?"

This was a nightmare. All Chad wanted to do today was hang out at the mall and pretend he had enough courage to introduce himself to a random woman. Instead, he found himself not only in the middle of someone else's family drama but needing to choose sides in a war. Either stay true to his humanity or swear fealty to his animal side. One woman betrayed him while he betrayed the other. Kat lied and manipulated, but she at least acknowledged him. The warning of a new lycanthrope pack coming to the area was just the tip of the iceberg, but at least she warned him. Wanda wanted to kill him, and she had power over his parents and most of his friends' parents. He doubted that would change if he told her what she wanted to know, so he said, "I do not."

Wanda crossed her arms and scowled. "You know everything she says is a lie, right? If you follow her lead, you'll be following her straight to Hell. That's if she doesn't eat you first."

Chad had faced down and killed a werewolf. He had to remind himself of this, but he kept his mouth shut. Nothing good could come from opening it, no matter how badly his eyes wanted to water from Wanda's fiery gaze. Just like her sister, though, she was fed up with Chad.

Wanda rolled her neck, vertebrae cracking like dry sticks, and stood. Her smile returned and this made Chad uneasy. "It just occurred to me that I haven't taken my new students on their first hunt yet. Maybe it's time to do that? After all, I believe they're ready to catch and kill their first lycanthrope."

After Wanda left, Chad gently placed his head on the table and mumbled, "Fuck."

CHAPTER 9

Heston watched his brother as nonchalantly as possible. The convenience store was small, the gas pumps and lottery tickets the most popular items, so when someone loitered outside, it wouldn't go unnoticed for too long. A quick stop like this beside a ten-room no-tell motel was the type of place where drug deals went down. Heston doubted anyone would ever mistake him for a drug dealer, and if he wanted any booze or pot, he'd just go to the barn and get some from Tyler, but he'd rather not draw attention or be dubbed a "suspicious character."

Leaning against the back corner of the cinderblock store, Heston placed his rucksack on the ground and slurped away at the root-beer-flavored slushie in the sixty-four-ounce cup. After classes he decided to follow his brother, which sometimes meant unleashing the beast within, so he wanted to make sure he had a change of clothes in reserve. Oxen weren't known for their speed, but they were certainly faster than people on foot. Chuck had tooled around town, meeting up with shady people, only one being a pot dealer for a quick score. Now dusk, Chuck was leaning against his car and smoking a cigarette in the motel parking lot. He didn't even flinch when the "VACANCY" neon light popped on, the "N" flickering.

Heston looked around to make sure no one threatened his position. Two cars at the pumps, the owner of one wrapping up the transaction. He was a younger man, overweight. Heston didn't pay him much attention until he noticed the young man's skin glistened. The snow hadn't melted one bit today, yet he was sweating. Wide-eyed, he focused more on the hotel than his transaction. Was he looking at Chuck?

Yes. Yes, he was. After paying for his gas, he got back in his car, drove the hundred feet across the shared gravel parking lot, and stopped about five parking spaces away from Chuck's car. He exited his car but left it running with the door open. Shaking like a fawn learning how to walk, he approached Chuck.

Heston thought this guy looked a lot like him, if not for the beard and thick hair, and then almost chuckled at the notion that Chuck had a "type" he liked to bully. In usual Chuck fashion, he didn't move from his car, making this scared individual come to him. Heston couldn't hear them from here, so he decided to move closer.

Hoping no one would notice his rucksack, Heston left it on the ground and crossed the parking lot to the nearest trash can. He tossed the empty container and checked over his shoulder one more time before he kept walking. Their voices were muffled; he was still too far away. He tried to be as quiet as possible, but the loose gravel sounded like collapsing mountains with every step. The edge of the motel was so close, if he could just get to the wall, but he swore each footstep was getting louder. The meeting wasn't going well, and Heston stopped moving, ready to run behind the motel.

The bearded kid handed over a regular white envelope and waited while Chuck looked in it. The kid's voice was shaky, bordering on squeaky, but Heston heard the word, "Money."

Chuck laughed as he crossed his arms and leaned back against his car. He mumbled something and the kid's eyes widened. He said "no" about a dozen times as he backed away. Chuck barked an order, something like, "Do it!" The kid yelled "No" one more time and ran to his car.

His half-brother was the reason Heston knew what "hubris" meant. Because Chuck was too cocky, the kid was able to get in the car, slam the door, and pull out of the parking lot before Chuck could catch him. All Heston's brother could do was yell, "Get back here!"

Heston was happy the young man had escaped. He wasn't happy that his escape caused Chuck to move away from his car.

"Fucking fuck!" Chuck yelled as he turned back toward his car, Heston now in his line of sight. "Who's there?"

Twilight had been quick to give way to night, and the lighting at this section of the motel was poor. Heston was confident Chuck didn't recognize him, and he ran to the back of the motel. A lone streetlight sprouted from the roof of the motel, like the antennae of an angler fish. It was just bright enough to show the edge of the sprawling field behind the hotel.

"Whoever you are, you better stop and tell me what you saw!" Typical Chuck logic, thinking there were people in the world stupid enough to follow his instruction. But he was chasing, and Heston couldn't outrun him. As soon as he got into the chest-high weeds of the field, he took his shirt off, kicked off his shoes, and dropped his pants. He transformed into full ox mode just in time.

Chuck rounded the corner and stopped. "Where the fuck did you go, asshole?"

Again, Chuck was stupid enough to think someone would answer him. He was also dumb enough to think an ox was a cow. He walked along the perimeter of the field, looking for anyone hiding within the grasses. No luck. Just a cow. "Moooooo!"

Chuck moved along the back of the motel, looking into the darkened field, still shouting, "Come on out, asshole! I know you're in there somewhere!"

Even though Heston's heart was bovine, it still thudded hard enough to rattle his bones from the fear that Chuck's voice caused. The sadness. The frustration. The *anger*. Heston didn't realize he was running toward Chuck until a tall weed smacked his face. He was *running* toward Chuck. He thought about stopping or turning to flee, but . . . he didn't *want* to. He ran faster. Faster! When Chuck turned around, Heston was no longer in his pure oxen form, rather a minotaur sprinting upright on two cloven feet, human arms churning. Head still in the shape of an ox, he bellowed and leaped into the air.

Chuck swore and jumped backward, falling just as Heston landed. Backlit by the flickering streetlight, Heston flexed his massive chest muscles and bellowed again, spraying spittle all over Chuck as he crab-crawled away. Whimpering, Chuck got to his feet and ran back around the motel. In less than a minute, his car started, and he tore out of the parking lot, flinging gravel in a fan.

Thick streams pluming from his mouth and nostrils, Heston returned to his human form and fetched his clothes. As he walked back to the convenience store to collect his rucksack, he reviewed what just happened. He felt like a stranger to himself, the act of standing up to his brother so foreign, the look of fear on Chuck's face so alien.

Heston liked it.

——— ✦ ———

Cooper watched Sanders. He watched how he ran when he had the ball, how his eyes locked onto the net, how he planted his foot and flexed his arms right before he took the shot. Cooper blocked the shot. Sanders swore while a few onlookers clapped or called out, "Nice stop." Sanders telegraphed his intentions so badly that Cooper felt confident he would have prevented the goal even without his enhanced speed.

The whistle blew and Coach barked, "All right, men! Good practice. We're gonna take a week off, so make sure you come back better than you are now."

"Damn, you're good!" Bryce said as he extended his gloved hand for a fist bump. A tiny sense of infidelity skittered through Cooper as he obliged, bumping fists with someone other than Heston. And to do so with no panache almost sickened him. But uncreative forms of interactive celebration came with the territory of being the team's star goalie, on his way to becoming star player. Of course, there was only one other goalie on the team—Bryce. And he had displayed zero complaints about being the backup.

"Many thanks. My skill is the product of a steady diet of Ambrosia and Pan Galactic Gargle Blaster."

"Ambrosia?" Tuck asked as he and Brandon approached. "Isn't that the fruit salad made with whipped cream and coconut chips?"

Brandon countered with, "Naah! Ain't it the one with mayonnaise and nuts and grapes?"

Tuck and Brandon were both sophomores and gravitated toward the younger players. Some of the older players hadn't warmed up to Cooper yet, and they usually followed Sanders, even though they ribbed him about never being able to score when Cooper was tending the net.

Cooper chuckled and said, "I hate to be the bearer of bad news, Brandon, but Tuck is correct. You're thinking of Waldorf."

"Isn't he one of those old muppets in the balcony who make fun of the other muppets?" Brandon asked.

"Yeah. Who do you think they named the salad after?" Tuck countered.

To keep from making a sarcastic and deprecating comment, Cooper bit his tongue so hard that a trickle of blood slid over his tastebuds. He hadn't been on the team long enough to dole out good-natured ribbing, especially since the statement he wished to unleash could be construed as insulting. He truly wanted to be a part of a team, to expand his horizons even if it meant doing so with individuals with such limited horizons. These conversations were nothing like those he had with Chad, Heston, and Kyle. Cooper missed those guys and looked forward to their next game night.

"Hey! New guy!" Sanders called to Cooper as he stormed closer. "We need words!"

Again, so many snarky, multisyllabic comments formed within Cooper's mind, but the gatekeeper of self-awareness kept them at bay. "Yes?"

Nostrils flaring, Sanders snarled, "You need to quit with the stupid nickname you came up for me. I'm getting real fucking sick of hearing it."

Oh-For. That was what the other guys on the team had started calling him because he had gone "O for thirty, O for fifty, O for a hundred" when shooting against Cooper. If Cooper had his druthers, he would have chosen a much more pointed epithet like "Aryan Wet Dream," but "Oh-For" worked just as well. "Sorry, Sanders, but I'm not the origin point of the nickname of concern."

"Don't give me that shit. I know you got a big fucking mouth, and you love to run it."

"My proclivities toward loquaciousness are mutually exclusive to what others say about you behind your back."

"That bullshit right there makes me think you're the one who came up with it and spread it around. I'm telling you to stop it." Sanders punctuated his statement with a poke to Cooper's chest.

Cooper tried. He should have searched for ways to de-escalate the tense situation, but it was Sanders's blue eyes. The windows to his soul sparkled with entitlement, a lifetime of getting his way with little to no effort. Handsome, financially well-off, naturally talented. A bully. After taking control of his lycanthropy, Cooper had decided never to be bullied again. "Well, if you want everyone to stop calling you Oh-For, then maybe you should score on me."

Sanders answered with a shove and a, "Fuck you!"

Thanks to his abilities, Cooper didn't fall; he merely took a step back. Thanks to his training from Tyler, Cooper avoided another shove by spinning out of Sanders's way. With another spin, he was behind Sanders. A few quick steps with a sprinkle of anticipation and Cooper remained behind Sanders no matter which way or how fast he turned.

Most of the team had gone to the locker room, but the dozen that stayed watched in slack-jawed silence as Cooper twirled and shuffled his way out of Sanders's grasp. Cooper held his stick by the neck, the bottom pointed at the ground, until he decided it was time to end this. A simple twist of his wrist and the end of the stick caught Sanders's ankles, sending him to the ground.

Cooper should have known that would not end Sanders's anger. Instead, it added fuel to the fire. Jumping back to his feet, Sanders went after Cooper again, this time with fists swinging.

As with the last round, Cooper dodged Sanders's attacks with ease. As effortless as stepping over a small puddle, Cooper sidestepped Sanders while angling the bottom of his stick to connect with his feet. Sanders hit the ground once more.

There was no third attack. The spectators became participants, four of them stopping Sanders when he got to his feet, the other eight gathering around Cooper. Even though he had never been a part of a team before, Cooper recognized the conflicted feelings of the others. They had known Sanders for two or three years, yet he was very clearly in the wrong. This time, Cooper opted to say his scathing words inside the privacy of his own mind, allowing the quartet of teammates to drag Sanders away, still red-faced and fuming.

Once Sanders had been escorted into the locker room, the players surrounding Cooper started to clap his back and swat his shoulder while showering him with adulation like, "Those moves were sick," and, "That was Matrix level shit."

Cooper liked it.

Kyle watched Janey. He was fascinated by her eating habits.

They had met up at the Student Union Center after class, as had been determined the night before. She was all smiles, and Kyle smiled too, unable to stop himself from matching her level of intensity.

"Hi!" she squeaked, her pitch so high Kyle had only heard what sounded like a vowel and assumed she had greeted him with, "hi!" Feeling safe with his educated guess, he said, "Hi!"

"Hi! I'm happy you showed up."

"Hi! I'm happy you're here."

She laughed. There was a nervousness to it. Kyle recognized it because his laugh was just as anxiety-ridden. Her cheeks were as red as his felt. Wringing her hands together, she asked, "How were your classes?"

"Good. How were yours?"

"Good, too. Mine were good. Good classes."

"Good." Kyle had a lot of fears, so many that he was self-aware that they were disallowing him to lead his life to the fullest. Fear of awkward silence with a girl was high on the extensive list, so he asked, "So . . . now what?"

Bouncing on the balls of her feet, Janey answered, "A date!"

"A . . . date?"

"Yeah! What people our parents' ages talk about, even though kids our age don't really do that until we reach some weird age between our ages and our parents' ages. It'll be fun!"

A date! Kyle had expected to spend an hour or so just talking about school and the esports team and then head back home or to the barn to ask Tyler for advice. But a date? He was so unprepared for any of that! "Umm, okay! That sounds great."

They decided on a movie, the new sci-fi thriller about an addictive street drug that allowed people to time travel by simply popping a pill. It was both thought-provoking and mind-bending. By the time Kyle realized he needed to pay attention to understand what was happening on screen, the movie was half over. He had spent the first half wondering if he was truly on a date or if he was dreaming this while in a coma, or this was an elaborate ruse and she was a robot designed to win his affections only to crush them later. He had come up with a dozen other scenarios that would lead to his demise or heartbreak until he caught a whiff of her shampoo. Something delectable and fruity. He spent well over twenty minutes with his eyes crossed, attempting to pinpoint the specific fragrance elements.

Kyle wished he had paid more attention to the movie, because now he sat with her at Rocket Lizard Pizza, attempting to uphold his end of the conversation regarding the movie while simultaneously cursing himself for not picking a restaurant better than a local pizza shop with statues of anthropomorphic reptiles catering to a family atmosphere. After the movie, Janey asked him which restaurant was his favorite, and in a moment of mind-blanking panic, he blurted out this place. She seemed to be enjoying herself, though, smiling as she used a fork and knife on her pizza, slicing it into one-inch squares. This fascinated him.

"Sorry. I'm being weird," she said when she noticed him watching her.

"It's awesome that you like such precision. It's not weird at all. Certainly not as weird as the movie."

"I know, right? It took my brain right out of my head, turned it a hundred and eighty degrees, and then put it back."

Kyle chuckled as she pantomimed her statement. "I'm not sure I believe in time travel, though."

Janey shrugged as she went back to eating her perfectly squared bites of pizza. "Why not? It's mathematically possible."

"You're a math major. You want to solve everything with math."

"That's because math is the language of God."

"Whoa. Wait . . . what?"

"Math. God. All but the same thing. No matter your religion, you're told that God is everything. Well, the same goes for math."

"Math is everything?"

Janey grinned at him over her soda. "Ev. Er. Ree. Thing. Ever. Math was used to construct this building. Math was used to make this pizza. You're seeing me and hearing me because of different wavelengths of light and sound, measured with math, because your brain has been mathed to translate these waves into useful information. We're nothing more than big bags of chemicals that move around because of chemical equations. Every thought, feeling, and memory you have, have had, will ever have, is a chemical equation. Equation equals math. Every atom in the entire universe follows a set of rules, all of them can be explained with math. God is everywhere. So is math."

"Wow. So, you're saying math determines everything about us, from who we are to how we think to how we look?"

"I wouldn't say determines. But it's the building block of everything. It's mathematically impossible to build a wall too high. It's mathematically probable that we'll look similar to our parents."

"Interesting. So, you're saying you're so pretty because of math."

Like drops of red dye in water, Janey's blush started at her cheeks and radiated outward. She dropped her silverware, covered her mouth with her hands, and looked away. *Oh no*! Kyle yelled at himself, fending off the all too familiar sting forming behind his eyes. He had said too much! He rarely felt comfortable in social situations, because he didn't have a firm grasp on the accepted and unspoken boundaries constructed around conversation. He let his guard down and became too aggressive. Now he offended her.

Kyle's heart melted when Janey turned back to face him. He didn't know how it was possible, but her smile was even wider and more beaming than before. Eyes glossed with the start of tears, she said, "Kyle, that was the sweetest thing anyone has ever said to me."

"No one ever told you you were pretty before?"

"No. And more than that, you understood what I was saying about math. You *listened* to me."

It was Kyle's turn to blush. He didn't know what to say, so he went back to his pizza. Janey did as well, glancing between her food and Kyle, still smiling with pink cheeks. Suddenly, the sounds of laser guns emitted from the table. Kyle almost ducked, but it was Janey's phone, her text notification.

"You should get that," Kyle said.

Janey looked nervous. "Are you sure?"

Even if it were something that ended the date, it would still end on a high note. "Absolutely. I'd feel bad if it were an emergency and I kept you from it."

"Thank you." Janey picked up her phone, and her eyes widened as she covered her mouth again. "Oh, God."

Shit! It was an emergency! "What happened?"

"It's Declan. His roommate just texted me that he got hit by a car. He's alive, but they're taking him to a hospital."

"Oh, wow."

"I need to call his mom. And then my mom. And then his sister."

"You know his mom and sister?"

"Declan and I are cousins."

A slight tremor asserted itself in her left hand as she looked around the restaurant. Kyle reached out and placed his hand on hers. The trembling stopped. "I'll tell you what. How about you go outside and start making calls and I'll take care of paying. The night may not have ended as we would have liked, but it was . . . I think it was a good first date."

Janey closed her eyes and took a deep, cleansing breath. After a few more, she stood. Her smile wasn't as big, but it let Kyle know he said the right thing. "You're the best." Janey leaned over, kissed Kyle on his lips, and then headed toward the exit.

Warm. Soft. More than just a simple peck. His first kiss.

Kyle liked it.

CHAPTER 10

"It all comes down to this," Kyle said. "Your quest is at an end. Hours of adventure, fighting, bartering, side quests, exploring, victories, and loss will now conclude in the Cavern of Eternal Bliss. Your party has performed admirably, especially against the cavern's guardian, the Frog of Forgotten Foes. He used his Croak of Confusion on your party members, yet you bravely fought him, taking him down to his last hit point while sustaining massive damage from the slices of his Razor Tongue. He hit you one last time for one d20 worth of damage. You have a mere two hit points left. How do you feel?"

Cooper stood from the gaming table in Chad's basement and rolled his twenty-sided die between his palms. He had it custom-made with a middle finger. "I, Floridian Musk, believe we shall be dining on *cuisses de grenouille* while rolling around unclothed in the massive stash of gold coins that shall be our just reward after I absorb his life-threatening blow."

He handed the die to Kyle, the Dungeon Master. With only two hit points left, the only way to survive would be for Kyle to roll the finger. Kyle flicked his wrist. The die bounced once and started to spin. Cooper leaned over and whispered to the die, "Come on, you know how glorious this victory would be. Only you can make it happen."

The die slowed, wobbled, and then stopped.

The finger.

Cooper, Kyle, and Chad laughed. Heston smiled. Cooper turned to him, ready to exact an epic high-five routine, but Heston didn't move. "Sorry, dude. I'm just not in the mood."

Something was wrong. When everyone had arrived this morning, Heston mentioned he didn't want to be the DM, and he was *always* the DM. He participated in the quest but lacked vigor. And now he didn't want to celebrate a high-five with Cooper? These two once had a high-five routine that involved a cartwheel, a donkey kick, and a spatula.

Cooper sat down and asked, "Hey, what's going on. You know this is part fantasy adventure, part therapy. Let's have it."

Heston used his index finger to flip a six-sided dice along the tabletop, one side at a time. "It's Chuck."

The temperature of the room dropped ten degrees. Kyle looked concerned and the question formed in Chad's mouth, but Cooper asked it. "Did he beat on you again?"

"No. But I almost beat on him. It was about a week ago, and it's been eating at me, because . . . I did it . . . as . . . my other self."

Heston's words blew the air out of the room. Chad couldn't inhale. It had been a busy week at school for everyone, always a ton of homework and projects during the beginning of the semester, so no one shared much more than "getting slammed." Barn time was all but nonexistent. Today's gameday was a welcome respite.

Cooper followed up with, "Does Chuck know . . . who you are?"

"No. He didn't see that it was me, but I came at him in my minotaur form."

Everyone breathed an uneasy sigh of relief. Part of their secret was safe and the exposed part was unbelievable. Cooper was still the only one capable of speech. "So, what happened?"

"Chuck has been hanging around campus lately. I suspected he was shaking down a few students. I saw him and followed him around. He met with someone, and they made an exchange of some kind, but he wanted more. The guy ran. I couldn't stand it, couldn't take the idea of Chuck invading my world, bullying other people."

Cooper nodded. "Okay. Yeah, I think it's obvious you were justified in attempting to mete out a form of justice. Obviously, it's fortuitous that he didn't see the minotaur was you. And I'm beyond sure that it was satisfying on many different levels for you to scare him."

Heston smirked. "Yeah, it was."

Cooper smiled and patted Heston's shoulder. "Nice."

Kyle opened his mouth to say something, but a pew-pew laser gun noise came from his phone. This struck Chad as odd. He didn't remember that sound being Kyle's text notification. On the other hand, he really hadn't heard his notification too often since the four people at the table were usually the only four who sent texts to each other.

Kyle checked his phone and his eyebrows rounded to a look of concern.

"Is that Janey? Everything okay?" Chad asked.

"Yeah. No. Well, better, I guess."

"Trouble in paradise?"

"No. Well, I don't think so. I mean, we haven't been able to get together as much as I'd like, but she's been pretty busy with her family. It's been pretty crazy since her cousin got hit by a car last week. But she texted me to say that Declan just came out of his coma. She's going to see him in the hospital tomorrow and asked me to join her."

Cooper made a face akin to biting a lemon peel. "Oooooh, not good."

"Why not?"

"Heading to a hospital to visit a relative coming out of a coma? Not very romantic. It sounds like she might be planting a flag in the Friend Zone."

"But . . . but we kiss each time we see each other."

"Are they long, passionate kisses?"

"No. But they're on the lips."

Heston rebutted Cooper. "Friends don't kiss friends on the lips."

Kyle turned to Chad and asked, "What do you think?"

Seriously? The one person who was the least qualified, as evidenced by spending his evenings at the mall trying to meet women, was now the ultimate voice in the matters of romance? However, a close friend asked for his opinion, and he wanted to help. "I think it's a good sign. She's turning to you as someone to lean on and asking you to be a part of her life."

Kyle smiled; what Chad had hoped for. If nothing else, his friend was happy for the moment. Kyle tapped away at his phone and said, "Yeah, you're right. It's weird, but you're right."

"Well, there has certainly been a lot of weird stuff happening."

Chad didn't mean anything by that comment, just a few words of support and solidarity. Everyone else read something more into it, especially Cooper. Flat-browed and thin-lipped, he said, "Go ahead, Chad. You may as well tell us, because it's obvious you wanted to ever since we got here."

"What?" Chad was genuinely surprised.

"That's what we're waiting for you to tell us."

"How . . . how did you know?"

"You're very easy to read."

"Like a two-page book," Kyle said.

"On audio," Heston added.

"You're such an easy book to read that the movie version needs to add content to make it more challenging," Cooper finished. "So, go ahead. What's the big, weird thing that happened in the world of lycanthropy that you view as a danger to all of us?"

Chad sighed. His quest for life transcendence had been a week old and it was taxing. He thought of defensive statements like "I didn't ask for this" or "I wasn't looking for trouble; it found me," but that was the old Chad. New Chad needed to think in new ways to become a new person. Instead, he just stuck with the unembellished facts. "I was at the mall last Friday and was approached by Kat. She told me a group of lycanthropes is coming this way from Mills Hook."

Cooper rolled his eyes and threw himself into a slouch in his chair. "I hardly need a scrying spell to see where this is going. Let me guess, she wants the four of us to risk our lives and go kill them while she and Dylan sit back and do nothing."

"No. She didn't ask us to do anything."

"Really?"

"Well, she didn't have a chance. Wanda showed up. She and Kat argued, then Kat left."

"So, now you're getting yourself pulled into the middle of family drama. Awesome sauce. I can only imagine how Natalia fits into all of this."

"I haven't seen her in weeks," Chad lied.

"How does Kat know about the lycanthrope pack?" Heston asked.

"The Ink Stains got two new members, and one of them came from Mills Hook."

Heston addressed Kyle and Cooper. "This sounds like it might be a thing."

"I truly believe this is a non-issue." Cooper sat back up and fiddled with the twenty-sided die, absently spinning it on the table. "Kat is posturing to piss off her sister and using her feminine wiles to manipulate our well-intentioned friend. The source of information regarding the supposed pack coming our way is highly suspect. There are at least two bigger cities closer to Mills Hook, so why come to The Bends? How many in the pack? What kind of animals are in the pack?"

Kyle jumped in before anyone else could speak. "It's not often I agree with Cooper, but there seem to be a lot of unknown variables."

Heston shrugged and turned back to Chad. "Do *you* think it's something to worry about?"

Yes! Very much so! We need to come up with different scenarios and plan and . . . and this is not the way New Chad should think. It was obvious Cooper and Kyle wanted to dismiss the information as immaterial so they didn't have to disrupt the momentum they were gaining in their new lives. Wasn't that what Chad was looking for? A new life with new motivations so he didn't have to keep rehashing the same concerns, hitting the same roadblocks? "Nope. I may have been concerned when I got here, but you guys make a lot of sense. No use getting upset over hypotheticals, right?"

Cooper became all smiles once again. "Excellent! So, thanks to my amazingness, I'll kill this troll, resurrect you guys, and then we'll clean out this cave."

Footsteps coming down the stairs gave everyone pause. Chad's father. "Hey, guys. How's it going?"

"Good," all four replied in unison.

The basement was divided in half with a small rec room to the left of the stairs and a workshop to the right. The rec room was nowhere near as game-centric as the one in Kyle's parents' basement, but there was a couch, two bookshelves of gaming manuals, and a table solid enough to support any game played upon it. Chad's father went into the workshop and gave a half-hearted, "Glad to hear."

The quartet of friends exchanged glances while Chad's dad remained in the basement. The noises of tools being shuffled around, with the occasional clunk of something falling on the floor, lasted a few minutes. Heading back up the stairs, he held up a heavy flashlight and said, "Probably won't need this for our . . . excursion . . . tomorrow, Chad, but just in case, right?"

Chad offered a weak smile. "Yep."

"You're going with them?" Cooper asked after Rick left.

Chad's parents were the only ones to share the existence of lycanthropes with anyone outside the hunting group and what they planned on doing about it. Cooper's mom wasn't participating, so the topic never came up. Kyle's parents were too worried about their son's frail psyche to expose him to such things, while Heston's dad simply didn't bother to share anything with his son. But they all knew that Wanda was taking most of her new recruits on a hunting expedition tomorrow. They didn't know that Chad was joining them. "I'm just going to observe."

"Are you sure your presence won't perpetuate their ridiculous notion that lycanthropes exist?"

Kyle laughed. "Dude, we *do* exist. And how would Chad going along perpetuate anything?"

"Yes, but *they* don't know that. Chad being along is like taking a match to a kerosene convention. All it would take is one strike and everything goes up in flames."

"I think you're reaching," Heston said.

"Am I?" Cooper countered. "Chad has a habit of looking for conspiracies. If you devote a hundred and ten percent of your available time to conspiracy quests, you'll eventually find one, real or not."

Chad pressed his palms together and gestured toward Cooper. "I promise I'm not looking for a conspiracy. I've heard you. I've heard you all about getting a life outside of lycanthropy. I'm only going along tomorrow to observe. If there's an opportunity to guide them down the path your mother followed regarding this, I'll do my best to give them a nudge. I'm not looking for trouble. I swear."

"I think it's a good idea," Kyle said.

"Me, too," Heston added.

Cooper rubbed his eyes and ran his hands through his hair. He then nodded and placed the twenty-sided die in front of Chad. "Okay. You're right. I believe you and I agree with the logic behind the decision. The only thing left for you to do is roll for luck."

Chad rolled the finger.

CHAPTER 11

The snow-covered twigs and leaves crunched beneath Chad's feet as he maneuvered through the forest.

"Shhh!" Wanda admonished him with an angry whisper. "You're way too loud, Barelli."

Chad bit his tongue. He wanted to point out that he was by far the quietest of the seven people traipsing around the forest, but the discord he'd create wouldn't be worth it. Instead, he simply accepted her words and muttered, "Sorry."

"Try to be more like your father," she said with a shit-eating grin before moving ahead, crossbow at the ready. It burned Chad behind his chest that she could get under his skin so easily.

"Come on, son," his dad whispered from behind him. "I know you're along for observation, but you gotta keep up, stay focused."

"Got it, Dad." Chad struggled to keep his eye roll from altering his tone of voice.

His father hurried away, jogging like a one-man herd of bulls to hide behind a nearby tree, the equipment hanging from his belt clanking against the equipment within his pockets. Small first aid kit, two hunting knives, small metal bottle of water, military-grade compass, flashlight. He, too, had a primed crossbow with a dozen bolts in a holder strapped around his right thigh. To complete the ludicrous look was his head-to-toe white and gray camouflage jacket and pants. The only two that looked more ridiculous were Bud McCurdy and Anna Sedgeweck.

Heston's dad was the farthest from the group but the easiest to see, even as he crouched behind the thick curls of a bush. There were no leaves on the bush, and he wore a camouflage outfit similar to Chad's father, except with swaths of fluorescent orange. Bud assumed all animals were the same, hunting lycanthropes no different than hunting deer. When in rabbit form, Chad could see the entire spectrum of color. After exhaustive research about his animal self, he knew he shouldn't be able to see red in his rabbit form, yet he did. Not sure why. He had been a lycanthrope for about four months, and everyone who could answer that question wanted to kill him, so he assumed a best-of-both-worlds situation.

Kyle's mom stood out for different reasons. She dressed appropriately for the occasion—white jacket, ski pants, boots, and gloves. However, her outfit did nothing to hide that her chest was larger than average, each bra cup twice the size of her head. In her younger days, she had been a topless model. Thanks to the age of the internet, the decisions a person made in their youth could have repercussions for them as an adult, such as pictures from her modeling days being used against Kyle to coerce him into turning the jocks into lycanthropes. Currently, she hid behind a tree. Most of her, at least. From Chad's viewpoint, the tree thirty feet away was shaped like the letter "P."

The last two members of the hunting party were the only two doing a good job moving through the forest—Chad's mother and Donovan Butera. His mother had a natural talent for this sort of thing. At first, it disturbed Chad, but it wasn't that she was freakishly good at this while being terrible at everything else. He had no idea what she could be good at. Pregnant by the end of high school with no aspirations for college, she and Rick married. Chad had always assumed that his father had to work so hard because she was docile, incapable of surviving without him. Thanks to Wanda inserting herself into their lives, his mother showed an aptitude for learning, for critical thinking, for hunting. What other areas in life could she excel at if given the opportunity? And why was this opportunity her first to become something more? This was the twenty-first century, the age of opportunity! Was there something holding her back? Was *his father* holding her back? As smoothly as the breeze, his mother glided from one tree to the next.

Donovan was good at this as well, smart attire, effortless movements. Chad knew little about the Buteras, just that Justin, Donovan's son, had gone missing at the start of last semester. That event started this misguided path to lycanthropy.

The Ink Stains had made Justin the same promise they had made Chad—a way to solve his bully problem—but lied. Chad had escaped the clutches of the Ink Stains. Justin hadn't been so lucky. Donovan looked similar to Kyle's father. On the shorter side, thin, with shoulders rounded a bit from the weight of the world pressing down on them. But he was angry that his son felt the need to seek strength, protection, from a cruel world and unwittingly sought help from monsters. He wanted vengeance. He was the one Chad worried about most.

Cooper's reasoning that the interest generated by Wanda telling the parents about lycanthropes and teaching them to become hunters would fade seemed valid. Chad felt certain that traipsing around the snow-coated woods for a few hours would be enough to discourage them from their newest hobby. Not Donovan, though. Chad could tell that it would take more than a few cold hours of failure to dissuade his motivation.

Patience. All Chad needed was a little patience. All he needed was for the sun to go down, and they'd call it a night. He'd review the mission with his parents at dinner to gauge their enthusiasm. He also needed a little luck, but as history had proven to him time and time again, he'd get none of that.

Wanda stopped and raised her fist the way soldiers did in movies when they wanted everyone else to stop. Looking down, she waved everyone over to join her. As she crouched down, everyone else formed a loose circle around her. She whispered, "Tracks."

Bud grunted. "Just deer tracks."

"No. They're different."

Easy to see, the tracks wound among the trees and went deeper into the forest. Bud grunted again and raised his crossbow, equipped with a massive sight. He panned to the left, to the right, turned some knobs. "I see it. Kinda small."

Wanda stood and pulled a handheld sight from her pocket. After a few seconds of adjustment, she concurred. "I see it, too. That's definitely no deer. That . . . yep, that's a gazelle."

No! Of all the times for the mysterious gazelle to be roaming around this part of the woods!

"So, it's a gazelle," Chad's father said. "All but the same thing as a deer, right?"

"Maybe in Africa," Wanda answered, "But not in the American northeast."

"Oh," Anna whispered. "Oh, wow. So . . . so that is one of them? That is a . . . a lycanthrope?"

"Unless a gazelle escaped from a nearby zoo, I'd say odds are it is one."

"What's the plan?" Donovan asked, a soldier ready for his orders.

"Simple flanking maneuver. We keep it simple—women in the middle, men on the edges. We spread out as we move forward. And for fuck's sake, don't shoot each other."

Donovan and Chad's father went to the left, while Bud and Chad went to the right. Chad had to do something. Only one idea came to mind, and he didn't like it. Didn't like it all.

Everyone was too amped up on adrenaline to remember that Chad was unarmed. Bud was too focused to care about anything else around him or notice that Chad crept backward as everyone moved forward.

Chad knew exactly where he was in this part of the woods. The one corner of the campus was a mile behind him, and Tyler's barn was a half-mile to the right. Should he get into too much trouble, he could make it to the barn in minutes. He also knew of a fallen tree that made the perfect place to hide his clothes. By the time he undressed and stuffed his clothes into a rotted-out alcove, he was losing sight of everyone, the hunters spreading out as they advanced toward the gazelle.

"Here goes nothing," Chad whispered as he shifted into full rabbit.

Chad raced through the woods, parallel to the line the hunters created, making as much noise as possible. The distraction worked. The forest came alive with the sounds of people running and shouting.

"I see something!" Donovan yelled.

"What is it?" Bud called out.

Anna screamed.

"I see it too! It's going that way!" Chad's father called out.

"Don't break formation!" Wanda yelled, but no one listened.

Step one, complete. The hunters were too new not to break formation by a simple distraction. Now, to find the gazelle. Chad hoped to meet the other lycanthrope and find a safe place to talk, but if he could encourage it to flee, that would be good too. He looped around the end of the line and tried to find the gazelle's tracks again. There! He followed and found the gazelle eating a small fern. It looked up as he rushed to it, but before he could say anything, a crossbow bolt whistled through the air and sunk into a tree between him and the gazelle. His mother! As she reloaded, the gazelle took off. Unfortunately, it was running toward the other hunters.

Chad followed the gazelle as it put enough trees between it and his mother. But it ran right in front of Donovan. Anna ran toward Donovan, so Chad broke off his path and ran at her. Perfect! He startled her and she changed course, colliding with Donovan hard enough to knock them both to the ground.

Bud ran to the scene, his heavy wheezing giving away his position, his prodigious girth slowing his steps. But he was an avid hunter, knowing how to wield and use weapons effectively. He dropped to one knee and propped the crossbow butt against his shoulder. A clear shot right at Chad.

The element of surprise was a powerful tool, and Chad hoped he could use it properly. He raced toward Bud, and about twenty feet away, he leaped into the air. At the apex of his jump, he shifted into his half-human, half-rabbit mode. Fur covered, his arms were human-shaped, and his right fist reeled back.

Bud's jaw dropped and he failed to shoot. It felt good—no, *great*—to clock Bud right in the cheek as Chad landed on him. He wasn't sure how Heston would react, though. Undoubtedly, he'd agree that his father deserved to be knocked out, but Bud was still his father.

Chad stood and held his breath until he saw Bud's chest lift and fall. *Thank God I didn't kill him.* Now for the rest of them. A blur rushed toward him and slammed him to the ground.

Donovan! Brandishing a hunting knife, Donovan knelt on top of Chad and screamed, "You killed my son! You killed my son!"

Chad shifted into full rabbit form and easily squirmed out from under Donovan. He ran. Ran away from danger. Ran away from the unintended consequences of being a lycanthrope. Ran away from the heartbreaking sobs of a father in pain. But Chad couldn't run from the sudden bleat of a wounded animal.

Shit! No, no, no, no! Chad raced toward the cry. He really wanted to run away—the prey animal screamed in his brain to run away. He silenced it and ran toward the animal's cries for help, careful of potential threats, the biggest being his mother. She was reloading her crossbow, and Chad assumed she was the one who shot the gazelle. No body nearby, so it might not have been a critical hit. Wanting to buy as much time for the wounded gazelle to escape, he stopped fifty feet in front of his mother. Motionless, she stared at him. He was in rabbit form, but he was still as big as a human. The sight of him was enough to give his mother pause, but after a few breaths, she went back to reloading, never taking her eyes off him. How was he going to take his mother out of the equation? Luck finally threw a scrap to Chad today in the form of his father.

"Ow! Fucking fuck, Rick!" Wanda called out from somewhere in the woods. "You fucking shot me!"

"These things are everywhere!" Rick's voice bounced around the woods.

Chad's mother returned the bolt to its quiver and stared at Chad for a few more heartbeats before running toward her husband. With a sigh of relief, Chad went to find the gazelle.

Spatters of crimson highlighted the trail of hoofprints in the snow. Chad thought that was a good sign. Small splashes were preferable to large puddles. There! The gazelle was up ahead, stomping around in small circles, occasionally snorting with a head shake.

It hadn't seen Chad yet, so he crept closer. Closer. He stayed behind a tree, trying to figure out what to do next. The bolt was stuck in the bottom half of its left front leg. *I have to help,* Chad thought as he stepped out from behind the tree. He stepped back when the gazelle reared up.

Body thinning, its limbs morphed into legs and arms. The gazelle transformed back to human—a female human. The injured leg turned into an arm, streams of blood flowing from the wound. The horns retracted while her snout retreated into her face. The fur disappeared, replaced by long, blonde hair. Chad had been excited to meet a new lycanthrope coming into the area, like the newest addition to the Ink Stains, until he saw who it was.

Brittany.

Gritting her teeth, she grabbed the crossbow bolt and pulled it out of her arm. "Fuck!" She dropped the bolt and squeezed her forearm to slow the bleeding.

Chad stepped out from behind the tree. He didn't know why, but something in his gut told him to do it. They had known each other since elementary school, but she had always been a cool kid and evolved into a bitchy cheerleader who dated the high school quarterback, Mason. He was why Chad had taken the Ink Stains' offer to become a lycanthrope. The Ink Stains ate Mason, taking him from Brittany. It had been months since Chad had last spoken to her, but she seemed lonely. Maybe Chad made his presence known to connect with her, to show her that they were a part of the same unique tribe, to show her that she wasn't alone.

When Brittany noticed Chad, he turned back into human form.

They stood frozen in time, just looking at each other. Chad didn't know what he thought her reaction was going to be, but he would have wagered there would have been some reaction: surprise that Chad was a lycanthrope too; relief that she knew someone else who was one; fear that she had been shot by hunters. Instead, there was . . . nothing. A blank expression. Chad opened his mouth, but she quickly transformed back into a gazelle and took off. He thought about pursuing or calling out to her, but he heard his mother's voice echoing through the woods, "Chad? Chad, where are you?"

Confused, Chad changed back into a rabbit and sprinted to where he had left his clothes. As he got dressed, he answered his mother, "Over here! I got all turned around! Sorry!"

What the hell was he going to do now? Brittany was a lycanthrope. And injured. How did she become one? And when? Which pack did she know? All questions he should have thought about before exposing to her that he was one as well. Now pissed at himself for being so stupid, he'd quickly check in with his parents and devise a plan to ditch them. He needed to follow Brittany while the trail was still fresh.

CHAPTER 12

Kyle was spent. He wasn't used to this much activity, not that he had experienced much physical activity today. The way he had been training with Tyler and the guys these past few months, he might have welcomed something physically challenging. It had been four hours since meeting up with Janey, but it felt like ten.

It wasn't a bad thing. He enjoyed spending time with her, especially since he hadn't had many chances all week until today. His exhaustion didn't even stem from meeting Janey's aunt and cousin—Declan's mother and sister—nor the comical set of events that led to him spending over three hours in a car with Janey instead of the thirty-minute estimation from the GPS.

Kyle had met up with Janey at her apartment, and the original plan was for her to drive them to the hospital to visit Declan. Halfway there, her aunt called and said she had a panic attack and could no longer drive herself, so Janey changed course and headed to the other side of town. By the time Kyle and Janey arrived at her aunt's—Aunty Martha, as she introduced herself even though Janey addressed her as Aunt Marty—she was better and decided to reward Janey's efforts by insisting that she drive so Janey and Kyle could ride with her. Janey and her aunt drove back to Janey's apartment to drop off Janey's car. Right around the same halfway point to the hospital, Janey's cousin called in tears. Her car had broken down. Aunt Marty altered her course to rescue her daughter, Janey's cousin Del, short for Delaware. With Del in the passenger seat, they followed the tow truck that came an hour after Del called for it all the way back to a garage near Aunt Marty's house. Kyle held his breath when they got to the dreaded halfway point for the third time. The idiom was the charm; they drove right past it, doing five miles below the speed limit.

The experience itself didn't drain Kyle. The women were talkative and full of life, though Aunt Marty and Del seemed to be a little more dramatic than necessary. Kyle laughed along and felt comfortable around them. They talked a lot, which he appreciated. The more others talked, the less he had to; the less he had to talk, the less chance he'd say something stupid. No, it wasn't the nonstop conversations happening around him that tired him out. It was the way Janey introduced him each time. "This is Kyle Sedgeweck." No other descriptor. No title. It was the not knowing that sent his brain into overdrive. What was his role? Boyfriend? Friend? Teammate? The nonstop debate with himself as he analyzed everything Janey said and the way she said it. Cooper's voice was in his head with a constant, "Dude, meeting a girl's aunt and cousin on the second date while going to the hospital is soooooo unromantic." Yet Janey would randomly squeeze his hand to confuse him further. Was that connection? Support? A nervous habit? He needed an FAQ section!

Wanting to be a good person, Kyle would have come along no matter his role. He wished he knew what it was so he could better anticipate what to do next and what was expected of him. Now that he was alone with her in the hospital lobby, he was about to find out.

Declan's visitors were limited to two at a time, so Aunt Marty and Del went first. Finally, alone for the first time all day, Kyle started with the standard, "So . . . ?"

Janey threw her arms over his shoulders and kissed him.

With tongue.

Confident that this was more than a peck, more than a friendship smooch, Kyle closed his eyes and reciprocated as best as his inexperience allowed him. After hours—or seconds? Minutes? The concept of time no longer wished to communicate with him—they came to a nice conclusion, and Janey stepped away, smiling. Her teeth were a blinding white to the radioactive levels of red her face had become. She bounced on the balls of her feet and clasped her hands as if she needed to do that to keep them under control. "I'm really sorry I just pounced on you without asking for permission first, but I reallllllly wanted to do that all day because you're basically the coolest person ever for enduring my aunt and cousin for countless hours, and I know it's weird to kiss you in a hospital because it's a super unromantic second date especially after meeting my aunt and cousin, but thank you for not running away."

Kyle now had all the information he needed and showed his appreciation by returning her wide smile and blushing. He reached out and held her hands. "So . . . this is a second date?"

Janey's nods were quick and numerous. "Yeah! Well, as long as you want it to be."

"I do. I would like that very, very much."

She glanced over his shoulder and gently removed her hands from his. "Okay, Aunt Marty and Del are getting out of the elevator. So, after we visit Declan, you wanna blow this popsicle joint?" She punctuated her question with a long, awkward wink. She covered her mouth with her hand and said, "Sorry. I don't know why I did that or what I thought I meant by it. I have impulse control issues and get weird quickly."

Kyle chuckled. "Weird is awesome. You're awesome. And yes, I'm all for blowing popsicle joints." He didn't know what he meant by that either, but Janey laughed, and it sounded like heaven. The sound resonated in his head the whole way to Declan's room.

Kyle didn't know Declan well. They had a class together last semester. Been teammates for less than two weeks. Shared a conversation here and there. The limited time together didn't stop Kyle from feeling horrible seeing him like this.

Declan's left arm and leg were in casts. Face bruised and still slightly swollen, Declan smiled. It seemed like it hurt, but he did it anyway as Janey and Kyle approached the side of his bed. "Hey," he said, his words barely louder than the soft noises of the machines helping him. "Good to see you, cuz. Hey, Kyle."

Kyle offered a piteous smile and a weak wave, uncertain if Declan could even see that far.

"How are you feeling?" Janey asked.

"Sleepy. Good meds here." Declan licked his lips and closed his eyes. His smile faded and he took a deep breath. "Don't . . . don't tell Mom or Del, but . . . I know who hit me."

Janey looked at Kyle, her eyes wide with fear. He grabbed her hand, and they leaned closer to hear Declan better. She asked, "Who?"

"Don't know his name. Big guy. Scary looking, like a movie thug."

"Was he the one who tried to talk to you before practice last week?"

"Yeah. Him. He . . . he asked me if I could make . . . make fake IDs. First, I said no, then . . . then I thought about it. And he offered me money . . . lots of money for six IDs. I did it. Then I . . . I got scared. Scared of getting . . . getting caught, but I did it. I gave . . . him the IDs, but . . . he didn't pay. Wanted more . . . I said . . . no. I drove away . . . but stopped . . . to get burgers. I stress eat. He found me . . . and did this."

"Okay," Janey said. She was breathing faster and petted Declan's hand as he spoke. "Okay. Okay, okay, okay. Okay, so . . . is there anything you can tell us about him? Anything we can take to the cops?"

"No cops yet. So . . . tired. But . . . Pixel Ro-Ro-Ronin saw him the first time . . . and . . . and I have . . . backup files . . . files . . . my apartment . . . loose ceiling tile in . . . my closet. Thumb . . . drive . . . blue unicorn . . . don't judge me . . ."

Declan lost consciousness, his breathing rhythmic and strong. Janey's breathing became rapid and shallow. She still petted his hand. Kyle put a hand on her shoulder, and she leaned into him. Her voice was small, timid. "That's . . . that was a heck of a story, right?"

Kyle stood straighter. He had many, many fears, so he understood what Janey was feeling. Declan got involved with someone he shouldn't have, and this frightened Janey. Kyle would have been scared, too, but not now. He had abilities. Skills. Power. Whoever did this to Declan should be afraid of Kyle.

With a reassuring squeeze, Kyle said, "Let's leave him sleep. We'll head over to his apartment tomorrow, get the thumb drive, and come back to see what he wants to do with it."

Janey nodded and wiped tears from her cheeks. "Yeah. Good idea. I like this idea. This is a great idea. Let's do that idea."

As they left the room, Kyle's phone vibrated. After a few more steps, it vibrated again. By the time they got to the lobby, it had vibrated a third time.

Janey squeezed his hand and said, "Go ahead and check. I'd hate for you to miss an emergency because of me."

"Thanks." He had three texts. One from each of the guys, all of them said the same thing: "Emergency meeting at the barn."

Heston was tired. He'd been helping his father since early in the morning. Bud was terrible with numbers and worse with planning. A mulch supplier offered a pre-season deal, less than half the cost it would be in a few months, so

Bud ordered a few tons. Of course, he had forgotten he also ordered a few tons of salt in case the parking lots of the local business froze within the next couple of months. He also ordered a few tons of split wood for the fireplace.

The salt delivery was the easiest. All the driver had to do was back up into the oversized barn and drop his load. It was the dance he had to do with the other two trucks that made it complicated. The ground was hard from the mid-winter temperatures, but the snow and truck tires caused just enough mud to elicit profanities. No fights broke out, and there was no damage to any of the trucks, but after they delivered their commodities and left, a seething silence remained as Bud and Heston pitchforked mulch and stacked firewood. Heston knew better than to call attention to the fact that Chuck stayed in the house all morning and afternoon instead of helping. It wouldn't solve anything and possibly lead to a backhand or two. And it would have disrupted Chuck's plans. Heston wanted to make sure Chuck was left to his own devices so he could follow his brother again. Maybe even scare him again. One could always dream, right?

After the mulch was where Bud wanted it, tarps were on the salt mounds, and the wood stacked against the barn walls, they called it a day. Since Bud had to leave to join Wanda's hunting party, Heston had the rest of the day off. Perfect. A quick shower and then to his room until Chuck made his move.

It took a few hours, but Chuck finally began his day. He grabbed a couple beers from the fridge and the keys to the F-150. Time to follow him. It was a challenge, but Heston had done it before. Rucksack slung over his shoulder, he slipped out the door after Chuck drove away.

Late afternoon was sliding into early evening, so there was still plenty of light left. Heston had to be creative. Past the barn, a field stretched to the forest. Once he hit the forest, he turned into his minotaur form and sprinted. His T-shirt and shorts were tight but didn't hinder him. He carried his shoes in one hand and rucksack in the other. Unlike Cooper and Chad, Heston could only shift into his minotaur mode or become one hundred percent ox. The other two could shift individual body parts. He was getting better at slimming down his human form, but he had yet to learn how to change specific body parts. Kyle could focus his eyes in different directions at once, but he could only be human or animal, no in-between. Except for that . . . *whatever* . . . he turned into months ago at the coal depot.

The road Chuck was on looped around the forest. Cutting through the forest, Heston could get a little ahead of him and prepare for any direction Chuck chose at the intersection. Right. Toward the college. Why was Chuck spending so much time at the college? Did it have anything to do with the student Heston had seen him harass? Or Kyle's friend, Declan?

Heston had seen Chuck washing his car around the same time Kyle told everyone about Declan. He kept this information to himself and didn't ask questions. Chuck was an asshole, but if he crossed the line into that level of violence, Heston wanted proof before stirring the pot. And God only knew how his friends would react. After joining the lacrosse team, Cooper was becoming a dismissive dick, not wanting to listen to anything anyone had to say. Kyle listened but tried to rationalize that there were no monsters in the closet while hiding his head under the pillow. And Chad . . . Christ, Chad would be the exact opposite, creating complex theories that linked Chuck to Declan to lycanthropes to the JFK assassination. No. Mouth closed until he had something to say.

The tree density thinned, giving way to small copses between backyards. He had to be more creative, shifting between human and minotaur while scampering along, but he never once lost sight of Chuck's car.

Large Tudor houses lined each side of the street, random trees and trimmed bushes interspersed. Chuck parked along the street and walked down an uneven sidewalk that had been cleared of snow. Fraternity row. *Why the hell was Chuck here?* More questions formed when Chuck went into one of the houses. *What the fuck?*

Attempting to look nonchalant in shorts and a T-shirt, Heston crossed the street to be on the same side. No one else was out and about, but he remained vigilant. The house was the last one on the street before the road took a soft ninety-degree curve in front of the forest. Heston slipped through the leafless branches and found a good spot to observe. He never thought he'd be on a stakeout, so he regretted not bringing any food. When the nearby bushes rustled, he quickly forgot about his hunger.

Something was coming closer. Had he been seen? Did Chuck have a lookout? A dangerous one? *No, don't think like that*, he reminded himself. He had abilities. Skills. Power. Whoever crept closer should be afraid of him. Fists clenched, he readied himself to turn into a minotaur. Until he saw what was making the noises.

Chad.

And he looked just as surprised to see Heston.

"Dude," Heston whispered. "I almost gored you."

"I'm glad you didn't, but what are you doing here?"

"I followed Chuck. He went in that house. Why are you here?"

Chad pointed to the street. "Her."

Brittany.

Wearing a sweatshirt and shorts, she hurried along the sidewalk while clutching her arm. She went into the same house that Chuck had gone into. "What's going on, Chad?"

As Chad told him about their parents' misadventures in the forest, Heston's stomach dropped. There was a certain humor in Chad's dad shooting Wanda in the leg, but it was erased by the cold feelings of Chad being right to be paranoid. Brittany was a lycanthrope, and Chuck was somehow involved. He wasn't thrilled about Chad punching his father, but it needed to happen.

"Now what?" Heston asked.

Chad shrugged. "I don't know. We don't really know anything. It's too light to really snoop around the house, so . . . I guess we wait?"

Heston nodded. "Did you bring any food?"

"Ummm . . . no."

"Too bad."

They watched the house in silence for almost fifteen minutes before, predictably, Chad could no longer tolerate the silence. "So, how's this semester going for you?"

"Good."

"Yeah? Good. Good for me too."

"Cool."

"As a side note, I noticed you dropped a few pounds. Have you been working out with Tyler more?"

"No. Joined a gym."

"Yeah? Fit World? That's the one closest to your house, right?"

"It is, but not that one."

"Club Circulation? By campus?"

"No." Heston didn't like to lie, but it was a one-and-done cut to his moral fabric that could be easily repaired. Using his animal side to alter his human appearance felt like cheating, a long, elaborate con that didn't feel good. He rationalized that he was experimenting, testing his abilities. The ends would justify the means. Even though he truly believed that, it didn't feel good to lie to his friend, but he wanted Chad to stop the interrogation. "It's a small place, no big deal. So, what's our plan?"

Chad looked offended, but he stopped pressing the issue. This bought an-other fifteen minutes of silence. Then came the fidgeting and the mumbled jokes about the dirt and rocks not being very comfortable to sit on. Heston checked his phone to see what time sunset was and how much longer he had to wait until they could sneak closer to the house under cover of darkness. Then the door opened.

Chuck exited, laughing and joking with the person following him out of the house.

Brick.

Chuck gave Brick a fist bump and walked toward his car. Brick turned back to the house but paused and looked up and down the street. Frowning, he went back inside.

Heston and Chad looked at each other, their faces as white as the snow around them. In unison, they said, "We need an emergency meeting at the barn."

———

Cooper was exhausted. Not only from a rigorous practice but from being the new mayor of the team. He wasn't team captain, but his popularity grew to him being the undisputed best player. If he could limit opposing offenses to minimal points scored, it benefited the whole team. Some of the seniors, Sanders among them, didn't see it that way, viewing him as an eclipse of their potential stardom. The vast majority of his teammates appreciated his skills, but he felt the need to converse with as many players as possible to reassure himself of his perceived standing within the team dynamics. After all, this was the first non-LARP team he had ever been on. However, due to his exuberance to con-nect with as many teammates as possible in the locker room, he found himself the only one left in a towel while everyone else was dressed and either gone or getting ready to leave for pizza at Mortelli's. Cooper preferred Rocket Lizard Pizza, but he wasn't about to share that information; Mortelli's was just fine.

"We'll meet you over there," Bryce said, slinging his gym bag over his shoulder.

"Indubitably," Cooper replied.

Bryce laughed. "You talk like a fuckin' weirdo."

"That's half my charm."

"Only if it works on the ladies. Later."

After Bryce left, Cooper went to his locker and contemplated the limita-tions of his imagination. Never in a million years would being on a sporting team enter his mind, let alone being so popular within that team. Then he opened his locker. The feelings of inadequacy and terror he thought he left behind in high school gym class had returned, twisting his gut.

His clothes were gone.

Not all of his clothes, though, just his shirt and jeans he wanted to change into. Nothing else in his locker was missing or even disturbed in the slightest. Sweat-soaked T-shirt and shorts from practice were still in his duffel bag, where he had tossed them. Keys, cell phone, and wallet on the top shelf. Was he being paranoid? Did he have such mistrust in humanity that he instinctively blamed the malfeasance found within a person's soul instead of making any further hypotheses, such as misplacing his clothes? He mumbled, "Well, fuck."

Cooper checked the lockers next to his. Both empty. Then he checked the neighboring lockers to those and the ones across the aisle. Nothing. Wet feet slapping on the concrete floor, he checked the other banks of lockers. He was the first to admit that once his mouth started moving, his focus tended to skew toward the details of his story rather than the details of the world around him. Maybe he hadn't been paying attention and wandered down the wrong bank of lockers? Nope. Now his mind went back to being a victim of someone else's malice rather than a victim of his distraction-induced ineptitude. He checked more lockers, then stood on a bench to check the tops of the lockers, then the trash cans. Nothing. Until the showers came on.

"Hello?" Cooper called out. "Who's there?"

He felt stupid for following the horror movie recipe for becoming the victim of a slasher, but he couldn't stop the primal unease fluttering within his heart when he stepped out from the bank of lockers and watched a wall of steam billow out from the shower area. This fear was irrational, though. He had abilities. Skills. Power. Whoever lurked within the steam should be afraid of him.

Fists clenched, he started toward the steam. "If you're attempting to elicit some form of fright from me, let me assure you that your plan isn't working. I'm more than what you think."

A voice flowed out of the showers along with the steam. "Oh, that's what I'm hoping for."

Sanders.

He strode naked from the steam as if he were a monster of perfection conjured from a cauldron by locker room witches. Wet blond locks framed his face, and rivulets of water streamed over his rolling muscles. He was holding the missing shirt and pants. Cooper sighed. "Seriously, Sanders?"

"I wanted to make sure we were alone, and I had your attention."

Anger turned into confusion, then understanding. The animosity Sanders had shown to Cooper now made sense. Poor fellow probably came from a world where an individual with such feelings was not allowed to express them, not allowed to be himself. Pity.

Cooper slowly waved his hands in front of him, erasing the misunderstanding. "I feel I must apologize profusely if I may have sent conflicting signals, but I do not fall anywhere along the GLBTQA+ spectrum. I love all people, and I'm very flattered that you—"

"Oh, for fuck's sake," Sanders laughed. "I get pussy eight days a week, you egotistical schmuck."

"Oh. Then . . . why did you want to get me alone? And naked?"

Sanders didn't stop walking toward Cooper, his smile like a scimitar, wickedly curved and ready to kill. "To see what you got."

Cooper kept his hands out in front of him, now palms out, a sign to Sanders to stop. "Sorry, I'm not dropping my towel, but you just stated you weren't gay, so I have yet to grasp why you'd want to see anything I've got."

Sanders stopped within one pace of Cooper and stared at his outstretched arm. "To see who's bigger."

Sanders bit Cooper's arm.

But not as a human.

It happened too fast. A muzzle full of teeth clamped down on Cooper's forearm. The pain was blinding, all-consuming. He barely heard his screams over the thunderstorm within his body, lightning striking every nerve from his arm to his skull. Survival reflex took over, transforming him into a hybrid of his other self. The right side of his body went into ferret mode, his arm shrinking into a front leg, while the left side stayed human as he drove a knuckle into the Sanders's animal eye. It was enough to yank his arm free and shift into full ferret mode. He skittered away, but in his panic, he didn't realize it was down a bank of lockers to a dead end.

The Sanders animal snarled and shook his head, dealing with the effects of getting poked in the eye. Triangular head, short brown fur, body low to the ground, curved claws long enough to scrape the floor. A wolverine.

Recovered from the eye poke, the wolverine hissed and opened its mouth to expose two rows of glistening teeth. It wasted no time and continued its attack, claws clacking as it rushed at Cooper.

Wounded leg drawn close to his chest, Cooper scurried under the bench in the center of the aisle as Sanders leaped into the air. Cooper tried to flee, but the wolverine was fast enough to recover and swiped at him, connecting with a hind leg. It didn't hurt, but it was enough to alter his trajectory, sending him running into the showers.

Cooper slid along the wet floor, claws skittering in failed attempts to shift momentum. No luck. He bounced off a wall and slid to a stop in the middle of the floor. His fur protected his skin from the scalding water, but the heat was unbearable. And it didn't stop Sanders from pursuing him.

Mouth open and teeth ready to latch onto any unprotected body part, Sanders found enough purchase to run straight at Cooper. This gave Cooper an idea. A risky one, but he'd take any suggestions his brain had to offer.

The shower water didn't slow Sanders down, his fur matted and dripping. He even picked up speed. Closer and closer. The teeth. The opened mouth. It was that open mouth Cooper wanted to exploit. At the last second, Cooper shifted his right leg back to human and kicked out. Foot first, he shoved his leg into Sanders's opened mouth.

Just like him, Sanders in wolverine form was still as large as a human being. Cooper's leg slid down Sanders's throat and stopped thigh deep. The wolverine's gagging vibrated Cooper's whole body, and the momentum from the attack spun Cooper in a half-circle. Timing it perfectly, Cooper shifted his right leg back to that of a ferret while his left leg went human to kick Sanders in the head. Physics sent them sliding across the floor in opposite directions, Sanders deeper into the shower, Cooper toward the exit.

Cooper didn't know what he had done to Sanders, and he didn't care. The showers couldn't drown out the horrid noises of retching and phlegm-filled choking. Cooper threw on his clothes and ran to his locker. He tossed the rest of his stuff in his gym bag and wrapped a towel around his bleeding arm.

He ran out of the locker room with only one destination in mind—the barn.

CHAPTER 13

Chad and Heston entered the barn and were greeted by Cooper's cry, "Chad is right! Chad is right!"

Just once, Chad wanted to go a whole day where he knew what everyone was talking about. Cooper was slumped forward in his hay bale chair, elbow on the table with his forehead resting against the back of his hand like a half-fainted antebellum woman. There was a teacup in front of him. Chad asked, "What's going on?"

"What's going on is you're right. Not only were you so, so right, but I was so, so wrong. I curse my narrow-minded and limited viewpoints! I apologize for ever eschewing your words."

Just last year, Chad had mentioned that once upon a time, Coca-Cola had halted production of their main cola product and completely replaced it with a new formula. Cooper didn't believe him and argued against the concept until he was blue in the face. Once he realized he had been "embedded in the bunker of wrongness"—his words—he apologized so dramatically that it bordered on patronizing. Although, Chad had to bring sufficient evidence before he was believed. So if Cooper was now admitting that Chad was right about something, something must have slapped Cooper in the face.

"Uh-oh," Kyle said as he walked into the barn, the last to arrive. "Is this a New Coke meltdown?"

"Looks like it," Chad said.

"What were you right about this time?"

"I honestly don't know. We haven't gotten that far yet."

"The jocks," Cooper moaned, his head sliding down his arm and finishing with his forehead on the table. "The jocks are up to something."

Chad, Heston, and Kyle exchanged worried looks as they sat at the table.

Cooper lifted his head from the table and snatched the teacup. He took a sip. "Dear Lord, this is panacea."

"Good tidings, fellow universe travelers," Tyler greeted everyone as he stood up from the couch. "Tea?"

"You should accept his offer. It's both tasty and comforting." Cooper backed up his statement by taking a long sip.

"What kind is it?" Chad asked.

"Cannabis," Tyler answered.

"Pot tea? No thanks."

Cooper extended his arms, still holding the cup as if it almost bit him. "Pot tea? You gave me pot tea?"

"To calm you down. And I told you it was cannabis tea when I gave it to you."

"Obviously, I was too mentally distraught from my recent trauma and misunderstood what was being offered to me. I thought you said, 'Can of cactus.'"

"Can of . . . ?" Chad started to repeat. "Why would you possibly think Tyler was offering you cactus?"

"First of all, this is Tyler we're talking about. His teatime proclivities are vast, enigmatic, and unpredictable. Second of all, I thought maybe there was a tea made from agave."

"Agave?" Tyler chuckled. "You mean the cactus that tequila is made from? So, in your mind, tequila tea is more acceptable than pot tea?"

"Mentally distraught!" Cooper yelled and then slugged back the remaining tea. He then handed the cup to Tyler. "May I have some more of your medicinal elixir, please?"

Tyler took the cup. "Anyone else?"

"No, thank you," Kyle said.

"I'd like some cannabis, but in its natural form," Heston said.

"Excellent choice. Step into my office," Tyler said. He handed Cooper a full cup of tea, then joined Heston on the couch. Close enough to the table to be a part of the conversation, they started rolling two joints.

Chad cleared his throat and said, "Okay, so it seems like we each have a story, so how about Cooper goes first."

"I'm sure it won't matter who goes first, because I'm sure all our stories are interconnected, entwined by the fates as predicted by Chad, who is somehow attuned to the very—"

"Cooper!" Heston snapped right before he brought the freshly rolled joint to his lips.

As if snapping out of a glitch, Cooper continued, his words more meaningful. "After practice, I was the last one in the showers. Or so I thought. Lurking to lure me into a trap was my on-team rival, a blond he-who-has-everything named Sanders. Truth be told, I don't know if that's his first name, last name, or only name." He paused to take a breath and wave his hand. "Actually, that information doesn't matter for this tale, just that his name is Sanders. Well, he transformed into a wolverine and attacked me."

"Whoa," Kyle said, rearing back as if the wolverine might appear because Cooper mentioned it. "Then what happened?"

"We tussled and I escaped." Cooper extended his arm to show the bite marks, healed to the point of minor scabs. "There are two things that continue to stick in my mind. One: He knew I was a lycanthrope. The way he talked and taunted me before springing his trap. And two: He was full wolverine the whole time. I think he was *recently* turned."

"And you think the jocks did this?"

Cooper shrugged while taking a sip of tea. "I think the connection is there. Sanders is a jock's jock; it doesn't matter what sport he's playing. I would find no surprise if we ascertained knowledge that he knows Brick."

Upon mentioning the name "Brick," Heston started coughing, smoke shooting from his mouth and nostrils. Cooper took notice and frowned. "So, what might have happened to you, Heston?"

"To us," Chad said. He decided to tell the story so Heston could compose himself. "Well, today was the first hunt Wanda took our parents on. Long story short, they found a lycanthrope to hunt. The gazelle."

"I don't like where this is going," Kyle mumbled.

"Nor do I, my friend," Cooper added. "Nor do I."

Heston continued to cough as Tyler patted his back.

"The bullet-point version," Chad continued. "The gazelle is Brittany. My dad shot Wanda in the leg with a crossbow bolt. My mom shot Brittany in the arm, also with a crossbow bolt. I followed Brittany and ran into Heston along Frat Row because he followed Chuck. Chuck and Brittany went into the same house—the one Brick was in."

Cooper and Kyle had the same wide-eyed, gape-mouthed stare on their faces. Finally, Cooper snapped out of his stupor. "Holy shit!" He turned to Kyle and said, "Can you top that?"

Kyle shook his head. "Thank God, no. Janey's cousin, my esports teammate, is in the hospital. She and I went to visit him now that he's awake. He said the hit and run was on purpose. Some thug paid him to make fake driver's licenses. He said the thug wanted more, but he told the guy no."

Cooper sat straight, more attentive. "Okay, so if I'm hearing correctly, that actually doesn't seem like it has anything to do with our lycanthropy issues, does it?"

Everyone in the barn looked around at each other, shaking their heads.

"Good," Cooper continued but quickly expanded, "I mean, it's horrible that your friend is in the hospital, but that just means it's one less piece in this surreal puzzle."

"I understand," Kyle said. "I feel the same way."

Cooper shifted in his seat to address the couch. "So, Heston. Was there any specific reason you were following Chuck?"

"He's a suspicious asshole," Heston said before taking another hit.

"That's the best answer you could have given, far better than 'he's a lycanthrope, too.' God, could you imagine Chuck as one of us? Nightmare. Anyway, Chad . . . did your parents or anyone in the hunting party see that the gazelle was Brittany?"

"No. But Brittany knows that I know, and she knows that I'm one of us, and like with Sanders and Cooper, it seemed like she knew that before today."

"And you and Heston saw her hanging out in a house where Brick was. It's abundantly clear that Brick and his cronies are involved."

"But that's kind of good news, right?" Kyle asked. His whole demeanor was different. Instead of shrinking back like he used to, he now sat up, attentive. "They used one of their vials right after The Morrigan gave them to us at the coal depot, and if they turned Sanders and Brittany, then that means they used all three of their vials."

"Unfortunately, that doesn't seem too likely," Chad said. He hated to burst Kyle's bubble. "First of all, we're assuming Sanders is new to being a lycanthrope. Second, I can't really imagine Brick using his vials so quickly, especially since we don't know how close he is to Sanders or Brittany."

"So . . . that means they have another source of Elder Blood?" Kyle asked.

"Fuuuuuuuuuuck me inside out!" Cooper moaned as he buried his face in his hands.

"Oh my God . . . how many more of them are there?"

Heston's eyes went wide as he held his breath.

Not good. Chad might not have embraced the brave new world of "no bullies" with as much verve as his friends, but he certainly liked the premise. Plus, they were his best friends, and he could not let them slip back into old ways of thinking. "Let's wait to freak out. Like Tyler had said before, there is always time to panic later. Now isn't later. We're reacting to phantom data, variables we haven't substantiated. Yes, there are now two new lycanthropes in the area, and the jocks might have turned them, but we also know you can't just buy a case of Elder Blood online. It's not easy to get, or else the Ink Stains wouldn't have struggled like they did to summon The Morrigan."

Chad's speech worked. Everyone calmed down, even Kyle, as he asked, "What do you think we should do?"

"What we've been doing. Enjoying life. We just need to stay vigilant. Heston, keep an eye on Chuck. See if you can figure out what he's up to."

"Suspicious asshole," Heston said.

"Kyle and I will watch our parents with their hunting."

"Sounds good," Kyle said.

"Cooper . . . what are you thinking? Are you going to quit the team?"

Cooper sighed, staring at something a million miles away. "No. The whole reason we chose the path of lycanthropy was to gain the means to explore opportunities. A way to bolster our confidence levels. A viable alternative to running away. Well, I'm enjoying this sportsball thing more than I thought I would, and I want to stick with it to its natural fruition. I'm not running away."

"So, you like lacrosse?" Kyle asked, his voice warbled with a hint of trepidation. "And your new friends?"

Cooper smiled and leaned over, close enough to Kyle to pinch his cheek. "Don't worrwy, wittle buddy, you'll always be my fwiend!"

Kyle used both hands to slap away Cooper's. At first, he frowned, then he laughed. "Ass hat."

Laughing as well, Cooper sat straight and sipped his tea. "Seriously, you guys are my best friends. My teammates aren't as bad as I thought they'd be, most of them anyway, but you guys far surpass them in every conceivable way. You are like *The World of Glark*. Complex, deep, rich, inviting. Those guys are like *Pong*. Simple, completely different, fun for a few laughs, but really boring after a while."

"It sounds like Cooper wants a group hug," Tyler suggested as he stood from the couch.

"Wait. What? How did you possibly hear that?" Cooper asked.

Everyone stood, Kyle with a delightful smirk, ready to exact the same level of discomfort he felt from the cheek pinch. They ambled to Cooper like zombies. Despite the eye rolls and grunts of disgust, Cooper stood as well.

Tyler put a hand on Cooper's shoulder. "Of the four, you are the most and least in touch with your feelings. You know what's inside of you, all the various pieces to the puzzle, but no final picture of what you're trying to assemble. You're trying to grab water, dude, hands splashing and arms wet to the elbows. Articulating your feelings to everyone the way you just did was a step closer to using a cup to scoop the water. Congratulations are in order."

The four other people swarmed Cooper, arms pinned to his sides and eyes crushed closed. The grimace of disgust remained until Kyle reached up and mussed his hair. "Okay, okay, okay! I feel appreciated, but you're knocking my chakras out of alignment!"

Everyone laughed as they separated. As Cooper ran his hands through his hair, he asked, "What's everyone doing tonight?"

"Dinner with the parents," Chad answered.

"Same," Kyle said, "Plus, I need to call Janey. Declan asked us to get something from his place, so we need to schedule a time for that."

"Oooooh, schedule planning!" Cooper said, waving his hand in front of his face as if it were a fan, "Sounds hhhooooottt!"

"Ass hat." Kyle blushed, but he laughed. He was getting better about not letting little things bother him. Maybe he needed a congratulatory group hug as well?

Cooper addressed Heston. "How about you?"

Heston shuffled back to the couch and sat down. "I'm gonna stay here for a bit."

"Rock on," Tyler said as he sat next to him and started to prepare two more joints.

"Okay. Next weekend. We need some *D&D* time. Right here."

Everyone agreed. Chad pulled out his phone to put it in the schedule, and an idea struck him. He sent a text.

Cooper saw what Chad had done and crossed his arms over his chest. Scowling, he moaned, "Please tell me you didn't text who I think you texted."

"I just want to pass on this information."

"No. You want to hook up with her. You want to spend time with her and try to convince her that we're the good guys so she'd stop hating you and open the doors to falling in love with you, and you two could live happily ever after. Chad, you need to recognize that she is so not into you that she is out of you."

"What? Eww. What does that even mean?"

"I don't know, but your heart does."

"Did he just text Natalia?" Kyle asked.

"C'mon, man!" Heston shouted. "Have some dignity."

Chad pinched the bridge of his nose and closed his eyes to keep them from shooting right out of his head. "It's not that at all. We've all said we don't want any more trouble. I want to steer us out of trouble's way. We tell Natalia and Wanda that there are two more lycanthropes in the area and that both of them know Brick. We let them do the leg work and deal with the danger."

His cellphone went off; his text had been answered. He held up his phone to show the group. "Look, I'm going to meet her at the mall. I'm just passing on information. That's all."

"No misguided attempts at romance?"

"None. I promise."

Chad promised his friends, but could he promise himself?

CHAPTER 14

Chad pressed his index finger on the salt grains piled together on the paper plate. He waited a few seconds, then put his finger in his mouth. The pretzel had been surprisingly tasty.

The food court pretzel shop had been there about a month and was met with mixed reviews. Being named "A Salt and Buttery" with the "A" done as the anarchy symbol made it stand out, but it seemed more suited for the downtown area by the college instead of a family-friendly mall. They displayed hard and soft pretzels in a bakery-style display case with bad puns for the names of their whimsically shaped pretzels. When the shop first came in, Cooper viewed half of the puns as vaguely sexual, while the rest of the group believed that only people like Cooper would view the puns as sexual, the level of vagueness not-withstanding. Tonight was the first time Chad tried them.

The food court would close in ten minutes, and Natalia still hadn't arrived. Dinner was waiting for him at home, but when he arrived at the mall an hour ago, he needed a snack to justify sitting by himself in the food court, waiting for someone who was probably going to stand him up. The new pretzel shop was the best option, and he became the second person in a line of two.

The customer in front of him was easily twice his age and extremely focused on receiving the best possible pretzel experience, having spent five minutes just asking questions about the different offerings. The girl behind the counter—Selma, as named by her badge—was running out of patience. The sleepy-eyed aloofness of a fashion model from the '80s, she had a cold beauty, like art in a museum offering catharsis from a distance. Jet black flowed from her scalp and ombred into bright blue tips around the middle of her back. She had a smooth, husky voice, the kind of voice Chad imagined a piano lounge singer from the 1940s would have. Her disenfranchised expression never changed, but her tone became increasingly clipped after every inane question.

"May I see the 'Knot on my Watch,' please?" the customer asked.

Selma gestured to it in the case.

"No," the customer followed up. "Can you pull one out of the case so I may view it more closely?"

Even while in a silly T-shirt that read "Knotty by Nature" that displayed a cartoon pretzel with two knots instead of the traditional one, she conveyed a rather frightening level of annoyance with her glare. Chad tried to remain distant from the conversation by taking one of the three-inch pretzel sticks from the small cup of samples on the counter, careful not to do something stupid like knock over the cup. The last thing he wanted was for her impending wrath to miss the appropriate target and hit him instead.

Selma pulled the pretzel in question from the case and rested it on a paper plate. It was a simple foot-long length of soft pretzel with two tight knots in the center, giving it the overall appearance of a watch. The customer stroked his chin while scrutinizing it like a real watch in a jewelry store. "Does the 'Knot on my Watch' have a soft core or a hard core?"

Selma exaggeratedly moved her head to look at the pretzel, then back at the customer. "It's a soft pretzel."

"But the interior of it, is it soft or hard?"

"It's a soft pretzel."

"I understand the concept, but sometimes the intersections formed by the knots create patches of hardness within the core. May I see the interior?"

Selma broke off one of the arms.

"Hmmm. I mean, it *looks* like the center is soft, but I don't trust that it is. I'm sorry, but I'm going to have to pass. I feel like there is some hardness in that core, and a soft core is just better."

"Wow," Chad said after the man left, not realizing the word left his mouth until Selma looked at him. He worried she might verbally tear his head off, but she said, "Shit like that happens all the time."

Chad felt bad that such experiences were commonplace, so he said, "He's wrong, though."

She squinted, a predatory look. "How do you mean?"

"He said soft core is better. Some things are meant to be hardcore."

She crossed her arms, her steel-blue eyes boring into his soul. "I'm sure you have an example to support such a wild proclamation?"

"Heavy metal. I mean, think about it. Could you imagine a soft-core metal band? How terrible would they be?"

Selma's intensity withered as she chuckled. "I must confess, they sound like they would be awful."

Chad grabbed two pretzel sticks from the sampler cup and rhythmically tapped them on the case. "Their drummer would sound something like this."

Selma's smile grew as she picked up the larger piece of the pretzel she had broken. She held the stem with her left hand while strumming the knot with the fingers of her right hand. "And I'm ready to go as the guitarist."

"All we need is an agent to sell our souls to and a manager to embezzle our millions. What's the band name so I can come up with concept art for our over-priced merchandise?"

Still smiling, Selma put the pretzel on the plate and then put the plate on a tray. She handed the tray to Chad. "I'll work on that while you work on the merchandise. In the meantime, chow down on my lightly used guitar that may or may not have been breathed on by a lonely man with a pretzel fetish."

"Are you sure?" Chad asked as he accepted the plate.

"Free of charge to a fellow band member. Although, if you were asking if I'm sure if that man has a pretzel fetish, then the answer is yes, definitely yes."

"Thanks. For the pretzel, not the nightmare-inducing images you've given me by sharing that information. I'm Chad."

Selma pointed to her left breast, where her nametag rested. Chad didn't need to look, so he simply said, "Bye, Selma," and walked to a table at the far corner of the food court. That had been twenty minutes ago, and the pretzel went quickly. Now all that remained were ten grains of salt. Once those were gone, he'd consider the night a bust and head home to come up with a different plan.

Running his finger over the plate, he corralled the last bits of spice and pressed down on them. An embarrassing amount of satisfaction tickled his brain when he managed to get all ten grains with one try. Natalia appeared out of nowhere and sat across the table from him right when he shoved his finger in his mouth. "Are you always a perv, or is it something you can turn on and off. Or is that all just for my benefit."

Chad removed his finger and wiped it dry with a napkin. "So not a perv and . . . you know what? Never mind. I didn't ask you to meet me for that."

Natalia leaned back in her chair and crossed her arms over her chest. She wore a red hoodie with the hood down, her auburn hair flowing over her shoulders. Green eyes, so pale they bordered on yellow, demanded answers. "Well?"

Chad leaned in. "It's Brick."

"I don't have time for this." Natalia started to stand.

"I know who the gazelle is."

She stopped and returned to her seat. "The gazelle?"

"Yes. Your aunt told you about the hunt, right?"

Chad didn't know how it was possible, but she looked even angrier. "She told me your father shot her in the leg. She told me she can't walk for a week. But, yes, she told me there was a gazelle. She was upset and confused that there was another lycanthrope in the area. She wasn't sure if it was a stray or if my mother's ridiculous story about another group coming into town might be true."

"You don't believe others are coming in?"

"I don't believe my mother. And neither should you. It's obvious that all she has to do is show you some cleavage and you'll do anything for her."

"That's not true," Chad lied. It was very true. He wished he wasn't so weak when it came to Kat. He knew she led him on and had used him for her personal gains. But . . . "She hasn't asked me to do anything."

"Yet. I'm sure she will, and I'm sure you'll do it."

"I don't think—"

"Who's the lycanthrope, Chad?"

There was no point in arguing. It wouldn't solve anything, and he wasn't entirely sure what he was arguing for or against. It was better to stick to the information he wanted to share. "She's another college student, someone I've known since elementary school. She hangs around with Brick and—"

"Jesus, Chad." Natalia rolled her eyes and shifted in her chair, ready to stand and leave again.

"And there's another one. Someone who might know Brick."

Chad didn't know how it was possible, but her glare made him sweat and freeze at the same time. "Another one?"

"Yes. A wolverine. Cooper got . . . the ferret got attacked by it. The wolverine is a lacrosse player, another jock. It's not outside the realm of possibility that he knows Brick. The gazelle used to be a cheerleader, and she definitely knows Brick. I think Brick is making more lycanthropes."

"How? You told me the ceremony at the coal depot was unsuccessful."

Chad had lied to her about that. It was no wonder she and her aunt Wanda didn't trust him. But he couldn't have them know there were three different groups with the means to make more lycanthropes. When he had asked her what happened to her that night, she said she didn't see a low beam and hit it hard enough while running to render herself unconscious. But he wasn't lying when he said, "I don't know how Brick is doing it. All I know is he and the gazelle were seen at the house at the end of Frat Row. Do you know where it is?"

"Frat Row? I do, but I need more to go on. Give me the human names of the two new lycanthropes."

"No. I have no idea what you and Wanda will do with that information. We need to work together if we're going to solve this problem. I thought you and I should go to Brick's house and gather intel."

Natalia laughed, a sick and piteous chuckle of watching the obvious consequences ravage someone who attempted something stupid. "You keep forgetting you are part of the problem, especially through my aunt's eyes. Even if the 'jocks' are somehow involved with this, they would still be last on her priority list because they never betrayed her trust. She is very pissed at you and your friends, in case you've forgotten. And so am I. The days of us working together are long gone. If you give me the human names, it might buy you a little leniency with my aunt."

"No."

Natalia stood and pushed her chair in. "I think it's a sad kind of funny that you can say no to me, who is trying to help, but yes to my mother, who will undoubtedly hurt you."

Chad had no retort as she left, content to wallow silently in his shame. He sighed, somehow feeling even more empty when he looked at his plate and saw no more salt grains. As he stood, he almost bumped into Selma. "Oh! Sorry about that."

"No worries. I should have announced my presence. I'm cursed with cat-like stealth." Selma gestured for him to give her his tray.

"No, it was my fault. I make it a rule to beware of ninjas. I let my guard down." Chad handed her the tray, and she dumped the paper plate into the nearby trash can. "Thanks, but I could have done that."

"Actually, you're the one who did me a favor. Very limited number of trays for the food court restaurants, so it can get like the fuckin' Hunger Games around here sometimes. Just last week, the pizza place got into it with the salad place. What made the moment so much extra is that both franchises are owned by the same guy."

Chad chuckled. "That sounds . . . just utterly ridiculous."

"It was. I almost witnessed a real-life 'who would win?' scenario involving heads of lettuce and a baseball bat of pepperoni. Anyway . . ." Selma nodded to the seat Natalia had been sitting in. "Trouble with the girlfriend?"

Chad couldn't stop a snort from escaping. "No. She is not my girlfriend."

"She looked mad."

"She's *always* mad."

"About your girlfriend? The one you met here last week?"

"Last week?"

"Yeah, the biker looking hottie in the black leather pants. You two were talking to Whacky Wanda."

Chad snorted again. "She's not my girlfriend either."

"Then obviously, you and Whacky Wanda are dating."

Chad laughed, a shoulder-shaking guffaw. "Sorry to laugh like that, but Wanda doesn't like me very much. And I, sad to say, do not have a girlfriend."

"Hunh," Selma grunted and squinted, a look of trying to figure out a puzzle. After a few seconds of scrutiny, her expression softened. "Okay. I'm done for the night, but it's dark out, and I wondered if you would walk me to my car?"

Chad shrugged. "Sure."

He followed her back to the restaurant front. She placed the tray on the stack, slid the security gate out from the side, and locked up. All the while, he mulled over what she said—she saw him last week. He always assumed he was unassuming, able to be forgotten after a first glance. If she remembered him and his whereabouts, others might as well. Brick was obviously branching out of his little circle by associating with Chuck. Was he also associating with others that Chad didn't know about? Unseen others who saw him?

As he and Selma aimed for the exit, he said, "So, you remember me from last week?"

"Not just last week. You're here quite a bit more than the average person."

Chad felt his cheeks warm from a blush, but the blast of night air helped cool them down when they got outside. A lone car was parked by one of the mall's many streetlamps in the first row of spaces, not more than fifty feet from the mall entrance. "Yeah. I'm not twenty-one, so I can't legally binge drink in public yet."

"Neither am I and neither can I."

"Yeah, I noticed you seem to be working a lot."

"I am. And before you ask, I'm not a model just doing this until my career takes off."

Chad cocked his head, confused. "Umm, okay."

Selma sighed. "Sorry. That was rude and uncalled for. At least four guys used a lame variation of 'are you a model?' line with me today."

"Well, that's because you're gorgeous." As soon as the words left his mouth, Chad realized how stupid they sounded and quickly followed with, "Sorry. I didn't mean to mansplain."

Selma laughed, rich and melodious. "Thank you. I appreciate that."

"That must be difficult for you sometimes."

She squinted, this time a look of bewilderment. "What is? Being gorgeous?"

"Yeah. Well, more specifically, the compliments that come with it. If you admit you know you're pretty, then people think you're conceited, but if you try to play it off, it comes across as false humility, which in itself is just another form of conceit. On top of that, there's the assumed value of what you place on that beauty. I'm sure people believe you prioritize your beauty more than you probably do. Those four guys are probably not the only ones who think you're a model."

"Do you?"

"No. It's obvious to me you're the lead guitarist in a soft-core metal band."

Selma laughed the rest of the way to her car. Chad didn't know one car from another, but he guessed the electric blue car under the streetlight to be some kind of muscle car from the seventies. Hand on the door handle, she turned to Chad and said, "It's my parents' place."

"The pretzel shop?"

"Yeah. That's why I work a lot. They have big, bold dreams, but they're not the greatest when it comes to business sense. A shop like this isn't good for a mall food court. I want to help out and learn what works, so after this location fails, I can help them find a better one."

Chad felt guilty, knowing he'd never taken an interest in his parents' dreams to this extent. Not that they would ever share their dreams with him if they had any. How would he know what their dreams were? He never asked. They never created an environment where he felt comfortable enough to ask. Or care? Chad shooed away the useless game of mental finger-pointing and returned Selma's smile. "That's . . . that's really cool."

Selma gave an "it's nothing" shrug and said, "Eh, they're my parents, right?"

"Right. So . . . I believe I fulfilled my contract regarding 'journey to your car accompaniment.' It was nice meeting you, Selma. Have a good night."

"You, too, Chad."

He walked away, hands in his pockets, but stopped when Selma called out, "Chad?"

"Yeah?"

"Wanna grab a light lunch and a coffee? There's a great organic café on Third Street. I'm busy tomorrow, but the day after?"

Chad didn't know what his friends were doing, but he assumed they'd be busy. "Sounds good. See you at noon, day after tomorrow."

"Is there a word for that? Day after tomorrow?"

"No, but that's the beauty of the English language, isn't it? There's a word for something as obscure as being pushed out of a window—defenestration—but there is no word for something as common as day after tomorrow."

Selma laughed again, the sound drowned out by the engine's roar. Chad waved as she drove away.

That was a fun distraction. Now, though, it was time to consider what to do next regarding Brick and his friends.

CHAPTER 15

Cooper looked out the passenger-side window. As the only one of his quartet who owned a car, the driving duties usually fell upon his shoulders. The other three had access to their parents' cars, but the use always came with a price: extra chores for Heston, a lecture for Chad, and a fifteen-point checklist and soul-crushing anxiety for Kyle. Cooper never minded driving, but it meant it was rare to observe life through the passenger window and let his mind wander. So, when Bryce had offered to drive to the get-together, Cooper gleefully accepted the offer.

Bryce met him at the mall. They might be teammates and Cooper liked Bryce more than any of the others, but after being attacked by Sanders in lycanthrope form, he felt particularly paranoid and opted to keep his home residence a secret from the rest of the team. Plus, it gave him a chance to grab a pretzel from the new place and flirt with Selma. Or attempt to, at least, since her usual reaction to his cleverness was a dead-eyed stare and a mumbled, "Enjoy your anarchy-infused pretzel."

Today was no different. He ordered the "cross my heart and hope to chive," a standard pretzel with a more defined loop at the top to give the pretzel an appearance of a person crossing their arms over their chest and served with a side of sour cream and chives. As she tucked the pretzel into a wax-paper sleeve, he said he might change his mind because "Crossing my heart doesn't chive with my belief system." Selma's silence was extra deathly as she took the change from the twenty-dollar bill he had handed her and dropped all of it into the tip jar. *Need to work on my material*, Cooper thought as he slunk away.

He had finished his pretzel by the time Bryce pulled up, Brandon and Tuck in the back seat. Cooper got in the front to a chorus of whoops and shoulder punches. When he closed the door and Bryce sped away, Cooper concluded that none of these three were secretly lycanthropes, doubting they could call forth anything more pernicious than a belch. But his mind quickly slipped out of the conversation held among the beats of the thumping music as he stared out the window and created a checklist of teammates' names to examine for other potential lycanthropes. A handful stood out, but he didn't associate with them well enough to decide one way or the other. The only evidence was their friendship with Sanders. Cooper shifted to get a better look at his car mates. "What's Sanders like? You know, outside of lacrosse?"

Brandon shrugged. "I dunno. He's cool, I guess," he said, his words as enticing as tap water, making the statement akin to "I dunno. He breathes oxygen, I guess." Tuck and Bryce both nodded in agreeance.

"Is he descended from affluence?" As soon as Cooper asked the question, he decided to reword it for his audience. "Are his parents loaded?"

Again, all three nodded, Bryce giving details. "Hell yeah. His dad is a big-time something-something for a big-time investment firm. He must have given up his lacrosse dreams because Sanders had a stick in his hand since birth, and his parents bought him the best coaches since he could walk. His dad all but built one of the best attackers on the east coast."

"If Sanders possesses that level of talent, why isn't he at a Quad-A school? No offense to our favorite institute of higher learning."

"Grades," Tuck grunted. "He ain't what you'd call smart. Got busted for cheating on tests and paying others to take tests for him. Daddy paid off a lot of people, but not enough for any Quad-A school to take him."

"Interesting." Cooper debated about his next question. Should any of the other three in the car be even remotely friendly to Sanders, this conversation would assuredly make its way to his ears. Cooper decided the risk was worth what his teammates could offer. Any answer held the potential of figuring out how Sanders became a lycanthrope. "So, why doesn't he like me?"

The three chuckled at varying intensities, but all implied that the answer was obvious to everyone other than Cooper.

"You're the new guy on the team," Bryce said.

"A freshman way smarter than him," Tuck offered.

"You represent all that he fears, a disruption in his perfectly balanced world where he placed himself on top by prioritizing only his achievements as an infantile measurement to success and happiness and subsequently minimizing the importance of growth by ignoring any outside stimulus unrelated to his myopic views," Brandon answered.

Bryce put the car in park, and everyone turned to stare at Brandon, their mouths agape. Brandon looked around. "What? I think I heard something like that on Dr. Phil or something, and . . . fuck yeah! We're here!"

Cooper forced down his laughter as they got out of the car. Brandon's unusually articulated assessment of Sanders made sense. It was more than just a nerd entering the world of a jock—it was a nerd potentially upending that world. If Sanders puts his whole life into one identity, what would happen if an outside force made him doubt that identity?

Cooper shook his head. That contemplation would have to wait. They arrived at the house designated as a place to hang out. The street looked familiar. Nice tree-lined neighborhood right by the campus. Tudor houses with Greek letters adorning the fronts. Frat row! Were they going to a frat house? A thought punched Cooper in the brain hard enough to make him wince as he walked up the porch steps to the front door. *Which house were we discussing at the barn?*

Bryce rang the doorbell.

The door opened, releasing the noises of a party.

Brick stood in the doorway.

Kyle looked out the passenger-side window. His face ached from smiling so much. He needed to rest it, or he might pull a muscle, but first, he turned to display it to Janey. Both hands on the wheel and sitting straight to the point of almost leaning forward, Janey returned his smile, then went back to bopping her head from side to side while humming along with the music. It was a good day, even though it started a bit weird in the food court.

They had met at the mall and bounced from store to store, not buying anything, just having fun with comments, stories, and jokes. After an hour, they decided on a light lunch before heading to Declan's apartment. Kyle got four slices of pizza while Janey grabbed a couple soft pretzels. They found an empty table at the same time and sat down. As they distributed the food, Janey said, "Some disgusting creep was hitting on the poor pretzel girl. He ordered two pretzels by pointing at her boobs and saying, 'I'll take two of those.' Did he actually think he would score points with her? Creeper. I mean, she is drop-dead gorgeous, and her boobs are huge. I wonder if they make noise when she walks? I'm thinking something like an AT-AT crushing rebel infantry. *Vrrrrr, ka-bloosh. Vrrrrr, ka-bloosh.* God, if I had boobs like hers, I'd need my brace again. *Vrrrrr, ka-bloosh.*"

A warm flush bloomed across Kyle's face, but before his cheeks could go nuclear red, one word caught his attention. "Brace?"

Janey had her hands by her chest, mimicking the movements of her theory, but froze mid *ka-bloosh*. Face turning fire-engine crimson, she brought both hands to her mouth. "Oh my God, you have to think I'm a psychopath. I'm so sorry. I really like you, and I just want to share with you, so any thought that pops into my head, I just let it fly right out of my mouth, zooming right past the filter I should be using to stop me from being a psychopath."

Kyle's heart thumped against his chest and carved her name into his ribs. "I really like you, too," he replied, his words coming out faster than he wanted. "It's awesome that you want to share whatever pops into your brain with me. I'd like to encourage that."

Janey dropped her hands to the table and smiled, her teeth almost glowing in contrast to her scarlet face. "You don't think I'm some sort of psycho?"

"Nope."

"Then what the heck is wrong with you? Psycho."

They both laughed and finished parsing out their lunch. As the mutual redness of their faces subsided to a shade of pink, Janey continued, "So, I had scoliosis and needed to wear a back brace for all four years of high school. You can only imagine how fun that was. My dad was a line worker at the candy plant and had really awful insurance, so he couldn't afford the surgery to straighten my back. Being a single parent raising three girls is tough, you know? There was so much I wanted to experience in life, but my brace held me back. Well, it only held me back from a few things, but I blamed it for everything because I had no confidence. It's weird, right, that you need confidence to try new experiences, but you can only gain confidence through experience. Anyway, right before graduation, my dad got promoted from line worker to management. He got better insurance, so I was able to get the surgery. Now I have the confidence to experience life, but not the experience yet, so I feel like I'm behind everyone else, like I'm fourteen instead of eighteen."

Feeling fourteen instead of eighteen. Kyle was never able to articulate that feeling of being behind everyone else. He felt safe and confident with his friends, but they were in the same situation due to the same circumstances, so he couldn't grow any faster than them. How could he learn from someone who had no more information than he? "I completely understand."

Janey smiled as a form of appreciation. "Thank you for not thinking I'm crazy. I guess I just get too excited sometimes, and my mouth runs away without telling my brain where it's going. There's so much I felt like I was missing out on. I would never have tried out for an esports team, even though my back brace didn't hinder me from that. I'm sure I would have gone to college, but I'm not sure I ever would have stepped foot on campus. I never went on a date before the surgery. I wanted to date a lot now that I'm discovering what confidence is. I even went out with Pixel Ronin."

"Really?" That explained why he kept close personal proximity to her any chance he got.

"Well, it was just a lunch. Guh, longest of my life. It was awful and I was worried that all dates would be like that and started to doubt the benefits of dating and wondered if there was such a thing as mail-order boyfriends and if it was even remotely legal. Anyway, none of that matters because you came along."

Kyle liked the way she said that, as if he were a knight in shining armor. "Yeah?"

"Yep." Janey sighed, almost a swoon. "You're so freaking awesome. I know we haven't been together that long, but it feels like you're a missing piece to the puzzle of my life."

"Wow. I feel the same way, too."

Janey took another bite of her pretzel and did a little happy dance in her chair. "I actually canceled a date with Stanley Lester."

"You had a date with Stanley Lester?"

Janey pointed at Kyle and crinkled her nose. "No judging. I said I canceled it. I told you I wanted to experience all that life had to offer. After spending so many years in a back brace and then having it removed? God, it was like . . . like I had received superpowers. I mean, imagine one day waking up with soooooo many more abilities than you had the day before."

Kyle smiled at the secret joke within. "Believe it or not, I understand. But Stanley Lester? That guy is even skinnier than me."

Janey waggled her finger at Kyle again. "Still no judging. And you shouldn't put someone down by comparing how awesome you are to them."

"Umm, you kind of did the same thing when you compared yourself to Selma."

"That's different. I didn't put her down. If anything, I put myself down. You're superior to Stanley; Selma is superior to me."

Kyle set his pretzel down and reached across the table to hold Janey's hands. "I think you're superior to Selma. In every way."

Janey's face turned pure red again. "Oh my God, Kyle. You are the sweetest!"

Kyle felt good, happy. And a bonus level of happiness that it seemed he made another human being happy. They both went back to eating their lunch, but one last nettle from the conversation dug into his brain, one more question. He was terrified of the answer, but all this talk about confidence pushed away his insecurities, so before he changed his mind, he asked, "You said you wanted to date a lot. Does that mean you still want to date other people?"

"Oh, God, no. I want to do the boyfriend-girlfriend thing." Janey paused mid-chew, eyes growing wide from surprise, and slowly looked at Kyle.

Kyle wanted to play it way cooler than he did, his smile wide enough to hurt, but he couldn't contain his excitement. "Me, too!"

Now in Janey's car, he replayed the whole scene in his head again and again. He thought about texting the guys, but he could wait until later. First, he and his new girlfriend had to retrieve a thumb drive from her cousin's apartment.

The small building was a boring square stack of bricks. A small lobby and a set of stairs greeted them. Three one-bedroom apartments per floor, and Declan's was the one on the right. The door opened to a modest-sized living room that led to the bedroom, the two rooms hugging the kitchenette and bathroom on the left. The living room had a couch and television with three gaming systems hooked up to it. An empty pizza box and a six-pack of crushed Red Bull cans resided on the coffee table.

A cold discomfort settled like a rock in Kyle's gut, making him feel like he was snooping. As he followed Janey into Declan's bedroom, he reminded himself that he was invited, doing a favor for the person who lived here.

Janey giggled as she kicked the dirty clothes strewn across the floor into a pile. "Boys!"

Milk crates lined the base of Declan's closet. Kyle slid one out and turned it upside down to use as an ersatz step stool so he could reach the ceiling. Just as Declan had described, there was a loose tile that hid his secrets. Not wanting to learn anything more about his girlfriend's cousin, he grabbed the blue unicorn thumb drive and ignored the rest of the items. "Got it."

"Awesome. Let's go before these smells become an indelible part of my brain."

"Knock, knock!" came from the living room. The voice sounded familiar.

"Pixel Ronin?" Janey whispered to Kyle. Cautious, they left the bedroom to investigate. Janey's suspicion was correct. "Ronin? What are you doing here?"

"Janey! How great to see you." With a colder tone, he finished with, "You, too, Kyle."

"Umm, yeah," Janey replied. "You didn't answer my question."

"Oh, yeah, sorry. I just swung by the hospital and saw Declan. He mentioned that he had a thumb drive he needed and asked me to pick it up for him."

"I highly doubt he asked you to do that since that's why we're here."

Something didn't seem right. Pixel Ronin shut the door behind him and took a couple steps closer. "Cool, cool, no worries. So, did you find it?"

Janey clenched her fists but stepped back and moved closer to Kyle. "I don't think that's information you need. So why are you really here?"

Ronin smiled like he just drank vinegar and enjoyed it, making Kyle's skin crawl. "I told you—to get the thumb drive."

Janey grabbed Kyle's hand, and they started to walk around Ronin to get to the door. "Sorry, but we looked and it's not here, so I think we should all just—"

Pixel Ronin moved to block them, his speed baffling. "Oh, I think the thumb drive is here, and I think you found it already."

"Move, Ronin! This isn't funny!"

"I'm not trying to be funny. I'm trying to be scary. Here, maybe this will help."

Feathers sprouted along Ronin's neck as his eyes yellowed and his nose turned into a beak.

———— • ————

Heston looked out the passenger-side window. Nothing much to see other than fields, farms, and forests. He rolled his eyes every time Chuck sucked his fingers, a slobbering smack of his lips. He finished his pretzel minutes ago. How the hell could there still be any salt left?

Another drooling slurp and Heston squeezed his eyes closed as if they were shutters to keep his emotions from escaping. Frustration consumed him. All he had wanted was a quiet semester to temper the excitement from last semester. He deserved that. All of his friends got to reap the rewards of surviving the peril of eliminating their bully problem, even though Chad went out of his way not to enjoy it. Now the bully problem might be back, thanks to Heston's brother.

Bud had tasked Chuck to go into town to the small hardware store to pick up some new tools. The owner gave Bud steep discounts, so there was no other place he'd go for tools and supplies. Bud also needed Chuck to talk to a farmer right outside The Bends regarding a past due bill for snow removal work Bud did for him the prior year. As much as Heston hated to take his father's side in anything, fair was fair. Bud did the work, so he deserved to be paid. And as much as Heston loathed to do it, he asked if he could accompany Chuck.

Of course, Chuck resisted the idea, but Bud told his oldest son to let his youngest ride along. It wasn't often that Heston took that much interest in the business, and he knew Bud would never deny Heston an opportunity to participate, no matter how menial the tasks. Heston didn't care about the business; he just wanted to keep an eye on Chuck.

Their first stop was the hardware store. It was small, tucked comfortably between a bank and shoe store. Next to the shoe store was a jewelry store, the main window boarded up with plywood. Heston found it odd that the hardware store's gate was almost closed, open just enough to expose the front door.

"Sorry about that," the shop owner said as a greeting when Chuck and Heston entered. "There's been a few robberies in the area."

"Like the jewelry store?" Heston asked. Chuck ignored the conversation, moving around the store with purpose.

"Yep. Just last night. Another jewelry store six blocks away a week ago. That antiques and collectibles place a block up a couple days ago. I ain't got anything as valuable as that, but you never know. These degenerates could get desperate."

"Any suspects?"

"No. Police are looking into it but no leads. What they got on the security cameras is real confusing. The bastards are smart, taking out the cameras first, but what's confusing is what can be seen of them. They're large. Real big but moved fast. No getaway car neither."

"Come on, let's go," Chuck said to Heston as he aimed for the exit with a pitchfork, a shovel, and a posthole digger in his hands. To the store owner, he said, "Put this on Bud McCurdy's tab."

Heston wanted to yell at Chuck for being a rude prick, but it dawned on him . . . was Chuck involved with the break-ins? He was vile enough to rob stores, but what part could he be playing? He was big, but the owner implied that the perpetrators were even bigger. And Heston had *never* seen Chuck move fast! The only value he'd be able to add was getaway driver, and the owner said there was none. Maybe Chuck was just being a dick as usual?

The mall was on the way to the farm they needed to go to, so they stopped for a quick bite, meaning a half-dozen greasy burgers followed by a couple soft pretzels from the new place in the food court. Of course, Chuck ordered by pointing at the pretzel on Selma's shirt and saying, "I'll take two of those."

Heston rolled his eyes and shook his head. Luckily, that was enough to exonerate him from his half-brother's words. While Chuck was looking at his hand to count exact change, Selma buried her left hand in her right armpit and pulled it out just before he looked back up. She gave his pretzel to him with her left hand, Heston's with her right.

Now, Heston was trapped in the pickup's passenger seat while Chuck tongued the remains of the pretzel from his fingers. Another lip-flapping slurp. Heston tried but couldn't stop himself from shooting a sideways laser-beam glance at Chuck. Eyes forward to guide the pickup over the rough terrain of a dirt road, Chuck still caught Heston's action. "What?" he asked, his laugh warbling with the gurgle of phlegm. "I can't stop thinking of pretzel girl. Her tits are fuckin' amazing."

Heston sighed and went back to looking out the passenger window. He knew he shouldn't have shown his annoyance because that only encouraged his half-brother. "That is," Chuck continued, "if you like girls. How about it, Heston? You like girls?"

"Yeah," Heston snapped, then the words flew out of his mouth before he even realized he said them. "Do you? Or are they just faceless pieces of meat to jerk off to?"

Chuck growled. "What a fuckin' response from a liberal sissy." He finished his statement by shoving his index finger into Heston's ear.

"Fuck off," Heston barked as he slapped Chuck's hand away.

Chuck retaliated by moving his hand back to where it was, dancing between smacking Heston's shoulder and slapping his cheek. Enough was enough! Heston made a fist and backhanded it into Chuck's chest, a fleshy smack filling the space in the cab.

All noise stopped, not even a thump from Heston's heart. He had never struck his half-brother like that before. Some pushing and shoving, just enough to get away whenever Chuck was wailing on him, but he never *punched* him before. Instinct told him to apologize as many times as possible to mitigate the payback, but he consciously kept his jaws clenched, brow furrowed, eyes angry. No. No apology.

Both hands on the wheel, Chuck laughed. It wasn't a regular laugh, though, and Heston didn't know how to interpret it. Was he laughing to cover up his embarrassment? Or was it in response to a joke only he understood? Heston took the victory and went back to looking out the window. The awkwardness didn't last long. One more turn and the farm was at the end of a long driveway.

Nothing special. Two-story farmhouse with a thin streamer of smoke from the chimney shifting with the wind, a dull red barn, and a duller silver silo. Chuck pulled up to the house and parked next to a pickup truck twice as rusted as this one. Heston got out but stayed beside the door, ready to get back in after Chuck talked to the farmer. Chuck knocked on the front door and then came back to the pickup. Arms crossed, he leaned against it the way he did when he met that man in the motel parking lot. Heston didn't like this.

A gray-haired man in a blue flannel shirt and jeans, exited the house, hair thinning and beard scraggly. His waist was larger than his chest, but there was no doubt in anyone's mind that he was sturdy enough to run a farm by himself. "Hello?"

"Hey, Mort," Chuck said in an overly familiar tone, almost threatening. "My old man sent me by to discuss some late bills."

Mort walked onto the porch and squinted. Still unsure who Chuck was, he stepped off the porch onto the packed dirt parking area. "Sorry, son, I don't recognize you. Who might your father be?"

"Bud McCurdy. Did some snow removal for you last year."

Mort spread his hands out and took a more relaxed stance. His smile exposed a few missing teeth. "You're Bud's boy? Nice to meet you, son. But I think your pop mighta mixed up some numbers. I already paid him."

"Don't think so, Mort. You're in the hole with him for seven hundred bucks. It ain't millions, but seven hundred bucks is seven hundred bucks."

Mort frowned and snapped, "Ain't no seven hundred! It's only four hundred I owe him!" He then paused and slouched, realizing he had said too much. "It *was* only four hundred. Paid him already, like I already said."

Heston was conflicted. Obviously, Mort owed money, but he didn't like the way Chuck smiled, the way he pushed himself off his pickup and sauntered over to the old farmer. Surely Bud wouldn't approve of Chuck's tactics. Would he? Bud was a mean old cuss, but wouldn't he try to work out a payment plan of some sort? That would make sense. There was no reason to try to extort an old man. Sometimes Bud just didn't make sense, and right now, neither did Chuck.

Cracking his knuckles, Chuck asked, "So, you're saying you can't pay the seven hundred you owe to my old man. Is that correct?"

"Chuck!" Heston called out. He wanted to walk right over there, grab Chuck, and drag him away. Frightening an old man wouldn't solve anything! All he could do, though, was yell, "Quit it! Let's go home and talk to Bud."

Chuck slid closer to Mort and put his arm around the old man's slumped shoulders, angling him so they both faced Heston. "Settle down, sissy. My father sent me here to work something out with Mort, and he gave me full authority for negotiating. My ways are just different than your sissy ways. I'm gonna ask you again, Mort. Are you gonna pay the seven hundred bucks?"

"I can't," Mort sighed.

Anger. The feeling that Heston had been taught over and over again to suppress for all of his life. He had to. There was nothing he could have done with it; he was too weak to use it. Now he had power. Now he could be angry. Now he was strong enough to do something, to stand up to Chuck, to stop him from hurting people. Heston clenched his fists and stepped forward.

But stopped.

Something was wrong.

With Chuck.

His fingers changed, growing shorter and wider. His skin became a sickly, pale gray. His eyes went black.

Chuck pushed Mort to the ground. All warmth left Heston's body as Chuck turned into a hippopotamus.

The hippo opened his mouth, an endless abyss of despair.

It slammed shut on Mort, his blood spraying in one gush.

CHAPTER 16

Chad hated this café. He had tried their fair-trade, non-GMO, locally sourced, chi-aligning, no-chemicals-added artisan teas and had yet to find one that was remotely tolerable on his tastebuds, let alone one he liked. Trying to figure out which one he wanted from the menu was like trying to choose which demon he wanted to torment him for eternity. The line was four people deep, so he had plenty of time to figure out how he wanted to torture himself.

When he settled for the newest tea on the menu—an experimental blend of Alaskan mint, California blueberry leaves, and zest from the legendary durian fruit sure to have an exhilarating ripple effect on his chakra (their words, not his)—the ambient noises of the crowded café lowered in volume. The rustling of paper faded, the clanking of silverware stopped, conversations went from talking to whispering. Chad instinctively checked his pants to make sure his zipper wasn't down, and after determining that it wasn't, he looked around. Selma had entered the café, and many of the patrons paused what they were doing to watch her. The entire establishment fell into a hush when she walked up to Chad and said, "Hey, it's finally totomorroworrow."

"Totomorroworrow . . . ?" Chad had researched and discovered the word for day after tomorrow was "overmorrow." He decided that her made-up word was funnier and less stuffy. "Oh, yes, the elusive and mythical word that means the day after tomorrow."

"I spent a lot of time tracking it down."

"Surfed the dark web to find it?"

"Worse. I had to turn to the black-market linguistics mafia."

Chad made an exaggerated "oh, that must have hurt" face. "Yikes. I heard they are vicious, nasty, mean, hurtful, venomous, malicious, rancorous."

"Indeed, they are. As a price to learn the secret word, totomorroworrow, I have to do some illegal verb conjugation for them."

"Wow. Your determination to learn this word is admirable."

Selma did a faux-curtsy and they both laughed. She touched his arm and said, "I'll go grab a table if you could order the turkey sandwich for me and whatever-you're-having tea."

"Sure. No problem."

Shit! Chad thought as she went to find a table. He had forgotten it was "lunch" at the organic café, not just a tea or two. Back to the devil's menu. He hadn't tried every fair-trade, non-GMO, locally sourced, chi-aligning, no-chemicals-added artisan sandwich they had to offer, but he tried enough to know they were just as tantalizing as their teas. His stomach flopped in an effort to discourage Chad from putting anything from the menu into it. By the time it was his turn to order, he had decided to keep it simple, two turkey clubs, two new teas.

"You got a turkey sandwich, too?" Selma asked when Chad sat down with lunch.

"I didn't know what to get, so I went with the whatever-you're-having sandwich."

"My favorite sandwich in the area."

The description of the sandwich haunted Chad, as if he could see the words written on the table: turkey breast rubbed with leak ash, topped with a generous helping of blanched amaranth aioli, a slathering of thrice smoked bulgur jam, and a heavenly dollop of bleached quinoa paste, served on Danish rugbrod bread, dried to give it extra texture. Selma bit into the sandwich with gusto, so Chad decided to try it. Half of the bread crumbled away as he picked it up, while the other half immediately turned to paste and coated his fingers. The first bite was a disaster, the second even worse, but by the third bite, he actually tasted what he was putting in his mouth. His eyes watered and he swore that somehow his tongue had turned inside out. He continued to munch away as quickly as possible, not having any other options, though he did side-eye the closest trash can in case of a gastrointestinal reversal of fortune. Done in record time! Now to choke down the tea.

"That was fast," Selma chuckled. "Did you like it?"

"It was special." His voice sounded funny, raspy. To deflect the need to lie about liking the sandwich, he asked, "Are you a townie?"

She was. By the time she explained that she was from West Bend and didn't participate in any extracurricular activities in high school—she didn't see the point in joining a club for the sake of joining if she didn't like the impetus behind the club, and she hated sports—Chad's voice had returned to normal, so he could ask her more questions and commiserate about high school and how happy they were to be out of it. She was a self-described homebody and didn't get out much. Her circle of friends was small and tight, content to hang out at each other's homes. They exchanged random, innocuous stories about their friends and discussed shared interests, including light gaming, heavy comic book reading, and a near obsessive love of movies.

Three hours later, when the topic of music came up, they decided it was time to come up with a name for their soft-core metal band. After rejecting Featherallica, Cloth Maiden, and Five Finger Life Tickle, they decided to go with Totomorroworrow. Since they pronounced the first part of the word as "Toto," they decided the band should be dogs dressed as various Wizard of Oz characters. To bring the vision to reality, Selma pulled a small notebook and a pen from her purse. Chad watched in amazement as she sketched away. After she finished drawing a corgi as Dorothy and a poodle as the scarecrow, Chad said, "Those are really impressive, especially for whipping them up in a few minutes. Do you do art for fun or profit or both?"

"Right now, for fun, but I wouldn't mind someday making a few bucks from it. I do all the art for the pretzel shop. My dad comes up with all the dumb names, but I come up with the merch."

"Hunh," Chad grunted. He forced a frown, but he could feel the corner of his mouth twitch in an effort to become a smile. "That's disappointing."

Selma looked up from her notebook and scowled. "Really? And why is that?"

"Here I thought I was hanging out with a hardcore artist doing what she does as a deep, unstoppable desire to show how she views life through her art-work, but it turns out she's just a soft-core corporate shill, working for 'The Man,' blindly doing 'His' bidding for a few gold pieces."

Laughing, Selma flicked a pinch of breadcrumbs at Chad. "You take that offensive comment back right now, sir."

Chad shrugged and made a goofy face while rolling his eyes. "Sorry, but I can only call it like I see it."

"Yeah? You want a hardcore artist? How about this?" Selma tore the two pages from her sketchbook. Using both hands, she showed Chad that she was ready to rip them up. "I'm so hardcore that I'd rather see my art die than be accused of being a corporate hack. So, either take it back, or the bassist and drummer of Totomorrroworrow will be joined together forever by decapitation."

"Fair enough. You passed the hardcore artist test. I take back all implications made that you sold your soul to Corporate America." Chad reached across the table and gently took the papers from Selma. Admiring them, he asked, "Dorothy's the bassist and not the lead singer?"

Selma placed her hand on his wrist. "It's the twenty-first century, Chad. She can be both."

Chad's attention went to her hand. Fear, anxiety, and concern joined together and whispered into his brain about how this would look if the wrong person happened to see. Fear, anxiety, and concern replayed all the times in school when an innocent glance at Brittany got him beat up by Mason. There was only one way to calm fear, anxiety, and concern. "So . . . do you have a significant other?"

Selma removed her hand and squinted at Chad. The look turned his spine to jelly, the feeling of saying something stupid. The right corner of her lips twitched, uncertain if laughter was called for or not. "Are you serious?"

"Yeah. If you do, my follow-up question would be if they would get overly jealous of you hanging out with me. I already have enough people who want to kick my ass. I don't need another one."

Selma leaned back in her chair and regarded Chad with utter disbelief. After a few seconds, she chuckled, possibly at something she thought of. She squinted again, studying him. His discomfort level rose to somewhere between having lettuce in his teeth and sneezing without covering his mouth. *What the hell could I have said to deserve this scrutiny?*

Satisfied with whatever judgment she passed in her mind, Selma leaned forward, elbows on the table, and asked, "You really don't know that we're on a date, do you?"

Chad somehow felt insanely hot and brutally frozen all at the same time, like a volcano erupting at the North Pole. Reality pulled itself apart one atom at a time until he could see nothing other than Selma. All one million words of the English language jumbled together into a screeching ball of white noise, except for one. "Why?"

"Did you just ask why?"

"Yes, why? I mean, why me? We have already established that you're gorgeous, and when I say, 'we,' I mean the entirety of society, so why would you possibly want to be on a date with me?"

Still leaning forward, Selma closed her eyes. "What does my shirt say?"

"Umm . . . ? I-I don't know."

"What color are my eyes?"

"A cold, light blue, like a cloudless winter day right before twilight."

Selma smiled and then slowly opened her eyes while sitting up straight. "Go ahead and read my shirt."

Chad glanced down just long enough to read: *This shirt works better than Hooked on Phonics*. He immediately looked back into her eyes. He still needed an explanation, and he must have contorted his face in a way that she understood. "You turned my shirt into a liar, Chad. And that is amazing. I've been on a lot of dates with a lot of men. A lot of *first and only* dates, some I ended after half an hour. You were a hundred percent right the other night. I know I'm pretty, and I know what most men think when they look at me. Most of the dates I've been on were nothing more than an opportunity for a man to try to crack the code and solve the puzzle of getting into my pants. Hell, I've had more than a handful of dates where a guy conversed with my tits more than with me. But you . . . you talked *with* me, not *at* me. You told me about things you enjoy, not things you'd think would impress me. You listened to me. So, why wouldn't I want to go on a date with you? You're nice, funny, smart, and you make me feel like a human being."

Chad wanted to look around to see if anyone heard that, for verification that this amazing woman said those things about *him*. Or to see if he was being recorded for a reality show where they get nerds to believe that women like this could be into them. But he didn't because now she waited for him to respond, which was the perfect time for his mind to go blank. "Well . . . cool."

Selma laughed. "You are adorable."

"Umm . . . thanks?"

"Okay, now that you *just* learned this was a date, please don't be weird."

"No weirdness. I am super awesome at not being weird." *Stop talking!* Chad was screwed. Weird was both the wallpaper and screensaver on the computer known as his life. It was his default factory setting.

"Good. And since half the people involved with this date didn't even know it was a date, how about we try again?"

Breathe. Just breathe like a normal human being for once in your life. He had a good time. She had a good time. The conversations were real, and he didn't have to try to impress her. In fact, she had explicitly stated she didn't like when guys did that. *This is simple— just keep doing what you did, be who you are.*

Chad smiled. A genuine, unforced smile. "Absolutely, I promise to pay better attention."

"Good. How about totomorroworrow we go traditional? Dinner and a movie. We can see that new sci-fi movie about time travel in pill form."

"Yeah, that sounds great."

Selma stood and dug around in her purse. A business card. Her name, number, and website for A Salt and Buttery, along with her title listed as "Baked Dough Anarchist." Chad stood as well and accepted her card. "This is my cell. You make fun of my title, and I may have to literally murder you. Again, my dad's brainchild."

"Now I can show everyone that I'm dating an anarchist because, as you know, nothing screams anarchy like putting it on a business card."

Selma smiled and then kissed his cheek. "See you totomorroworrow."

As she left, Chad became hyperaware that everyone in the café was staring at him. The women looked confused, while the men looked either amazed or angry. Feeling like the entire building was about to implode on him, Chad hurriedly threw everything away and left the opposite way Selma did.

He took the long way home, meandering through campus, walking in at least one circle. He thought he was trying to analyze what the hell had happened, but he found himself at the front door of his house, mind blank and utterly unaware of how it took him two hours to complete a thirty-minute walk.

No one was home. He thought that was odd, but he heard voices from the backyard. Grabbing a banana as he passed through the kitchen—*God, this is the best banana I ever ate in my life*—he headed outside.

Natalia. With a wicked, wicked smile on her face.

His dad was gearing up while his mother did some target practice with her crossbow. There were five bolts in the bull's-eye.

"Oh, hey, son," his father said. "We're going to train for a bit, then Natalia is taking us on another hunt. You're just in time to join us."

Natalia's smile grew and Chad's stomach dropped out of his body.

CHAPTER 17

The snow had melted, creating a layer of slimy leaves on top of the dead, crunchy ones. Not only did Chad have to risk slipping with every step he took, but he also had to endure an angry "Shhh!" from Natalia despite being quieter than anyone else in the hunting party.

"C'mon, son, try to be better," his father whispered as he tromped past, despite slipping twice. It had been a day of mixed emotions for Chad.

It started nicely enough, having a lot of fun with Selma, then became amazing because she declared they were on a date. Then came a period of uncertainty, self-doubt, and introspection because he had no idea he was on a date until it had concluded. That was followed by pure euphoria realizing he had made a future date with her. Well, she had made the date, but that didn't diminish the feeling of euphoria. However, Chad's happy feelings were crushed by the existential dread of returning home to find his parents training to kill him with a woman he had wanted to date. Not anymore, though, due to the whole she-wanted-to-kill-him thing.

Chad tried to focus on what happened at lunch. The laughter. The conversation. It was difficult, though, under the constant glare of Natalia as she criticized his every action. The drill for the day was target practice; his parents used crossbows while Chad was relegated to a bow and arrows. After an hour of, "Your chin's too high, your chin's too low, your feet need to be farther apart, your feet are too far apart," Chad finally asked, "Why are you doing this?"

"You need to learn how to walk before running, and right now, you can barely crawl."

Bud had pulled up in his pickup, pock-marked with primer gray, so Chad's parents paused in their training to greet him. Chad had no fear of them accidentally overhearing the conversation. "No, I mean training my parents and my friends' parents to hunt and kill me and my friends."

"I already told you—"

"Yeah, I remember. You and your aunt are pissed at us for not following your rules. I get it. But we haven't done anything since the coal depot, so this seems really petty."

Natalia's jaw muscles rippled like waves in an angry ocean. The fire behind her eyes desperately begged for release, but she kept her voice low to avoid unwanted attention. "Petty? Let's not forget my aunt has had *two* leg injuries since meeting you. On top of that, you sought her help and betrayed her trust—*twice*. But more importantly, she and I had a plan that involved killing Hunter and forcing my mother to move on to new hunting grounds. A plan *you* somehow screwed up."

Hunter. The lycanthrope leader of the Ink Stains who had promised to take care of Chad's bully problem like some leather-clad, tattooed faerie godmother. The bully problem had been solved by the Ink Stains eating Mason and the other football players who had been tormenting Chad. Then Hunter made him an offer. An offer that would allow Chad to control his destiny. It had been a lie. Hunter turned Chad into a rabbit so the Ink Stains could have fun with the chase before eating him.

"Hey, I killed Hunter." Something Chad still didn't know how to feel about. The idea of taking a life gave him occasional nightmares. But did he take a *human* life? If he didn't, it meant Chad wasn't human, an idea that sometimes made him feel worse than killing someone. Either way, it was irrefutable that it was in self-defense and Hunter, human or not, was a monster. "Something you and your aunt weren't able to do."

"We were trying to break his hold on my mother. Now that he's gone, she hasn't moved on. My aunt and I still have no idea why she's staying around and bringing on more members of the Ink Stains."

Chad knew why, but there was no way he would share that information with Natalia. "She's probably preparing for the lycanthrope pack coming from the south."

"If she were concerned about a pack of lycanthropes coming to The Bends, she would be leaving, not staying."

"Either way, you and your aunt should be concerned about this new pack."

Natalia smiled, an act Chad had rarely seen. It was unnerving. "But, Chad, we are."

Now Chad was tromping around the woods with her, his parents, Bud, Donovan Butera, and Mrs. Sedgeweck. He still hadn't the foggiest notion of what Natalia's plan was. She didn't share anything more than "Aggressive reconnaissance." The ride in his parents' packed minivan was quiet and awkward, everyone smashed together in the seats with their gear packed in the back. Bud made it considerably more awkward by staring at Mrs. Sedgeweck's chest, failing miserably at his attempts to be nonchalant about it by pretending to look out the window. Even when they found a place to pull over along the road running through one of the forests, the only instruction Natalia gave was, "Follow me."

The group stayed together, close enough that everyone could be heard without raising their voices. After half an hour of walking, they finally came to their target. A house. A house that Chad recognized. He had been at the very spot recently. This was the frat house he and Heston staked out because Brittany had gone into it.

It was barely visible through the trees, still plenty of woods to go before getting to it, but Natalia stopped and pointed at it. "One of my sources told me there are at least two lycanthropes in that house over there."

Bud stepped forward, his grip on the crossbow so tight the wooden shaft creaked. "What's the plan? Charge in and shoot 'em all?"

"No. You don't chase after deer, do you, Bud? You flush them out." Natalia removed her backpack and dug around inside it. She pulled out three canisters and handed them to Bud, Rick, and Mr. Butera. "These are simple smoke grenades. Just toss them through the first-floor windows, and we'll see what we flush out. If any of them are dumb enough to turn into their animal selves, we'll take care of them as quietly as possible."

"You can't be serious," Chad said. "Mom, Dad, this goes beyond vandalism. She's talking about *assault*."

Rick looked at the canister in his hand and said, "Son, she's talking about dangerous *creatures*. You saw one with your own eyes last week. We *all* did. If there is a chance that the house over there is some kind of den for these things, it's worth the risk."

Chad turned to his mother, looking for an ally. She wasn't one today. "Chad, I know it seems extreme, but when you become a parent, you'll understand. We want to protect you and your friends. All of us do. I agree it's vandalism, and if there aren't any lycanthropes in the house, we'll be scaring innocent people. But Natalia said these are smoke grenades. They're harmless. And I'm sure the building owner has insurance to pay for the broken windows."

"This is Frat Row, kid," Bud grunted. "There ain't no one in any of these houses who's innocent. Believe me. Fuckin' weirdos, all of 'em."

Mrs. Sedgeweck shrugged and tilted her head, implying Bud wasn't wrong. Chad didn't even bother with Donovan. He was so desperate to understand what happened to his son that he'd be the first to scream, "Burn the witch!" about any innocent girl brought to trial in Salem.

Chad tried a different tactic with his parents. "What if her source is wrong? What if there are zero lycanthropes here and you can no longer justify the vandalism and assault?"

"Then I'd go back to my source," Natalia said to Chad in a tone so pointed that it almost drew blood. "And have a serious conversation with them, one they would *not* like, possibly not walk away from."

"We're at the back of the house," Chad said. "Everyone will be running out the front door, so we won't see anyone."

Natalia replied, "Only the innocent ones who believe they have nothing to worry about. The ones trying to avoid getting caught will come out the back and any side doors."

"What about the cops? As soon as people run out of a smoking house, the neighbors will call the police."

Natalia's face melted from icy stern to gleeful as she reached into her backpack again, pulling out two half-globes of clear plastic. Inside each one was red and blue lights. "Not if they think they're already here. We're going to move closer and find good positions. Remember, it's important to be as invisible as possible. I'm going to place one there and the other one over there and start them remotely. When I do, count to three and throw the smoke canisters. Do you think you can handle that?"

Rick snorted. "I used to be an all-state quarterback. I think I can handle a can of smoke."

Natalia smirked at Chad before she disappeared into the forest.

"Wow," Mrs. Sedgeweck whispered. "I don't see her at all. She's really good at this."

"C'mon, let's move," Bud barked as he moved toward the house. Donovan followed him for a few yards, then split away. Mrs. Sedgeweck followed Chad's mom as they took a direct route to the house, then hid behind separate trees once they got close enough.

Chad followed his father, still trying to change his mind. "Dad, please. This isn't a good idea."

"Sometimes, we have to get through the bad ideas to get to the good ones."

"Come on. This makes no sense."

Stopping behind a tree less than ten feet from the house, Rick turned to Chad and whispered. "I know it doesn't make any sense. There are a lot of things in life that don't make sense at the time but turn out right by trusting your gut. I trusted my gut my whole life. On the football field, when a play didn't go according to plan, the only thing I could do was trust my gut. When I meet a new customer, I have to trust my gut, and that's why I'm consistently the top salesman."

"Dad, this is a completely different—"

Red and blue flashing lights surprised him. They were brighter than he had been expecting. A canister launched from the woods through one of the first-floor windows. Another canister crashed through a different window. Rick's turn. He pulled the tab and threw. His canister hit the back of the house and fell to the ground, the smoke pluming up the siding. Chad's father glared at him, the inference being it was Chad's fault he missed.

Commotion erupted from within the house, people yelling about a police raid. Chad had mixed feelings. An uneventful hunt meant that the parents could come out of this unharmed and they'd lose faith in Natalia. On the other hand, if no lycanthropes fled from the house, Natalia would lose what little faith she had in him, possibly enough to follow through with her threat of pain.

As Rick advanced, Chad moved away to get a better view of the house. He still couldn't see the front, but he had a better view of the street as people poured out. They all looked healthy, big, strong. Most likely athletes. Emmanuel was among the crowd, jogging away from the house with everyone else. After a minute, Brick joined him, and Chad wondered how brazen Natalia would be. Of course, if she were going to make a move, it would be with the people coming out the back door, not the front. Six, seven, eight people stumbled out the back door, wobbling as they made their way through the smoke cloud. Another joined them and Chad's heart sped up. Orlando. So far, he was still in his human form, and Chad repeated, *stay that way, stay that way*, over and over in his mind. Then a second-floor window at the back of the house opened and someone crawled out.

Chad's heart seized.

It was Cooper.

In ferret form.

CHAPTER 18

Chuck chewed the farmer. Entrails dangled from his teeth. Hippopotamus.

Like Heston's animal self, Chuck's was smaller than the real thing. Heston didn't know a lot about hippos, but he had seen enough adventure movies set in the jungle to know they were huge beasts. But being smaller than the real thing didn't diminish how imposing Chuck was in hippo form. He was certainly large enough to pulverize the farmer.

With slobbering grunts, the hippo's jaws worked like macabre pistons, his dull teeth pulping the farmer. The cracks and snaps of shattering bones gave way to wet smacks of grinding meat. One last chomp and the hippo shook his head, sending ground hunks of farmer this way and that. Looking as if he had just raided a butcher's shop, sloppy chunks slid over Chuck's nose as he turned his attention to his half-brother.

Sweat rolled over Heston's forehead, down to his trembling lips and chin. Dread rooted his feet to the packed dirt as Chuck charged. He fought with his legs, demanding they move; they gave him half a step back and stopped again when he bumped into the front of Chuck's truck.

This was it. This was how he would die. He always assumed it would have been from Chuck being stupid with a piece of landscaping equipment, but he always knew his half-brother would ultimately kill him. Pressing against the truck, Heston was disappointed in himself for allowing Chuck to make him feel this way despite having the power to do something about it. No, not disappointed. Annoyed. Angry! Heston changed his mind about dying.

Over the past few months, Heston practiced using parts of his abilities better. Minor changes to his muscles to make himself leaner. Now he needed a major change. Increasing the bulk of the musculature of his legs, he launched himself over the hood of the truck to avoid Chuck.

Heston hit the hood just as Chuck slammed into the side of the truck and tumbled to the ground, shoulder slamming the dirt first. It hurt, but not enough to stop his transformation. Bursting through his clothes, he shifted into full ox and ran.

One other hippo fact Heston knew was that they were a lot faster than they appeared. He remembered this just as Chuck clamped down on one of his back legs. Heston hadn't gotten very far with his escape, and Chuck threw him against the truck.

Too much pain to concentrate on holding his form, Heston went back to being human. At first, his head hurt, but grenades went off within his left leg. Thanks to the lycanthropy, he'd heal faster than normal—what would take days to fix now only took hours. If he survived.

Chuck took his time approaching Heston. *Why wouldn't he?* Heston thought. *He's a sadistic asshole, enjoying this.* After a slow, waddling trot, Chuck stopped ten feet away.

Heston worked himself into a sitting position, back against the truck, and pulled his right leg close to his body to plant his foot. He planned to shift into his minotaur form and push off with his good leg when Chuck charged again. It was not a good plan, but it was all he had.

Even from this distance, the hippo's hot breath washed over Heston. Pawing the ground with his right front foot, like a bull getting ready to charge, the hippo squinted its black, marble eyes and twitched its tiny ears. It smiled. Launching his girth, Chuck started to charge, but stopped within a few steps. Before Heston could form any questions, the truck shook and the windows blew out from something massive landing on the roof.

A gorilla.

Its roar vibrated through Heston as it pounded its chest. It wasn't the only animal to join the fray. A bear on all fours lumbered around the truck from the front while an alligator high-walked its way from the rear of the truck. A large cat leaped into the truck bed, silent and graceful. Heston recognized the tawny-furred mountain lion and the brown bear—Kat and Dylan. The other two were undoubtedly the newest members of the Ink Stains that Chad had mentioned.

Heston slumped against the truck; all hopes of survival dashed. As slim as it was, he had a fighting chance to escape Chuck. Not the Ink Stains, though. Not with all four of them joining Chuck.

The gorilla jumped from the roof and landed next to Heston. He wasn't sure which god he believed in, but he prayed anyway, for a fast death, one as painless as possible. But the gorilla didn't face him. It faced Chuck.

The bear and the alligator advanced on the hippo, making their intentions known with rumbling growls and a hiss that made Heston's skin crawl. Kat jumped out of the truck bed and landed on the other side of Heston. She gave him a wink before turning her attention to the hippo.

Chuck shook his head while taking a few steps back. Heston thought he'd retreat, but this was Chuck, his anger fueling his engine of stupidity. With a chest-rattling groan, Chuck opened his mouth to expose two spike-like bottom teeth and stomped his feet, a posture of aggression. He snapped his jaws shut and charged.

He aimed for the bear and gorilla. Dropping his head and turning to throw his bulk, the hippo crashed into the other beasts with the heavy slap of meat hitting concrete. Chuck slammed the gorilla into the truck and knocked the bear off balance. He didn't let up, shoving his body into the bear and stomping his feet. Heston's heart fell from his chest as he watched the scourge of his existence fight off the Ink Stains, the scariest creatures on the planet. Before all hope was lost, they showed why they should be feared.

Kat pounced on top of the hippo, sinking her front claws into his back and digging with her back claws. The alligator whipped across the dirt and sank its teeth into the hippo's back leg. The gorilla recovered and joined in the fight, bringing both fists down on the hippo's head, driving the beast's bottom jaw into the ground. Chuck dropped and rolled, pulling his leg from the alligator's jaws and forcing Kat to jump away.

Heston grit his teeth so hard his neck hurt. He almost cheered when the Ink Stains attacked Chuck and wanted to swear when Chuck fought back, but all he could do was sit and watch. Sit and watch. That was what he had always done in life, almost like it was his mantra. That was his default reaction. He had strength. Chuck having strength didn't diminish his own. He could do something to help. He *needed* to do something!

Getting to his feet, Heston turned into his minotaur self. His leg hurt, but he fought through the pain. Shifting his balance from one hoof to the other, he watched the fight, waiting for a chance to join in. A glint of sunlight off something metal from the pickup's bed caught his eye. The tools. The pitchfork.

Chuck groaned and snapped his jaws at his attackers but missed every time. The Ink Stains were gaining the advantage, biting and slicing his hide with coordinated attacks. Bleeding from multiple wounds, Chuck finally decided to retreat. With one last hip check to the gorilla, the hippo fled the skirmish.

No! Heston needed to stop Chuck. How could he live in the same house after Chuck had murdered someone? It was no wonder Chuck's inner animal was a hippo, a massive beast capable of deadly disruption. That was what Chuck did. Disrupt. He'd appear from out of nowhere in Heston's life and disrupt it. Trample it. No more! Heston was not about to let Chuck simply run away. He raised the pitchfork over his head and started to run after the hippo. A hand reached out and grabbed his arm, stopping him.

Kat.

She was in her half-human, half-cat form. "Slow down, cutie. We can't let you do that."

"What?" Heston barked, the voice coming from his oxen face, deep and unnatural. He clenched his fists and turned to address Kat directly. The other three Ink Stains moved behind her, the alligator in a half-human form. They had helped Heston with Chuck, but they'd turn on him in a second should he continue his threats toward Kat. He yanked his arm from her grip and threw the pitchfork back into the bed of the truck. Partially from apathy, no longer caring if they ate him or not, and partially to show he wasn't a threat, he turned back to human and slumped against the truck. "Why?"

Kat turned human and the other three followed her lead. Dylan, the bear, had the shortest distance to cover between animal and human. Over six-and-a-half feet tall, a layer or two of fat covering muscles Heston wanted to have, thick curls of black hair covered his body except for his head, bald and shiny. The alligator was a slimy-looking man with tight muscles wound around a thin frame marked with faded black tattoos all over his body. Long wavy hair, tinted green like moss, draped like sweaty curtains over much of his sneering face. Surprising Heston, the gorilla was a woman. Taller than he was, she had thick arms and legs and a layer or two of extra cushion. She was nowhere as big as Dylan, but she could cause some damage should they get into a fight in their human forms. Sweat matted her long black hair in uneven strips against the shaved sides of her head. Like the rest of the Ink Stains, she had a plethora of tattoos, including a crow on the left side of her head, the mark of The Morrigan. Heston's only tattoo was The Morrigan's crow on his back.

Kat put her hand on his shoulder. "Hey, I get it. He's your brother, right? I'm sure you want to shove that pitchfork right up his ass. But he's involved with something big. Something bad. We were following him and decided to lend a hand when he ambushed you. We need him alive, though, to keep following him and see who he's been meeting with. In fact . . ." She looked over her shoulder and said, "Tasha, Kicks, if you wouldn't mind."

A forest bordered the farm and covered the nearby mountain. Heston watched Tasha and Kicks turn into their animal selves and pursue the hippo into the forest. "What is he involved in?"

Dylan walked over to the farmhouse and grabbed a large duffel bag. He brought it over as Kat continued, "Not entirely sure. But Kicks came from Mills Hook and warned us that a lycanthrope pack was coming our way. Coincidentally, stores are getting robbed and some scumbags have been disappearing."

"Scumbags?"

"The kind that counterfeit. The ones you see when you need fake passports, credit cards, social security numbers."

Heston took deep breaths and blew them out through pursed lips to calm himself. He paced in a small circle while running his hands over his head. "What about the farmer? What about my dad's truck? What the fuck am I gonna tell my dad about Chuck?"

Dylan had something else in his hand other than a duffel bag. A cell phone. He tossed it to Heston. Kat said, "The truck looks like it should still run. Take it back to your old man and show him what's on the phone."

Heston looked at the phone. And smiled.

———

Pixel Ronin turned. Beak, feathers, deadly talons. A golden eagle.

Janey screamed.

Where Ronin had stood was now a human-sized bird with a body of brown feathers and a head full of golden ones, its wings spread wide. With one flap, the great bird launched itself at Janey.

Kyle grabbed Janey and dove between the couch and coffee table. Ronin's claws tore chunks from the couch back as he swooped by. Janey screamed again.

The coffee table. Protecting Janey, Kyle squirmed under the coffee table, a massive slab of sturdy wood atop legs thicker than Kyle's. It shook as the eagle landed on it. Ronin released an ear-splitting cry, then slammed his beak into the top, his talons digging at the wood. Feathers hit Kyle in the face with every frantic flap of the eagle's wings.

Janey cried and trembled in Kyle's arms. He wanted to cry, too, wanted to close his eyes and wish away this problem. He'd be torn to shreds if he did that, though, as would Janey. He needed to change into his animal self, but he needed to get out from under the coffee table, get Janey out of this mess. He wished he could transform into a half-human, half-animal like the guys could. It didn't seem like Ronin could do that either, or he'd have done so to flip the coffee table over. Maybe his becoming a lycanthrope was a recent event? Experience. Kyle had experience being a lycanthrope. Time to see if he could use that to his advantage.

The television. From this angle, Kyle noticed that the seventy-inch television was perilously close to the edge of its stand. Could he launch himself from under the coffee table into the bottom of it? No, not possible. He looked around for anything to throw. A couple game controllers were close by. Both of them were attached to their respective systems by cords, recharging. Perfect.

Kyle reached out from under the table and fought back tears as the feathers from the slapping wings cut his arm. *Deep breaths. Don't look at the blood. Reach!* Kyle grabbed the controllers and pulled them closer. A few more cuts to his hand, but Kyle pushed through the pain to get a good hold on the cords and yank.

The cords were plugged into the systems tight enough to tug all three consoles. Kyle pulled again, harder. The consoles moved closer, and the cords connecting them to the television drew taut. One more pull and the front of the feet holding the television slipped off the stand. The television toppled on Ronin.

The flurry of screeches and scrapes stopped. Kyle hurried out from under the table and pulled Janey with him. Walking in small circles, Ronin held his left arm and grimaced, back in human form. "You fucking asshole! That fucking hurt!"

Kyle didn't waste time trying to think of anything to say. Instead, he guided Janey back to the bedroom while she yelled, "What's happening? What's happening?"

"I'll explain later." Kyle was right behind her but didn't make it into the room. Talons dug into his shoulders. Pain blasted from the puncture points, and he flailed about, reaching for anything. He grabbed the handle just as Ronin pulled, slamming the door shut.

Good, Kyle thought as he flew through the air. *She won't have to see me die.* He landed on his back. More pain searing everything inside his chest. He opened his eyes just in time to see Ronin back in eagle form launch across the room, leading with his talons. *No. I can't let this noob beat me!*

Kyle rolled out of the way as talons shredded the carpet. He turned into his animal self, a pheasant, and swiped at the eagle with his own talons, wings out for balance. Kyle wasn't sure where he connected, but he slashed Ronin enough to elicit a squawk.

Kyle in pheasant form was a little smaller than Ronin in eagle form. One was a predator, the other prey. One was built to hunt and kill, the other to run and hide. There was no place to run, nowhere to hide. And Kyle didn't want to! He was done with "run and hide." He had stood up to other lycanthropes, fought them, and even . . . killed one. He had no memory of that, though. From what everyone had told him, he mutated into something even more than a half-human, half-pheasant. Some kind of wicked bird monster. What he wouldn't give to be able to do that now.

Ronin spread his wings and screeched. Kyle did the same, though his wings were smaller. The eagle lunged forward and snapped his beak. Kyle jumped back and pecked Ronin's exposed neck. He connected twice but did little harm through the thick coat of feathers. The two danced around, both sets of wings fluttering, as they swiped at each other. Nothing more than superficial grazes until Ronin hopped onto the couch.

One leg on the back. One on the armrest, Ronin extended the tips of his wings forward. With the motion of a swimming stroke, he snapped his wings back and shot forward. Kyle couldn't dodge the collision, the impact sending him to the ground. Ronin straddled Kyle, talons on either side of his body. A stuttering chirp came from the eagle's mouth, an unusual noise that Kyle interpreted as laughter. The eagle brought his curved beak closer to Kyle's face and opened his mouth.

The sound of clanging metal filled the air. Ronin's eyes went wide, and his tongue flopped out his mouth. The metal clang sounded again. This time the eagle jumped off Kyle and staggered to the closest wall for support. Kyle was overjoyed to have Ronin off him, but what happened?

Janey. With a cast-iron frying pan.

Kyle, still in pheasant form, got back to his feet. Eyes wide, Janey gasped and took a step back, wielding the frying pan like a baseball bat. She had already hit a couple of home runs, judging from the way Ronin, in human form, leaned against the wall and struggled to stay on his feet, so Kyle didn't want to take any chances. He shifted back into human form.

Janey gasped again and took another step back. Shaking, she tightened her grip on the frying pan. "Wha . . . wha . . . What are you?"

Kyle recognized his nudity when Janey inspected his body. Despite the dire situation, the warmth of a blush bloomed across his cheeks. He covered his privates and inspected his clothes. Rags, now useless. The bedroom.

Kyle took quick sidesteps toward the bedroom, making sure to face Janey the entire way. "I'm a lycanthrope. I know it sounds crazy. Believe me, I'm living it and I still don't believe it. I didn't know Pixel Ronin was one, and I have no idea how he became one, but it's pretty obvious he wants to kill us, so we need to get out of here. But I need pants first."

Janey followed him into the bedroom and looked back at Ronin before she entered. He swayed back and forth on his knees, holding his head with his hands.

Kyle ran to the dresser and opened drawers, rifling through them for viable options. Declan was much larger than Kyle, so nothing would fit well. Sweatpants and a sweatshirt were Kyle's best options. He hurriedly put on a pair of socks and pulled the drawstring of the sweatpants as tightly as he could. "Okay, we need to get out of here before Ronin comes to."

As if his words were a spell that conjured what a person wished for the least, Ronin appeared in the bedroom doorway. "Too late, bitch!"

The golden eagle returned, and Ronin was gone. Kyle stepped in front of Janey and readied himself for round two of his fight with Ronin. The eagle opened his mouth to screech, but sirens sounded instead. Faint but quickly growing louder, red and blue lights flashed on the other side of the windows. Like the sirens, they started small but grew in intensity as the police cars sped closer.

Ronin backed out of the bedroom, his intense eyes locked on Kyle the entire way into the living room. Close enough to the door, Ronin fluttered out of the apartment. Kyle couldn't fly, and even if he could, he doubted he'd be able to carry Janey.

Three police cruisers turned the final corner, one stopping by the curb outside the bedroom window. Having no other option, Kyle grabbed Janey's hand and ran into the living room to grab his shredded clothes and destroyed shoes. He didn't want any evidence, and he absolutely did not want to leave his phone behind. As fast as possible without hurting her, he pulled Janey out of the apartment. The tiny foyer flashed red and blue. The other two cruisers came to a stop in front of the building.

Stairs. Up the stairs.

They made it to the flat roof and peeked over the edge. Despite the fast arrival, the officers took their time getting from their cars to the building. Kyle moved away from the edge and slumped down, drained, shoulders hurting from the fight.

"Kyle?" Janey whispered. Cross-legged, she sat next to him as two streams of tears flowed over her cheeks and splashed against the black rubber rooftop. "What's going on?"

He told her. Everything.

— • —

Brick answered the door. Cooper saw Sanders as well. He thought he was fucked.

Bryce, Brandon, and Tuck entered the house, doling out smiles and high-fives. Brick glanced at Cooper and smirked. "Hey, weasel, welcome to the party. Beers in the kitchen. You're responsible for getting your own pussy."

Brick showed no signs of aggression or hostility; he simply handed Cooper a red plastic cup of beer and mingled with the crowd. Sanders behaved as well, offering a sneer and then plodding his way up the stairs. Brandon and Tuck gleefully joined the crowd. Bryce tapped his red plastic cup against Cooper's and said, "C'mon, man."

There were other members of the lacrosse team here and people from other college sports teams. Cooper recognized a few individuals from the baseball team and a couple from the soccer team. There were an equal number of female athletes, if not more. Cooper recognized more of them than their male counterparts. What sent klaxons blaring in his mind was the appearance of Orlando and Emmanuel, teammates of Brick's and fellow lycanthropes. Emmanuel was an offensive lineman and a bull but favored his half-animal, half-human form of a terrifyingly massive minotaur. Orlando was a wiry wide receiver, his animal self a greyhound Cooper had tangled with on more than one occasion. Cooper's stomach knotted when Orlando noticed him from across the room. The knot tightened when Orlando smiled pleasantly and raised his cup as if saluting an old friend.

Cooper needed to let the gang know what was happening. When he reached for his phone, it was no longer in his pocket. Panic threw a lightning bolt through his chest, thinking someone had swiped it but realized the reason for his missing phone was nothing more nefarious than his own foolishness. He had sent a text to his mother during the drive over and put it in the passenger door pocket instead of returning it to his back pocket. Feeling vulnerable, he had no other choice but to follow Bryce into the crowd.

The party went on in every room in the house. The front door opened to a massive living room large enough to accommodate two full couches, one love seat, and three recliners. The carpeted stairs disappeared into the second floor while creating space for a closet. A dining room, designated "The Chug Emporium," lay beyond the living room and had two beer pong tables. The kitchen was next with an empty fridge and full keg, neither seemingly ever changed status. Another long, thin room shot off from the far side of the kitchen and went along the side of the house and back to the front, giving access to the stairs.

Cooper flowed with the crowd, letting the party take him through the house, tempering his drinking with awareness, which wasn't too difficult since he just now discovered that his palate wished to reject the beer that sloshed over it. Thanks to the cup's opacity, it was easy to feign a big swig while merely taking a sip. Having lost Bryce somewhere within The Chug Emporium, Cooper floated from conversation to conversation through the rooms. A smile, a nod, a witty statement or two, another nod, move on. Vigilance was key if he wished to survive this soiree.

He didn't know how many people here were like him, a dangerous variable considering that at least four of them had tried to kill him. How many more were skulking through the crowd, ready to pierce his back with a claw or rake a talon across his neck? Everyone else here? No one else? Was there a way to tell? A physical feature? A smell? That idea intrigued him. Smell was an integral part of the animal kingdom, something humans no longer prioritized for survival. Lycanthropes, no matter what the inner beast may be, had to possess a different aroma than humans. Could he detect it? Ferrets had a keen sense of smell, so Cooper decided to use that to his advantage the same way he used his inner animal's quickness in front of the goalie net. Slowly, carefully, he focused on shifting on a micro-level, just his olfactory senses. The smells of alcohol and body odor punched him in the face. He shifted his sense of smell back to the dullness of a human and thanked various deities that there was a wall close enough to lean on after being thrown off balance by the assault of disgusting stenches. Not that they were terrible, it just felt like the entire party had been shoved up his nose all at once. He'd have to experiment with this at a later date and time. For now, he continued to meander his way through the house.

Despite his enthusiastic façade, he was not having fun. The conversations were vapid at best, few containing any form of topic he found interesting. Even if he did stumble upon one that had threads begging for him to pull and unravel, he didn't want to spend too much time in one place. He stumbled upon one group discussing the latest happenings on some reality television show, so he made a hasty retreat that led him upstairs.

Six bedrooms and a bathroom. Two of the bedrooms' doors were closed, and he assumed tawdry dalliances within them. He drifted in and out of one room, then another. The third had a conversation about the latest sci-fi movie. He couldn't resist joining a group speculating about overdosing on a time travel drug. The conversation moved on from the initial topic but stayed in the realm of movies, a nice change of pace from the other conversations Cooper had suffered through. Over the next twenty minutes, the group dwindled to five, then three, then Cooper found himself alone in the room. And savored the moment.

Drawing another sip of warm beer, he wandered over to the window and gazed out upon the forest behind the house, the dense conglomeration of trees coming right up to the building. Twilight shadows danced with each other, merging with the trees to create a web of darkness upon the ground. Soon enough, the sun would set, and he wondered how much longer he had to stay at this party. What was the etiquette regarding contacting the person who brought him? Why were a couple of those shadows outside moving?

Cooper moved closer to the window and squinted. Something didn't seem quite right outside. Something didn't seem quite right inside the room either when the door shut. Cooper turned, wondering at first if it was another party-goer looking to escape the mayhem for a moment or two. He was wrong. So wrong.

Brick and Sanders.

Fuck!

Cooper swallowed the lump in his throat and tightened his abs to control the roiling within his guts. He placed his cup on a nearby desk and crossed his arms, making sure his hands were hidden so he could form claws. Ferret claws weren't the deadliest in the animal kingdom, but they could do some damage if slashed across the eyes of an attacker. "It's quite a shindig you have brewing below us, Brick. Isn't it considered a faux-pas to abandon your own celebration while still in progress?"

"Not my place. Not my party," Brick said. "We need to talk."

Sanders scowled at Brick. "Talk? This isn't what you and I planned. We said we were gonna mess him up."

"Still might, but I need to know something from him first."

"You wish to ascertain the quantity of vials we have left, since it's obvious you used all of yours," Cooper said.

"We haven't used a fuckin' one of them since the night we got—" Brick stopped himself. Shaking his head, he chuckled. "Clever way to figure out how many we have left. You might be too clever for your own good."

"Let's fuck him up now," Sanders said as he clenched his fists and stepped forward.

Brick extended his arm, dropping it in front of Sanders like a parking garage gate. Sanders fit no definition of the word "small," but Brick's arm was so large it almost hid Sanders's chest. "Not yet. I want to know what he knows about the upcoming storm."

"Upcoming storm? What are you talking . . . do you mean the pack of lycanthropes coming up from Mills Hook?"

Brick nodded slowly. "Yeah, so you do know. I think we need to talk about that."

"I assume you have some pertinent information about them?"

"I do. Not quite sure what to do with it yet."

The situation took a turn from dire to fortunate. Not only might Cooper make it out of this alive, but he'd have gained information about a variable involving potential doom. Of course, fate being the fickle anthropomorphic personification of a higher-level concept, it flipped the metaphorical middle finger to Cooper and changed the fortune of the situation. Red and blue lights flashed outside, followed by the sounds of breaking glass. Footsteps thudded along the hallway outside the door. Screams emanated from the first floor. Muffled voices called out, "Cops!" and "Tear gas!"

"Fuck!" Sanders yelled as he yanked open the door and fled. Brick followed but not before scowling at Cooper and slamming the door shut.

Dicks!

Cooper assumed that if he tried to follow, there would be a punch to the face in his future. He opened the window and took off his clothes. If the shadows he had seen earlier were caused by the police moving closer to the house, he'd aim right for them. Smoke rolled along the back of the house. Tear gas or not, it offered cover. He shifted to his ferret form but kept his left arm a little more human so he could hold onto his clothes and shoes. As he climbed down the outside of the house, he hoped that all the police had rushed into the house. About halfway down, the situation became more confusing when a crossbow bolt struck the wall, mere inches from his head.

Mind racing as he dropped into the spreading smoke below him, he heard the thunk of another bolt hitting the house. Natalia and the hunters were here. Staying in his current form, he crept through the haze. He considered changing back to human and dressing, but there were way too many problems with that, the biggest being the potential for someone seeing him turn. No, he'd stay the course, ready to sprint away as soon as he saw a clear path to freedom.

All he could see and smell was smoke; thankfully, it wasn't tear gas. He heard random voices, people yelling. Footsteps around him, running through the forest. Into the forest. They had to be partygoers fleeing into the woods.

Cooper scurried deeper into the woods, picking up his pace but still cautious. The smoke thinned and his confidence grew that he was heading in the right direction, away from the house. Shapes. Shadowy figures moved about, cutting holes into the smoke. Suddenly two of them changed course. "Over here!" That voice was familiar. Chad's father!

The hunters were too close, and Cooper had no idea how many there were. It was a calculated risk, but one he decided to take. Run!

Left front leg clutching his belongings, he couldn't reach top speed, but there were too many trees to attempt to run that fast. Shadows shifted, appeared, and then disappeared. The smoke was gone, but it was now nighttime. Chad's father kept yelling. Heston's father joined in, shouting things like, "There! Over there!"

Ahead, something rushed toward him, too fast to be any of the hunters. The terrain didn't allow him to veer. It was fast, way faster than he was running. In no time, he saw it was a greyhound. A human-sized greyhound. Orlando. They ran past each other in opposite directions. In a split second it took to pass, they each shot the other a look of recognition, of solidarity. As soon as they passed each other, Cooper realized he was now running toward whatever Orlando was running from.

Cooper made a hard cut and thanked his instincts as two bolts struck the ground right where he would have been. The shouts grew louder all around him. He couldn't see them, couldn't determine if he was running away from them or toward them. The survival part of his brain told him to run serpentine, zigzagging among the trees.

Leaves crunching, twigs snapping, Cooper tried to use the noises to determine where other people were. Was it just him making those noises? Something zipped across his path in front of him. A rabbit. A human-sized rabbit. Chad!

You beautiful bastard, Cooper thought as he tried to keep an eye on Chad but lost sight of him quickly. He stayed his course, running straight ahead. He wanted to help Chad but didn't know how. Or maybe Chad was helping him? After a couple minutes, relief came over him, an instinctive sense letting him know danger was gone.

Stopping behind a large tree, Cooper scanned the area, nostrils flaring to take in as many smells as possible. He was not alone—something else was nearby. Something not human.

"Cooper," came from behind him.

Cooper spun to see a rabbit peeking out from behind a nearby tree. "Chad! Are you harmed?"

Chad hopped over to Cooper with no signs of injury. "I'm good. You?"

"I came out of this unscathed, many thanks to you. I assume that was Natalia and the parents?"

"Yes. I tried to talk them out of it, but they obviously didn't listen."

"You're right again, my friend. They're becoming a problem we need to address. However, a more pressing matter arose today at the party. Brick and the jocks know something about the Mills Hook pack. And they didn't use their Elder Blood to turn either Sanders or Brittany."

"Meet at the barn tomorrow?"

"Indubitably. Do you have clothes?"

"I do. I'll go change and play dumb. I tried texting you and the others but no response."

"I left my phone in a teammate's car. I'll get it tomorrow."

"Okay. I'll keep trying the others. See you soon."

"Salutations, friend Chad."

His house was far from the woods, but Cooper could easily cover it in his ferret form. What was not at ease was his mind, wondering what could have happened to Heston and Kyle, stopping them from texting back.

CHAPTER 19

A shower always helped Chad sort out his thoughts. Sometimes he felt like the water washed away the muddiness in his mind as it did the dirt and dried sweat from his body. And his mind was certainly muddied right now.

The car ride home was nothing but chatter among the parents, and Chad wouldn't have been able to get a word in edgewise even if he wanted to. They had seen *three* lycanthropes tonight, one of them being the rabbit from their first hunt, but no signs of the gazelle. It was an epidemic. The town, if not the world, was being overrun. Bud was so agitated he didn't once look at Mrs. Sedgeweck's chest during the trip home.

Natalia had opted to stay behind and collect the flashing lights and crossbow bolts to conceal the hunters' existence. Chad asked if she would retrieve the empty smoke grenade canisters. She'd leave them behind, saying it would add to the misdirection. It'd look like a prank gone wrong. If people had an answer, no matter how dumb, they'd stop asking questions.

Once home, Chad went right upstairs to shower. He needed to talk to his parents about what the hell happened tonight, but he knew it would do no good to try with Bud, Mrs. Sedgeweck, and Donovan Butera around. He'd shower, let them have their frantic and misguided discussions, and figure out what he wanted to say.

What he had seen tonight was unnerving. Not only did they not lose interest as they had done with so many other hobbies, but they embraced this with such gusto that they were willing to do whatever they deemed necessary. This was getting out of hand.

What were they thinking? Property damage. Shooting weapons around innocent civilians. Sure, it was a frat house full of jocks, but that didn't mean it was acceptable for his parents to do what they did. His parents! In front of him—their son! What kind of example was that? He was just a kid, after all! Okay, he was an adult, but he had been one for about a year and hadn't been very good at it. It wasn't like an adulthood instruction manual came with the cake on his eighteenth birthday. If there were such a thing, one of the top ten rules would probably be, "Don't become a lycanthrope."

As he scrubbed the remaining suds of shampoo out of his hair, he knew his last thought translated to "Don't try to take the easy way out," with a subsection of "Communication." As much as he didn't want to have this conversation with his parents, it was the adult thing to do. No good would come from ignoring the problem.

Done, dried, and dressed, Chad went downstairs. His parents were inside the kitchen by the opened door while talking to Bud as he stood outside. Their whispers were exaggerated enough for Chad to hear with ease.

"We could have used her tonight." Bud's whisper sounded like his regular speaking voice, only raspier.

"You don't believe those rumors are true, do you?" Rick asked. "About what she used to be."

"Don't matter if they're true or not . . ." Bud paused to look over Rick's shoulder at Chad, then continued, "We need to strengthen the group."

Rick and Samantha looked over their shoulders at Chad. Samantha smiled as if Chad had walked in on them sharing pie recipes. Chad returned a look of earnestness and sat at the dining room table, the place for family discussions. Samantha caught the meaning and turned back to Bud. "We'll try to contact her before the next hunt, whenever that may be."

Bud grunted at her answer, then left.

Chad assumed they were talking about Wanda but couldn't imagine which rumors were in question. Not that Wanda mattered at the moment, just the nonsense her interference had wrought. "Could we talk about what happened tonight?"

"Yeah, that was pretty crazy, right?" Rick asked as he took a seat.

Samantha sat between father and son, the demilitarized zone meant to keep the peace. "What's on your mind, son?"

"Ummm, tonight?" Chad asked, incredulous that either of them even had to ask.

Rick frowned. "What exactly about tonight are you referring to? Us flushing out a den of deadly creatures? Or us fighting those deadly creatures?"

"How about the recklessness involved? Not only could you have been hurt, but you were blatantly breaking the law."

"Breaking the law? My friends and I would do way worse in high school. And I'm sure laws are being broken every hour on Frat Row."

"Jesus, Dad, this isn't high school. You're almost forty, not a teenager. There are real consequences to your actions. And just because someone else is breaking the law doesn't mean it's right for you to do it, too. I mean, didn't you and Mom teach me that in kindergarten?"

Rick frowned. "You need to watch your tone."

"Now, Rick," Samantha said, placing a hand on her husband's clenched fist. The act had a calming effect, and his hand softened to a more relaxed state. "He's not wrong. Whenever you're faced with new stimuli, your first instinct is to draw experience from your high school days." She turned to face Chad, a warm smile on her face. "And you should listen to your father. We know you're an adult now, but you need to remember that no matter how old you get, we'll always be older, more experienced." She then put her other hand on Chad's, her tone almost playful. "You also need to learn the difference between 'almost forty' and 'halfway through our thirties.'"

Chad took a breath. "Sorry, Mom. Sorry, Dad. I didn't mean for my words to have that tone. What I meant to express is that you two are breaking the law, something you spent the first eighteen years of my life telling me not to do."

"Sometimes you have to do a little wrong to do a lot of right," Rick said, undoubtedly quoting from some coach.

Samantha held her smile and subtly squeezed Chad's hand, telling him to pay attention to her words. "As I'm sure you've learned already, you can't always color the world in black and white. You have to use a lot of grays. Part of being an adult is looking at a topic or an issue and figuring out how much shading to use."

"I get that, but don't you think you used a lot of shading? You damaged property. You scared dozens of people. You shot crossbows very close to a residential area."

Rick's eyes widened. Over his lifetime Chad had seen all varieties of frustration, confusion, and anger on his father's face. On occasion, he'd see contentment and joy. The two expressions he had never seen his father express were sympathy or fear. Chad could now cross the latter off that list. Not only did he look afraid, but he spoke faster. "Son, you saw those . . . those . . . *things*. They are so far outside of being gray that I don't even know what color you'd call it."

"I don't know what I saw. In the forest, I saw a deer with strange antlers. By the frat house, I saw a greyhound, some kind of weasel, and a really large rabbit. Everyone keeps saying they're . . . lycanthropes? I mean, they're supposed to turn into people, right? All I've seen are unusual animals. That's weird, but I'd hardly call them lycanthropes. Has anyone seen one of these animals turn into a person?"

"Bud said during our first hunt, the rabbit turned into half a human. Wanda and Natalia have seen lycanthropes change many times. And they showed us the video. You saw it, Chad. You saw the video, saw how those thugs . . . the . . . what are they called? . . . the Ink Stains turned into those creatures and slaughtered Mason and the other two football players. That's some crazy shit, son. It . . . I'm gonna be honest . . . it scares me. It scares me that there are these . . . *things* . . . out there that could kill and eat any one of us at any time. Aren't you scared?"

Chad was definitely scared. Of his parents. "I am. But that doesn't mean we should join some homeless woman's cult of crazy animal killers. We know nothing about Wanda and her niece. Doesn't it bother you that one day they show up with a crazy video and ask for your help hunting mythical creatures? Do we even know if the video is real?"

"Is it real? Of course it's real. Mason was in it. The Ink Stains were in it. How could Wanda fake that? Why would she fake that?"

"I don't know. Maybe her niece is a CGI wizard? Maybe they want attention? Or recognition? Or to be heard? Or money? You haven't given them any money yet, have you?"

Chad was starting to get himself worked up. He never thought it would be so difficult to convince his parents not to join a crazy woman and shoot up the town with crossbows. Why did they feel the need to do this?

Samantha released her husband's hand and stroked Chad's, a sensation that propelled him right back to being a kindergartener scared of closet monsters and beasts under his bed. The soothing effect of her maternal calm shooed away his concerns with a tender touch. "Do you really believe that? I know it's difficult to believe some people can turn into animals, but I think it's even crazier to believe that Whacky Wanda and her niece somehow created a video involving local thugs killing someone you grew up with. Don't you?"

Chad sighed. He was losing this battle. He so desperately wanted to tell them that Wanda was using them to get back at him. If he could only get them to see that. "Why does it have to be *you*? Why has Wanda come to *you* and not the police? No offense, but you're just a couple of middle-class suburbanites. What about her lycanthrope hunter friends?"

"The police," Rick snorted. "The only thing they're good for is catching taxpayers in speed traps. If they were any good at their jobs, deviants like the Ink Stains wouldn't be allowed in public."

Another hand squeeze from Samantha. "What I think your father is trying to say is they aren't the right people for the job. If Wanda—*Whacky* Wanda—went to the police with stories of people turning into animals, even with the video as evidence, they'd probably lock her up for psychiatric purposes."

"If they knew what they were doing," Rick continued, "they would have found out about these lycanthropes already. Three high school kids and three college football players vanish in a year because of the Ink Stains, and the police did nothing."

"Their investigations were inconclusive," Samantha corrected. "Those are the exact words that Mr. and Mrs. Butera used regarding the police investigation into their son's disappearance. Justin was their only son, and they were devastated, gutted by not knowing what happened to him." Samantha's bottom lip trembled slightly, and her eyes shimmered from the start of tears. "Then Wanda approached them, told them what happened to their son and the other two missing high school boys. Justin and Kyle knew each other, so Wanda got in touch with the Sedgewecks. Since the missing boys were a lot like you and your friends in many ways and like the things you enjoy and the . . . way you all are. It's obvious the Ink Stains—that lycanthropes—target kids like you and your friends. I wouldn't know what to do if something happened to you, Chad. I really wouldn't. Your father and I can't put our fates . . . your fate . . . in the someone else's hands, even the police."

Chad's heart broke as his mother sniffled and turned away to wipe her tears. It was his fault that they were doing this. Justin was a nerd and lycanthropes ate him; his parents were powerless to protect him. Chad was a nerd. A equaled B equaled C, so his parents wanted to change the equation. Kyle's overprotective parents felt the same way. Bud probably just wanted to express his xenophobia in myopic and violent ways with his gun, but on some level, he might also want to protect Heston. Chad speculated that Cooper's mom cared but felt too broken to contribute.

Having no other argument, Chad stood from the table. "I understand why you're doing this. I don't agree with it, and I don't like it. You're putting yourself in danger. At the very least, you're willingly breaking the law. Obviously, I can't stop you, but I can't be a part of this. Please just tell me what you're doing and when you're doing it."

Rick's face hardened; all semblance of fear gone. Or maybe that was just how his father dealt with fear, by converting it to anger. "Chad, you need to train with us. You need to learn how to defend—"

Samantha cut her husband short, once again needing only to place her hand on his to stop his words. "Rick. It's okay. Protecting our children is why we and the others are doing this."

Protecting his parents was why Chad told them to no longer include him on their hunting missions. He needed to know their whereabouts and their plans. He was thankful he was along the last two times, but he—the human—was too close and almost too slow to act. He, the lycanthrope, could do far more good if he was there and no one knew about it.

Samantha turned to face Chad, looking at him with her warm smile. "That's okay, Chad. We will always tell you where we are."

"Sounds good. I'm going to head up to my room."

"I'll let you know when dinner is ready."

Chad forced a smile for his mother's sake, but when he got to his room, the tears of frustration rolled over his cheeks.

CHAPTER 20

Cooper snapped his wrist, snapped his whole body. The die shot from his hand and bounced twice before settling into a blurry spin among the pewter figures on the table. Unblinking, four pairs of eyes watched until the numerological fate was revealed.

Twenty. The exact number needed to kill the wraith. Had it lived past this turn, it surely would have created three corpses deep within the Cave of Damaged Souls.

All four people around the table erupted with glee. Cooper extended his arms, ready to embrace all of the congratulatory remarks sent his way. "Feel free to write songs about the inhuman accuracy of the one, the only, Sir Floridian Musk, the great slayer of the nearly impossible to slay."

Chad clapped and laughed along, happy that today came together. Yesterday had been intense, everyone living through nightmares caused by either lycanthrope or human the day before. They had met here in the barn first thing yesterday morning before class. Chad was a little surprised by how calm Kyle and Heston were. Kyle sat with his knees pulled to his chest, but he wasn't hiding his face or rocking back and forth or whimpering. Heston was quiet, which wasn't unusual, but his eyes weren't bulging, and he wasn't quaking as Chad had expected. Maybe they were getting used to being attacked?

After everyone shared their stories, Cooper nervously worked his scalp with his fingers, his hair getting bigger by the minute. "This . . . this is insane. The measurement of sanity involved in this situation is nil."

"There's no need to panic now," Tyler said as he approached the table with four mugs of tea. After setting them down, he handed each one out with purpose, obvious that he had crafted four different mixtures for each person. Chad assumed what was in his cup was tailored to his specific need, which was rather interesting because he didn't know what he needed. Not caring what the concoction might contain, he accepted it with a "Thank you" and drank deeply. It tasted . . . nice. Chad expected the flavor of dirt or tree or gravel. It had an earthy but comforting flavor, laced with a mild sweetness. He felt focused.

Tyler joined everyone at the table and said, "Each of you added some bitter ingredients to a murky soup. Before we dole any of it out and sip from it, let's take a moment to reflect."

"What are you proposing?" Cooper asked.

"Let's connect some dots to see if it starts to form an image. We know there are six new lycanthropes, and there are four packs. I think a good place to start would be to figure out which pack each of these new lycanthropes belongs to."

The other four at the table nodded and sipped their teas. "That's a good idea," Cooper said. "The most obvious thing to do is take our pack off the table. We're not affiliated with any of the new ones, and we're in possession of all three of our vials. At least we hope we are."

Kyle cringed, reacting to the reminder that he was why the jocks had their own pack.

"You are," Tyler said. "I checked while I was heating the water for the tea. So, six lycanthropes, three packs."

"Well, we know Tasha and Kicks are with the Ink Stains." Cooper looked at Heston for more details.

Nodding, Heston added, "True. We can assume Kat used one of her vials to turn Tasha into a Lycanthrope. I saw a crow tattoo on the side of her head."

"Thanks to my verbal exchange with Brick, we know that Sanders is a part of his pack. Even though it wasn't expressly stated, I can think of no reason why Brittany wouldn't be as well. What's confounding is that he explicitly stated he used no vials of Elder Blood to turn either Brittany or Sanders."

"So, the jocks obviously have another source of Elder Blood," Kyle said.

"Oh, shit!" Heston sat up straight as if the answer bit his toe. "My brother!"

"Whoa," Cooper reeled back as if Heston threw his tea at him. "Your brother is supplying the jocks with Elder Blood?"

"I don't know. Maybe? Kat told me they were following him because he's involved with something big. Have you guys heard about some of the local businesses getting robbed?"

Four nodding heads.

"He's involved in that. She also said that the 'scumbags' who make counterfeit documents have been disappearing. And . . ." He reached into his back pocket and pulled out a phone. He continued as he tapped away at it. "I think he might have been the one who hurt your friend, Kyle. Here. I just sent a picture of Chuck to your phone for the next time you see Declan."

Kyle gave a thumbs-up to show he received the text.

"We saw him go in the frat house our folks all but raided," Chad said. "But what's the connection between him and the jocks? Why would he be robbing stores or getting fake IDs for them?"

Kyle added, "We looked at the six IDs Declan made and cross-referenced them with the different sports teams on the school's website. Neither the faces nor the names matched any of them."

"So, we're back to square zero," Cooper moaned.

"Not necessarily," Tyler said. "You've certainly connected a few dots and answered a few questions."

"But we still have more. Including which pack or packs Pixel Ronin and Chuck are involved with."

"Well, there is a potential connection between him and Chuck if Chuck really was paying Declan to make fake IDs," Chad said.

"You're suggesting they're somehow working together?" Cooper asked. "Which means that either or both could be part of the jocks' pack."

"Even though that thought sends terror through my veins, Declan told me Ronin saw the guy who approached him," Kyle said.

"And we still have no idea how the Mills Hook pack fits into this, if at all," Cooper said.

"We also learned the Ink Stains are on our side," Chad said.

Kyle and Cooper glared at him, their eyes set on laser-beam destroy mode. Realizing the error in his statement, Chad waved his hands as if that would erase his words. "No, no, no. I didn't mean we try to team up with them or anything like that. I meant that it's obvious the jocks aren't working with them, and neither is Chuck nor Ronin."

"That's a big ol' mound of supposition you got there, Chad," Cooper said flatly.

"I think he might be right this time," Heston said. "The Ink Stains could have hurt me, or worse. They did me a favor."

"Yeah, but they made you let Chuck go," Kyle said. "They might be setting us up for something."

"For what? And why?" Chad asked. "It doesn't make any sense. If they're working with Chuck, it would make sense that they have the same access to more Elder Blood like the jocks have. I think we can all agree that if they did, there would be way more than just four Ink Stains."

Cooper ran his hands through his hair one more time and sighed. "Okay, that is a valid point. I think we're all concerned about your eagerness to work with them, which by extension means we're concerned about your eagerness to see Kat again."

"That is something you no longer have to worry about. I really do not have any interest in seeing Kat again."

"Promise us you won't meet with her. Or Natalia. Or Wanda. Or anyone from that whackadoodle family. Even if it's some long-lost distant second cousin twice removed from a long-lost great uncle stating he can revert all lycanthropes back to human and end this nonsense."

"I promise."

Tyler stood and asked, "What's your comfort level moving forward? Kyle and Heston, do you two feel safe now that Pixel Ronin and Chuck have revealed themselves to be kindred?"

Kyle shrugged. "We can work under the assumption that if Ronin's in the jocks' pack, he's following the same rules. I mean, Cooper saw Sanders, and he hasn't tried anything since his initial attack. Plus, Ronin ran like hell when the cops showed up, so he's clearly not looking to go on a psycho murder rampage."

"I'm good, too," Heston said.

"Are you sure?" Tyler asked. "You can always stay here if you'd like."

"Thanks, but I'm good."

That was all Heston had to say about that. After another hour at the barn, most of it spent exercising and following Tyler in martial arts training, the group left and went about their classes. Chad spent yesterday trying to relax by painting a few new pewter figurines.

Now, after saving the group from certain death from the wraiths found within the Cave of Damaged Souls, Cooper danced under the shower of adulation until Kyle stopped clapping and suddenly looked confused. Still smiling, he asked, "Hold on. You called yourself 'Sir' Floridian Musk. When did you get knighted?"

"Ummm, just now, obviously," Cooper replied. "After what I did? My improbable accomplishments deem me to be knighted on the spot."

"As great as that roll was, I don't think a five percent chance is insurmountable. Plus, you can't knight yourself."

Cooper contorted his face to suggest that Kyle's statement was insane. "Of course I can! I'm chaotic neutral, so it's well within my character to do so."

"Who's chaotic neutral?" Heston asked. "You or Floridian Musk?"

"Both," Kyle answered.

Chad added, "That's Sir Chaotic Neutral to you."

Cooper sat down and cocked his head as if deep in thought. "You think I, myself, me personally, am chaotic neutral?"

"You're the very definition of chaotic neutral," Heston answered.

Cooper stroked his chin while contemplating Heston's words. "Interesting. I always thought of myself as lawful good."

The other three at the table burst into laughter, and even Tyler laughed from the couch. Kyle gained control of himself first. "Cooper, I'm not even lawful good. If anything, I'm lawful neurotic."

"Okay, okay, maybe I'm not exactly the textbook definition of lawful good, but am I truly chaotic neutral? I could even possibly maybe concede that at times, infrequently, I lean slightly toward chaotic. But neutral? I believe I align myself on the side of angels."

"Douchey ones," Heston said. "There's your alignment—chaotic douche."

More laughter. The corners of Cooper's lips twitched as he fought with himself not to laugh. Straightening and tightening the knot of an invisible tie, he said, "I resemble that remark and shall wear it as a badge of pride."

Chad touched his index fingers and thumbs together to form an idea of a rectangle over the left side of his chest. "Kind of like a conference greeting badge? Mine could say, 'Hello, my name is Lawful Doofus.'"

Cooper's eyes lit up. "Exactly! I love this idea. I say after we get out of this Cave of Damaged Souls, we head over to the nearest office supply store, preferably one in the vicinity of Rocket Lizard Pizza, where we can enjoy a tasty dinner."

This was it, the moment Chad was nervous about. He was more nervous about this than the conversations he had with his friends yesterday, unnerved that their lives being in peril was a much more common occurrence than the good news he was about to share. "I can't tonight. In fact, I gotta leave in about an hour because . . . I . . . have a date." The final word felt foreign, a word from another language he tried to pronounce correctly. The looks on his friends' faces told him he had indeed mispronounced it. Then, all smiles. Even Heston.

"A . . . date . . . ?" Cooper asked. Chad could see through his friend's eyes, directly into his brain. The gears and cogs turned and burned, seizing up with all the potential comments he wanted to make. Zingers, pithy comments, puns, questions all clogged his internal mechanisms. "Awesome!"

Kyle perked up, sitting straighter, excited that another member of the group had entered this strange new world he had found himself in. Chad guessed he was formulating a dozen questions, all starting with, "What does it mean when . . . ?"

Heston asked the next logical question as he rubbed a d20 between his hands. "What's her name? Should I roll for luck?"

"Rolling for luck won't be necessary," Chad answered. "And it's Selma, the girl from the pretzel shop."

Heston dropped the die. Cooper dropped his jaw. Tyler jumped up from the couch and raced over to the table. He took a seat and a character sheet. Pencil in one hand, he rolled six d20s and wrote the numbers down as the traits of his character, none lower than fifteen. "My character's name is Cannabis Maximus. I'm a mist-elf cleric that uses smoke magic to heal characters' chakras. Did you say you have a date with Selma, the girl from the pretzel shop in the food court?"

"I did."

"I have taught you how to center your thoughts, view the planet as one living organism, and a variety of self-defense martial arts, but it appears you have knowledge to impart upon me. How did you get a date with her?"

What he said was true—Tyler had taught all those things and more to Chad. Disappointment laced Chad's words when he said, "I honestly have no idea."

Tyler steepled his fingers together and bounced the tips of his index fingers against his chin. "Interesting. I've asked her out on more than one occasion, and she politely declined. Yet you aren't aware of what you have done to secure her interest. You may have more than one animal locked inside of you, Chad. One we should find. Are you opposed to hypnosis? How do you feel about psychogenic hallucinogens?"

Chad chuckled. "Sorry, I'm going to have to say no to both. You're acting like you've never been shot down before."

"Well . . ." Tyler let the word hover in the air long enough for everyone to catch the underlying meaning.

Chad and his friends scowled at Tyler and snapped in unison, "Seriously?"

Tyler shrugged. "We all have our strengths and weaknesses. We should neither glorify nor besmirch."

Heston shook his head while Kyle rolled his eyes. Cooper moaned, "I feel besmirched by your glory."

Kyle followed it up with, "You seem besmirched by Chad's glory."

Tyler frowned. "Upon a quick introspection, I believe you are correct. Even though I am your spiritual shaman, it's obvious that I, too, need to find better ways to navigate this cosmos. I apologize and feel nothing but peace, love, and respect for you all, my fellow travelers."

Chad and his friends accepted. Chad pointed to the character sheet in front of Tyler and asked, "So, do you actually want to join in the quest, or did you just fill out a character sheet to sit at the table."

Tyler looked at the pewter figurines in the center of the table. "It would be my honor to join. It appears that the group is in dire need of healing, so I will pull out my magical pipe of toking plus five."

A bolt of indignation struck Cooper in the spine, and he sat straighter as he said, "Waitaminute. As much as I would love a character to appear out of nowhere with the ability to heal us, this goes well beyond what the rules are capable of—"

Heston placed a hand on Cooper's forearm to get his attention. "As DM, I'll allow it. This is the Cave of Damaged Souls, after all, and Floridian Musk could use his soul to be healed. Everyone could."

Cooper looked around the table and smiled. "When you're right, you're right. I welcome the efforts of Cannabis Maximus, the newest team member."

Everyone clapped and cheered. Chad didn't know what the future held, what problems the new lycanthropes would bring, but he knew he was part of a good team of adventurers who would figure things out.

CHAPTER 21

Chad was on a date. Heston went home. Kyle was with his girlfriend. Weirdness sped unbound along the highway of life. *Might as well treat myself to some dinner*, Cooper thought.

If he went home, it'd be another night of nothing with his mother, her plans of sitting in her chair in front of the television not varying one iota. Cooper was caught up with his homework and didn't feel like contacting Bryce or his other lacrosse comrades. He wasn't interested in the shift in gears necessary to slow down from his earlier high-quality fun while gaming with his friends. Not necessarily in the mood for human contact, more like observation to stave off boredom. No better place than the mall for that.

A plate of Chinese, followed by a gyro, and a soft pretzel for dessert. A pang of disappointment twitched behind his chest when there was no Selma at A Salt and Buttery, even though he knew she wouldn't be there. No matter. Cooper wished his friend well and lounged in the food court chair while enjoying salted baked goodness.

All was good with the universe until the other three chairs at the table suddenly became occupied.

Brick. Orlando. Emmanuel.

None of them had food, just bringing their stone-carved faces.

Before Cooper could react, could even begin to hypothesize how to react, Brick nodded as a form of acknowledgment. "Wassup, Pencil."

Orlando frowned at Brick and reprimanded, "Dude. We talked about this."

Brick frowned back with such intensity that Cooper worried that the shockwave of his anger would crack the table in half. "What? I gotta call him something, and it's not like I know his fucking name."

"Cooper," Orlando responded. "It's Cooper."

"Fine. Cooper. Wassup, Cooper?"

Cooper's default setting was caustic sarcasm, but he had a secondary process that ran in the background, ready to switch off his default setting whenever it might interfere with his primary directive of life preservation. The secondary process kicked in, commanding him not to be a smartass. He raised the last bit of pretzel and answered, "Just enjoying a little dinner."

"Oh, shit." Brick snapped his head in the direction of the pretzel shop. "Is that chick working? She's got tits for days."

"Sorry, she's not working tonight." Cooper wanted to tell Brick that Chad was on a date with her so badly that a spot behind his eyes burned. He could only speculate how amazing the look of disbelief on Brick's face would be. But it's the information age, knowledge being the supreme currency of this era. It made little sense to give away currency for free, especially to someone he didn't like. To make sure he didn't slip, he shoved the remaining piece of pretzel into his mouth.

"Damn," Brick grunted. "Anyway, we need to talk about the pack coming from the south. Do you know anything about them?"

"Why would I know anything about them?"

"Because you nerds know a lot about a lot."

"Yo, c'mon, man," Orlando snapped.

Brick grunted again and rolled his eyes. "I meant you and your 'pack' always seem to know what's going on. Sometimes even more than us."

Now Cooper needed to exchange currency. Trying to lie would be dangerous, the ramifications of getting caught too great. But he didn't need to share everything. "We know that a migratory pack is coming into town from Mills Hook. We plan to keep our heads down until they move on through." He paid a tithing; now it was his turn to collect a fee. "At the party, you said you knew something about them."

Brick peered over his shoulders as if spies lurked within the shadows, then looked at Emmanuel and Orlando. They each nodded and Brick leaned forward. "They got no plans on moving on. And they know about us."

"They know about you and your pack?"

"They know about all the packs. Us. You guys. The Ink Stains."

Cooper had learned that sometimes Brick wasn't the best at keeping his coins in his purse and could be tricked into tossing a few away for free. He quickly asked, "Is your pack working with the Ink Stains?"

"Fuck no!" After he barked his answer, his expression went flat, clearly upset with himself for sharing that bit of information. The anger he felt for himself quickly turned back to Cooper, as evidenced by his growl. "No, Cooper, we are not working with the Ink Stains. Happy?"

"Like, right now? Or with my life as a total picture in general?"

"Don't be a dick."

Cooper looked at Orlando to observe his reaction. Orlando shook his head and replied, "Sorry, don't got your back on that one. That was a very dick response."

"Fair enough," Cooper said. Orlando had been standing up to Brick, and Cooper needed to find the limitations. "So, to what do I owe the pleasure of this meeting?"

"We wanted to see what you know and where you stand," Brick answered.

"Okay, well, I think we already covered that."

"You ready to fight the pack coming from the south?"

"We wish to fight no one."

"You might not have a choice."

"Why do you think they're looking for a fight?"

"Think about it. They're coming into an area where they know there are other packs. Why? To take the territory. They're gonna want us to fight them or follow them. You guys are followers—we're not."

Cooper inhaled deeply and exhaled slowly through puffed cheeks, an exaggerated display of contemplation designed to stall and think about what Brick had said. Unfortunately, he was right. Whatever thoughts Cooper and his friends had about laying low were reduced to optimistic fairy tales. "Are you asking us to stand by your side should the need arise?"

Brick relaxed, though it was difficult to tell, just that the striations in his muscles diminished. "Sometimes our football team has to pull for our most hated rivals because if they win a certain game or two, it will help us out for playoffs."

"The enemy of my enemy is my friend."

"Yeah," Orlando chimed in. "Exactly that. Look, we're coming to you because of what you did for me when the party got raided. I had two psychos shooting at me, and you got them off me. That took major balls, dude. I was able to get away with ease. I appreciate that."

It was borderline hysterical that Orlando not only thought Cooper saved him on purpose but complimented his testicles as well. He couldn't wait to tell the guys! He needed to play it cool for now. "No problem. We need to have each other's backs when it comes to lycanthrope hunters."

All three of Cooper's tablemates shifted in their seats, straightening their posture to be more attentive. Brick frowned and asked, "Hunters? Do you know them?"

Shit! Cooper accidentally devalued the information currency. "Of course not. You fellows need more nerd friends, because they'd tell you that there are always hunters hunting lycanthropes."

"Why would the hunters have come to the house?"

"You tell me. You're the one making all kinds of new lycanthropes."

"I already told you, we didn't make any new ones."

"You said you didn't use your stash, but I'm pretty confident you made them. I'm guessing you have a supplier. Who is it? Chuck?"

"Let's just say I have a supplier. How do you know Chuck?"

"Let's just say I know who Chuck is."

Brick leaned forward and scowled. Cooper didn't blink. Somehow Brick turned Sanders into a lycanthrope, but he was only one lacrosse player. The rest of the team would surely seek revenge if a football player harmed the star goalie. After a few uncomfortable seconds, Brick's expression softened as best as it could. He nodded and then stood. "All right, Cooper. We're gonna assume you're on our side unless you prove otherwise."

The other two stood to leave as well; Emmanuel snorted in Cooper's general direction, and Orlando flashed him the peace sign.

Cooper sighed and slumped in his chair. They were trying to set him and his friends up for something, that much was sure. But what? And how was Chuck connected to them? If he were their supplier, where was he getting the Elder Blood? Too many questions to tackle, too many scenarios to ruminate about. First, he needed another pretzel. Or two.

———

Chad was on a date. Kyle was with his girlfriend. Cooper went to the mall. Life was weird. *Might as well get ready for this shit*, Heston thought.

As he approached the door to the doublewide, he heard the voices through the open kitchen window. His father and Chuck.

After the incident at the farm, Chuck disappeared. He stayed away from the doublewide, stayed away from the college, stayed away from anywhere Heston was. Of course, Heston didn't go out much other than to classes, to the barn, and on whatever errands his father had him run. He wasn't sure if Chuck would come back. His half-brother had a habit of running. A year and a half ago, Chuck stiffed a local drug supplier. The idiot thought the guy dealing on the street was the one he'd have to deal with, not considering that the street pusher worked for someone else who also had a boss. Chuck disappeared for eighteen months. If Heston had any connections to drug dealing, he'd have sold Chuck out for free. Alas, Chuck didn't run this time, which meant he was into something big, even bigger than owing money to a faceless drug lord.

Heston drove the truck home after the incident at the farm and explained to his father that Chuck was behind the robberies in the downtown area, and he ran when he was confronted about it. Bud swore and threw a beer can against the wall. That was the end of the discussion. Now, Chuck was back.

Taking a deep breath, Heston opened the door. His father and Chuck sat at the small kitchen table. The talking stopped and the glaring began. Then came the aggression.

Before Heston could shut the door, Chuck leaped from his chair. Rattling the entire doublewide, he stomped over to Heston and grabbed two fistfuls of his shirt. "Why'd you lie to Dad, huh? Tryin' to ruin my name?"

Bud just sat at the table, brows furrowed, the look in his eye implying that he favored this altercation ending the way it had ended many times before. Whimpering, crying, pleading. Well, Heston was out of tears.

Heston stepped forward with his hands on Chuck's chest and pushed with all his might. Chuck was large enough to absorb most of the impact, but he let go of Heston and stumbled backward. He caught his balance, and he and Bud looked at Heston as if a stranger were standing in the living room. The act of such rebellion caused pinpricks behind his eyes and at the back of his throat. Making sure to speak with purpose so his voice didn't crack, he said, "You did that all on your own."

Chuck stepped closer to Bud, who remained seated like a judge presiding over a courtroom and pointed at Heston. "You don't fucking believe him, do you, Dad? All that stupid shit he told you about me? He's lying! You're not going to believe a Klesky over a McCurdy, are you?"

Bud didn't utter a word, not needing to. He conveyed his every thought by crossing his arms over his chest and shifting in his chair while accusing eyes settled on Heston. Proof. He wanted proof. Fair enough.

Heston walked over to the kitchen table, leaving the door to the outside open. He might need to make a hasty retreat depending how the other two men reacted after he provided Exhibit A to the court.

He had two cell phones in his back pockets. One was his and Kat had given him the other. He pulled out Kat's, and as he tapped away at the screen, he said, "Chuck was right. I lied. We made it to the farm."

Still cloaked in anger, Bud's expression shifted to concern, confusion. Heston set the phone on the table; a video queued up.

"What the fuck are you—?" Chuck started but cut himself short when Heston hit "play."

The camera work was perfect. It caught every moment of Chuck talking to the farmer and included his transformation into a hippopotamus. Not a second of his attack on the farmer was missed. And Heston wasn't included in a single frame.

For the first time in his life, Heston saw fear on Chuck's face. It only lasted for seconds, but Heston would remember it forever.

Bud stood and grabbed the phone, a slight tremor running along his hand. Chuck backed away, shaking his head. "That wasn't me. That couldn't have been me. That's . . . that's . . . what you saw is impossible. No one can do that, right?"

Holding the phone, Bud stared at it yet addressed Chuck. "I know what's possible and what's not. I know about . . . things . . . like you."

"It's fake! That video's fake! Heston's nerd friends did this!"

"You're one of them. You're one of those . . . those . . . things." Bud exited the kitchen and crossed through the living room to the couch. Knee on the cushions, Bud kept his eyes glued to the screen while he reached over the back of the couch and didn't look away until he procured what he was looking for.

A shotgun.

Heston couldn't believe his eyes. Everything he knew about his father's exploits as a lycanthrope hunter came from the stories Chad shared. He never saw it with his own eyes, never realized his father's true feelings until now. Eyes as slick as glass, Bud pointed the gun at Chuck and growled, "Get out of my house."

"Dad, you can't be serious—" Chuck started to step forward, but Bud pumped the twelve-gauge.

"The only reason I ain't shot you yet is 'cause you got some of my blood in you, boy. You best take advantage of my kindness and get the fuck out."

Chuck's mood darkened as if a shadow passed over his soul, implying that he'd be willing to stand against the shot from the gun. "I suggest you change your tone. You know what I can turn into."

Bud stepped forward and raised the gun to aim at Chuck's head. "You will not change into that thing here! You will not destroy the house you was born and raised in!"

Heston hated his brother, the secret whispers of wishing him dead were now full-blown shouts in his mind, begging his father to pull the trigger. A weird mix of relief and disappointment stirred within his gut when Chuck walked toward the door. He paused and looked at Heston. "I'm not done with you yet. You better—"

"No!" Bud barked. "You will *not* threaten my son!"

Even though Bud didn't kill him, the look of shock on Chuck's face was a satisfactory consolation prize for Heston. The real prize was to hear his father refer to him as "son." It had been years since he last heard that.

Chuck shut his mouth and left the doublewide, slamming the door behind him.

Bud tossed the shotgun onto the couch and approached Heston. The last thing Heston wanted to do was show weakness by crying right after showing strength, so he tightened his throat and fought back the sting of tears.

His father's eyes looked small in his large head, sad from his jowls pulling his face. He put his hand on Heston's shoulder and said, "There's a lot going on that you don't know about. What me and your friends' parents have been doing."

Bud explained everything. There wasn't anything Heston didn't know, but it was nice to hear his father talk.

———

Chad was on a date. Cooper went to the mall. Heston went home. These were weird and exciting times, indeed. *Might as well get this over with*, Kyle thought.

He had received the we-need-to-talk text from Janey about a half-hour after he and the guys left the barn, then he cried for another half hour. His practical experience with girls had been nil until he met Janey, but even he knew what "we need to talk" meant. Now, he stood on the sidewalk in front of her apartment building, trying to muster the courage to cross the threshold.

Man up, he told himself. *This is just one of the many experiences you missed during high school. You can do this, because it has to be done.* It didn't hurt any less as he entered the building.

The building was a three-story rectangle, an old office building converted to near-campus apartments. Kyle stood in front of her door, knuckles hovering in front of it, ready to knock. He didn't know what to do. Should he try to play through every possible scenario the conversation could take to prepare for what was to come? Or should he clear his mind and just react to the moment? Neither option seemed compelling—there were too many forks in the conversational road to think of all of them, and if the conversation went down a path he wasn't prepared for, then he'd panic and possibly blurt out things he didn't mean; however, if he decided to rely on his improvisational skills, he'd find himself in the same situation of panicked babbling.

Looking for a clue about how bad this might go, he thought of the last time he saw her—on the roof of Declan's apartment building. By the time he finished telling her everything, the police had left. Janey told him she needed a couple days to process and she'd text him when she was ready to talk. She kissed his cheek and walked away. He didn't know what to make of that. She had stared with wide-eyed amazement but remained calm throughout his entire story. His first thought was to ask the guys what a kiss on the cheek might have meant, but telling them about Pixel Ronin took precedent. After finding out about the parent-driven anti-lycan-thrope militia and Chuck's involvement, his love life didn't need to be discussed.

The time at the barn today was fun, everyone focused on the game and no other topics of conversation arose, so he didn't want to ruin it by asking for opinions about the mysteries of women. Chad had dropped a bombshell about going on a date with the hot pretzel girl, and Kyle wanted so desperately to ask for an opinion about his situation. Then Janey's text came, and he realized he was on his own.

Knock, knock, knock.

Kyle stared at his fist as if it knocked on the door without his command. *Why the hell did you do that?!* he admonished his hand.

"Come in, it's open!"

Kyle opened the door and slowly entered as if navigating through a field of set mouse traps. Her greeting had been in her usual sing-songy voice, which confused him. There was still a lot he wanted to learn about her, but he never imagined she would take such glee in breaking up with him. She was a monster!

As a money grab, the owner renovated on the cheap, making twenty-four identical studio apartments, no walls to separate the living area from the sleeping area from the kitchenette. With the blinds closed, there was no chance of the waning twilight making its way into the apartment. A few lit candles on the end tables were the only source of light. Janey appeared out of nowhere with two glasses of red wine and handed one to him. "Don't just stand there. Come in, come in. You look like you're sick. Are you okay?"

"Umm . . . yeah? You . . . uhh . . . you said we need to talk."

"We do, we do. Come on." She led him to the couch, the only place to sit in the cramped apartment. She was barefoot and wore a thin T-shirt that wasn't long enough to touch the top of her shorts.

Her movements were quick, and she was talking fast. That meant she was nervous about trying something new. She had never had a boyfriend before, so she never broke up with anyone before. Even though she was her usual upbeat self, Kyle took a weird solace in knowing she was at least nervous about breaking up with him.

She sat facing him, wine glass in her hand. He didn't know how to sit. Facing her to take the news head-on? Or sit straight ahead so he could hide his tears better? He decided on an angle somewhere in between.

He looked at her without saying a word and waited for her to start. She placed her elbow on top of the couch back and did a quick twirl of a lock of hair, then quickly moved her arm, her hand falling to her lap but then moved her elbow back to the top of the couch and leaned her head against her hand. That pose lasted two seconds, and then she sat straight. She glanced at her wine glass and then did a double-take as if she had forgotten she was holding it. She raised the glass and smiled. *God, I'm going to miss that smile.* After a big gulp, her left eye closed, and she puckered her lips. A quick shake of her head and she was back to smiling. "Smooooooth."

Kyle took a swig from his glass, hoping the alcohol would ease his pain as it so often did for characters in movies and television shows. Grape juice from a juice box that had been lurking in the back corners of the fridge for years stabbed the back of his jaw. He simultaneously fought back tears and the urge to twist his face in unnatural and frightening ways. He didn't say anything, patiently waiting for Janey to start the breakup process.

She fidgeted for a few more seconds, then leaned over to the coffee table. She set her wine glass down and picked up a tin of hazelnut-cream-filled cookie rods. Offering the opened tin to Kyle, she asked, "Pirouette?"

Kyle was thankful he hadn't wasted any time exploring all the different scenarios about this evening, because being offered a tasty snack wouldn't have been one of them. Of course, as predicted, his improvisation skills left him floundering to the point of his best response being, "Ummm . . . ?"

Janey's body went limp, and she sighed. "You're a pocky stick man. I know that. We spent an hour analyzing the different flavors, and I know you love the classic chocolate-covered stick, and that's what I should have gone with instead of this, but I just wanted to be fancy, and these are just fancy versions of pocky sticks. Okay, maybe not, but they're at least in the same rod-shaped cookie and chocolate family and—"

"It's okay," he said, grabbing her hand. "I love these things. Stupid embarrassing secret—I've eaten a whole tin by myself in one sitting."

She didn't pull her hand away; instead, she squeezed his. Quite the opposite reaction he was expecting. The tiniest reflection of candle flame danced in her eyes as her smile returned. "Me too!"

Kyle smiled, but it quickly faded as he realized little moments like these would be ending soon.

Janey sighed again. "I'm so sorry, Kyle. I'm totally making this awkward. It's what I do. I take something a normal person can do and make it awkward."

This was hard for Kyle, but he realized this was hard for her, too. Even though he knew it was coming, he was never once mad at her. He thought she was a monster for being so cheerful about it, but she was no demon or fiend, just an inexperienced girl trying to do what was right for herself. Deep down, he knew it was the right thing for her to do. He had dumped a lot of information on her, exposing her to a life that not only went far beyond the norm but moved into dangerous territory. Short of saying the words for her, Kyle said the next best thing. "It's okay. You said we needed to talk."

Eyes widening, she perked up. "We do!"

Kyle debated about thinking of her as a monster again. "Okay."

"Well, more like a continuation of our talk on the roof. I guess more like my turn to talk. You shared a lot, and I feel like I didn't give the proper responses while you were opening up to me. I can't *truly* understand what you're going through, but I know it's been difficult for you. Standing up to bullies and taking the risks you did and fighting. I've never been in a fight in my life with a human being person, let alone with lycanthropes, and you did that. And you have to keep it a secret from your parents, who, in a bizarre twist of fate, are hunting you alongside the town weirdo. I can't believe Whacky Wanda is a lycanthrope hunter. Scratch that. I can believe it. I can believe it very much. But what I think I'm trying to say is that I need to see your other form."

Kyle cringed. "Are you sure? It's . . . it's really . . . weird. I mean, you've seen it already and . . . it's really weird."

Janey smiled. "First of all, Kyle, if you hadn't noticed, I excel at weird. And awkward. And embarrassing. And spastic tendencies. I saw your other form at Declan's, but things were happening so fast that I didn't know how to process what I saw. Now, we're in a good space. Plus, your other form is a part of you, and I want to know the whole you."

This no longer felt like a breakup. Kyle didn't know what this felt like, but it felt almost like the opposite of a breakup. Did he misinterpret "we need to talk," or did she? Keeping that to himself, he placed his wine glass on the table and stood. Still holding his hand, Janey stood as well. He said, "Are you sure? Last chance."

"Show me, show me, show me, show me."

"Okay, but if I change right this second, I'll ruin my clothes, so . . ."

Janey cocked her head and squinted, confused. Her eyes went wide when she finally caught his hint. "Oh! Yep, sorry, yep." Folding her hands together, she turned around and shifted quickly from one foot to the other, a small dance of excited anticipation.

Kyle's face went ablaze as he took his clothes off. With no effort, he changed into a human-sized pheasant, thankful Janey wouldn't be able to see him blush. Upon ruffling his feathers, Janey stopped fidgeting and slowly turned around. Wide-eyed, she looked at Kyle with the same awe and glee a kindergartener would have if discovering Santa by the family Christmas tree. She took a step forward and reached for him. Instinctively, Kyle took a step back. No one had touched him in this form. Kicked, punched, and tackled but never touched.

"It's okay," Janey whispered as she stepped closer. Kyle didn't move this time.

Her fingers glided along his beak and ran through the short feathers of his face. Circling under his eye, her hand swooped up to his head and back down. Seconds bled into minutes as her hands caressed his face.

"Okay, change back," she whispered.

Kyle went back to his human form, forgetting he'd be standing naked in front of a girl, but her hands on his cheeks felt so nice that he'd follow her into a lava pit if she asked. He would have never guessed what she did next, not in a million years—she removed her T-shirt.

"My boyfriend is a superhero!" Janey squealed right before she threw her arms around him and kissed him.

What happened next, he never thought would have happened in a million years either.

CHAPTER 22

"God, my hair sucks," Chad muttered to himself. Standing in front of the mirror on the back of his bedroom door, he reevaluated his hairstyle choice, which could only be described as a "mop." It was one he had for about half a decade, ever since puberty asserted itself by giving him an uncontrollable wave and random curls that refused to be tamed. He had used half a bottle of gel to mold it; he lost all hope of "sculpting" ten minutes ago. His only hope now was to make a blood sacrifice to a Hell demon for the fleeting ability to create an organized clump.

He ran his comb through a few more times and checked to see if it did any good. Two curly locks fell over his right eye and down to his cheek while a wavy chunk of hair touched his left eyebrow. "I'm going to change my major to genetics so I can understand who peed in my gene pool."

Comb in his right hand, a tube of gel in his left, he contemplated his next attack. *More gel? Comb attempt number seventeen? Take another shower and start all over?*

"Oh my," a familiar voice came from behind him. "Some choices were made."

Kat rolled her hips as she sauntered across his room. He wondered if he should put bars on his window. No need. They wouldn't keep her out. Nothing could stop her, so Chad just rolled with it. "You're not wrong. My next choice will be how short to shear it once I get the clippers."

Kat chuckled. "No need to be so extreme. Hot date tonight?"

165

"I don't know how hot it will be, but I do have a date."

Kat stopped and blinked a few times, her face awash with confusion. "Really?"

Chad shook his head and flatly replied, "You can at least pretend not to be surprised."

A soft smile was her form of apology. "You're right. So, who's the lucky girl? Anyone I know?"

"I doubt it. She works at the pretzel shop in the mall."

Chad didn't know why he shared the information. He had promised the guys that he wouldn't talk to Kat, but he wanted her to leave as quickly as possible so he wouldn't get himself in trouble. They were rightfully concerned since she had a power over him. She knew what to say and, more importantly, how to say it to get him to do her bidding. He secretly hoped she knew who he was talking about as a way to show her that her hold on him wasn't as great as she thought it was. It worked.

Wide-eyed and slack-jawed, Kat said, "Jesus, Chad. Swinging for the fences, aren't you?"

Chad shrugged. It was petty, but he added, "It's our second date." He paused to give his words a chance to impact Kat. But like the idiot he was, he continued, "Which is why I'm making failed attempts to control my hair and harboring thoughts of burning it off."

Kat squinted. Chad knew what she was thinking—weighing odds and running scenarios. She smiled wide enough to expose her pointed canines but not wide enough to imply wickedness. "No need for extremes. We can fix this."

Klaxons blared between his ears, and internal warning systems screamed directly into his brain, *Too close! She's getting too close! Cognitive shut down imminent!* Too late. She grabbed the towel from his bed and tossed it over his head. Surprisingly gentle, she rubbed and removed most of the gel from his hair. The towel fell to the floor, but she continued to work her fingers through his hair. Ecstasy raced along his body, leaving a trail of goosebumps. He needed to get her out of here. "So . . . why are you here?"

"I was going to invite you to Clinty's for drinks, but now that you have a big date with a hottie . . ."

"Ha, ha. Why would you do that?"

"To share information."

"I'm afraid I don't have much to share."

Kat stopped massaging his head and held her hands in front of his face. Golden fur grew from her skin as her nails extended into hooked claws. Every bit of ecstasy within Chad turned into fear. Rabbit instinct yelled at him to flee from the predator and her sharp claws. She surprised him and his fear instinct when she ran her fingers through his hair again. As locks fell away, she asked, "Have you talked to Heston?"

"I have. Not only is Chuck a lycanthrope, but you said he's involved with some pretty shady dealings."

"That's right. I was going to tell you he's been hanging around Factory Park, but since you have plans, there's no reason for me to bring it up. So, where are you going for your date?"

"Don't know yet," Chad answered. It was the truth, but since Selma had picked the movie, she demanded he pick the restaurant, which he had yet to do. Factory Park was a revitalization initiative in South Bend. The Snaking River formed the northern borders of West Bend and East Bend. The river curved around East Bend and then ran along the east side of South Bend, creating plenty of opportunity for industry to set up shop along its banks at the end of the nineteenth century. Times changed and facilitated the fall of some of those industries and the rise of others, the tectonic shift of capitalism. The factories along the shores of South Bend were hit the hardest, going from thriving to a blighted eyesore. A decade ago, the city council teamed up with investors who had deep pockets to revitalize a section that contained three defunct factories. There were now plenty of trendy restaurants in that area for Chad to pick from.

He must have had a tone in his voice because Kat reacted as if she knew his thoughts. "Don't do anything stupid, Chad."

Any comeback he could think of would be disingenuous. Instead, he changed the subject, "Why are you doing this?"

Kat's gaze went from his hair to his eyes, and she smiled, the wicked one. She curled her fingers, pulling his hair. He gasped as she stepped closer, her chest almost touching his, warm breath flowing over his face. "Doing what, exactly?"

Chad tried to quantify the danger of this conversation, but being this close to her created static within his brain. "Helping me get ready for a date."

Kat remained close to Chad as she went back to cutting his hair. "Isn't it obvious? I'm grooming you."

"I know you're cutting my hair, but I asked why."

"Not that kind of grooming, Chad. I mean the psychological kind. The kind of grooming the rich men who run Hollywood do to young girls. Hook 'em when they're young and turn them into the women they want. Why should rich men have all the fun? I stole their idea and decided I would groom you. Even though we lycanthropes don't age the same way as regular people, I don't want to invest the time in trying to find a suitable man. It's faster and easier if I take a chunk of clay and mold it into a suitable man."

"I'm the clay? You're going to turn me into a man you find suitable?"

Kat stepped back and brushed her now human hands together, strands of hair falling to the floor. Her smile went beyond wicked, now evil. She gestured to the mirror behind him. "Take a peek and tell me if you see anyone familiar."

Chad turned around. At first, he didn't see it, but when he recognized who she was talking about, he couldn't unsee it.

Hunter.

Not a spitting image, but there was a resemblance. Hunter had dark, deep-set eyes, strong cheekbones on either side of a solid nose, and a powerfully square jaw. Not as dark or intense, Chad's eyes had a similar shape and placement on his face. His nose was a hint smaller, and his cheekbones and jawline were softer. Hunter had wild, black hair. Chad's was brown and shorter, but the gel darkened it by a shade, and Kat's handiwork made it into a similar style.

Chad remained silent, not wanting to spring any kind of trap she might have set for him. She wasn't going to let him off the hook, though. Pressing her chest against his back, she placed her chin on his right shoulder as she reached around to run her fingers over his face. Sickle-shaped pupils like cuts in the centers of her yellow eyes. More of her teeth were pointed and glistened as she spoke. "We still have work to do. About forty . . . sixty . . . pounds of muscle need to be added. Hunter had a nice scruff on his face, so maybe go a few days without shaving and see what you think. Of course, your wardrobe has to change. More black, more leather. Let me know when you'd like to go shopping, and I'll dress you up like my own personal Ken doll."

Chad squirmed his way out of her clutches and moved away from the mirror, away from her, away from the insanity. "So, you're doing this because I look a little like Hunter? Because I *could* look like Hunter?"

"Not just look like, Chad. Hunter was an amazing man. Cunning. Driven. Dedicated. He was the leader of the pack, cared for each of us, and ferociously defended us. And he was more than that to me. He was the one who showed me the light, who opened my eyes. He freed me. He was my lover and my partner. And you took him from me."

"You told me to kill him!"

"Right. My next command is for you to go to the Fourth Street Bridge and jump off it."

"I'm not going to—" Chad tried to cut himself off, but his brain was nothing but tires spinning in mud right now. Why did she have this effect on him?

"See? You can say 'no' to me."

"I wasn't following your command to kill him. You told me that if I killed him, I'd no longer be a lycanthrope. That and *he* was trying to kill *me*, so I was defending myself."

"But you still killed him. Whatever the reason, there's something inside you, be it born from logic or instinct, that you tapped into to do what you did. That's what I see in you. Not just that you could look like him, but you could *be* like him. Cunning. Driven. Dedicated. Leader. That's what I want to bring out of you. That's why I'm doing this."

"But . . . but aren't you like my mom's age?"

Chad phrased his question inappropriately, the look of complete disgust on Kat's face told him as much. It was her fault, really, coming into his room and purposely twirling him out of control. She should have known well enough that if she spun his mind too hard and too fast that his brain would barf out stupid words.

Kat's expression softened as she glanced away, hurt. After a moment, she looked contemplative, almost as if wondering about leaving and cutting her losses with this failed investment. She shook her head, chuckled, and then considered Chad with the slightest hint of anger in her eyes. "You're in a phase. An awkward phase where you just can't stop yourself from making situations awkward. So, fine. You want to make this awkward? Let's make this awkward."

Kat kissed him. A deep kiss, her sandpaper tongue dancing with his while she cupped his face with her hands. It lasted longer than the creation of a galaxy, yet simultaneously as short as one flap of a hummingbird's wings. Chad's vision was blurred when she stopped and let go of him. Taking one step back, Kat pointed at his crotch and said flatly, "Enjoy your date tonight, Chad, but you should take care of that first so you can leave the awkwardness at home."

As soon as Kat left through the window, Chad ran to the bathroom to do what she had suggested.

CHAPTER 23

The restaurant was locally owned and specialized in seafood. This wasn't Chad's first choice, but when his parents found out he was going on a date, his dad gave him a credit card and this place as a suggestion. On the bank of The Snaking River in Factory Park, the eatery offered an amazing view from their deck, weather permitting. Mid-January prohibited deck usage, so Chad and Selma sat across from each other in a comfortable booth in the center of the restaurant. Chad felt exposed, as if a spotlight were shining upon them for the amusement of all the other patrons. Those feelings dissipated after appetizers; he was too focused on her to notice anything else happening around the restaurant.

After discussing if they were Team Alien or Team Predator and why, they slipped into sharing some of their favorite cartoons from when they were children and which of those they still watched. Selma pulled out a small notebook and sketched various mashups of cartoon characters as Aliens and Predators, complete with blood splatter and chests bursting.

"Well, I'll never look at a pineapple under the sea the same way ever again," Chad said as he stared at an illustration of Patrick Star as a face hugger.

"I feel, as an artist, it's my duty to disturb and entertain."

"You've succeeded. Very successful with both the disturbs and the entertains."

"Okay, we all know what I want to be when I grow up, so how about you? What's next for Chad?"

Chad opened his mouth, but nothing came out. He didn't seize up or forget how to speak; he just didn't have an answer. Accounting was his major, but he viewed it as a future job, nothing more. Numbers were easy and learning how to keep track of money seemed like a good life skill, but having a future accounting career hardly set his soul ablaze. Before becoming a lycanthrope, his only goal was to get a decent job and move away from all of his problems so he could do better than his father. Not exactly how one would define a dream. "Ummm . . . ?"

"Whoa!" Selma held out her hands to shield herself and sat back in her seat. "Slow down, chief. That's a pretty hardcore aspiration you got there. Are you sure you'll be able to accomplish that within one lifetime?"

Chad chuckled, sad that her sarcasm was valid. "Sorry for not having an answer."

Selma leaned in and reached across the table to grab Chad's hand. "Nothing to be sorry about. We're all just wandering along the path of life. It's just like they said in *Lord of the Rings*, right?"

"Not all those who wander are lost."

"That wasn't at all what I was thinking of. The quote from the movie that best fits this touching moment is obviously, 'Never toss a dwarf,' but whatever you said might work as well."

Chad laughed, but the truth was that her joke might as well have been his life's credo. He wasn't wandering. He was following a path, yet he was still lost. His friends might be lost as well, but *they* were wandering, exploring the world around them. Chad still felt limited, still felt chased by the boogieman, still felt unable to move past being a lycanthrope. Or was that it? His purpose?

After his last trip to Clinty's, he declared that his purpose was to find a girlfriend. He didn't know exactly what the relationship status with Selma was, but it certainly seemed to be moving in the right direction. But even if they ended up getting married someday, would that be his purpose in life? Especially since he stumbled into the situation, not even realizing their first date was exactly that. But being a lycanthrope? That was something he wanted and then not wanted, but it was a part of him, a part of his life. His friends had embraced this element of their lives, so why was he so desperate to deny it? Thinking about it, he knew nothing about lycanthropes. The real ones, not the ones from fictional outlets. Was that his purpose? To be the best lycanthrope possible?

A gurgle rippled through Chad's stomach at that thought. Luckily, it wasn't audible. Just in case his guts decided to demand more attention, he said, "Excuse me. Nature calls."

"When she calls, you can't put her on hold," Selma replied.

"So very true."

On the way to the restroom, he wondered if being the best lycanthrope possible would make a good dream. It'd be unique, solely his. Whether it was his dream or not, it was still a part of him that he hid from Selma. Should he tell her about it?

He once told Brick that they were on the same team. The concept was nothing more than words to keep Brick from killing him, but there was truth there. The Morrigan bound three packs to this area, and two of those packs were growing in number. This was part of Chad's life now, and he needed to stop pretending it wasn't. From this moment on, he would be the best lycanthrope possible! He *needed* to be. Now that he discovered his calling, should he share it with Selma?

Chad exited the men's room and got his brain ready for another debate. As he wove his way through the people milling about in the waiting area, he saw something through the windows.

Chuck.

Outside, Chuck ran by the restaurant, looking behind him as if being chased. For good reason. Natalia ran past the window after him.

The voices of everyone he knew screamed at his brain to forget what he just saw and continue back to the table. But it was Chuck—the number one suspicious character who could tie so many loose ends together. Chad had to risk it.

He slipped out of the restaurant and ran in the same direction, toward the river.

Between the restaurant and the water was a patch of manicured grass and a paved walkway. Natalia tackled Chuck. A white envelope dropped to the grass when he slammed into the ground. Chad hurried to grab it, then shoved it in his back pocket before anyone noticed he was there.

Chuck backhanded Natalia across the face. It didn't seem to hurt her, but it was distracting enough for him to push her away and get back to his feet. Chad clenched his fists, ready to join Natalia in fighting Heston's brother. However, Chuck patted his pockets and spun in circles while looking at the ground. "Fuck. Fuck, fuck, fuck. Where did it go?"

Natalia brandished a hunting knife and stepped toward Chuck.

There were no bystanders, this time of year not conducive for a nighttime walk through the park, but Chad couldn't let Natalia kill someone out in the open like this. He grabbed her arm and said, "Chuck! Get the fuck out of here."

Chuck stopped fussing and looked at Natalia. Eyes wide, sweat slicking his face, he turned and ran.

Natalia yanked her arm free and pointed the blade at Chad. "Are you working with him, too?"

"No. He is definitely the enemy. But I couldn't let you kill him in public, out in the open like this."

"I wasn't going to kill him, you idiot. Just interrogate— Your hair. It looks different. Styled like that, you look like . . . Oh, God, did my mom cut your hair?"

". . . No . . ." Chad tried to lie, but from the look of disgust on Natalia's face, he doubted it was convincing.

"Hey, is everything okay?" came from behind Chad. Hands in her pockets, her breath visible in the cold air, Selma walked closer. "Dinner came and I was beginning to wonder if you were ditching me."

"No! Not at all. I . . . I . . ." *am at a loss for words.*

Everything inside Chad shriveled like a bunch of slugs, each second that ticked by another dose of salt. This was it, the end of the relationship before it even began. Then Natalia surprised him by asking, "Did you see that big guy who ran by?"

"Yeah," Selma replied.

"Drunk asshole harassing me. Chad saw and he came outside to help out."

Selma squinted, her glare boring into Chad's soul. "Really?"

"Yeah," Chad squeaked. He cleared his throat. "I saw her outside and thought she needed some help."

Selma turned to Natalia and held out her hand. Smiling, she said, "Hi, I'm Selma."

Natalia shook her hand, but her expression never changed. "Natalia. Nice to meet you."

"So . . ." Selma started. She looked at Natalia, but Chad felt like she was talking to him. "It seems like you two know each other?"

"We do," Natalia said. "We're in chemistry class together."

She was playing along! Chad wasn't sure why or what kind of price he'd have to pay later, but she didn't rat him out. Of course, he wasn't out of the woods yet. Selma turned to Chad, her eyes windows of suspicion. "You need chemistry as an accounting major?"

Chad shrugged. "Science credits. I like chemistry because it's basically accounting with elements."

Then Natalia said, "I'm so sorry. I didn't mean to interrupt your date. I was just walking home, and that guy came out of the restaurant and started catcalling me. Chad, thank you for the help. Selma, it was very nice to meet you. Please, enjoy the rest of your night."

Before Chad could say anything else, Natalia disappeared into the night.

"You saw she was in trouble and helped?" Selma asked.

"Yes."

"And I have nothing to be suspicious about?"

"Nope."

She placed her hands on his cheeks and kissed him. "You're lucky I'm so awesome."

"I am."

She then pressed his face, squeezing his cheeks. "But you better never fucking lie to me."

"Never." The word sounded funny coming from fish lips, but the fear was obvious.

Selma released his face and gently took his hand in hers as she led him back to the restaurant. "Good. Let's get back to dinner. I told the waiter if we weren't back in five minutes he needed to spit in your food."

"Good to know the variables." And he couldn't wait to learn about the variables in the envelope in his back pocket.

CHAPTER 24

Heston walked along the railroad tracks. The text had read, "We need to talk," and included an address. Heston was curious, so he texted back, asking for a time to meet. It was early in the morning, but Chad had texted him last night that they needed to meet at the barn. Something about seeing Chuck and getting a bunch of driver's licenses. This meeting first, then to the barn.

Heston rarely came to this part of town, even though it was walkable. No one did. Two blocks away from downtown East Bend, the scenery changed from two-story buildings to vacant lots of gravel overgrown with weeds. Rows of seldom-used railroad tracks ran from horizon to horizon, a few abandoned carrier cars rotting away on unused tracks.

Equidistant between the edge of town and the tracks stood a Cape-Cod-style house on a small plot of brown grass. The wood siding had once been dark blue, accented by cream trim and shutters. Now everything was faded and tinted green. This house was the meeting place. The people he needed to meet with were out and about.

The Ink Stains.

Heston was surprised to see all four of them. He always thought of them as creatures of the night, and never would he have guessed they were awake and active this early in the morning. Three of them worked on an old-style Dodge Challenger. Tasha's legs poked out from under it while Dylan and Kicks examined what was under the hood.

Holding two metal travel mugs, Kat strolled over to Heston and handed one to him. "It's a 1970. I'm not much of a car girl, but it's a favorite of the others. They found it in the junkyard and pushed it over two miles to get it here."

"Cool," Heston said, debating if he should drink what was inside it or throw it and run away.

"Just coffee," Kat said and then took a sip. "Trust me; if I wanted to cause you harm, it wouldn't be through coffee."

Heston had a hard time reconciling the most feared group of individuals in the tri-city area doing such pedestrian activities as drinking coffee and fixing cars. *I guess they're just regular people*, he thought as he tentatively sipped the coffee, *who can turn into bloodthirsty killing machines.* "You really don't want to harm me?"

"No."

"Then why'd you invite me here?"

"Why'd you come?"

Heston demonstrated that he had no answer by looking away and taking a bigger swig.

Dylan looked up from under the hood. He wiped his hands on a rag, then walked over to Kat and Heston. "Hey, kid. What's up?"

"I literally don't know."

Dylan and Kat chuckled, but it was inclusive rather than sadistic. Kat said, "You can relax. We're not going to hurt you. In fact, quite the opposite. We want to give you sanctuary."

"Ummm . . . ? What?"

"You heard her correctly," Dylan said. Heston had never heard him talk before and was surprised at how smooth and inviting his voice was. The voice of a concerned uncle who wanted nothing but the best for everyone he cared about. "You're a bit of an outsider with family drama. Trust me, we all know something about that."

"I'm still not following."

Kat gestured to the house. "We're offering you a place to stay."

"A place to stay?"

"Yes. We know your brother is dangerous, and we also know who your father is. You have your friends, but are they enough? If not, you can hang out here as long as you need."

"So . . . you're recruiting me to become an Ink Stain? Is there any kind of ritual or hazing I have to go through?"

Kat laughed. "Do you really think we call ourselves 'the Ink Stains?' I mean, do you and your little group of friends have a name for yourselves?"

Heston really did believe "the Ink Stains" was something they called themselves. "No. We don't."

"Neither do we. Someone around town called us that, and then that's what people saw us as. Just a bunch of stains covered in ink. That's how people are, aren't they, Heston? People will always see what they want to see, not what actually is. That's how you feel, right? The people in your life, at school, around town will never see you for who you are, no matter what you do or how you grow."

Kat wasn't entirely right, but she was nowhere near being wrong either. His father only accepted him as a son because he created a void for that part of his heart when he kicked Chuck out of the house. Since kindergarten, Chad, Cooper, and Kyle had been a part of his life. He loved them dearly—like brothers. Had they ever viewed him as anyone other than the pudgy, shy kid they needed to coax out from hiding places? Chad was the only one to notice Heston using his abilities to make himself thinner, but he did so with questions and an accusatory tone. The only time they truly let him have a voice was as the DM for gaming campaigns.

"I already have a group of friends—a pack—and school."

"That's fine and something we'd encourage. We're not asking you to give anything up. We just wanted to extend an invitation to add more to your life with others who can truly understand what you're going through."

"But you eat people."

"The last time we did that was with Mason and his shit heel friends. And that was to save Chad."

"You ever taste people? Terrible. Taste nothing like chicken," Dylan added.

"You turned Chad into a rabbit to *eat him*."

Kat shrugged. "True. But things have changed. That thought process was driven by Hunter and reinforced by Viper. Who, by the way, was a fucking psycho. Yes, I loved Hunter, and yes, Dylan and I went along with it, but it's no longer a part of our vision. Thanks to the pack coming from Mills Hook, we need to stick together. Even before what went down with The Morrigan, we wanted to make The Bends our permanent home. Since Hunter is no longer the leader of the pack, we can do things differently, embrace the overall community and not focus on pack superiority."

Heston squinted, focusing his gaze in an attempt to see into Kat's head and determine if she was lying. She smiled and continued, "You're wondering if I'm lying. I'm not. This is an open offer, and you really don't have to make a decision. Hang out whenever you want, leave whenever you want."

Heston nodded. He took one final gulp of coffee and handed the mug back to Kat. "Thank you for the coffee. And the offer."

"Any time. Come back whenever you want."

"See you around, kid," Dylan said as he turned back toward the car.

Backpack slung over his shoulder, Heston walked all the way to the barn with one thought in his mind: *What the hell does all this mean?*

———

Kyle hurried into the barn, anxious for a story. "Is Chad here yet?"

"Not as of yet," Cooper replied. He and Heston were flowing from one Tai-Chi pose to the next, following Tyler's lead. Before Kyle could ask a follow-up question, Cooper added, "We, too, are excited for him to arrive and tell us a tale, hopefully one of joy, not of woe."

"He should be here soon," Kyle said as he sat on a hay bale at the table.

After a few more moves, Tyler pressed his palms together and bowed to Cooper and Heston. They mimicked the gesture. Cooper joined Kyle at the table while Heston and Tyler adjourned to the couch, each cracking open a beer. They didn't have to wait long—Chad finally arrived.

"How was your date?" everyone asked in unison.

Chad stopped in his tracks, wide-eyed. "Ummm, good?"

Kyle was happy to hear that. He was euphoric about taking his relationship with Janey to the next level, and he wanted his friends to experience the same levels of happiness. Hell, he wanted everyone in the world to experience the same levels of happiness. It would certainly be a better place! That was a macro-level wish, though. On a more micro-level, Kyle wished that at least one of his friends would get a girlfriend so he could discuss shared experiences. And do "couples' things." He wasn't entirely sure what "couples' things" were, but he knew that women liked to do them and that at least two couples were needed to do them. But first, he needed Chad not to screw things up.

Cooper frowned. "Okay, first and absolutely foremost, what is up with your hair?"

Shorter and styled, no hint of the moppy mess it once was, it looked good, modern, but ultimately unusual on Chad. He shrugged. "I wanted to try something new. And coming from a guy who changes his hairstyle once a month, I'm not entirely sure you're the one to pass judgment."

Cooper placed his hands out in supplication. "Touché, correct, and you're right. However, judging from the raise in octave as you answered, you're making me think things actually didn't go well."

Chad continued to the table and took a seat. "Sort of? Sorry. The date was great. She's a really cool person to be with. Smart, funny, fun, an extremely talented artist. And she loves to do wild mashups. On the back of a placemat, she did a whole *Game of Thrones* scene using only muppets. But then . . . I ran into Natalia."

Kyle groaned, but he could barely hear it over everyone else's groans. Even Tyler groaned.

Waving his hands around in a panic, Chad hurriedly continued, "No, no, no. It's nothing like that, I swear. After dinner, I went to the men's room, and I saw Chuck outside, running past the restaurant. With everything that's going on right now, I had to follow him. He was running because Natalia was chasing him. She caught him and started to whoop his ass, but he got away. However, he dropped this."

Chad placed a regular white mailing envelope on the table. Cooper, being closest, opened it. "Whoa."

Kyle leaned in while Heston and Tyler came over from the couch.

"More driver's licenses," Cooper said. "Six more and a business card."

"That's a total of twelve licenses," Chad said. "Since we know the other six are counterfeit, we can assume these are as well."

"Does the name on the business card match any of the names on the licenses?" Tyler asked.

Cooper flipped through the licenses, but Chad answered. "No. The business card is for a salesman named Scotty Chapman from a property management company. It's pretty close to the waterfront, close to Factory Park."

Heston grabbed his backpack and pulled out his laptop. He sat on a hay bale at the table and booted it up. "I'm guessing this is why you wanted us to bring our computers? To research the names and faces on these licenses?"

Chad grabbed his laptop as well and started it up. "Yeah. I mean, as long as you don't have other plans."

"Nah, I'm good."

Tyler strolled over to the couch and sat down. He grabbed his tablet from the hay bale coffee table. "I am more than willing to help, so toss me a license or two."

Cooper tossed one to Tyler and handed out one to everyone else while keeping two for himself. Kyle looked at the one he got, and his blood stopped moving through his veins, a cold sweat percolating along his hairline. His hands trembled as the world around him fell away, leaving only the license in his right hand.

"Kyle?" Cooper asked. "Kyle? What seems to be the dilemma?"

"Th-th-this . . ." Kyle pushed his words out as if trying to speak underwater. "This is Justin Butera."

Everyone gathered around him. Cooper asked, "Are you sure?"

"Yes," Kyle answered. His mind loosened up, getting over the initial shock of seeing a dead friend. "I'm absolutely sure."

"Timothy Hanover?" Heston said, reading the name on the license. "Why is Timothy Hanover using a picture of Justin?"

Chad added, "And does that mean all of the pictures on the other licenses are of people who are . . . umm . . . who . . . umm . . . are . . . ?"

"Dead," Kyle finished his friend's question. Justin was dead. Killed and eaten by the Ink Stains. Kyle could have shared the same fate had he decided to join Justin when he accepted the Ink Stains' offer to help him. When Justin first disappeared, Kyle's guilt made him wish he would have joined Justin. But now . . . now Kyle fostered a new emotion while holding the image of his dead friend. Anger. "He's dead. And Chad's onto something. Maybe the people who want these licenses are using the faces of the recently deceased."

"But why?" Cooper asked. "Unless the people using them look like the people in the licenses, they're useless."

"Maybe they just want some form of identification?" Chad said. "The concept of something is better than nothing."

Cooper nodded. "Okay. With the last set of licenses, we researched the names and came up with nothing, and none of us possess any form of facial recognition software. All we did was access and peruse student directories on the off chance we'd get lucky. We did not."

"Obituaries," Kyle said. "If these are the faces of people who died within the past few months to a year, then let's start looking at obituaries."

Cooper rolled his neck and cracked his knuckles. "All right, boys, it seems we should prepare ourselves for a long afternoon."

"Actually," Kyle said as he picked up the business card and handed it to Cooper. "I have an idea, should you choose to accept this mission."

"I accept!" Cooper gleefully snatched the card from Kyle. "I could use a partner-in-crime. Chad, would you be up to the challenge?"

Chad shrugged. "Sure. Sounds like fun."

"Splendid! I always love a good side quest. I shall now roll for luck."

The finger.

"Damn it!"

While Cooper and Chad discussed their plan, Kyle stared at the driver's license. Who wants this license? Why would they want to use the picture of a dead teenager? How is the realtor involved? *What the hell does all this mean?*

———

Cooper strolled up to the property management offices with Chad in tow. "Come on, keep up, and walk with authority. Don't forget the root word for 'con' is 'confidence.' We need to exude confidence to be believed."

"Con? We're not in *Ocean's Eleven*, you know."

"We are. The little-known sequel called *Cooper's Two*, so don't mess this up, or we'll be a box office disaster."

"You worry me," Chad whispered as they entered the building.

A quick internet search had told them the company owned four upscale apartment buildings in The Bends. All smiles, Cooper aimed straight for the receptionist and launched into his cover story. "Greetings and salutations to you on this fine January afternoon. My associate and I would like to meet with Scotty Chapman."

"Do you have an appointment?"

"No. A friend referred us to Mr. Chapman and suggested we see him about renting an apartment."

The receptionist tapped away on her computer keyboard. "Well, he usually doesn't see walk-ins, but let me check his . . . okay, so it looks like he doesn't have anything until later. I'll take you to his office."

Perfect! Cooper high-fived himself in his mind as he and Chad followed the receptionist to Scotty's office. *Hopefully, he'll dawdle, which will afford us a moment to snoop about.* No such luck.

As soon as the receptionist left, Scotty entered, leading with his perfectly coiffed hair and impossibly bright smile.

"Hey, guys! How's it going? I'm Scotty Chapman," the salesman said as he attacked them with handshakes. Open-mouthed and full of glistening teeth, he had a hyena's smile, ready to elevate to a laugh at a moment's notice. This man was all about feeding on others. Cooper wasn't entirely sure they would make it out of his office without signing a lease on a river-view luxury apartment. *No, focus.* They had a job to do.

Barely after Cooper got out, "I'm Larry, and this is Steve," Scotty gestured to a pair of chairs for them to sit in while he took his chair behind his desk.

He pressed his fingers together and said, "I gotta be honest, guys. I'm not entirely sure I'm the best choice for you. The apartments I find are high-end, not usually what college students are looking for. You'll have better success finding your price range using the internet. Unless, of course, you have parents willing to foot the bill. You don't happen to have parents willing to foot the bill, do you?"

"Ha! College students!" Cooper snorted as he smacked Chad's shoulder and then pointed to Scotty. He continued with a thick southern accent. "Ya hear that, Steve? He thinks we're college students. Oh, tarnation, Scotty, that's a good one! Can't wait to tell the ol' boys about this one. See, Scotty, we're just a couple of dentists from Kentucky, lookin' to move up here and become Yankees."

Scotty squinted and tapped the tips of his index fingers against his lips. Cooper wagered that he was trying to choose his words wisely, careful not to upset the potential clients in his office just in case they weren't lying. "Now, I know the world keeps getting younger and younger around me, but you two seem too young to be dentists. I'm not sure what you're playing at, so either you be upfront with me now, or I'll have to ask you to leave."

Chad looked like he was fighting incontinence, so Cooper charged forth. "Well, shoot, Scotty, we only came by because your name was referred to us by our good friend, Timothy Hanover."

Silence. Scotty's face went stone cold for just a second, but it was long enough for Cooper to realize that he had struck a nerve. But the smile came back, and Scotty stood. "Timothy Hanover? Well, why didn't you say so in the first place? Any friends of Timothy are friends of mine. I'll tell you what, let me get everyone some waters, and then we can get down to business."

"Sounds great," Cooper replied, his smile just as big as Scotty's. It fell away as soon as the salesman left his office.

Cooper jumped from his chair and ran around to Scotty's computer. "He's on to us, my friend, he's on to us. We have two minutes—three tops—before he comes back to do nefarious acts upon us."

Chad shot out of his chair and joined Cooper behind the desk. "What? What are you talking about?"

"Have you never seen a thriller or suspense movie? He reacted mightily so when I mentioned Timothy Hanover. Scotty is probably contacting Timothy as we speak." Cooper moved the mouse, and the screen asked for a password. "Damn. What do we think it might be?"

"What are we even looking for?" Chad asked as he opened a drawer.

"Anything that can link Scotty to anyone from the driver's licenses. It's abundantly obvious they're in cahoots. If I can't hack into his computer, we might just have to follow him after he leaves the office." Cooper tried *1234, scotty,* and *iamgod* with no success. "Damn."

"How about his calendar?"

"That'd be perfect, but if I can't access his computer, I can't access his calendar."

"How about this?"

Frustrated, Cooper looked over to see what Chad was pointing at. Scotty's desk blotter was a giant calendar. Cooper pulled out his phone and took a picture. "Perfect! Excellent job, Chad. Now let's act like a tree and get the flock out of here."

They followed the hallway in the opposite direction they had come. It led to an exit, and they ran to Cooper's car. They wasted no time celebrating, aiming straight for the barn to share the information they garnered. *What the hell does all this mean?*

CHAPTER 25

Chad glanced over his shoulder at the restaurant's entrance and then watched the waiter, uncertain why he was pouring olive oil onto the plate in the center of the table. The waiter sprinkled some spices into the oil, left a small bread basket, and then disappeared. Chad assumed the two items went together, but he wasn't sure how. Pour the seasoned oil onto the bread? Dunk the bread into the oil? Use a fork and knife or his hands? He looked around at the other tables in *Il Cibo* Italian restaurant for clues. Thank God for Selma.

While listening to Janey tell the table that she found a place that hosted square dancing lessons, Selma used her hands to break off a small piece of bread and gently dipped it into the spiced oil. Chad marveled at how cultured she was.

"Square dancing, you say?" Selma asked. Chad mimicked what Selma had done, and so did Kyle, probably just as clueless about working the appetizer properly.

"Yeah, I know it sounds lame, but I want to experience everything I missed out on, no matter how bad the perceived experience. No one liked square dancing in high school, but I never really experienced it. When the first step is 'Bow to your partner,' and it's an all but insurmountable challenge, the rest of the process would be tainted. Now that I'm physically able to do everything needed for the process to be successful, I want to try it again."

"Even if this process has been openly, widely, and vehemently criticized by all who have participated before?"

"Yes."

Selma raised her glass of complimentary ice water. "To a woman far braver and more driven than I could ever be."

The other three at the table raised their glasses, Janey blushing as she did so. After a clink and a gulp, Chad returned to scoping out his surroundings. Nothing unusual about the restaurant itself—rustic décor, table clothes made from cloth and unaccompanied by crayons, stucco walls with murals of happy people in old-country Italy. Cobblestone roads, houses with opened windows, smiling faces, bicycles with baskets full of bread, grapevines more plentiful than Alabama kudzu. Chad had no measuring stick to determine if this place was up-scale or not, but the prices on the menu were higher than the seafood place he and Selma visited two nights ago, and theirs was the only table without a bottle of wine on it. He wondered if the I-left-my-ID-in-the-car password would work at the bar across the room like it did at Clinty's. Judging by the plush barstools looking more comfortable than any chair he had ever sat in before and the fact that the bartender wore a clean shirt and tie, he doubted it.

He peeked over his shoulder again at the door.

A buzz tickled his leg, and he glanced at his phone, resting on the booth's seat.

Dude you;re being obvius.

Chad looked up and Kyle shot a stern look at him before turning his at-tention to the conversation between the girls. The sudden warmth of embar-rassment ran up Chad's neck after being scolded about societal decorum by the most socially awkward person ever to walk the Earth. But Chad couldn't help it—espionage made him uncomfortable. Yesterday was a blessing and a curse having Cooper along. There was no way Chad could have done that while flying solo, but Cooper thought himself way smoother than he really was. What the heck accent was that? It was most likely an attempt at a vague southern accent, but it drifted into Jamaican more than once. They didn't find anything that tied Scotty Chapman to any of the names on the fake driver's licenses nor to Heston's brother, but they found a meeting date, time, and location for his next appoint-ment. Here and now. Chad looked over his shoulder again. This time it paid off.

Scotty Chapman walked in.

Chad's breath hitched and he snapped his head back around. Too fast. He caught Selma's attention, and she squinted, her eyes drilling into him. That smoldering look told him she knew he was up to something. "You okay?"

"Yeah. Yep. Sorry," he answered. "Just nervous. This is the fanciest restau-rant I have ever been in, and I feel like everyone's staring at me."

"And you figured that being a twitchy spaz is the best way to avoid attention?"

"It's not? Damn. I've been trying that tactic all my life and never realized it wasn't the way to go."

Selma's gaze softened and a slight smirk touched the corners of her lips. "Well, now that I've enlightened you, I feel accomplished."

"You should. There are quite a few layers of pure brick between enlightenment and the center of my skull."

"Good to know."

As soon as Selma turned, Chad glanced toward the bar. Scotty sat next to another man, the person he was scheduled to meet. Chad didn't like being duplicitous, but he couldn't tell Selma about the ulterior motive for having a double date at this restaurant. Kyle told Janey, but that was because they had been thrown into a situation where there was no other option than to tell Janey everything. Now she was in on the operation. Before dinner, they had game-planned different scenarios, one of them being what to do if Scotty met with someone at the bar.

"So, Selma," Janey started, "Chad tells us that you're an amazing artist."

"I doubt the superlative is necessary, but I do a bit more than dabble."

"Oooooh, I love art. I'm so not good at actually arting, but I'm really awesome at admiring it. Do you have a portfolio I could see?"

"Yeah." Selma pulled out her phone and leaned forward. Janey leaned forward and the two met at the center of the table. Janey "ooh'd" and "ahh'd" at every piece Selma swiped through. Chad had seen her portfolio and had the same reactions, which was why this was part of the plan. The distraction.

After a quick text exchange with Kyle, it was time to enact the next step of the plan. He leaned close to the center of the table and said, "Kyle and I are going to see if we can find our waiter."

"Okay," Janey replied and went back to asking questions about Selma's artwork.

Chad approached the bar carefully so Scotty didn't notice him. The group had discussed that Janey should join Kyle while Chad stayed back at the table, but as much as he hated espionage, he liked the idea of putting Janey in the line of fire even less. Plus, he would have been a complete mess, agonizing about the mission and wondering what was being said between Scotty and the other guy. Luckily, there was no one else at the bar, so Chad could hear Scotty's half of the conversation, even with a barstool between them.

Scotty turned toward the other man at the bar and said, "Everything is good to go with Empty Island."

Kyle sat beside the other man to catch his end of the conversation, but Chad had already heard plenty. Empty Island, a failed attempt for South Bend and East Bend to generate revenue. The Snaking River flowed from the north but made a sharp turn to the east for a few miles along the northern parts of West Bend and East Bend before hooking back to the south, running along the eastern parts of East Bend and South Bend. A mile-long island sat in the middle of the river, half claimed by East Bend, the other half claimed by South Bend. In a joint effort, the two cities built a bridge leading to it and dubbed the land Rec Island. That was where their collaboration stopped.

South Bend wanted to turn their half of the island into a high-end residential area, hoping to capitalize on luxury taxes. Meanwhile, East Bend hoped to turn their half of the island into a family fun entertainment getaway. Thanks to neither city's development committee being open or honest with their communications, both projects moved forward simultaneously, neither succeeding. Now, Empty Island—or Wreck Island, as some locals referred to it—housed one five-story graffiti-covered, dust-filled luxury apartment building and a fully functional, never-once-used baseball stadium—the perfect size to host a single-A minor league team that never came to fruition.

Since the other man was turned toward Scotty, Chad could see his face. Sure enough, that face was on one of the fake driver's licenses.

"What'll it be?" the bartender asked Chad.

If Chad could hear Scotty, then Scotty could hear him, so he didn't want to say anything that would bring attention to himself. Whining about the waiter or asking for water refills didn't seem like background conversation heard at a bar, so he said, "What's your specialty?"

The bartender chuckled. "Shirley Temple."

Chad had zero knowledge of any mixed drinks, their names, or what went in them, so he said, "Never heard of it, but I'm intrigued. I'll take two."

"Coming right up."

Surprised that the bartender didn't ask for ID, Chad was happy to pay, grab the drinks, and hurry back to the table.

"What's this?" Selma asked as Chad slid the drink to her.

Chad mustered up all the swagger of James Bond and answered, "Shirley Temple."

Selma replied with a soft laugh and a slow headshake. "Weirdo," she said as she took a sip and went back to answering Janey's questions.

Kyle returned, wide-eyed and with two waters. In between furtive glances ar the women, he texted: theyr talking about empty island

Chad replied: IKR but why????

I didn't hear. What do u think its about?

"Okay, what is going on?" Selma asked.

"Ummm . . ." Chad replied.

"You two have been acting really twitchy and weird. More than usual. Like you're trying to hide something."

"Ummm . . ." Kyle added.

"They're playing a game," Janey said, tapping away at her phone screen. "I'm sure you've heard plenty about *The World of Glark*, the game Kyle and I play for our esports team. Well, there's an augmented reality version of the game called *Glark World,* where each player has a stable of characters they can find in the real world. Some characters are harder to find than others, and there happens to be one in this restaurant."

Janey held up her phone, the screen showing whatever she pointed the camera at. She slowly panned across the restaurant and then stopped at the neighboring table. Standing on top of the table was a wolf in the overly muscled form of a human. Fear splashed within Chad's heart like a pebble dropping into a lake when he saw the werewolf, but the ripples dissipated quickly as he realized the cartoonish image wasn't Hunter. Not only was there a difference in fur color, but this werewolf had an eye patch, green Mohawk, steel teeth, and wielded an ax with a head bigger than its torso.

"This is Cezomir," Janey explained. "He's an extremely powerful general in *The World of Glark* and very, very, super, extremely rare in *Glark World*. It would be well over two hours before he returns for any other player once he's captured, if he even returns at all. None of us have him in our stable, so the boys were trying to determine who should capture him in a very clumsy, awkward, distracting manner."

Selma stared at the phone screen in silence for a few seconds before whispering, "Cezomir?"

At first, Chad thought she was repeating a word she had never heard before, but then she pointed her phone at the same table. Cezomir appeared on her screen as well. Chad had no idea she played *Glark World*, and judging by how fast she captured Cezomir, she played the game well. She said, "There. I answered your question for you."

"You most certainly did!" Janey squealed. "Who else do you have in your stable?"

Conversation flowed around the table for the rest of the double date, and many laughs were shared, especially after Selma explained to Chad what went into a Shirley Temple. But Chad couldn't get Kyle's last question out of his head. What was it all about?

CHAPTER 26

The walk home from campus was long and hard, as if Chad were walking through three feet of snow instead of a mostly melted half an inch. The snow came while everyone slept, but the morning sun shooed away the clouds, creating a warmer day than usual. The snow on the sidewalks, walkways, and roads was gone, leaving behind darkened spots as shadows of its existence. The weather wasn't what weighed Chad down—it was the weight of his Pinocchio nose.

All through dinner two nights ago, he lied to Selma. It was stupid and he felt childish. Why hadn't he told her about the most unique aspect of his life? Fear, obviously. On top of her reasons-to-leave-Chad list might be, "He turns into a freaky mutant rabbit thing." But Kyle was forthcoming with Janey, and not only did he support that aspect of his life, but she was almost downright enthusiastic about it. Selma was cool like that, too, right? As an artist, she'd have an open mind, ready to accept Chad for who he was. Wouldn't she? What if she didn't, though?

Chad sighed as he tromped through the forest shortcut, an occasional dollop of snow hitting him from the branches above. Whether she accepted him or not was moot compared to her safety. He would be asking her to venture with him into a world he knew so little about. The jocks and the Ink Stains were question marks in regards to safety. Both packs were playing nicely for now, but either could turn vicious at any moment. And what about the pack coming into town? The danger level from them was unknown but assumed to be high. How were they connected to Scotty Chapman and Empty Island?

Yesterday, Chad and his friends debated and researched. Sure enough, the man Scotty met with had his face on one of the fake driver's licenses, but the name on it—Brendan Druthers—had died ten months ago. And what was the connection to the island? There were rumors about both East Bend and South Bend looking to get rid of the ownership of the island. Was there a connection between this and the Mills Hook pack? Too many questions, too many variables. No. Chad couldn't tell Selma about the other part of his life, at least not yet.

Thanks to Fate making Chad into its personal squeak toy, a squeeze in his gut made him look up.

Brittany.

Fully clothed and in human form, she walked through the forest toward him, a backpack slung over her shoulder. Too stunned to move or speak, Chad stood like a statue—as mute as one, too.

"Hey, Chad," she said, stopping a few feet away from him.

"Hey," he replied, wondering about this interaction. She wasn't smiling, but she wasn't wearing her usual scowl either.

"So . . . You're mom's a pretty good shot." She rubbed her forearm for emphasis.

"That was . . . she . . . my parents . . ."

Brittany waved her hand and shook her head. "Chad, stop. You're going to hurt yourself. It's obvious that your parents, and a few other people, including Whacky Wanda, are hunting . . . us."

Chad had no idea how to read her, and panic set in when he remembered she knew his parents. "Don't tell Brick!"

"Brick? Why would—"

"Please! Please don't tell him that my parents are lycanthrope hunters."

The scowl he had come to expect was in full force. Another head shake followed by an eye roll, she said, "I'm not going to fucking tell Brick."

"Okay. Okay? Okay. Promise?"

"Jesus, Chad! I was hoping to talk to you about who we are, but clearly that's not going to happen. I was hoping you had changed."

"Changed? I changed a lot since high school."

"You still see athletes as enemies, Chad. You still see me as a bitchy cheerleader. You still yourself as a victim." Brittany started to storm away.

"That's . . . that's . . . not entirely true! I *have* changed!"

"Just because you're dating the hot pretzel girl doesn't mean you've changed. And just because we weren't friends in high school doesn't mean we couldn't have been now."

She was trying to connect with him, trying to bond with a shared experience, and he scared her away. "Brittany, wait."

She paused long enough to turn around and look him square in the eye as she said, "Goodbye, Chad."

He had no reply and could only watch in silence as she walked away.

Good job, moron. He scolded himself for the rest of the trek home.

Chad exited the woods onto his parents' back lawn, treading carefully in case they were target practicing. The skill level of his mom was terrifying and getting better. But his parents weren't practicing; they were in white and gray camouflage loading weaponry into their car. He hurried over and asked, "Where are you going?"

"Out," Chad's father said.

"Rick!" Mother snapped.

"It doesn't matter where we're going—he's going to be judgmental and fussy."

"We promised to tell him where we were going, and you don't have to be so snappish about it." She emphasized her point by slamming the car door closed after placing a compound bow on the backseat.

"Fine." In a more even tone, Chad's father said, "We're meeting with everyone to do a safety patrol."

Safety patrol. That could mean a meeting, practice, or hunting. Chad didn't like any of those options. He debated rescinding his rule of not joining them, feeling compelled to sabotage their efforts, but instead reminded himself that he was as good at sabotage as he was at espionage. Someone would get hurt. Anyway, he doubted they had any good information to act on. All the lycanthropes he knew were cautious, and if they had a bead on the Ink Stains, he was certain Natalia would contact him. Not to share information, but instead make snide comments to him about his relationship with her mother. He was confident that their safety patrol would be fruitless.

"You'll never believe who we ran into at the farmer's market today," Chad's mom said, a sing-song quality to her voice as if she were packing groceries into the trunk of their sedan instead of crossbows and bolts.

To keep the peace, Chad asked, "Who?"

"Brittany McNamara."

Chad almost laughed at how his mother's tone implied that this was good news. Playing back the exchange he just had with Brittany mere moments ago, he wondered why she didn't mention that to him. It wasn't like he gave her a chance. Or was she withholding something from him? Or was she setting him up? Maybe she was planning on telling his parents about him, especially after he was such a jerk to her. Could she do that in a way that wouldn't incriminate herself? He couldn't think of one, but that didn't stop him from assuming she could do it. "Yeah?"

"She's doing well. Have you seen her on campus at all? She goes to the same college you do."

"I've seen her around."

"You should get in touch with her, son," his father said.

This time Chad did laugh. "Dad, I'm dating someone."

Rick crossed his arms and leaned against the driver's side door. Frowning, he said, "I didn't say ask her out. I just said you should contact her."

"Why?"

"You two have known each other since kindergarten. That's more than two-thirds of your life. Now that you two are in the same college, you have a lot in common. I'm sure there's a lot to talk about."

"Dad, she's a cheerleader and I'm a nerd. We've *never* had anything in common or anything to talk about."

"Now who's still stuck in the past? She's not a cheerleader anymore, and you aren't in high school."

Chad's mother followed with a gentle throat clear and a translation. "What your father is saying is Brittany seems lonely. She went through a heck of a trauma a few months ago when Mason went missing. She doesn't know that he was murdered, but everyone around her suspects he's dead. Grief like that is difficult to deal with. Any contact from people she knows would probably help."

Leave it to his mother to make him feel guilty regarding the feelings of someone who hated him. Though, he started to suspect as much after his recent run-in with her. "She's upset?"

"Yes," Rick jumped back in. "Very. Teared up while talking about Mason. It was sad and it added to our resolve—your mother's and mine. Brittany is why we're doing this, Chad. We want to protect you and make the world a better place, but we also want to protect the Brittanies of the world. The people who have had people stripped out of their lives. No one should lose a loved one the way she did. And that's not including Mason's other friends or his family. We know you don't approve of our methods, but you can't argue that we're not trying to do the right thing."

Chad bit his tongue hard enough to taste blood. His father was right. There were evil lycanthropes out there, but not all of them. He wanted to stop his parents' quest of misplaced heroism, and the only way to do that was to tell them his secret and that he understood what they were trying to stop. There were better ways to accomplish what they wanted without putting their lives on the line. That meant they'd have to accept their son risking his life instead, and that was even if they could accept that he was a lycanthrope. Bud McCurdy made mortal threats once he found out that his favorite son was a lycanthrope. Chad's parents were different, but that didn't mean they wouldn't react in a similar fashion. Logic going impotent, Chad could only say, "Please be safe."

"Always are," his dad said as he and his mom got in the car. Chad waved as they drove away.

Before heading to the barn, he microwaved some leftovers and shoveled them into his face. Halfway through his meal, his phone chimed, letting him know someone wanted to video chat. Selma? Odd, because she usually texted.

It was Selma's phone, but it was not she who had called.

Chad stripped, shoved his clothes into a rucksack, and went full rabbit to sprint to the barn.

CHAPTER 27

Heston cranked the ratchet wrench in time with the music in the background. He never considered himself a big car lover, but he could appreciate the appeal of the 1970 Dodge Challenger he worked on. "Done."

"Nice work, kid," Dylan said, inspecting the brake drum Heston had finished installing. "You got a talent for this."

"Thanks. My dad has a landscaping business, so I've worked on vehicles before. Nothing like this, though."

Tasha walked around the car, her hand running along the sides. "She's pretty sweet, isn't she?"

There wasn't much to the car at the moment. Hood, trunk, and doors gone. Tires off. But Heston understood what Tasha meant. The mess of metal and components had the potential to be powerful, and there was always a certain beauty within power. He saw this car's appeal and of helping rebuild and fix this machine. "Yeah. What's next?"

Dylan pulled out a set of keys from his pocket and flopped himself in the driver's seat. "That depends. Tasha's been working on the engine all week. Let's see if she has a little necromancy in her."

Dylan turned the key.

The engine roared to life.

Tasha whooped, then delivered loud high-fives to Dylan and Heston. He had only spent an hour working on the car with them and hadn't touched the engine, but Heston still smiled from the sense of pride.

Chuckling, Dylan turned the car off and stepped out. "All right. We're gonna hunt for a transmission. You comin' along, kid?"

"Ummm . . ." Heston replied.

"Don't worry," Kat said from behind him. She was always sneaking up from out of nowhere. "They'll go shopping and actually pay for it, if that's your cause for hesitation."

It wasn't. He hadn't done anything in a social manner with anyone other than the guys. It was time he started, which was why he was here. Cooper joined a sports team. Chad got a girlfriend. Kyle somehow joined a sports team *and* got a girlfriend. Heston didn't have those kinds of outlets. He associated with other students in his classes, but he only communicated with any of them after normal school hours to work on group projects for school. There was Tyler, but their interactions were always at the barn and limited to either training or lounging around, smoking pot and drinking beer. The Ink Stains had invited him to hang out, but he never expected to get invited to join them in a run to get a car part. "Sorry, that wasn't it. Just trying to remember when I said I'd meet the guys."

Kat smiled, making Heston feel as apprehensive as a mouse. She had power and she knew it. "I kind of figured it had something to do with Chad and the boys. Speaking of . . . how is Chad?"

Heston shrugged. "Good, I guess."

"I'm guessing he's spending a lot of time with his new girlfriend."

"Yeah."

"What's she like?"

What the hell? How did Chad do it? His girlfriend was hot and seemingly awesome, and now Kat—hot and awesome in different ways—was asking about him? That didn't include whatever the hell might be between him and Natalia as well as his random interactions with Brittany. Was he bitten by a radioactive gigolo? "I don't know. Haven't met her yet."

"Hmmm."

Heston didn't know what that meant. It sounded innocuous enough, but he knew Kat meant something more, something deeper, something nefarious by it. He regretted coming here and started thinking of excuses to flee. Luckily, one presented itself for him. Kat's phone buzzed. "Yeah? Yeah. Okay." She slid it back into her pocket and said to Heston, "Sorry, but we have to head out. Feel free to stay in the house if you'd like." To Tasha and Dylan, she said, "That was Kicks. We gotta go."

Heston didn't think twice about his escape. "Thanks for letting me work on the car with you."

"Any time, kid," Dylan said.

"Come back when you can," Tasha replied.

"Tell Chad I said hi," Kat purred.

Heston didn't know what was happening, but it wouldn't end well.

———

Kyle kicked the heavy bag hanging from the barn rafter. He delivered a hard blow right where he had been aiming, his form perfect. The bag swayed as if a light breeze caressed it. This was why he wanted to train, to get stronger, better. He felt comfortable working the heavy bag with no one else at the barn. Yes, Tyler created an environment where Kyle felt he was part of a team, where everyone worked on using their unique strengths to improve upon their weaknesses. But everyone else got the bag swinging while Kyle could barely move it. Tyler always encouraged Kyle by saying he had great speed and accuracy, which he appreciated, but he desperately wanted to add some strength to his attacks. Taking cleansing breaths, he focused on his punches and kicks, aiming for a singular spot on the bag. He kept hitting and kicking, commanding his arms and legs to move faster. Faster. Again. Again! Harder! Faster!

The bag was finally swinging back and forth.

Winded, he placed his hands on his knees to catch his breath, fatigue similar to when he transformed into a pheasant and back again. Had he tapped into his bird self without transforming into a pheasant?

"Greetings and salutations!" Cooper shouted as he entered the barn. "Using some downtime to add to your skill level? Admirable. Very admirable. By the powers that be, I know I need to do more of that."

Kyle wiped the sweat from his brow. "I thought you hit the gym and exercised with your teammates?"

"I do. That certainly aids my physical fitness but does little to aid my lycanthropeness. And it does zero to aid my interpersonal bonding with my main crew." Cooper extended his fist to Kyle, and Kyle bumped it with his.

"Yeah, the four of us haven't had a lot of group time together this semester. I feel like it's partly my fault, spending so much time either practicing with my esports team or hanging out with Janey."

"Nonsense!" Cooper snapped. "Never feel bad for pursuing opportunities to enrich yourself! Don't forget, each and every one of us is finally exploring the world around us now that we've freed ourselves from the yoke of tyranny."

"Yeah, that's true. Even Chad is finally moving past some of his hang-ups."

"As unbelievable as that may sound, you are correct. I just wish Heston could get more opportunity to stretch his legs in a metaphorical sense."

"Don't worry about him," Heston said as he entered the barn. "He has a few opportunities here and there. In fact, I just came from hanging out with the Ink Stains."

It would have made more sense had Heston said he met the Pope. Kyle couldn't articulate how confused he was. "Ummm . . . what?"

"I agree with Kyle," Cooper said. "Isn't that Chad's line?"

"No," Heston answered. "Chad's lusting after Kat—he doesn't know the others."

"Know them or not, they tried to eat us not too long ago."

"Technically, they tried to eat Chad. And that was when Hunter and Viper were with the pack. Chad killed Hunter and Kyle . . . uh . . . took care of Viper."

Kyle had killed Viper. He didn't remember it, but he woke every once in a while from a nightmare about eating snakes. The other three had told him that he had shifted into half-bird, half-human, half-monster, but they became fidgety when talking about it. Too afraid to learn the truth, he accepted whatever they said and moved on, although he would love to learn how to shift into his half-bird, half-human form. "Even though they might not have tried to eat us, they did try to kill us."

Heston shrugged. "We tried to kill them. And the jocks. And the jocks tried to kill us, yet we're coexisting with them. Cooper even hangs out with them. People can change . . . no lycanthrope pun intended."

"Well, I wouldn't say I've been hanging out with Brick. We just happened to be at a party together and held a conversation with him and . . . You know what? You are absolutely right to say that people can change."

"Guys! Trouble!" Chad yelled as he ran into the barn, shifting from his rabbit form into his human one.

"Is it the Ink Stains?" Cooper asked.

"Dick," Heston said.

This was bad. Chad didn't take the time to put any clothes on. Instead, he placed his phone on the center of the round table. "Kyle, did you get a call from Janey's phone?"

"I . . . I don't know. My phone's in my bag," Kyle said as everyone gathered around the table.

Chad pulled up a video and hit play. It started with a close-up of Scotty Chapman's face and his bright white teeth. "Hey, guys, Scotty Chapman here. Sorry, I know you know who I am. Thanks to a little bit of research, I now know who you are. You know who else I know you know? Them."

Scotty panned the camera across a baseball field and stopped at home plate. Sitting in chairs were Selma and Janey. The man pretending to be Brendan Druthers stood behind them, grinning, more evil than the devil himself. Scotty Chapman continued, "I think you also know where we are."

The screen went black.

Kyle lost control of his hands, shaking them as if trying to air dry them. His mind was static as darkness encroached from his peripheral vision. "This is bad. This is bad. We gotta go. We gotta go get Janey."

"Kyle's right," Chad added. "We have to rescue the girls. We need to leave now."

"This is bad. This is so bad."

"Gentlemen! Calm down!" Cooper yelled. It worked. Kyle's tunnel vision subsided. Ants still crawled under his skin, but he could concentrate enough to register what Cooper was saying. "Scotty and the fellow posing as Brendan did not harm your lady loves. They weren't even bound to the chairs. Janey looked angry and Selma looked positively freaked out, so I surmise that at least one of their captors is like us and must have shown the women."

"We can't go in guns blazing," Heston said. "We need to think this through."

"He's right," Chad said. "This feels like an ambush."

"By whom?" Cooper asked. "We have different pieces of the puzzle, but we don't know how to assemble them properly. We don't even know what the finished image will be."

"They kidnapped Janey and Selma," Kyle said, his words flying quickly from his mouth. "I agree with Chad that this seems like an ambush."

"Should we try to contact Tyler for help?" Chad asked. "What about the Ink Stains? Should we contact them?"

"The Inks Stains are busy," Heston said.

Chad winced. "How do you know that?"

"Long story," Cooper said. "But we don't need to contact Tyler or the Ink Stains or any other outside help. Trust me, I can't fathom the level of panic you two are experiencing, but I understand why you're experiencing it. However, we all need to take a collective deep breath and think about this. Why would they set an ambush? To do so implies we're at odds with someone, and the only reason anyone would view us as enemies is if we were being the antagonists in someone's story. Even though I now have a personal nemesis in Sanders and Kyle is not in the good graces of Pixel Ronin, it doesn't seem like they're involved with this."

"We don't know what they're involved with," Chad said.

At odds with. Being the antagonists in someone else's story. Cooper was right. The quartet hadn't hindered anyone's plans. Except . . . "The driver's licenses," Kyle said. "We have their fake driver's licenses."

"Maybe they just want them back?" Heston asked.

"There we go," Cooper said. "It's a fact that one of the fake licenses has the image of the lout with the oh-so-sleazy Scotty Chapman. Let's grab the counterfeit identifications and give them back. Even if they hadn't overtly asked for them, it would be viewed as a gesture of goodwill."

Chad grabbed his rucksack and went to the safe where they kept the licenses. "Should we bring a vial of Elder Blood in case something goes wrong?"

Kyle liked the idea. As lycanthropes, they now healed faster than they did as mere humans, but Elder Blood accelerated the process. Should one of them get severely injured, the Elder Blood would keep any wound from being mortal. Before he could voice his opinion, Heston said, "No."

"I agree with Heston," Cooper said. "Our mission is to procure the women and flee. If there is a physical confrontation, we simply grab and run."

Kyle didn't know what was happening, but it wouldn't end well.

———

Cooper pulled the car off the road and came to a stop. The island was easy enough to access; two lanes led to it, and two lanes went from it. A few signs stated that the island was closed and there was no outlet, which deterred motorists from turning off the main road and heading toward Rec Island. The barricade spanning all four lanes didn't appear until the island itself. There was plenty of room on the gravel turnabout for Cooper to park.

"Okay, gentlemen, let's polish our shining armor and rescue some damsels," Cooper said.

Heston got out of the car and changed his appearance, but not in a way Cooper expected. Heston's belly no longer stretched out his T-shirt; now his arms and chest did.

"Whoa!" Cooper exclaimed. "How is it possible that you did a year's worth of steroidal enhancements in a few seconds?"

Heston flexed and stretched, twisting back and forth at his waist. "Something I've been working on for the past month or so."

"So, you haven't really been losing weight?" Chad asked.

"No. I've been shifting a little here, a little there, slimming myself down. I can hold that shape all day. This shape? Maybe half an hour, but I thought it could help with the intimidation factor."

"Good thinking," Cooper said as the four started down a paved path leading to the stadium.

"Umm, guys? Isn't the island supposed to be totally abandoned?" Kyle asked.

"It is," Chad replied.

"Then why are the lights on?"

Quaint lampposts lined the path. A few remained dark, the bulbs long since burnt out, but most of the lamps were lit, the soft glow almost unseen. They'd be much more noticeable after the sun set in an hour. Behind the rows of lampposts were small buildings, tiny single-story shanties with wood siding, the paint jobs once bright and colorful, now dulled by neglect. Each building housed one product; the words streaked with rain created mold. Hot dogs in one building, burgers in another. Memorabilia in the blue shack, novelty T-shirts in the green one. The intention was an upscale, Mediterranean fishing village, but the result was a ghost town resort.

The path split. The left fork was the last leg of the journey to the stadium, while the right led to other island attractions, the first being the mini-golf course. The eighteen-hole course was a replica of The Bends, each hole a different landmark or area. The buildings were worse looking than a middle school production of *Godzilla*, and that was before nature had its way with the golf course. A shrunken, post-apocalyptic landscape. The college took up holes eight and nine.

They hopped the turnstiles next to the ticket booth into the baseball stadium and continued along the restaurant-lined concourse. Even from this distance, Cooper could see the women were unharmed. Physically, at least. Lord only knew how Scotty and Brendan threatened them.

Getting to the field was as easy as walking down a few stairs, but a chill ran down Cooper's back. It was more than being ill-dressed for the cold weather or his sneakers threatening to slip out from under him as he walked across the snow-coated outfield. It was as if he were stepping into an arena. He wished to fancy himself the star gladiator with gleaming sword, who the crowd cheered for, but he couldn't shake the feeling that he was the sacrificial slave ready to be disemboweled to warm up the fans.

"Took you guys long enough to get here," Scotty said when they were within ten yards. "I was starting to think you didn't love your girlfriends."

"Fuck you!" Kyle said, shaking. "Let them go!"

"We have what you want," Chad said as he rooted through his rucksack. He pulled out the fake licenses, bundled together by a rubber band. "I guess you recognized me at the restaurant?"

"You're nowhere near as smooth as you think you are, Shirley." Scotty gestured to the women that they were free to go, then waggled his finger to Chad, indicating he wanted the licenses. As Selma and Janey ran to the guys, Chad tossed the licenses to Scotty.

Janey ran to Kyle, and they hugged.

Chad extended his arms to Selma, but she stopped and asked, "What the fuck is going on, Chad? What the fuck have you gotten me into?"

Chad reeled back, looking surprised by her outburst. "Ummm . . . I'll explain everything. Let's get out of here first."

"I don't think you and the guys want to leave yet, Shirley," Scotty called out.

"Fuck you!" Kyle yelled back.

Scotty invitingly spread his hands, looking every bit the salesman he was. And that smile. That smile brought the chill back to Cooper's spine. "Didn't you guys figure out what this meeting was about? After snooping through my office and spying on me at the restaurant, didn't you figure it out?"

"Quit being coy, Chapman," Cooper said. "You don't wear it well."

Scotty chuckled and shook his head. "Guys, guys, guys. They're coming. The pack from Mills Hook will be here any minute."

Cooper didn't know what was happening, but it wouldn't end well.

CHAPTER 28

"Guys, guys, guys. They're coming. The pack from Mills Hook will be here any minute."

Chad froze. They started to leave, but what Scotty said piqued Chad's curiosity and offered him a way to put the puzzle together. He was beginning to see how the pieces fit. Chuck was involved with the pack from Mills Hook; Chad felt it in his gut. Now it was confirmed. Chuck had the fake IDs and Scotty's business card and somehow became a lycanthrope from an unknown source. The mystery of the source was now solved; the next question was the "why" of it all.

"Chad?" Selma said. "Why'd you stop?"

"Dude, you absolutely, utterly, unequivocally cannot be serious at this moment in time," Cooper said.

"Why not? I mean, this is a chance to meet them, talk to them, understand their motivations," Chad explained.

"This isn't some social mixer or speed dating opportunity. The enemy is coming, so we should vamoose, skedaddle, and run away before they get here."

"Why are they the enemy?" Heston asked. "We know nothing about them other than what town they've come from."

"We know they turned others into lycanthropes, including your brother," Kyle snapped.

"Hell yeah, they did!" came from one of the dugouts. Chuck strode from the shadows with a beaming smile and puffed-out chest. Sanders and Pixel Ronin exited the dugout behind him.

"I surmise that the one with his own face emblazoned on his T-shirt is the infamous Pixel Ronin?" Cooper asked.

"It is," Kyle replied. His tone was angry with no hint of fear. That concerned Chad.

"See?" Cooper addressed Chad and Heston while pointing to the three newest animals. "The enemy. They are the enemy; ergo, the new pack is the enemy."

"How do you even know each other?" Heston asked the trio.

"Funny story," Sanders started. "Chuck is my hookup. Not just for my party stuff, but everything a growing boy like me needs to do the body good. We had a good system until you came along, weasel. One day I was bitching about you, and Chuck told me you're a friend of his brother's and he had a way to make me better than you. Better than anybody."

"And you?" Kyle asked Pixel Ronin.

"Also, a funny story, Mi Not Amigo. That day Declan got accosted by Chuck? Yeah, I totally witnessed it and heard what he asked Declan. I decided to see if I could help Chuck get what he was looking for, and he said he saw you talking to me, said you knew his brother. One thing led to another."

"You are a fucking psycho!" Janey yelled, looking like she was ready to tear Ronin apart.

Heston shook his head. "Do I even need to ask?"

"How about you take a guess," Chuck laughed.

"You owed money to a drug dealer, so you ran. You ran to Mills Hook and found the pack of lycanthropes."

"Close. The guy I owed money to is a pack member. He actually caught me, but he dragged me to Mills Hook instead of killing me. A few months ago, there was a shakeup in their pack's upper management. A new alpha took over, someone who came from The Bends. This leader wanted to do things a little differently. Once he found out I'm also from The Bends, he came up with a plan, one I could get behind."

"You're the one behind the recent downtown robberies, too, aren't you?"

"Yep. I needed some cash to buy the fake IDs."

"Why do they need fake IDs?"

"Like I said, the new alpha wants to do things a little differently."

Sanders started to undress. "Can we skip over this bullshit and start killing them? I'm tired of looking at the weasel."

"Before anyone tries to kill anyone, I still have questions," echoed from the concourse above the field. Kat. Once she had everyone's attention, she leaped onto the field and sauntered toward Chad and his friends. The rest of the Ink Stains took the stairs. "Number one—what the hell does a cheesy rental property salesman have to do with this?"

Selma grabbed Chad's arm. "Chad, tell me what the fuck is going on. Tell me now."

Chad's guilt was crushing, but too much was happening, too many answers being given to questions that had bugged him for days. But pride assuaged remorse when the Ink Stains stood with him and his friends, though he wasn't sure why Heston fist-bumped Dylan and Tasha. "I will. I promise I will, but there's just too much to get into at the moment."

"Chad, that guy with the salesman . . . *changed* into a creature. A . . . a . . . *thing* with a shell and claws, like . . . like a man-shaped lobster. You're one of them, aren't you? You and your friends, right?"

"Selma, I can't get into it right now. This isn't the time."

Scotty held his hands over his heart and said to Kat, "Cheesy? Oh, you hurt my heart with your harsh words. Standing on a piece of real estate the owners want to dump should give you some idea of why we're here."

"Jesus," Kat said. For the first time since Chad had met her, she didn't seem confident. In fact, a look of worry played across her face. "They're going to buy the island?"

"Once the deal goes through, they'll make me one of them," Scotty said. His laugh held a touch of mania. "They're very generous with their Elder Blood."

"Yeah, it seems that way," Brick said as he walked out of the other dugout with Emmanuel and Orlando behind him.

"Well, *now* it's a party," Cooper mumbled.

"You've been helping them?" Chad asked.

Brick smirked and shrugged.

The lines had been drawn. The Ink Stains stood with Chad and his friends while everyone else made some kind of deal with the new pack. Chad knew this new pack couldn't have been on the side of angels, considering who had aligned themselves with them. What were they offering? Why were they so interested in coming to The Bends? What did they want?

"So much for being a leader," Cooper said to Brick.

"Watch yourself, weasel," Brick said. "You don't know how big this is."

"Obviously not, so why don't you tell me."

Brick chuckled and looked behind Chad and his friends. "I'd say about eight, maybe nine feet tall."

Everyone turned to the back of the ball field. The new pack entered through the right-field door. Eleven creatures were walking on two legs, led by a massive orca. Brick hadn't exaggerated about the height.

The tunnel to the field was designed to allow easy access for vehicles. This beast made it look like a tube from a child's playground, head almost hitting the ceiling, shoulders going nearly wall to wall. Chad wondered if it wasn't a true whale somehow walking like a human. How could this lycanthrope be so large?

The largest lycanthrope Chad had ever seen was Brick, but that was because he was the largest human he had ever seen. From what he understood, it wasn't possible to add or subtract mass, only rearrange it. This lycanthrope broke that rule. In fact, they all did.

Ten other lycanthropes in half-animal, half-human forms, followed the orca, with Brandon, Scotty's accomplice, being the twelfth member of this pack. All of them were much larger than Chad thought possible. A dolphin and a crab were only a few inches shorter than the orca. Not as muscular, but they certainly had the appearance of being able to singlehandedly reduce this stadium to rubble. The other creatures were just as ferocious looking. An eel, a shark, a crocodile. Even the shrimp, goldfish, and seahorse looked terrifying. The anemone and urchin looked like things from nightmares.

"Welcome," the orca said, his voice rumbling the ground, "to our new home."

"Who . . . Who are you?" Chad asked.

"You can call me King. That's my name and that's who I am to you. But you might not recognize me in this form. Here, let me change."

The orca's body shrank, his muscles diminishing. He turned back into his human form.

Chad knew him. He hadn't met him or ever talked to him, but he knew who this person was.

Justin Butera.

CHAPTER 29

Justin Butera, the individual who started Chad down this crazy path. He had never met Justin, but when his face adorned a "missing person" flyer, Kyle had a breakdown. Justin had confessed to Kyle that the Ink Stains offered to turn him into a lycanthrope to give him the power to change his life. The same offer they made to Chad. The Ink Stains turned Justin into a lycanthrope, not to give him power but to make him tastier. They did the same thing to Chad. But Chad escaped, whereas Justin did not. Though, that was according to . . .

Chad turned to Kat. "I thought you said you ate him?"

Kat smiled, but it wasn't her usual act of wickedness. It was forced and lacked confidence. "I told you that what he did with his abilities was his choice."

"And that he chose poorly. It looks like he chose pretty wisely if he escaped."

She shrugged. "It's called perspective, sweetie."

"Oh, I escaped all right," Justin said with a tone in his voice and swagger in his step, unbefitting his size. Shirtless, he wore a kilt with pockets, the same kind of kilt the other half-human creatures wore. His muscles were tight, but his size was somewhere between Kyle and Chad. "The Ink Stains were a lot cockier then. If they had known what animal I would change into, they wouldn't have lured me to an area by the river."

"This is very true on all levels," Kat said.

"Well, it's a good thing they did," Kyle said. "I'm happy to see you alive."

Justin frowned. "But not happy enough to come along with me to meet the Ink Stains when I asked you to. Yet, it seems you met with them anyway."

"What? No. It's not like that."

"Sure, it's not. You let me go by myself to die. But I didn't die. I got lucky; I'll admit that. I washed up a little north of Mills Hook and was discovered by one of the awesome dudes in this pack. Instead of trying to eat me, they took me in." Justin glared at Kat. She shrugged off his statement and moved closer to Chad.

Becoming more animated as he spoke, Justin started to walk around as if on stage giving a TED Talk. "They taught me about who I was and what I could do. They taught me about their pack and allowed me to join. They taught me about Elder Blood and what it could do. They taught me how to use it."

"How did you convince The Morrigan to give you so much?"

Justin laughed. "Dude, you gotta start thinking past the boundaries of these towns. The Morrigan might be your elder, but they aren't ours. Proteus is and he is very giving. But he's a water being, just like the members of my pack, and the problem with flowing like water is the lack of permanence. I suggested to the pack leader that we come back to The Bends and stay awhile. He disagreed, so I killed him. Now I'm the King."

"Why?" Chad asked. "Why come back here?"

"It's still my home. But If I'm going to be honest . . . revenge. I want revenge. I want to kill the Ink Stains. And I want to kill you guys."

"Us?" Chad didn't like the way his voice squeaked. "Why the hell us?"

"Haven't you been paying attention? I already said that Kyle dicked me over. You guys are now guilty by association."

"Justin, this isn't like you," Kyle said. "What about the life you had? What about your parents?"

Justin sneered. "You don't know me well enough to make that statement! Whatever you think you know about me is long gone. I've changed, Kyle, in ways you can't comprehend. And my parents? They'd try to kill me on sight. Yeah, I know how you guys teamed up with Whacky Wanda, then fucked her over, and to get back at you, she turned our parents into psycho hunters. Heard all about it."

"How did . . . ?" Chad's question faded as Brick and his friends moved closer to Justin and his cronies.

Justin spread his arms wide, a messiah preaching to heretics. "See, I easily killed the original leader of this pack because he was so one-dimensional. He kept the pack flowing with the current because he couldn't conceive a way to establish permanence. I could. Get Chuck to do some leg work for the fake IDs.

Get Scotty Chapman to work a deal for this property. Get Brick to give me all the dirt he could about the other packs in this area. I still needed some size to take out the leader, but I could get it using my brains."

Justin reached into a kilt pocket and pulled out a thin, plastic tube, about a foot in length. It reminded Chad of those yogurt-to-go treats his mom would give him as a child. He ripped the top off and squeezed the tube slightly, causing pink goo to ooze from the top. "Then I developed this. A massive amount of protein and carbs condensed into a special fish paste. The effects are temporary, but . . ." He paused as he sucked down the entire tube worth of paste and shifted into his half-orca, half-human form. Back to eight feet tall and muscled, he finished his thought with a rumbling growl, "It's such a rush!"

The other members of his pack laughed and whooped, some pumping their hybrid fists in the air. Justin spread his hands again, this time as a gesture of victory. "Now I'm the King. Not just the king of my pack, but the king of all lycanthropes. But I'm a benevolent king. We're still going to kill the Ink Stains, but I'm feeling generous with you guys. Chad, you're right about you guys not doing anything, so I'll give you four one chance. Kneel. Kneel to me and declare your fealty, and we'll let you live."

All at once, five voices shouted at Chad. They blurred together, but he caught bits and pieces from each.

Cooper wanted to bow to them and let them do their thing.

Kyle wanted to make amends, or at least make an effort.

Janey agreed with Kyle and saw this as a good opportunity.

Heston was concerned about the Ink Stains and how the group couldn't let Justin kill them.

Selma wanted to get out of here, no matter what it meant.

One thing bugged Chad about this situation. A lot of things bugged Chad about this, but one item topped the list—the conversation Cooper had the other day with Brick. About not wanting to be followers. Chad stepped a few paces away from the ruckus of his friends and addressed Brick. "I think it's interesting that you're willing to kneel to someone. Especially a nerd."

Brick laughed. "See, *nerd*, you assume everyone has the same motivations as you. You also assume that only you guys are smart. I will give you crazy respect for having a hot girlfriend, and I get why you think you're smart and where your motivations are. But when I first saw an eight-foot whale, I suddenly wanted to turn into an eight-foot rhino. I tried. I practiced and kept trying but couldn't break past my size." Something was weird about Brick right now. Loquaciousness wasn't a top ten characteristic for him, yet now he was monologuing, speaking slowly and deliberately. Wait. He was pacing, too, but it was uneven. Emmanuel and Orlando slowly moved, almost imperceptible compared to Brick's grand hand gestures. All three were aiming for one spot, one lycanthrope. The shark? "So, I buddied up with him and waited until I figured out his secret."

All three of them changed into their half-animal, half-human forms. Brick and Emmanuel punched the shark at the same time while Orlando clawed the kilt away. Only needing a few seconds, Orlando reached into the pockets. He pulled out the tube-shaped packets of boost and tossed two each to Brick and Emmanuel. Each of them squeezed the contents into their mouths.

Orlando's greyhound mouth stretched into a horrific smile, pulling well past his back teeth. Muscles grew, stretching his fur-covered skin taut. Laughing, he looked like Anubis with rabies. Emmanuel and Brick roared as they grew taller. Not to the eight-foot height Brick had wished for but impressive enough. Not only did their muscles stretch the limits of biology, but their horns extended and grew thicker.

"This," Brick started, his voice deep enough to shake the ground. "This is better than 'roids!" He punctuated his statement by sucker-punching Justin, the uppercut devastating enough to lift the orca off his feet.

Justin rolled as soon as he hit the ground, quickly getting back to his feet. "Nice betrayal. Good thing I've got one of my own."

Kicks shifted his arms into alligator legs and raked his claws across Dylan's back. Tasha transformed into a gorilla and swiped at Kicks but grabbed only air as he dropped to the ground in full alligator form.

"Kill everyone not loyal to us!" Justin yelled.

"Get behind me," Chad said to Selma.

"What the fuck is happening?" she screamed.

Chad didn't know how to answer that. He had fought with other lycanthropes before, but it was still difficult to register what he saw. Brick exchanged blows with Justin while Emmanuel and Orlando attacked anyone who tried to help Justin; the greyhound bit at the dolphin while the minotaur threw the crab at the eel and shark. The urchin with legs charged at Chad and his friends.

"Urchins are poisonous!" Cooper yelled. Everyone scattered as the creature shifted into a human-sized rolling ball of poison-tipped spikes. Those who could transform into something more did so, and Chad shifted into his hybrid form to push Selma out of the way. He lost his balance and rolled along the ground. By the time he got to his feet, Selma had run up the steps leading to the first-base-line bleachers. Brandon was chasing her in his lobster form.

"No!" Chad yelled as he chased after the lobster. The stairs posed no problem for the crustacean as it scuttled up them with ease, almost catching up to Selma. But the metal of the bleachers caused the lobster to slip sporadically. Chad tore across the infield and up the steps in full rabbit form. Getting between Selma and her pursuer, Chad kicked. His aim perfect, the lobster flew off the bleachers and back onto the field. Selma continued to run up the bleachers.

"Selma!" Chad called out to her. "Wait!"

Not looking back, she sprinted once she hit the concourse. Storefronts of various food offerings lined the concrete as it curved around the field. Chad changed back into his human form and chased after her, slowed by using both hands to cover his privates. "Selma!"

She was too fast, and he lost sight of her as she rounded the corner. "Selma, wait!"

A scream. Selma's scream.

Chad turned back into a rabbit and sprinted around the curve. Brandon, as a human-sized lobster, claws snapping, scuttled toward Selma, her back pinned against the security gate of a taco shop. Fast and silent, Chad raced to the lobster and turned half rabbit at the last second to deliver a kick to its side. Selma ran.

Suffering no visible effects from the kick, the lobster raised its open claws and came at Chad. The gate rattled as Chad backed into it. Small metal bars ran in uneven ladders, strong but flexible. Perfect.

Chad stepped forward and jumped straight up, which made the lobster react. Hoping the mutant crustacean would repeat its actions, Chad jumped again, only a few inches off the ground. The lobster arched its back again and snapped its claws, exposing its underside. Chad took advantage, turning human just long enough to slide underneath the beast. On his back, he shifted into his hybrid form and kicked, driving the full power of his rabbit legs into the lobster's chest. As Chad had hoped, there was enough force behind the lobster crashing into the gate to tear a part of it from the ceiling. The lobster thrashing about was enough to rip the remaining part of the gate from the ceiling and turn it into a net.

The lobster rolled and twisted, its shelled legs caught within the gaps of the gate's fencing. Brandon went back to human form, but Chad was ready. As a rabbit, he leaped into the air, and by the time he came down, he was in his hybrid form, the knuckles of his fist connecting with Brandon's cheek, a hit hard enough to render him unconscious. Chad hoped he didn't give him severe injuries, but he had no time for those thoughts. He needed to find Selma and make sure she was unharmed. As a rabbit, he got in front of her and turned human. With one hand over his privates, he held out his other and said, "Selma, stop. Wait. It's me, Chad. I can explain."

"No!" Selma yelled, tears flowing from her bloodshot eyes. "Stay away! Stay away from me!" She ran from him, down the stairs to the field.

Chad shifted back into his hybrid form. It probably freaked her out more, but he couldn't run while covering his crotch. As he ran, he caught a glimpse of the field below, different animals fighting each other. One split away and ran toward the bleachers. In a flash, the half-human, half-goldfish leaped from the field onto the stands, landing between Selma and Chad.

The mutant goldfish grabbed Selma's arm and backhanded Chad, sending him sprawling. Pain blasted through his shoulder when he slammed into the metal bleachers. Stars burst all around his world, making the goldfish hard to see. His vision came into focus as the goldfish leaned down and said, "Got your girl. She's mine now. Don't worry, I'll treat her real ni— hhuurrk!"

The half-goldfish released Selma and brought both hands to the knife sticking out of his neck. He yanked it free and tried to run away, but another knife zipped through the air and lodged itself in the goldfish's back. Chad wanted to thank his rescuer but suddenly felt more afraid than facing a mutant goldfish creature.

Natalia.

CHAPTER 30

Kyle turned into a pheasant, wrapped his wings around Janey, and dove out of the way as the urchin rolled by. He got to his feet and gawked at the chaos ensuing around him. A lobster chased after Selma as she ran to the bleachers, and Chad chased after the lobster. As his oxen self, Heston avoided the urchin but ran toward the Ink Stains. Dylan squirmed in pain on the ground while a gorilla and Kat, in hybrid form, fought with an alligator. Cooper, in ferret form, dodged the urchin attack but, in doing so, now needed to weave among wolverine, shrimp, and eel hybrids as they slashed their claws at him.

"I have to get you out of here," Kyle said to Janey as he pushed her away from the madness.

"No!" she shouted. "Don't worry about me. There's a clear path to the dugout. I'll hide there. You need to help Cooper."

"But—"

"No 'buts,' Kyle! Your friend needs help, and the man I love is just the superhero to help him. Now, go!" Janey kissed his feathered cheek, just above the beak. She pointed to Cooper while running toward the dugout by third base. "Go!"

Spurred on by inspiring words from the woman he loved, Kyle ran toward center field, where the bulk of the fighting took place. In the middle of it, Brick and Justin exchanged blows. Kyle had hung out with Justin enough to know he had never been in a fight. He had been beaten up plenty of times, but he hadn't been able to defend himself. His lack of experience showed when Brick stopped swinging and charged. Wrapping his arms around Justin's chest, Brick twisted and slammed the whale hybrid to the ground as if they were wrestling in high school gym class. After an elbow to the whale's head, Brick pushed himself back to his feet. He then delivered punch after punch to Justin's head until Justin's cronies intervened.

Kyle always thought dolphins were cool, sleek, and intelligent creatures, at peace with the ocean environment. He no longer thought that as one shaped like a bodybuilder launched itself at Brick. Unlike Justin, the dolphin had the fighting skills to go toe-to-toe with the human-rhino. Emmanuel and Orlando tried to help, but every time they got close enough to be effective, the crab and the shark intervened. Kyle didn't care about the jocks; he just wanted to make sure he knew where Justin's cronies were. Two of them teamed up with Sanders to chase after Cooper.

Concerned about his personal nemesis, Kyle looked around for Pixel Ronin, but he was nowhere to be found, in human or bird form. This was it. Time to help his friend. Wings tight to his body, he rushed toward the confusion. The shrimp snapped its claws while the wolverine snapped its teeth. The eel was an expert at shifting, effortlessly slipping between full eel to wriggle ahead and a hybrid to corral Cooper and block his path. That was how Kyle could help!

Kyle saw an opening where Cooper could run and aimed for that. As he suspected, Cooper ran toward the potential escape route, but the eel squirmed its way there first. Kyle timed it perfectly. Before the eel could switch to its hybrid state, Kyle pecked at its tail.

The eel whipped around, shifting into its half-human form and snapping its needle-like teeth. Kyle jumped back, narrowly escaping the eel's bite. As Cooper flashed by, he swiped a claw across the eel's back. Kyle surprised himself by taking advantage of the distraction and attacking. Fluttering his wings, Kyle got off the ground enough to lead with his talons. A few good scratches here and there before the eel got its bearings. In full eel form, it wriggled out of Kyle's reach, then turned around to strike. Still maniacally flapping his wings, Kyle pressed forward. The eel got a mouthful of feathers, and Kyle sank his beak into the eel's neck, deep enough to taste blood. Deep enough to taste the familiar.

Not letting go, he flapped like crazy again and brought his talons to bear, digging into the fishy skin. Kyle was winning! Until he wasn't.

Much like Justin, Kyle had limited experience in physical altercations. Months ago, he and his friends defended themselves against the Ink Stains and the jocks. Since becoming lycanthropes, Tyler had been training them. But his real-world exposure to fighting had been limited. Even though it was wounded, the eel turned the tide. A punch. A bite. A slap with its tail. More punches. Woozy, Kyle dropped to the ground, holding one wing in front of his face to defend himself. The eel shifted into a hybrid form and sauntered on human-shaped legs toward Kyle. Its triangular head made its slimy smile more wicked.

The crack of wood against bone made Kyle's heart skip. Then it swelled when Janey screamed, "Get your slimy scales off *my man*!" She swung the bat again and landed a perfect hit across the eel-creature's jaw, dropping it to the ground. With a wide smile, she waved to Kyle and said, "Hi, sweetie! I found a bat!"

Still in pheasant form, Kyle laughed. It was a weird, scratchy sound, but it made Janey smile even wider. Their shared joy was short-lived when a flurry of golden feathers dropped from the sky and hit Janey. She lost her bat as she fell next to Kyle. Eyes wide, she looked at what knocked her down.

Pixel Ronin.

He had been practicing his transformations. Still more eagle than human, he stood before Kyle and Janey, his wings as arms spread wide. "Lost your bat, bitch!"

Kyle's heart pounded faster. He felt hotter, a heat pluming from within him. Anger. He had felt anger so many times in his life, but it always ended with him turning it back on himself, raging at who he saw in the mirror because he was powerless to stop whatever external force made him angry. No more. He had the power now to stop whatever made him angry. He had the power to stop Pixel Ronin.

A whistle and a whoosh of air. Something struck Ronin's wing, causing a burst of golden feathers. Another whistle, this one ending with a crossbow bolt tearing through Ronin's leg.

Turning to see where the bolt had been shot from, Kyle saw his worst nightmare—his mother with a crossbow, standing on the right-field concourse.

Heston turned into his oxen minotaur form and did a summersault to avoid the urchin. Momentum had him running toward the Ink Stains. When he saw Kicks whip his alligator tail across Tasha's head, Heston ran faster. Kat was capable of handling herself under most circumstances, but Heston wasn't sure how she'd do against an alligator, especially when it was going to be joined by the crocodile doing a sinusoidal belly crawl toward the Ink Stains.

Kat hissed and spat as she swatted her claws at the alligator. Kicks hissed as well, moving around with his mouth wide open, trying to position himself to clamp down on Kat. No luck as she was too agile. Heston now knew what to do. He changed into a full ox and picked up speed. Head down, he jammed his horns into the side of the approaching crocodile. With a bovine grunt, he lifted his head and flipped the reptile, two thin streams of crimson arching through the air. Heston's horns were small, nowhere near the skewers Emmanuel sprouted in his bull form, but they were long enough to draw blood.

Tasha regained her wits and quickly joined Kat in fighting with Kicks. Heston trotted over to Dylan. "Are you okay?"

Still in bear form, Dylan snarled. "I never trusted that fucker. He got me good, but I'll live."

"Okay. There's a crocodile around us. I hit him good, but—"

A flash of gray. Heston had no time to react to the hit. As he flew through the air, he shifted into his minotaur form, which allowed him to roll when he hit the ground. A quick headshake knocked his blurry world back into focus, and he saw what had hit him.

Chuck.

He had learned how to control his shape, striding toward Heston on two legs, stubby fingers curled into meaty fists. "Time we end this once and for all."

"Fine by me!" Heston's voice surprised him, deeper with an anger he had suppressed his entire life. What surprised him even more was his reaction. His arms and legs moved as if being controlled by someone other than himself, someone allowed to express himself. To be himself. To stand up for himself. To tackle his brother and drive him to the ground.

Chuck rolled and pushed and punched, muscling his way out of Heston's grip. Jumping to his feet, Heston smiled. It was awkward with the thick lips of an ox's mouth, but it felt so good to hit his half-brother. He wanted to do it again!

In full hippo this time, Chuck charged. Remaining in his hybrid form, Heston dodged with ease and even delivered a nice kick. It wasn't devastating, but he was satisfied when Chuck's head jerked. More!

Heston jumped on Chuck from behind, wrapping his left arm around the hippo's neck. Chuck shifted into his hybrid form, but Heston refused to let go. Because he had dreamed about a moment like this for years, Heston shifted his right hand into a hoof and dug it into the top of Chuck's skull, a noogie from Hell.

"Get off!" Chuck shouted as he pushed Heston away. It wasn't enough to stop Heston, to stop his anger. Planting his feet, Heston delivered an uppercut that lifted Chuck off the ground. That felt so good!

Chuck got back to his feet and swung, but Heston saw the punch coming a mile away and dodged it with ease, then delivered one of his own to Chuck's hippo snout. Another swing and a miss from Chuck, followed by a well-timed hit from Heston. Chuck went for a body shot this time and connected, but there was little force behind it. Heston absorbed it and released a flurry of head-shots, causing Chuck to stumble backward. Yes! Time to end this. He would have if not for the crocodile.

Coming from nowhere, the crocodile in human form tackled Heston. The fall was awkward, but he got his knees to his chest, then kicked the crocodile away. The three lycanthropes stood at the same time. Wiping a trickle of blood from the corner of his mouth, the crocodile said to Chuck, "Figured you could use a hand."

"Yeah," was all Chuck had to say. Heston knew his half-brother well enough to know he was confused. In Chuck's world, he was the toughest there was, which meant there could be no one tougher. He never did well when facts suddenly challenged his beliefs, especially when he believed his younger brother would *never* fight back, let alone win. Heston could tell Chuck didn't want the help but knew he needed it. Heston could do this. Feeling strong enough to live in this world, Heston could take on these two. Hell, he could take on all of the lycanthropes on the field! But none of them had guns, like some other people in this stadium.

A crack of thunder and chunks of dirt and grass exploded from the ground close to Heston. With both hands on his smoking rifle, Bud McCurdy ran toward the trio fighting with each other. The crocodile man looked at Chuck, said, "You handle the ox; I'll handle the meat," and ran toward Bud.

"No!" Heston shouted and chased after the crocodile.

Bud planted his feet and shot again but missed, the crocodile too fast. With one swipe of his reptilian claw, he knocked the gun away. Bud fell backward to the ground, helpless. The crocodile laughed and snapped his jaws menacingly.

"No!" Heston screamed again as he launched himself at the crocodile. He made it in time to save his father.

Much like when the crocodile tackled him, they slammed to the ground. This time, Heston took advantage of the situation. He got to his feet just long enough to drop his knee on the crocodile's head. He stood again and stomped his hoof repeatedly on the creature's head. Heston let up to see if the reptile was still alive. The crocodile stirred and tried to stand.

Big mistake, especially as Chuck charged closer.

Heston grabbed the crocodile man by his tail, yanked him from the ground, and started to spin. Two rotations. Three. On the fourth rotation, he released. The reptile smashed square into Chuck's chest. Heston wasted no time jumping on his half-brother, releasing a flurry of punches to his face. Thick keratin of hoof walls covered his fingers, his punches tearing away strips of skin. Blood streaked through the air, and Heston punched faster, harder. He stopped and looked up when a chunk of grass exploded next to him, followed by the thunder crack of a gun.

Bud trained his gun on Heston. "I recognize that you saved me from that monster on the ground over there. I don't know why you did, but I recognize the gesture. Me not shooting you now is returning the favor. We're even. Get off my son and back away, or we won't be even no more."

No. No, no, no, no! Heston wondered how he could finally win yet somehow still lose. Maybe if he turned back into his human self, his father would understand. Understand what? It wouldn't make Bud love him any more. If anything, Bud would find an excuse to shoot him and get him out of his life. Hell, Chuck might just blurt out who the ox minotaur really was and encourage Bud to shoot anyway. But seeing no other good option, Heston did as instructed, moving slowly.

Gun butt tucked under his right arm, Bud used his left to rouse Chuck. "C'mon, boy. Let's get you outta here. Let's get you home and cleaned up."

The half-hippo rolled over and coughed, blood spraying the grass. No matter what happened next, Heston was proud of himself for that. Chuck turned back to full human, most of his face slicked in crimson. Chuck put an arm around Bud's shoulders as Bud used his free hand to help his favorite son to his feet.

"Thought . . . you . . . hated . . ." Chuck gurgled.

"I gave it some time. I hate who did this to you, and I hate what you've become. But there's gotta be a cure, right? I'll help you find a cure. There's gotta be a cure."

Heston didn't move as they limped their way to the door in the right-field wall. Once they went through, he went to help the Ink Stains.

Cooper turned into his ferret form and skittered away from the urchin. Unfortunately, away from the urchin meant toward the thick of the fighting. The jocks tangled with Justin, the dolphin, the crab, and the shark. Cooper ran right at the eel and shrimp. The eel bit, the shrimp snapped its claws, and both missed. He turned to retreat but almost ran into Sanders.

Cooper saw only bristling fur, sharp teeth, and razor-like claws. Sanders cursed as he missed his target. Cooper had been a lycanthrope a lot longer than Sanders, much more coordinated as a ferret than Sanders was as a wolverine. But dodging Sanders's attack sent him right back to the eel and shrimp. Cooper could tell they had been lycanthropes for a long time. Their reflexes were fast and intuition accurate. They switched from full animal to hybrid and back with ease, capitalizing on their respective strengths. They worked together and used the occasional assistance from the nearby crab and shark to corral Cooper, pushing him toward Sanders. He felt confident that he could take Sanders one-on-one, but any time he spent fighting Sanders would be time the other nasties would use to converge. Escape was his only option. But how? Where?

Kyle!

Kyle ran directly toward the action. That went against his friend's nature, but Cooper needed all the help he could get. It was time he did some corralling of his own.

There was a gap between the eel and the shrimp, one that would surely close up. He aimed for it anyway but closer to the eel to make him react, to move into Kyle's path. Perfect! Kyle got the eel's tail, and Cooper swiped his claws across its back.

The maneuver helped greatly. Now able to get some breathing room, he could— *Fuck*!

Others from Justin's cadre joined the fray. Cooper hurt his ankles from changing directions while sprinting, narrowly missing the urchin as it rolled by again. Of course, he now had to contend with the anemone and the seahorse.

Extra careful to avoid the poisonous tendrils of the anemone and the spines of the urchin, Cooper overcompensated when they got too close. A punch from the humanoid seahorse. A hit from the shrimp's shelled claw. He still dodged Sanders's attacks, but they were getting closer.

It hurt to breathe, his lungs burning. His speed and endurance waned. Help. He needed help. Too focused on what was happening around him, he lost track of his friends. Hope fading, salvation came from an unlikely source.

In the form of crossbow bolts.

One sunk deeply into the anemone, another thumped impotently into the ground between the seahorse and the urchin. The only effect they had was garnering everyone's attention.

Rick Barelli and Donovan Butera stood along the first-base line and re-loaded. They each fired again. Mr. Butera hit the urchin, but the bolt shattered. Rick missed again.

Cooper welcomed the respite but started to worry when the seahorse, urchin, and anemone turned their attention to the lycanthrope-hunting parents. Rick kept missing, even as his targets got closer. *How in the name of all things holy and unholy was he a star quarterback?* No matter. Even if he hit his targets like Donovan, odds were it would be ineffectual. Cooper had to do something, but what? He was in no position to save himself, so how could he save someone else? Then a miracle fell from the sky.

Literally.

Clad in black tactical gear and eyewear, a woman dropped from seemingly out of nowhere. Her long, brown hair was pulled back into a ponytail, and there was something about her that rang familiar to Cooper. Who was she and why did he think he knew her? She then turned into a hero.

With a Glock in each hand, she blasted the three lycanthropes closing in on Rick and Donovan. Spines flew off the urchin while scales and blood sprayed from the seahorse. The urchin screamed and started to roll away but didn't get far. Shards of its exoskeleton twirled through the air along with sprays of murky liquid. The slower the urchin moved, the more the liquid looked like blood. Then it stopped.

The seahorse met a more dramatic end—its scaly, trumpet-like head was removed from its neck, one bullet at a time. The body collapsed, nothing but glistening strips of meat remained of its neck. Whoever this woman was, her aim was impeccable. But the best aim in the world couldn't affect the anemone, the bullets passing through the creature.

Waving its tentacles and cracking them like toxin-tipped whips, it rushed toward the woman. Cooper held his breath, wondering what she'd do. What she did made him drop his jaw.

She holstered the guns and reached behind her back to pull out a sword. A sword! Using two hands to wield it, she swung and slashed as if it were an extension of her body, lopping off tentacles, two and three at a time. After it lost a dozen tentacles, it tried to flee, but she wouldn't let it. As if pruning a gelatinous tree, she continued chopping off parts of the anemone until it was nothing more than an immobile pile of ooze.

"She's here!" Rick shouted. "She's here! Samantha! Bud! Anna! She came! I knew she would. Bud? Bud, where are you?"

"Wow!" Donovan said. "Who is she?"

"That's Trish Duper."

What.

The.

Literal.

Holy.

Fuck?

Cooper's eyes went so wide they hurt. He whispered, "Mom?"

CHAPTER 31

Chad lay awkwardly on the metal bleachers, looking up at his savior and potential death. Natalia trained a loaded crossbow at his head. Never once had he considered himself an expert on human expression, but he knew without a doubt that behind Natalia's glare was pure hatred. There was nothing she wanted to do more than kill him right now. He read it on her face, felt the desire radiating from her like a nuclear power plant ready to meltdown. Instead, she moved her aim and fired. The bolt blew right through the goldfish's skull.

She lowered her crossbow and reloaded it but continued staring at Chad with murder in her eyes. He wondered if she would choose to end his life with the crossbow or her bare hands. The question was answered when she raised it again and squeezed the trigger. However, the bolt wasn't meant for him. It whizzed past his cheek and blasted through the head of the human-sized lobster sneaking up behind him.

Natalia glanced at Selma and said, "Get her out of here." She then ran along the bleachers and jumped over the edge onto the field. From this angle, Chad couldn't see where she was going, but he knew it was close to where her mother and the Ink Stains were.

"Selma, please listen. It's me, Chad. I'd change back to human, but . . ." He didn't want to tell her that if Natalia was here, his parents and his friends' parents were probably here too. "It's complicated. You need to trust me."

Tears streamed over Selma's cheeks as she got to her feet. Eyes wide, she looked ready to sprint away again. "What the fuck is going on, Chad? What the fuck is happening?"

"I'll go over the details later, but the short version: Lycanthropes are real. My friends and I can change into animals. There are others, like the Ink Stains and a few jocks, that we knew about, but the others, the sea creatures, we didn't know about. They lured us here to ambush us. There are also people hunting us, but they're hunting us because they're afraid and don't know much about us, so they act blindly. But shit's getting real, and we have to leave."

Selma looked at the fighting on the field. "What about the others? Your friends. We can't just leave them."

Chad didn't know what to do, where to begin. The confusion on the ball field was overwhelming. Chuck was in human form and bloodied, Bud helping him escape through a door along the outfield wall. Heston helped the Ink Stains fight an alligator and a crocodile. Cooper tangled with Sanders and other creatures while the jocks fought with Justin and a few others from his crew. Dad! Chad watched his father and Justin's father run onto the field, almost overtaken by a trio of lycanthropes. Who was that woman? She came out of nowhere and killed the three lycanthropes with ease. Was . . . was that Cooper's mom? Chad found an opportunity. There was a clear path to Kyle and Janey. They fought with Ronin. "You're right. Follow me."

Chad reached for Selma's hand, but she yanked it away. "Just go. I'm right behind you."

No time to feel rejected, he reminded himself as he ran down the steps toward the field. He still glanced over his shoulder every few steps to make sure Selma was behind him and unharmed as he went. If they could get to Kyle and Janey, he could help Kyle with Ronin, and they could protect the women and act as a rally point. Alliances were ambiguous at the moment, and he didn't care. As soon as Heston and Cooper joined them, they could run away.

Cooper struggled to get away from his battle, Sanders working hard to keep him close to the jocks and some of the water creatures from Mills Hook. Crossbow bolts zipped into the scene. One passed through Brick's leg. Mom! A touch of pride tickled Chad's heart, seeing his mom nail one of his nemeses through the leg. However, fighting against Justin's imperialistic crew of water dwellers, Chad was no longer sure which side was which or even how many sides there were. The injury to Brick's leg allowed the dolphin to take advantage of the fight, landing devastating punches to the rhino's jaw. Sprays of blood accompanied the last few. Then a miracle occurred—Chad's dad fired his crossbow and hit his target.

The dolphin writhed as he reached for the bolt sticking out of his shoulder. Brick was back in the fight. His advantage didn't last long—Justin delivered a massive blow, knocking the rhino to the ground. This was it. Brick was going to die. Or so Chad thought. A crossbow bolt through Justin's arm changed everything.

Roaring, Justin wheeled around and stood within mere feet of his father, struggling to reload his crossbow. Unable to reload it in time, Mr. Butera threw it aside and pounded his chest. Tears running down his face, he screamed, "Go ahead! Go ahead, you monster! Kill me! Kill me like you killed my son!"

Justin curled and uncurled his fingers, reached for his father, then drew his hands back. He twitched and snarled as if he couldn't control his body, his animal self and human side fighting for control. Love versus blame. Chad could sympathize; his father was the major reason he sucked at life, but he still loved him.

"If you don't kill me, I will kill you, you freak!" Mr. Butera yelled, his voice cracking from grief.

With a pained growl of his own, Justin backhanded his father, hard enough to send him flying into Chad's father. Chad winced as his dad cried out in pain from his leg bending the wrong way.

Justin took a step toward his father, reaching for him. Despite having the head of an orca, Chad could see the guilt playing across Justin's face. But Justin stopped. He shook his fists and stomped his feet. Finally, he called out, "We're done! Let's go!"

Justin, the crab, shark, and dolphin stopped fighting and limped to each other, hands pressed on bloody wounds. Chad had seen Cooper's mom kill three and witnessed Natalia kill one right in front of him. The alligator and the crocodile lay in crimson-painted grass, their organs on the outside of their bodies courtesy of the Ink Stains. The eel lay unmoving, a few crossbow bolts in his head. The dead water creatures from Mills Hook slowly turned back into their human forms, even the ones that Cooper's mom dismembered or decapitated.

As Justin and his crew retreated, Scotty Chapman ran from the third-base dugout. "What about me? You'll still change me, right? The deal's still good, right?"

Justin paused long enough to grab Scotty and throw him down the third-base line, his unconscious body rolling to a stop on home plate. "Fuck no! The deal's off! We're done here."

"No!" Pixel Ronin shrieked. Wings spread wide, he flapped once, twice, three times. "It can't end like this! I won't let it!"

Ronin dove at Janey, pulling up at the last second to swipe his talons at her. A scream. An arc of blood.

"Nooooo!" Kyle yelled, his voice transforming into a shrieking beast as he screamed. His pheasant body transformed as well.

This change had happened once before, and Chad thought it was the most terrifying thing he had ever seen. Now, he was more frightened.

The human-sized pheasant grew taller as its wings shifted farther back to make room for the arms sprouting from the humanoid chest, talon-tipped claws for fingers. Its feet remained talons as well, but its legs thickened, muscles bulging under the dark blue feathers. The round eyes no longer looked panicked and fearful, now angry and insane. A barbed tongue pierced the air as it tilted its head back to release a screech so intense that the closest battle participants covered their ears. With one push of his legs and flap of his wings, Kyle launched himself into the air.

Ronin didn't stand a chance. He released an eagle cry as he furiously flapped to escape. No such luck. The mutated bird-creature Kyle had become wasted no time in capturing its prey. So much faster than Ronin, Kyle sped past, getting ahead of him to attack head-on. Kyle's hand-claws grabbed Ronin's wings while his other talons dug into his belly. Kyle released one more screech, then shoved his beak into the eagle's chest and pulled in four different directions. An explosion of blood and feathers sent organs raining on the field below. Face covered in blood, Kyle tilted his head back and gulped a few times to ingest a length of intestine. He still held Ronin's wings.

"Oh my God!" Selma cried.

"No," Janey said. "He's *my* god!"

Although Chad was happy Janey was alive—pressing her right palm against the cuts along her left forearm—he was more than a little disturbed by the glee radiating from her smile.

"Retreat!" came from the concourse. Chad's mom meant the order for the hunters, but everyone reacted to it. She and Mrs. Sedgeweck disappeared, while Cooper's mom helped Chad's dad and Mr. Butera to the exit past the first-base dugout. Brick, Orlando, Emmanuel, and Sanders hurried to the right-field exit. Justin and his pack fled up the third-base bleachers and over the stadium walls.

Kyle didn't pursue any of them.

He shrieked again as he tossed the eagle's wings aside, the noise echoing within the stadium. Like a lightning strike, he dropped from the sky and landed in front of Chad, Selma, and Janey.

"Hi, sweetie," Janey said, still wearing a maniacal smile that creeped out Chad, and approached Kyle. Chad didn't know how it was possible, but Kyle stood over seven feet tall. Did he have one of those tubes of mystery goo? He also feared for Janey's safety as Kyle moved closer to her. Globs of feather-covered meat slid from his beak and face as he lowered his head toward her injury. Chad prayed that his friend wouldn't kill her.

Kyle opened his mouth.

A chirping trill.

Janey nodded and shrugged. "Yeah, I'm okay. I have to learn to be faster."

Kyle extended his talons, reaching for her arm but stopped and brought them to his face. The claws receded; the gnarled skin softened. Feathers turned to hair while the creature diminished in size. Kyle was back to being human.

Woozy, he wobbled and struggled with his words. "You need to see a doctor. And I have a funny taste in my mouth."

Kyle dropped to the grass and passed out.

"He's right," Selma said as she put an arm around Janey's shoulders. "We need to get you to a doctor."

Janey protested. "But Kyle—"

"Is okay. He just passed out. His friends can take care of him."

Everyone remaining either knew his secret now or was dead, so Chad changed back into his human form, hands over his privates. "I can come with you."

"No!" Selma snapped. She offered nothing else as she guided Janey away, first to the torn clothes Brandon had been wearing to retrieve his car keys, then out the nearest exit.

"Is he okay?" Cooper asked as he ran over to Kyle, who looked peaceful, as if he were taking a nap—if not for the blood drying on his face and torso.

"I . . . ummm . . . I think so." Chad didn't know, too worried about Selma and how negatively she had been reacting to all of this. He wondered if he should have told her sooner.

"Yeah," Cooper said, kneeling next to Kyle. "Yeah, he's breathing normally. I don't think we can continue to use subterfuge to keep him in the dark about this drastic transformation like last time."

"You're probably right. Let's get Heston and get out of here."

In his half-ferret form, Cooper scooped Kyle up in his arms. "He's with the Ink Stains."

"Really?" Chad turned to where he last saw them. Something was wrong. Kat was kneeling next to someone and looked upset. No! It was Natalia.

Chad ran to the small group, two dead bodies on the ground, the human form of Kicks and the crocodile. Dylan and Tasha were bleeding, but they both watched Kat with concern on their faces. Heston paced in small circles, keeping an eye on Kat and Natalia. Chad knelt next to Natalia, who was half lying on Kat's lap. Natalia's breathing was shallow, hitched, and she held her waist, blood flowing over both arms. "What . . . ? What happened?"

"That fucker Kicks betrayed us," Kat said. A few tears rolled away from her bloodshot eyes, and she sniffled. "Natalia got involved and took a claw across the gut."

Natalia coughed; a glob of blood splashed her chin.

Chad couldn't believe what he was seeing. A woman so capable, so competent. Impossible. That was the only word he could think of. Getting a critical injury was impossible. Dying was impossible. She gave death, not received it. But she was still alive. That meant . . . "What if we turn her into a lycanthrope?"

Natalia jerked as if trying to sit up. She coughed up more blood and went limp. Still finding a way to look angry, she said, "No."

"It would work," Kat said. "The initial transformation would heal all her wounds. But we didn't bring any Elder Blood with us."

Hope bloomed warm within Chad. "Don't worry. We did."

"We did?" Heston and Cooper asked at the same time as Chad ran to his rucksack.

His heart almost exploded with joy when he saw the vial was undamaged. He rushed back and skidded to a stop on his knees. "Natalia. I know what you think of lycanthropes, but you're wrong. You'll still be you. I promise."

Even when dying, Natalia had a look of composure. No fear. No sign of weakness. If not for the blood flowing from the deep gashes, he would have never known she was in pain. A quick nod. "Okay."

Chad removed the stopper and poured the liquid, careful to get every drop in her mouth.

Blood flowing from a wound, Kat moved her hand toward her daughter's mouth. Natalia shook her head. "No . . . Chad . . ."

A strange feeling ran along Chad's spine, touching everywhere from behind his eyes to his chest. He assumed it was honor, an emotion he had never felt before. The taste of blood asserted itself, but kissing her now was inappropriate. He, too, had cuts on his hand and held it over her mouth. Drip. Drip. Drip. Chad wondered how long he should keep his hand over her mouth, how much blood was needed for the process to work. Not much, apparently.

Natalia lurched forward off her mother's lap. Still clutching her waist, she convulsed. Kat and Chad stood and backed away. Natalia's body twisted, muscles moving to accommodate her shifting bones. Hands and feet turned into paws as her mouth elongated into a snout. Brown fur tinted red flowed all over her new body. Natalia had turned into a fox.

No one moved, all eyes on the human-sized fox as it panted and shook each paw, one at a time. Its jaw opened and closed, muzzle rippling. It snarled as if Natalia were trying to speak. Chad knew from experience that speaking as an animal was a learned skill. After a quick head shake, Natalia in vulpine form ran toward the nearest exit.

"We gotta go," Dylan grumbled. He and Tasha started to limp away. Kat followed but turned to Chad and said, "Thank you."

A hero. He felt like a hero. He didn't stop the fighting, nor did he come up with a peaceful solution for what had happened here. But he saved Selma's life and Natalia's life. That was enough. However, the feeling was short-lived, dispelled by the looks of utter disappointment from Heston and Cooper.

"Come on," Heston said. "Let's go."

The situation was bad, but Chad felt hopeful. After a good night's sleep, he'd explain everything to Selma and apologize to his friends. After all, communication was everything.

CHAPTER 32

The mall parking lot outside the entrance to the food court. This was where Selma had asked to meet him.

After normal business hours, the lot was empty, and it was cold. Chad shivered, but his thick jacket protected him against the chilly air. The cold came from within, from the anxiety of the impending conversation. He'd have to tell her everything, then apologize. This conversation was going to suck.

A car pulled into the empty parking lot. Selma's. She pulled into her usual spot, next to the streetlight. Hands in his pockets, Chad sulked over. By the time he got close enough, she was out and leaning against the driver's side. With the exhaustion of recollecting a shared hardship, Chad said, "Hey. Yesterday, huh?"

"What the fuck, Chad? What the literal fuck?"

Her breath came from her mouth in thick white plumes, an angry dragon getting ready to burn a village. Chad felt he'd need some aloe after this. "So, yeah, I'm a lycanthrope. It all started—"

"You say those words like I'm okay with this concept, like we're discussing your eye color or height."

"You're . . . not . . . okay with this?"

"You can *literally* change into an animal!"

"I thought you'd think that was cool, maybe even badass."

Selma jerked back as if hornets came from his mouth instead of words. Blinking rapidly and waving her hands in front of her, she snapped, "Why the fuck of fucks would I possibly think that?"

"Your art. Everything I've seen you do, create, are characters from movies and aliens and zombies and all of that crazy stuff. You're into all of that and so am I."

"Jesus Christ, Chad, you can't be fucking serious. That's escapism. That's playing with creativity. Just because I draw zombies and aliens doesn't mean I truly want zombies and aliens. What sort of psycho would want that? Who the fuck would be enthused to be a part of a world like that?" Chad's mind immediately went to his conversation with Kyle regarding Janey loving him even more after learning the truth and her reaction when Kyle slipped into mutant hyper-murder mode. It was a mistake to assume Selma would have a similar reaction to learning he was a lycanthrope, but he had no other point of reference.

Tears slicked Selma's eyes as she continued, "The very first thing I did when you showed me a world like that existed was go home and cry my friggin' eyes out. The second thing I did was call my therapist and set up an emergency meeting."

"You have a therapist?" Chad wanted to rip his tongue out, pissed that his mouth was not on his side.

Selma sighed and wiped away tears. "Yes, Chad, I have a therapist. Just another thing you don't know about me."

"That's not fair. We just started dating. It would be rude to ask if you're seeing a therapist."

"That doesn't change that you'd probably never have known about it anyway."

"I . . . I don't even know what that means."

"It means that even though you're nice and fairly smart and never treated me like an object or prize, you still didn't view me as a person. I know everyone has a form of egocentricity where they can't imagine walking in someone else's shoes, and I know each human is the protagonist of their own story, but you've taken it to the next level, Chad. You're not looking for a girlfriend to be your partner, to share life experiences with, to explore the world around us, to learn with. You're looking for a girlfriend as a supporting character. You're looking for a manic pixie dream girl, Chad, someone to be that perfect blend of checklist cool qualities that validates who you are and encourages you to figure out who you could be without ever once asking you to reciprocate."

"That's not true. You are an amazing human being I care about. I want to spend time with you and learn about you. We just started something, something good, and I'd really like to continue with it."

"What's my dream?"

It was such an abrupt change in topic that Chad felt he was being set up for failure. "Your dream?"

"Yes. I know I've never stated it explicitly, but it should be pretty easy to piece together from our hours of conversation."

Chad knew this one. This was an easy one. "To be an artist."

"Not entirely true and very reductive, especially since I already consider myself an artist. You said it quickly, a reflex stemming from assumption. What's my biggest fear?"

She had him there. He didn't know, especially if he was incorrect about something he thought he knew. His heart was racing too fast, taking his mind with it. Too panicked to review conversations, to recall anything specific, or even to piece together clues, he went with the one most people had. "Ending up alone."

Selma crossed her arms over her chest and looked away, searching for the appropriate response to an answer that was clearly incorrect. Shaking her head, she turned back to Chad, and the pain of her bloodshot eyes made his sting. "That's *your* fear."

Frowning, he almost told her that she was wrong, but . . . was she? He had always thought his number two and three fears were clowns and spiders, number one being clown-spiders. But those were the fears of a child, fears of someone who needed to close the closet door before bedtime or use a flashlight to check under the bed. He was an adult. Even if he didn't recognize himself as one, other people did. Not only that, but she also recognized his true fear, why he made so many bad choices whenever a woman was involved. He blindly grasped at roses and never exercised caution for the thorns that sliced him deeply, never learning from any previous cuts. The women in his life clearly had no desire for his attention, but that never stopped him from trying to appeal to them: hoping a shared history would appeal to Brittany, hoping that feeling like an outsider would appeal to Natalia, hoping a sense of being a unique creature would appeal to Kat.

"You might be right, but that means that I'm living my fear now."

"Then why didn't you tell me about you being a . . . a . . . Jesus Christ . . . a lycanthrope?"

"I was trying to protect you from my enemies."

Selma laughed the sad, low chuckle from hearing an offensive joke. "That's the most fucking flawed explanation, Chad. How the hell is keeping me in the dark about something so huge meant to protect me? In fact, you put me in more danger by not telling me. When I got kidnapped, I had no idea who it was or why they were doing it. You don't understand what it's like to be female. I wasn't thinking, 'Oh, I'm going to be used as a prop to motivate the guy I'm dating into action.' I was thinking, 'I'm getting drugged and raped and sold to a sick fuck halfway across the world, and I'll never see my family again, and then I'm gonna get murdered.' Had you told me what you are, who you were dealing with, I could have been prepared. I might even have defended myself, or at the very least, I wouldn't have been frozen with fear, and I could have tried to run."

Tears flowed, one for every word she spoke. Chad hadn't thought of any of that. The villains he had were known; his tortures came in the form of wedgies and swirlies and bruises and broken ego. Her villains were unknown, her tortures undiscovered.

Wiping his cheeks with the back of his hand, he said, "You're right. I'm sorry. I'm really sorry I didn't think of that."

"No."

"No?"

"I can't accept that. I can't forgive you."

This hurt the worst of all the things she'd said, a dagger sliding into his heart. "I know I screwed up. I know that. But I'm really sorry I hurt you. I think we have something special, something worth working for, something worth moving past this."

"The offender *always* wants to move past what they did, Chad. Always. And this wasn't a screw-up. You didn't get drunk and say stupid things, you didn't forget to tell me something, you didn't look at some other girl and have stray thoughts. This was willful misdirection. This was withholding information to the point that you believed you needed clever ploys to keep it that way. There's no coming back from this. What happens if you forget my birthday? Or run late for a date? Or change plans at the last second? I'll tell you. I'll be thinking, 'What is he hiding from me now?'"

"But, I—"

"There you go, Chad. That's the fucking problem summed up in one word, one syllable, one letter. *I*. There's no doubt in my mind that you want to do better because you really are nice. But you're just trying to find ways for *you* to keep me. You're not interested in where to go from here; you're only interested in keeping me from going."

"I'm interested in keeping you here because I'm falling—"

"Stop! Don't say it, Chad. Don't you dare say it."

Chad clenched his jaw so tightly his teeth hurt. He didn't know what to say, so he said nothing.

"There," Selma said. "You're finally saying the only thing you can say at this moment."

After a few more seconds of giving Chad one last look with tears streaming down her face, Selma got into her car and rolled down the window. "I'm leaving town. I decided to go to an art school. I'm not telling you which one, and I'm not even going to tell you which city."

The car roared to life as she finished, "My dream is to matter; my fear is to not. Goodbye, Chad."

Selma drove away.

CHAPTER 33

Heston took a breath before he reached for the doorknob. Chuck must have been looking out the window because he whipped the door open. "'Bout time you got back. Dad's pissed at you for not coming home last night."

"Surprised he noticed."

Heston stepped forward to enter, but Chuck didn't move. "Watch your tone, or I'll let your secret slip."

Familiar feelings bubbled to the surface, like boiling soup made from fear and uncertainty. Soup ingredients were dead things, just like the feelings that went into Heston's concoction. Simmering, Heston stepped forward. Nose to nose, he locked eyes with his half-brother and didn't blink. "If that secret gets out, I'll be forced to share my other secret."

Chuck tried to look unafraid, but his dilating pupils and audible gulp betrayed him. "What secret?"

"That I can . . . and *will* . . . kill you."

Chuck didn't try to look intimidating anymore; he simply stepped aside.

Bud sat at the flimsy table in the kitchen, a mug of coffee in one hand and a half-gone cigarette in the other. "'Bout time you got back. Pissed at you for not coming home last night."

He wasn't. This was purely posturing. Thanks to Chuck being a lycanthrope, he healed faster than humans, so patching him up last night wasn't a big deal. Bud probably killed a six-pack and half a bottle of whiskey trying to figure out what to do next. Heston didn't care; he'd spent the night with the Ink Stains.

Instead of feeding into his father's abuse, Heston asked, "Why is *he* here? I thought you kicked him out for being a disgusting freak?"

Bud shifted in his seat, clearly uncomfortable with the words about to come out of his mouth. "He's . . . sick. He's sick and needs our help."

Chuck lowered his gaze, meekly staring at his feet. Despite how pitiful that looked, Heston said, "I'm not helping him."

Bud snapped back to his normal, angry self. "Don't give me no lip! He needs help! Don't you fucking liberals always spout off about helping everybody? He's your brother!"

While Buck threw his fit, Heston went to his room and grabbed the small suitcase from his closest. He filled it with pants, shorts, underwear, and socks, then grabbed as many hangers of shirts he could carry. He'd come back for the rest if his father didn't throw it out between now and then. When he re-entered the living room, his father yelled, "How dare you walk away from me! And what the hell are you thinking you're doing? Running away like a sissy?"

"I'm moving out."

"What? You can't—"

"You're right—I *can't* continue to let you make me feel like I need you. I *can't* continue to let you make me feel guilty for going to school on grants and scholarships. I *can't* continue to let you make me feel like I'm less than nothing. You need me far more than I need you. If you need help with landscaping, I'll help, but only if you *ask*. If you *demand* I help, then you get *nothing* from me."

Face reddening, Bud stammered, "You . . . You . . . You—"

Heston continued to the door but kept his gaze firmly affixed to Chuck. "Don't worry. I'll keep Chuck's secret. We don't want the wrong people finding out about him, do we?"

Blanketed by the stunned silence of his father and half-brother, Heston walked out of the house.

Now, to deal with Chad.

———

Kyle shivered. The quiet in his house was deafening. He got home last night after his parents. They were asleep, so he just snuck up to his room. He was almost nineteen, had mythical abilities, and had a girlfriend, yet he still felt obligated to sneak. This morning, no one said a word.

He thought they were giving him the silent treatment during breakfast, a penance he suffered through with his mouth shut. But neither of them wore their angry faces. Eyes down, sad. Nervous.

Voice quivering, his mother finally broke the silence with an innocuous, "How has school been?"

"Good," he replied. "But I just heard that the captain of my esports team has gone missing."

He didn't know why he said it, but it flowed from his mouth like any other part of a normal conversation. But he knew his parents wanted to talk about something bigger, moving from fussy to jittery. He asked, "Is something wrong?"

"Well . . ." Kyle's father started, but his sentence trailed off to nothingness with just one word.

"We . . ." his mother continued. "We have something to tell you. It's about what we've been doing with your friends' parents."

Icicles formed within his chest as he thought about his parents knowing his secret. They couldn't, though. He was certain that he and his friends were in some form of lycanthrope mode while the parents were there. His friends confirmed it with him and told him that he shifted into that weird bird-monster again, scaring away everyone with that transformation. He should be grateful, but a faint hint of raw meat smell lingered around him like last time.

His revving heart slowed when he realized his mom said, "something to tell you," and not, "We need to talk." He still didn't want to talk about it, though. Neither did they, by the way they avoided eye contact.

Then Janey saved him.

A sound of "pew-pew" laser guns shot from his phone. The ringtone for a text. A picture of Janey making devil horns with her left hand, her forearm wrapped in bandages. A tongue-flopped maniacal smile took up half her face. Hurrying to get the words out, he said, "I have something to tell you, too! I have a girlfriend!"

Anxiety melted from his parents to expose confusion. The corners of his mother's lips twitched, as if wanting to smile but too afraid to. "You . . . you have a . . . girlfriend?"

Kyle swiped through his pictures to find a nice one of her and showed it to his parents. There was no better way to change the subject. And it was a test. Did his mom see Janey? Or was she too far away? The huge smile forming on her face told him what he needed to know. "Oh, Kyle! She's beautiful! What's her name?"

Kyle shared all he could about her and how they met. This conversation was so much better than the one they tried to start. They weren't ready for *that* conversation yet. He knew it would have to happen, but not now. For now, they were happy to hear about his love interest. After an hour, he was satisfied with the situation and told them he'd be back before dinner.

Now, to deal with Chad.

———•———

Cooper's mouth was a desert. Dry. Cracked. Arid. His eyes burned from inadequate blinking for the past half hour. He had his hand on a glass of water for the entire time, but his mind was too overloaded for him to do anything until his mother smiled and said, "Cooper? You're looking a little pale. Take a drink."

With gulps so huge it hurt his throat, he drained the glass.

"I know I hit you with a lot, son. I'm sorry, but I thought it was time you knew the truth."

The truth. Cooper thought the truth was the opposite of a lie, but he was wrong. He had no idea what the opposite of the truth was, nor could he contemplate what the opposite of a lie might be. But his mother's statement was accurate: Even though she had never lied to him, she certainly withheld the truth. A lot of truth!

He had always assumed his father had left them because, on some level or another, he was a dirtbag. A man with a solid career leaving his preteen son and mother must have been a dirtbag. Especially since she had lost her office job shortly after that. Well, Cooper had been wrong.

His mother didn't have an office job. She worked for the CIA. Wet works. A fancy term for "government assassin."

When his father found out what she did for a living, he ran, too afraid to attempt custody of their child. At first, his mother's attitude was, "It is what it is." But she made a mistake. She didn't divulge to Cooper what that meant, but he comprehended the subtext. Due to her stellar performance up to that point, the CIA let her go quietly. This broke her.

She told Cooper that his dauntlessness inspired her to become a better person. She felt she had been asleep for six years, and now she was wide awake.

"Mom . . . I . . . I . . . I'm speechless. I literally cannot form words to properly convey my thoughts and feelings."

"I know, son. I'm sorry for that. I'm sorry I didn't tell you the truth sooner. I'm sorry . . . I'm sorry for a lot of things." Her smile was soft, comforting, while her eyes held sympathy. Cooper had always wished for a day when her default expression wasn't as blank as an unmarred sheet of paper. *Be careful what you wish for*, skipped merrily through his head.

"So . . . are you going to go back to the CIA?"

She chuckled. "No, not at all. I don't mean to drop a bomb and run, but I need to talk to Rick and Bud. And, of all people, Whacky Wanda. We have so much more to talk about." She stood, but before leaving, she placed her hand on Cooper's cheek. It was the first time she touched him like this, like a mother, in years. "You are such an amazing son, Cooper. Thank you for taking care of everything while I was gone. I'm so proud of you."

The CIA. The CIA. The CI fucking A. Those three letters haunted his mind as he walked through campus. They would have continued to be his only thought if not for Brick.

"Hey, nerd," the football player said as a form of cordial greeting.

"Well, this day is improving by leaps and bounds."

Brick laughed at a joke, and Cooper realized he was the punch line. "You can be such an asshole."

Cooper waved a hand to dismiss his prior statement. "You're right. Apologies. What great pleasure is in store for me due to your company."

Brick shook his head. "Fuckin' weirdo. Look, I just wanted to let you know that Sanders ain't gonna kill you. He says you ain't worth it. He still fuckin' hates you, and I'd suggest keeping your interactions with him at practice to a minimum, but he's over trying to kill you. I think your freaky little pheasant friend scared the piss outta him."

"Good to know, thank you. I believe you when you said you didn't turn him, but did you know he was one of us?"

"Yeah. Chuck, too. But not the gamer nerd who got his dumb ass eaten by your freaky little pheasant friend."

"And Brittany? You guys didn't turn her."

"We didn't turn Brittany."

"Then King and his crew did."

"Maybe. But she wasn't there last night. Sanders, Chuck, and the gaming nerd were all turned by King, and they were all there."

"That means she exhibited betrayal to the one who turned her."

"Or there's another pack out there dolling out Elder Blood."

Cooper's eyes widened.

Brick laughed. "Bet you didn't think I could think of that."

That was true. Cooper didn't believe Brick could follow the path of conjecture to any form of meaningful conclusion. "When was the last time you spoke with her?"

"A party the day before the party you came to."

"Have you seen her around campus?"

"Dude, we're not fucking dating. We hung out a bit after Mason disappeared, but that was only to figure out what happened to him. I don't give a shit what she does."

"Charming."

"Fuck you."

Cooper thought about his next words. He had a certain level of immunity, his mother being a super ninja killing machine, and it was clear that Kyle's other self inflicted fear. But Brick didn't know who the ninja killing machine was, so Cooper couldn't use that as a threat without exposing the truth. That would be costly. Fighting his antagonistic urges, Cooper stuck with a simple, "Now what?"

"Now what, what?"

"With regards to King and his pack?"

"We chased them away, dude. What more do you want?"

"You can't really think that's the last we'll hear of them."

Brick huffed, an expression of impatience with this conversation. "There are three 'packs' against them and a bunch of 'hunters' who kicked their asses. They'd be pretty fucking stupid to come back."

"Or they could come back stronger."

"I don't give a fuck. Orlando, Emmanuel, and I will be going pro in a couple years or less, and we're outta here. We do not give a shit about The Bends or who's living in them. The only reason we even interacted with King was because of how fuckin' huge he is. We wanted to know how he did it. Now that we know it came from some goop in a tube, we don't give a shit about King or his 'pack' anymore."

"Good to know."

Brick stared, and for a brief moment, Cooper swore he saw a flicker of weakness flash across Brick's stone face. He wanted something. Cooper asked, "Anything else?"

After glancing over each shoulder, Brick leaned in and mumbled, "Did you or your friends happen to grab any tubes of goo?"

Nothing about that question surprised Cooper, yet he was still disappointed. Strength molded Brick like a piece of artwork, now his weakness was an indelible blemish. "No, Brick, we do not have any tubes of goo."

With a mirthless smirk meant to cover his shame, Brick said, "Doesn't hurt to ask, right?"

"It does not."

"Later, nerd." Brick's parting words as he left, looking completely unaffected by the conversation. Cooper, on the other hand, had much more to mull over, especially the information about Brittany. But he had to put that on the back burner.

Now, to deal with Chad.

CHAPTER 34

Chad trudged into the barn, shoulders slumped and burdened by an invisible weight. Selma removed herself from his heart, yet instead of it being lighter, it felt heavier. His parents didn't help matters, telling him nothing about where they were last night. They didn't even bother to lie about it—they just ignored any question he asked with, "It's nothing." Even when he asked his father about the bruises and excruciating limp. But at least he could turn to the one constant in his life: his friends.

They contacted him individually to meet at the barn to talk. Strategizing about what to do next was the best thing possible. If nothing else, it would take his mind off Selma.

As expected, Tyler was lying on the hay couch, smoking a joint and drinking a beer. "*Que pasa, mi amigo?*"

"Selma broke up with me," Chad huffed as he dropped onto one of the hay bale chairs around the table.

"Sorry to hear that, my friend."

"She was an amazing woman."

"Hopefully, you've learned something about yourself and what you're looking for in your next relationship."

Next relationship? Chad didn't want a next relationship. He wanted this relationship. Why was that so wrong? He kept that to himself and just mumbled, "Maybe."

Cooper came strutting into the barn and greeted Chad and Tyler with smiles and flowery salutations. Chad perked up a little, excited to start the

241

meeting. As soon as Cooper sat down, Chad started, "Last night, huh? That was something."

"That it was, sir. That it was."

"Okay, so we now know the enemy. We need to—"

Cooper held up his hand and shook his head. With a slight chuckle to his words, he said, "Deepest apologies, Chad, but I feel the need to stop you before you get on a roll."

"Ummm . . . stop me from what? Planning?"

"That's not quite the term I'd use, but yes. You're one of my closest friends, one of my band, my tribe, my pack, my brothers, so I would be remiss if I didn't expose you to some truths."

The same gurgle in his gut, the same sourness in the back of his throat from when he spoke with Selma. "Truths?"

"Yes. You mentioned that we now know the enemy. Well, to be honest, I don't think there is one, other than maybe the person you see in the mirror."

"Wait . . . what?"

"Being a lycanthrope has turned into an obsession for you. I willingly admit it's a pretty big deal, but it's one aspect of life, not life itself. Now, I know you meant the enemy is Justin, or King, or whatever he wants to call himself, but I don't view him as some boss-level Big Bad. Yes, he lured us into a trap as part of his power trip. I just talked with Brick, and he's confident Justin won't return. I'm not one-hundred-percent sold on his theory, but I believe it has merit."

"You met with Brick?" Chad was upset with himself for how shrill his voice sounded.

Cooper's sigh was accompanied by a look of disappointment, like what a teacher would give to a willful student who hadn't learned a lesson after a dozen tries. "That right there, Chad. I'm staying on the lacrosse team. That means I will be hanging around other people who play sports, sometimes even crossing paths with Brick. And before you go off about me being a 'jock,' I need to remind you that individuals are far deeper than one label. Other than maybe Brick, but every rule has exceptions, right? The point is that you need to look beyond the one label. You need to see the bigger picture."

Chad didn't know what to say. His mind was a jumble of words, and none of them seemed to go together.

"You fancy yourself a leader, Chad," Cooper said, his quiet words holding the reverence of speaking in a church. "But you're not."

Chad never thought of himself that way. Did he come across as thinking of himself as a leader? "Is this about the Elder Blood?"

"Yes, and so much more. We voted to leave it behind, but you brought a vial anyway, in blatant disregard of that vote. You keep scaring up enemies and issues where there were none before, and then you pull all of us into the drama you created, the drama you keep looking for. I need to state expressly that I'm not mad. I don't know if you feel the need in your heart to apologize, but if you do, please know I forgive you. You're my friend, and I love you as a brother, so please hear me when I say this—even if nefarious individuals are lurking within the borders of The Bends, it doesn't matter. We'll be graduating in about three years, so it's unlikely we'll be around if anything comes to fruition."

"I hear you, I really do, and I admit I get a little . . . myopic . . . when it comes to being a lycanthrope, but what about our parents? They're hunting us."

"They will only hunt us if we give them something to hunt."

"But your mother is a ninja death murder machine!"

Cooper smiled and stood. "That she is, sir. That she is. She and I discussed that today, but that is a story for another time when all of us are together, not talking about lycanthropes. Maybe next game day. In a week, right?"

Chad slouched, the balloon in his chest deflating. "Yeah, okay," he mumbled, not paying attention to his words or Cooper's goodbye salutations as he left. Cooper was right; he certainly hit Chad with some truths. Chad heard his own words and what he said about himself. *Myopic.* Cooper chose the word obsessed. Yes, there was more to life than being a lycanthrope, but Cooper was dismissing its dangers. There were other packs out there. Hell, there was another Elder out there! How many more Elders were there? Chad needed to research Proteus, needed to figure out how water creatures could be away from the water so long. When Brandon was in full lobster form, his internal organs were still human, or at least human enough to allow him to function as well as he did out of water. Was that something that happened naturally, or did he have to shift his inner workings consciously? How could Cooper not be concerned about that?

Heston ambled into the barn next, and Chad felt a renewed vigor. If there were one person who would back Chad about the potential dangers, it would be the friend who had a murderous half-brother. Something seemed different about him, though. His shape. It looked like he had gained twenty pounds since yesterday.

"Hey," Heston greeted Tyler and Chad. He sat in the same spot Cooper had recently vacated.

"Hey," Chad replied. Too charged from his conversation with Cooper, Chad failed to practice any form of decorum and said, "You look . . . different."

A slight blush formed across Heston's cheeks. "Yeah. I stopped using my abilities to alter my shape. I realized I was trying to take the easy way out. The Ink Stains are going to help me be the person I want to be."

"The Ink Stains?" Chad was upset with himself for how shrill his voice sounded.

"Yeah. I'm going to be living with them."

Today was bombshell after bombshell. Up was down and black was white. "Why?"

"My dad took Chuck back, so I'm gonna live with them."

"*Mi casa es su casa*," Tyler called out from the couch.

"Thanks," Heston replied. "But I think my place is with the Ink Stains right now."

"You're leaving us?" Chad asked.

Heston chuckled and shook his head. "No. You guys are my brothers. And you need to stop thinking so linearly. We can like more than one thing at a time. We can need more than one thing at a time."

Heston's words stung just as much as Cooper's. "So, I've been told."

"Sorry to be blunt, but you need to change your way of thinking."

"I . . ." Chad tried to defend himself, but he didn't know from what. Was Heston talking about the same thing Cooper was? "In what way?"

"With Kat. I'm going to be living in the same house with her. You can't freak out every time I mention her name."

"Why would you think I'd—" Chad stopped himself when Heston's face shifted to a furrowed-browed pucker of consternation. "Are you referring to me saving Natalia's life?"

"Yes. Kat was going to save Natalia, but you swooped in to 'save the day.' You did it to impress either Kat or Natalia. It didn't work, and you betrayed the rest of us. You think of yourself as a knight in shining armor. But you're not."

His friends were two for two today. The truth was heavy, and it threatened to crush Chad now that Heston had put his on top of Cooper's. Truth also poked the stinging spot behind his eyes. The shame of not knowing who he was stifled his tears. "Got it. Thanks."

Heston stood. "Game day next week, right?"

"Yep."

"Later," Heston said to Tyler and Chad.

Today had not gone as he expected. He knew he had to apologize for taking one of the vials and explain why he did it. But his friends knew why he did it. What hurt was that they didn't think he needed to apologize. He had no idea what to do next. All he knew was that things would get worse when Kyle walked into the barn.

"Jesus, no," Chad moaned. "Cooper and Heston were already here."

Kyle sat down. "They were?"

"Yes, and they hit me with a ton of truth."

"How are you doing with it?"

Chad shrugged, the effort difficult. "It is what it is."

After a few seconds of awkward silence, Kyle said, "Janey and I want to hang out with you and Selma again. Sometime soon?"

Playing with a loose piece of hay, Chad didn't look at Kyle. Too beaten, too ashamed. He mumbled, "She broke up with me."

"No! Oh no!" Kyle was upset, his voice sympathetic. "I'm sorry. Really, really sorry. How are you feeling?"

Like a lava-filled balloon ready to pop. That was an immature response, and his apparent lack of maturity seemed to be the theme of the day. "Like I need to reflect upon my life."

"Yeah. That makes sense. I'm here for you if you need anything."

"Thanks."

After a few more seconds of awkward silence, Kyle asked, "Was it because you helped Natalia?"

Selma had taken Janey from the ball field before Chad saved Natalia. The comment could have been a passive-aggressive dig, but Kyle had never been so mean-spirited. Chad chalked it up to Kyle being unconscious at the time. "No. She left because of the whole me-being-a-lycanthrope thing. I'm guessing you're mad at me, too, for bringing a vial?"

"Well, yeah. Even though I wanted to bring one, we all agreed not to. All of a sudden, you have one. It's like you're living in a fantasy world where your actions have no consequences. You're not. But you're my friend, so I'm not mad at you anymore. And I certainly have no right to judge—I'm the one who turned the jocks into lycanthropes because of my bad choices. You forgave me and stood by me when I felt all alone."

"Thanks," Chad whispered.

"Anytime." Kyle stood, but before he left, he said, "Game day next week."

Only one person left could make Chad feel any worse today, and he had been here the whole time. *Might as well get it over with.*

Chad turned to Tyler and asked, "Do you have any truth bombs to drop on me?"

"Just that your friends love you, dude. It's more difficult to tell someone you love the truth than letting them live in ignorance."

Of course, Tyler made Chad feel guilty about wallowing in his self-pity by getting him to empathize with how hard it was for his friends to dig the hole and fill the pool. But he was right. Had roles been reversed, Chad would have felt awful about needing to tell any of his friends what they had to tell him. He had caused everything bad that had happened to him. His friends not only wanted him to stop hurting himself, but they wanted him to grow. Grow. That was one thing he hadn't done during his life journey over the past few months. Well, that was going to change.

Chad stood and stretched. "Got time for a training session?"

"Always," Tyler replied. He finished his beer and extinguished his cigarette in the ashtray.

Until Chad figured out how he wanted to grow, he would be the best lycanthrope he could be.

EPILOGUE

Chad walked into Clinty's and was greeted with an eye roll from the bartender. He was a regular now. That notion brought forth a weird mixture of pride and shame. The bartender scowled at Chad as he walked farther into the room, but his expression changed to jaw-dropping surprise when he saw who Chad was there to meet.

Kat.

"I'm glad you showed up," she purred.

Chad took the stool next to hers, and she immediately turned so their left knees were between each other's legs. The bartender's mouth remained open while he served Chad a beer.

Desperately trying to ignore her hand on his thigh, Chad asked, "Why'd you want to meet?"

"I told you I'd buy you a beer at Clinty's." Keeping one hand on his leg, she used her other to run her fingertips through his hair. She curled a lock around her index finger. "Dyed your hair black? I like it."

Chad tried to stay strong. He reminded himself that this was the very thing the guys were worried about. They flat out told him that this was self-destructive. He wanted to recreate himself, but he was trying to mold melting ice cream. "Thanks, but why'd you want to meet?"

"Just to catch up."

"I think you mean play me. I feel like you're playing me." Boom! Chad felt proud of himself for that one.

"Play you? I've been honest and forthcoming ever since our incident with The Morrigan. I was the one who told you about the pack coming from Mills Hook." Damn it! She was right.

"I still feel like the other shoe hasn't dropped yet."

"No other shoe, Chad. I'm barefoot here." Chad looked at her feet and instantly felt foolish. Of course, she was speaking metaphorically. She didn't make any reference to his stupidity and kept talking. "I mean it when I say we've changed. Dylan and I haven't eaten anyone since the football players we saved you from. Tasha never ate a single person. Very unlike your buddy Kyle."

"That's . . . different. He can't control himself."

Kat smirked as if she knew Chad was going to say that. "Uh-huh. Sure."

"If you changed, then why are you brainwashing Heston?"

"We offered him a place to stay, and he accepted it. That simple. Look, it's our way of extending an olive branch to you and your friends. We're not all that different. The normal masses accept neither of our packs—the human sides of our packs, at least. Dylan had a life a lot like Heston's, so we decided to help him out."

"I'm still dubious."

Kat's fingers over his skin made him even more suspicious, despite her saying, "You don't have to be."

Chad needed her to stop, needed to free himself from her clutches. But no fly ever escaped a spider's web, no matter how hard it tried. "How's Natalia?"

"I don't know. Pissed, I assume. You're not harboring any feelings toward my daughter, are you?"

Chad tried to play it cool with a lethargic shoulder shrug. "Don't forget, she chose me over you."

Kat laughed. It wasn't playful or flirtatious; it was bold, the kind heard from the audience at comedy clubs. "Oh, Chad. That is absolutely not what happened. There is no way she wants to stay a lycanthrope. Care to tell the class how one stops being a lycanthrope?"

"By killing the one who turned you." The words fell out of his mouth, lifeless as all forms of hope within him shriveled like a salted slug.

Kat reached into her cleavage and pulled out a card. Handing it to him, she said, "Here. This will help you forget about her."

"A membership to the gym?"

"Your fighting skills have been improving, so it's clear you've been training. To help you keep up the good work, I decided to get you a membership to the gym so you can add some meat to your bones."

"You really are trying to turn me into Hunter, aren't you?"

Kat leaned in and brushed her lips against his neck and ear. "Why is that a bad thing?"

"Because he's dead."

Kat pulled away and smiled broadly, her eyes gleaming. "There we go. That's the attitude I'm looking for."

"I don't get it. Why me?"

"I told you. I see potential, so I'm going to sculpt you into the man I want."

"What if you're not the woman I want?"

Kat's incredulous look hit Chad so hard he almost fell off the stool. Waving his hands as if trying to erase the words from the air between them, Chad shook his head. "Okay, okay, I heard how stupid that sounded. But what's your end game? You mold me into the man you want and we what? Live happily ever after? Live in a four-bedroom, two-story suburban house and raise little hybrid human-animal creatures?"

"How about you finish college first. I want my man to be educated."

"You didn't answer my question."

"Always so serious. Fine. If there's one thing the skirmish on Rec Island has taught us, it's that there are too many lycanthropes, and we, as a species, need strong leadership before the situation gets out of control. You and I could be those leaders."

Chad looked at his beer. He forgot it was even there. Still no expert, he took a swig and finally understood why people liked beer. The worse a person felt, the better it tasted. "I'm not feeling very leader-ly at the moment. Recently, I was told that I'm no leader, delusional, and living in a fantasy world."

Kat grabbed his hand and squeezed. For the first time since knowing her, this felt genuine. Nothing flirtatious or gimmicky. A real connection. "Hey, no one is born a leader. It's a skill learned through hardship and failure. Second of all, we're members of a group of people who can turn into animals. I legitimately can't think of anything more fantastical than that."

Chad wanted to pull his hand away. Every neuron in his brain told him to pull his hand away. Instead, he squeezed back. "If I believe you . . . which I still really don't . . . you need to be forthcoming with me. No more secrets."

"Open book, Chad. A book filled with scary shit and plot twists, but an open book."

"Why did it seem like you weren't expecting to see Justin turn into an orca?"

"Because I didn't."

"Why?"

Kat released his hand and turned on her stool, the weight of her sins resting on her shoulders. In a rare moment of not being in control, she stared off into the distance. A gulp of beer. A smack of her lips. Tone cold, she said, "We knew he would be a prey animal. The smell came off him in enticing waves. We did the same spiel with him that we did with you. Our mistake was meeting him at that park, close to the road leading to Rec Island. Right after he turned, we toyed with him. We got too cocky, as we so often did under Hunter's leadership, and he slipped into the river. But he wasn't an orca, Chad. He was a seal."

It clicked in Chad's mind. Everything fell into place, like he opened a brand-new puzzle and completed it by simply dumping out all the pieces. His friends were each moving forward with their lives and encouraged him to do so as well. He would move forward with his life, not by minimalizing his lycan-thrope self but by embracing it. Kat wanted him to be a leader? Fine, he'd be a leader, and he would do so by taking his animal self to the next level, like Kyle, and learning to change the animal within, like Justin.

Chad wasn't just going to become the best lycanthrope ever—he was going to become the most *powerful* lycanthrope ever.

ABOUT THE AUTHORS

BRIAN KOSCIENSKI AND CHRIS PISANO skulk the realms of south-central Pennsylvania. Brian developed a love of writing from countless hours of reading comic books and losing himself in the worlds and adventures found within their colorful pages. In tenth grade, Chris was discouraged by his English teacher from reading H.P. Lovecraft, and being a naturally disobedient youth he has been a fan ever since. They have logged many hours writing novels, stories, articles, comic books, reviews, and the occasional ridiculous haiku. To find out where they may be skulking next, visit them at www.novelguys.com. If you happen to see them at one of the various conventions they participate in, feel free to stop by their table and say, "Hi." They're harmless!